WILLING SEDUCTION

"Nay, I won't leave just yet," Troy murmured. "Not without first getting what I came here for this night."

"What do you mean?"

"I think you know."

The intensity in his eyes unraveled a knot of desire inside Elise. He took a step toward her, and she found herself retreating until the stones of the hearth were behind her, warm and smooth beneath her fingertips.

The warmth of his breath bathed her skin an instant before their mouths merged. Surrendering to the wild urges pulsing inside her, she pressed herself against him, conscious of the height and breadth of him, so commanding beside her petiteness.

Her hand sought his cheek, feeling the slight abrasion of stubble. He turned his head and kissed her sensitive palm.

Elise felt a rush of passion. Never before had she known the attraction between a man and a woman could be so overwhelming, so irresistible. . . .

DEFIANT SURRENDER

BARBARA DAWSON SMITH

ZEBRA BOOKS
KENSINGTON PUBLISHING CORP.

ZEBRA BOOKS

are published by

Kensington Publishing Corp.
475 Park Avenue South
New York, NY 10016

First printing: January 1987

Printed in the United States of America

To V J Melton
You live on in the hearts of those who loved you

ACKNOWLEDGMENTS

I would like to thank the following:

The people at the Colonial Williamsburg Foundation for their patient answers to my many questions

Dougless Strickland Bitler for teaching me the rules of whist

Melanie Catley for her valuable suggestions

Lu Wright for her help with the finished manuscript

AUTHOR'S NOTE

In the mid-eighteenth century, in the vast wilderness west of the Alleghenies, there were no roads other than a few Indian trails. The rivers were used by fur traders and other travelers as the swiftest and easiest means of getting from one place to another. Thus, whoever controlled the water routes controlled the land.

In 1753, France launched a campaign to challenge the colony of Virginia's claim to the frontier by building several forts along the major waterways. Governor Dinwiddie of Virginia wrote a letter to the commander of the French forces in the Ohio Valley, ordering him to leave these lands. Appointed to deliver the letter was a twenty-one-year-old major in the militia, George Washington, who eagerly undertook his first official diplomatic mission.

A number of people who appear or are mentioned in *Defiant Surrender* are true-to-life historical characters. They are listed below in alphabetical order:

Robert Dinwiddie
John Frazier

Christopher Gist
Captain Joincare
Captain Marin
Captain Legardeur de St. Pierre
Jacob Van Braam
George Washington

Prologue

May, 1741

A strange noise jolted the little girl awake.

Clutching the quilt to her chest as if it were a shield against the demons of the night, Elise propped up on her elbow and peered cautiously around the sleeping loft. What had she heard?

Though moonlight lacquered the center of the tiny room, unknown dangers lurked in the darkened corners. Stories spun through her head: tales of witches and wizards, of ghosts and goblins, told by her father while she had been nestled within the security of his arms.

Elise shivered as her fancy filled the shadows with monstrous creatures hungry for the taste of a little girl's flesh. But nothing moved through the gloom. Gradually her heart slowed its frantic beating and her small fingers relaxed their death grip on the quilt. She was about to lie back down when the sound came once more.

This time Elise wasn't frightened, for now she knew what had awakened her—it was the rise and fall of angry

11

voices lifted aloft by a breeze through an open window. Her parents were quarreling again.

Ever since that letter had been delivered by a passing missionary priest three weeks earlier, there had been many such arguments, though only when her parents thought Elise wouldn't hear. Tonight there was more tension than ever in their muffled words. She had to reassure herself that everything was all right.

The corn husk mattress rustled as Elise slipped out of bed. Slowly she stole toward the staircase, her bare feet silent on the cool plank floor. In her pale nightgown she might have been a tiny ghost drifting through the shadows. She tiptoed down the narrow steps and into the keeping room. Even without the faint light from the banked fire, she would have known the way past the dark lumps of furniture, for this cozy cabin had been her home for all seven years of her life.

Her hand brushed against the lush softness of a beaverskin, stretched out on a frame to dry. There was a musty scent in the air from the bundles of animal pelts piled at one end of the room. Papa was a trapper, and the fruits of his long winter's labor were ready to be transported to a nearby trading post.

Elise crept toward the chink of candlelight emanating from her parents' bedchamber at the rear of the log cabin. There, she crouched beside the partially opened door, listening to the hiss of low, angry voices. Though Maman was French, they were speaking in English, the language that Papa insisted they use at home.

"By the devil, Brigitte, you're a stubborn woman!" he said. "Why can you not see that what I propose to do is for the good of us all?"

"How noble you make yourself sound," Maman

retorted. "But I know the truth—you think only of your own selfish desires, rather than what is best for your wife and child."

"How can I make you understand?" he ground out in frustration. "The money I've inherited means that at last there's a chance for me to make something of myself. I'm thirty-five years old, Brigitte. If I stay here, I'll only be wasting what remains of my life!"

"There is naught wrong with our life here. What more could anyone want?"

"What more! Take a good look around you! We've both worked like slaves these past eight years, but what has it gotten us? One tiny cabin and a few hundred acres of uncleared land."

"If you've tired of dirtying your lily-white hands, North, then don't feel obligated to stay," Maman returned bitterly. "I don't need you."

"Don't you, now?" Papa's heavy footsteps thudded across the floor.

"Stay away from me—" Maman's indignant voice broke off in a choked gasp, and Elise heard the faint rustle of clothing.

She tiptoed closer to risk a cautious peek through the doorway to the candlelit room beyond. Maman was wriggling against Papa's broad frame, her long sable hair cascading to her slender waist as she tried to arch back from his kiss. Their lips met and for one long moment it looked as if she had ceased struggling. Then suddenly she twisted her mouth free. In one swift motion, her hand lashed out to strike his cheek with a loud *crack!*

Cursing, he let go of her, and she stumbled back a step, clutching at the bedpost for support, her chin lifted in defiance. Elise watched in bewildered distress as her

13

father clenched and unclenched his big fists.

"You make yourself perfectly clear," he said coldly. "I'll not waste my breath arguing with you any longer." He swung toward the door, his knee-high boots thumping purposefully across the rough plank floor.

Elise shrank into the shadows behind a nearby chair. Her heart was beating fast at the expression on her father's face. Never had she ever seen him look so enraged! And to her knowledge never before had one of her parents struck the other!

The bedchamber door banged open, and Papa strode out into the dimness of the keeping room, Maman at his heels.

"North, if you dare walk out on me now, don't ever come back, do you hear?"

Papa maintained a stony silence as he snatched his coonskin cap from a peg and clapped it over his dark red hair. He unbarred the door and jerked it open. Then he turned to face her, moonlight silvering the golden-brown of his buckskins.

"I'll send Jed by to pick up the pelts—he'll give you a fair price. The money ought to hold you until I can claim my inheritance and send you more." Pivoting, he headed out toward the barn.

"I don't want your filthy money!" Maman stood in the doorway, hands perched on her hips, her voice loud with spite. "*Sacré Dieu!* My father warned me—he said never to marry an Englishman. I should have listened to him . . . I should have listened!"

The last words were half-choked. She whirled back inside, slamming the door with such force that a pot hanging on the log wall clattered to the floor. Muttering under her breath, she jammed the wooden bar into place.

Then it seemed all the anger drained out of her, for her shoulders slumped and she laid her forehead against the door. The sound of soft sobbing drifted through the dark air.

Elise huddled in frozen silence, unable to make sense out of what had happened. Why had Papa stormed out so late at night? And why was Maman now weeping?

A few moments later, she heard the clip-clopping canter of a horse down the trail that led to the trading post some ten miles away. The sound faded until it could be discerned no longer.

Driven by a nameless fear, Elise crept out from behind the chair and scurried across the room to throw her arms around her mother's waist. "Don't cry, Maman, please!"

Brigitte turned with a muffled sob and sank down to hug her daughter without asking why Elise was out of bed. When she finally drew back, Elise could see in the faint fireglow the tears that glittered on her mother's cheeks.

"Are you sad because Papa left?"

"*Oui, ma chérie,*" her mother admitted.

"But he'll be back soon, you'll see," Elise said with childish confidence.

Brigitte drew in a shaky sigh as she reached out to smooth her daughter's copper hair. "Nay, not this time." She paused as if something had caught in her throat. "Oh, *ma fille,* never make the mistakes I did. You must remember always to follow your head and not your heart. Someday you'll understand what I say, but for now all that matters is that we do not think of your Papa anymore."

A dark dread twisted inside Elise. "But he always comes back, Maman!"

"Nay," her mother replied, shaking her head sadly. "From now on, our family will be you and I—and the baby I carry. You would like a new brother or sister, wouldn't you?" She hugged Elise, adding fiercely, "We don't need anyone else."

Even the news about the baby couldn't distract Elise. "But Papa—"

"Hush, *chérie*. What would you say to our moving to Montreal? 'Tis time for you to learn to speak French and to discover more of your heritage. Wouldn't you like that?"

Elise listened in bewildered silence as her mother painted a rosy picture of life in the city. She couldn't keep her mind off the numbing knowledge that Papa was gone for good. It couldn't be true, it just couldn't be! Why, he hadn't even kissed her good-bye!

Over the following weeks, as she helped her mother pack their belongings, Elise refused to let die the secret hope that her father would return. She spent every free moment watching the trail for his tall figure astride a horse. They were settled into their new home many miles away in Montreal when she was finally forced to face the terrible truth.

He was never coming back.

Chapter One

December, 1753

Englishmen!

As she peered out a window of the commander's lodging, Elise d'Evereaux felt a fury of hatred rise like bile in her throat. Imagine, four Englishmen prowling around inside Fort LeBoeuf, daring to venture onto frontier land that belonged to the French. In a short while, they would invade the very chamber in which she stood, and there was nothing she could do to stop them.

The small party of Virginians had arrived the night before and set up camp across the creek from the fort. This morning, under the escort of a French officer, they had entered the main gate. Now, the early afternoon sun glinted on patches of snow that scattered the hard-packed ground inside the garrison. The December day was bitterly cold, as evidenced by the icy draft that seeped in through cracks around the window. But Elise felt no sympathy for the Englishmen waiting outside. They could freeze to death for all she cared.

From what little she had been able to glean, they had been sent as emissaries from the British colony of Virginia to deliver a letter to Captain Jacques Legardeur de St. Pierre, the commander of Fort LeBoeuf. Though the Virginians had brought with them a man who knew French, at the moment everyone was awaiting the return of an English-speaking officer from nearby Fort Presque Isle, located on the shores of Lake Erie. Apparently St. Pierre trusted only a fellow countryman to translate the letter accurately.

Elise subdued a flash of guilt, her work-reddened fingers tightening around the homespun curtain. It hadn't been necessary for the commander to wait for a man from fifteen miles away, not when she herself was fluent in English. But only her brother Marc knew of her skill, and he was no more likely than she to advertise it. Shame prompted her deception. God forbid that someone should ask where she, a lowly servant who had spent most of her nineteen years in French Canada, had had the opportunity to learn English!

Her trim body taut with hostility, Elise continued to stare out the window through narrowed eyes a shade darker than the copper hue of her hair. A curse upon those British pigs! The commander adhered to a rigid military code of honor that required he respect the enemy emissaries. But did he have to carry it to the point of allowing the Englishmen free run of the garrison? Didn't it matter to him that they were studying the layout of the fort, and would carry back vital information of French defenses?

"Mademoiselle d'Evereaux!"

The sharp male voice made Elise spin around, her heart pounding. Standing in the doorway that led to his private quarters was Legardeur de St. Pierre, an elderly man with a black patch over one eye, whose stiff bearing betrayed his many years as a career officer. It had only been a week since he had arrived to assume command of Fort LeBoeuf, but already Elise had learned that he was a strict taskmaster.

And now she was in trouble! When she had work aplenty, he had caught her idly staring out the window. Fearing his reproval, she clutched nervously at the apron that covered the blue homespun of her skirt.

"Mademoiselle d'Evereaux," he repeated sternly, "I expect this chamber to be spotless when Lieutenant Larousse arrives. May I remind you that a housekeeper does not waste her hours in useless daydreams?"

"*Pardonnez-moi*. I assure you, it will not happen again."

"See to it that it does not."

"*Oui, monsieur*." Elise dipped a respectful curtsey.

To her relief, the commander said no more. His booted heels clicked over the wooden floor as he went to retrieve a stack of papers from the desk in the corner. With the documents in hand, he returned to his private quarters, closing the door behind him.

Mon Dieu, merci! Elise breathed fervently. Each day she prayed nothing would happen to jeopardize her employment, as it was the sole means of support for both herself and her twelve-year-old brother, Marc. Along with their mother, they had left Montreal the previous spring. Brigitte d'Evereaux had recently lost her position as maid in a prosperous merchant's home when the entire family had been wiped out by smallpox. Resolving to escape the pestilence of the city, Brigitte had begged a post as housekeeper to a distant cousin, Captain Marin, who was erecting a series of forts in the wilderness, which would give the French control of La Belle Rivière, the river that the English called the Ohio. But disease had followed the family to the frontier, and in August a fever had claimed Brigitte's life.

Having no other prospects, Elise had swallowed her grief and persuaded Captain Marin to let her take over Brigitte's role as housekeeper. He had been understandably reluctant to have an unmarried, unchaperoned young woman living in the midst of so many soldiers. But Elise had played upon his sympathies and had managed to secure a place at the fort.

Now, though, since Marin had died in late October and St. Pierre had taken his place, she was finding that she had to fight the same battle all over again. This new commander would use any excuse to ship her back to Montreal, away from the frontier she loved so much. That was why she must prove to him that she was indispensable.

After tying a linsey shawl more securely around her shoulders, Elise began clearing away the empty wine goblets and bottles left from a gathering of officers the previous night. Within half an hour, she had the spartan chamber swept and tidied. She was on her knees, adding a log to the fire, when a knock reverberated through the air.

She scrambled to her feet and hastened across the room. A smile dimpled her cheeks when she swung open the door and saw Lieutenant Yves Larousse, second-in-command at the fort, the man she had recently agreed to wed.

"*Bonjour—*" she began softly.

It was then that Elise saw the quartet of men crowding

20

the space behind Yves. All pleasure drained from her face. Her lips tightened, her brandy-hued eyes turning icier than the wind that whipped her skirts. How could she have forgotten about the Englishmen?

"*Bonjour, Mademoiselle d'Evereaux,*" Yves said solemnly, though his dark eyes flashed a more personal greeting. "I understand the commander wished to see me and these visitors as soon as I returned. Is he available to meet with us?"

It took an instant for his words to penetrate the bitter feelings fogging her senses. Recognizing her duty, Elise reluctantly stepped aside to invite the men inside. "Come in, *s'il vous plaît.* I'll tell Captain St. Pierre you're here."

But it was unnecessary to seek out her employer; the elderly officer must have heard the commotion, for he was marching across the chamber to greet the visitors.

Elise closed the door and turned to glare at the Virginians. The loathing that twisted her belly went far beyond that of mere politics; the cause of her fierce hatred was buried deep within the secrets of a past about which no one here knew but her brother, Marc. It was the first time in many years she had been near an Englishman, and her churning emotions made her feel faintly ill.

Her scornful gaze came to an abrupt halt on one of the visitors. An imposing man, easily over six feet tall, he rested his hands on his hips, thrusting back a thick beaverskin coat so that she could see the finely wrought garb he wore beneath—a forest-green waistcoat over a white ruffled shirt, tan breeches, and gleaming black leather boots.

And he was staring boldly at her, amusement quirking the corners of his mouth. As he caught her eye, he swept

21

his fur hat off his tawny-brown hair and gave her a nod, as if acknowledging her perusal.

Cochon! The stupid pig thought she was admiring him!

Rage rushed through Elise. Her fingers clenched and unclenched as she debated the wisdom of slapping that cocky grin off his face. Sanity advised her it was best to leave before she did something rash.

Before she could move more than a step toward the door, the commander's voice rang out in French. "Mademoiselle d'Evereaux, come take the visitors' coats."

Elise froze, tempted to rebel and make a dash for freedom. But to disobey was to sacrifice her employment. Gritting her teeth, she subdued her resentment and slowly walked across the chamber to the enemy. She reminded herself to keep a firm rein on the temper that had gotten her into trouble on more than one occasion.

The four Virginians were warming themselves by the fire. Yves was exchanging small talk with them, one by one, in the halting English he'd learned as a schoolboy. At first the words sounded foreign to Elise, but she discovered that even after all the intervening years, she still understood the language well.

Yves introduced himself to a rangy man in scarlet-hued military uniform who went by the name of Major George Washington. Though not precisely handsome, his face bearing the slight scarring of smallpox, Washington exuded a dignity that gave the impression he was older than his youthful appearance suggested. He handed Elise his greatcoat, affording her a grave nod before returning his attention to the conversation.

Stepping to Washington's left, she accepted a coat

from a blond Dutchman who spoke fluent French, and then a buckskin cape from a grizzled frontiersman who, she guessed, had been the party's guide through the wilderness.

Now there was only one Virginian left—that arrogant pig.

Schooling her expression into a mask of impassiveness, she stepped toward him with her armload of wraps and stopped, politely focusing her attention on his broad chest.

But the Englishman made no move to take off his beaverskin coat. Didn't the imbecile see her standing in front of him?

Irritated, Elise looked up to find him eyeing her with barely concealed amusement. Her gaze swept over him in contempt. Only with the greatest reluctance did she admit to herself that he was one of the most handsome men she had ever seen. In some bygone time, the chiseled symmetry of his features might have adorned a Greek coin. His thick, tawny-brown hair was drawn neatly into a queue at the back of his neck. There was an air of the rogue about him, a virility and a charm that were unmistakable, but also an overpowering authority that grated on her nerves. It was the kind of quiet force that could arise only from the certainty of his own worth.

His engaging grin deepened. Devilment danced in the depths of his green eyes, as if he had discerned the animosity behind her disciplined facade and found it most intriguing.

"Hello, lovely lady," he murmured in an intimate undertone. "Or shall I say, *bonjour?*"

His pronunciation of the French greeting was atrocious, but his meaning transcended any language barrier.

23

His gaze dipped to her bosom, lingering there with an expression of warm approval.

Elise realized her shawl had slipped, exposing the tightness of the bodice of her gown over her full breasts. The blush that bathed her body was inexplicable; it tingled every nerve, rippling over her skin in waves. She struggled to readjust the shawl despite her coat-laden arms. The turbulent emotion inside her was only anger, she assured herself. How typical of an Englishman to regard a woman as an object of lust! If only she dared hurl a scathing retort in his own language . . .

Scowling, Elise abandoned the futile effort with the shawl. If the stranger chose to stare rudely, she would have to grit her teeth and bear it. Knowing that she risked the wrath of the commander if she failed to treat the visitors with respect, she shifted the garments heaped in her arms as a blatant hint that she was still awaiting his coat.

The Virginian only gave a low chuckle.

Venom gushed through her veins. He was laughing at her! That was the last straw. If he wished to swelter, then so be it. She would be glad to see every one of these British pigs roasting—and preferably in hell! Spinning sharply, she started to step away.

"Whoa." The man's fingers bit into her arm before she could escape. "I believe I will remove my coat, after all," he stated, loud enough for the others to hear, for the commander was frowning suspiciously at them.

The Virginian wore a bland expression, though his emerald eyes sparkled with mischief. He tossed his hat onto the mound of garments she held, then shrugged off the beaverskin, draping it atop the heap.

"Mercy," he said. Then he turned to speak to Yves.

For an instant she stared after him, puzzled, before it struck her that he meant *merci*, the French word for "thank you." An unexpected bubble of laughter rose within her, but she firmly squelched the impulse.

Marching toward the commander's private chamber with the load piled almost to her chin, Elise heard the stranger introduce himself to the French officers. Troy Fletcher. She found the name ringing through her head as she deposited the coats on a bunk in a corner of the austere room.

Lingering beside the commander's cot, she absently brushed a hand over the soft beaverskin. It bore a trace of Troy Fletcher's scent, a blend of horses and leather and something exotic, sandalwood perhaps. She wondered if that same intriguing essence clung to his bare skin. . . .

Abruptly Elise banished the wayward thought. Troy Fletcher was her enemy!

Her lips curled in contempt as her hatred revived in full force. A typical Englishman, Fletcher sought to worm his way into a woman's good graces only so he could use her. But though his charm might entice other women, it would fail miserably on her.

Readjusting the shawl over her bodice, Elise headed back into the main room. She would see if the commander required anything more of her before leaving the building. It would be a relief to breathe air that held no stench of British.

But St. Pierre was engaged in conversation, and she was forced to cool her heels and wait. Pointedly ignoring Troy Fletcher, she watched as Major Washington withdrew a dispatch from his pocket and presented it to St. Pierre. The commander motioned to Yves, and the two French officers moved toward the adjoining quarters, apparently intending to peruse the letter in privacy.

Elise darted toward them. "Monsieur, may I go now?"

"*Non*," St. Pierre replied in their native tongue. "I wish you to fetch wine for my guests, and see to their comforts until I return."

Yves flashed her a distracted smile before the two men left the chamber, closing the door behind them.

Her heart sank. She was to stay here, alone, with four Englishmen? Never! But even as her mind rebelled, Elise knew she had no alternative but to obey.

Feet dragging, she stepped over to a pine table that held several bottles of wine. There, she dallied over the task of pouring the burgundy liquid into pewter goblets. It galled her to have to play the respectful servant around these foreigners.

But at last she could delay no longer. Picking up a tray holding the four tankards, Elise moved stiffly toward the men, now seated in chairs around the fireplace. One by one, she distributed the wine goblets. When it came time to serve Troy Fletcher, she kept her eyes trained demurely downward. Yet her gaze was drawn to the large masculine hand that curled around the pewter vessel. His fingers were long and well shaped, with a scattering of tawny-brown hairs. From out of nowhere came a curiosity to feel those fingers touch her skin. Heat washed through her and she looked up in confusion, to see him smile.

"To you, mam'selle," Fletcher murmured, lifting his goblet in a salute before putting it to his lips.

Elise felt her blush deepen and she scurried back over to the table to set down the tray. A peculiar blend of anger and bewilderment coiled her insides. What was wrong with her? Her heart was beating like a scared rabbit's! Then the sound of English voices penetrated her chaotic nerves and she froze, realizing the men were discussing her.

"Now, see here, Troy, you done scared off the poor gal with your teasin'," one of them said.

"Nonsense," Fletcher scoffed in amusement. "That shyness is all an act."

"Humph. I reckon she's shakin' in her boots right now."

Elise pivoted slowly to see that it was the grizzled frontiersman who spoke in her defense. Her spine rigid with tension, she folded her arms across her breasts in pretended nonchalance, reminding herself they didn't know she spoke their language.

Fletcher laughed. "You're a fool for a pretty face, Gist. Living in a fort with so many men, 'twould be a miracle indeed if she were as innocent as you seem to think."

His bold green eyes again sought her figure, and Elise was hard-pressed to keep from blurting an angry retort. The nerve of him to imply she had loose morals!

Major Washington stirred his lanky form in his chair. "Do you not think," he chided, "'twould be wise to first ascertain whether or not the girl can understand us before you continue this discussion?"

"Point taken." Fletcher grinned and turned to the squat, blond-haired man huddled near the fireplace, saying, "Van Braam, will you do the honors?"

The interpreter nodded, taking a gulp from his wine goblet before lifting a hand to gesture at Elise. *"Mademoiselle! Parlez-vous anglais?"*

"Non," she replied with an emphatic shake of her

27

head. Elise clamped her lips tight, hoping she didn't look guilty. There would be entirely too many discomforting questions should the commander learn she spoke flawless English!

"Well, now, Troy," the middle-aged frontiersman said in English, his dark eyes twinkling. "I reckon that'll make it mighty hard for you to sweet-talk her, eh?"

"Ah, but there are other ways for a man and woman to commune," Fletcher bantered back. Stretching out his long legs, he crossed the shiny black leather boots at the ankles. "Did I ever tell you about the French seamstress I once met in Fredricksburg? Veronique knew only a smattering of English, but I'll be damned if that stopped us. After all, who needs words to warm one's bed?"

Hearing the hoot of male laughter, Elise stewed in silence. Just let that strutting peacock try to charm his way into *her* bed! He'd soon find himself nursing a sore jaw!

The conversation drifted to other topics. Under the guise of indifference, Elise listened intently to a discussion of whether or not the Indian allies of the French could be won over to the British cause. The knowledge that they were plotting right in front of her filled Elise with frustration. If only she could relay what she heard to St. Pierre!

At last the bedchamber door opened and the two French officers emerged. It was decided that Van Braam would check the Frenchman's translation of the letter from Virginia's governor by reading it aloud in English, while Washington compared the words to the original. The interpreter cleared his throat and began.

"'*Williamsburg, Virginia, October thirty-first, seven-*

28

teen hundred and fifty-three. Sir, the Lands upon the
River Ohio in the Western Parts of the Colony of Virginia
are so notoriously known to be the Property of the Crown
of Great Britain that it is a Matter of equal Concern and
Surprise to me, to hear that a Body of French Forces are
erecting Fortresses and making Settlements upon that River,
within His Majesty's Dominions . . .'"

Listening unobtrusively from her stance near the wall,
Elise felt a resurgence of resentment. Who were these
arrogant Englishmen to claim the frontier as theirs?
French trappers and missionaries had explored these
forests long before the British had ever set foot here!
Incensed, she glowered at the group as Yves and Van
Braam argued over the translation of a certain phrase.

It was then that Troy Fletcher lifted a hand and
motioned to Elise. With a glimmer of an impudent grin,
he pointed to his goblet, making it plain that he desired a
refill. She was sorely tempted to ignore him, but the
presence of the commander made her reconsider.

Taking a deep breath that did little to calm her
vexation, she snatched up a bottle and headed across the
chamber, her skirts swishing impatiently about her
slender thighs. It infuriated her to have to humbly serve
a man who was her mortal enemy.

Haughtily, Elise reached for his goblet without
granting him so much as a glance. Their fingers brushed,
and heat seared up her arm and into her heart. The
disconcerting sensation made her hand tremble slightly
as she poured wine into the empty vessel. Flustered, she
looked up at Fletcher's face.

He winked. Taken aback, she stared at him, her fingers
paralyzed around the cold pewter. She felt an insane urge

to laugh. That impulse died in an instant, swept away by a tide of fury. How dare this filthy cur of an Englishman try to charm her!

Without thinking, she tipped the goblet and splashed its contents into his lap.

Fletcher leaped to his feet. "What the devil—!" he exclaimed, staring at the burgundy splotch that stained the front of his tan breeches. A trail of wine soaked down one leg and into his black leather boot.

But when he glanced back at Elise, she was startled to see a devilish grin steal over his handsome features. Her brief satisfaction soured. *Sacré Dieu!* Was there nothing she could do to put the man in his proper place?

It was at that precise moment she remembered they were not alone. She turned to look straight into the commander's angry face.

"Mademoiselle d'Evereaux! What is the meaning of this?"

"I . . . it must have slipped," she replied lamely, speaking in French as he had done. Suddenly realizing the enormity of her act, she quickly mumbled to Fletcher, *"Pardonnez-moi—"*

But her attempt at apology failed to placate St. Pierre. "Never have I seen a guest treated with such disrespect," he said coldly. "Take Monsieur Fletcher into my quarters and lend him a pair of my breeches while you clean his. Lieutenant, tell our guest what I have said."

As Yves dutifully repeated the words in English, Elise stood, mortified, her hands clenching the empty goblet and bottle. There must be some mistake! Certainly the commander couldn't mean she was to closet herself alone with this Englishman while he removed his breeches!

Her employer's implacable expression warned Elise to hold her tongue. Desperately she looked to Yves for support, but he was frowning at her, too. Didn't her fiance care that she was going off with another man, an Englishman? No, of course not, she reflected bitterly. Yves was a devoted military man and would never think of disagreeing with his superior's order.

She swallowed hard, reminding herself that she had a brother to support. She must do as St. Pierre said or risk losing her position as housekeeper—if she hadn't already lost it.

Pride sank beneath the burden of responsibility. She wheeled around and headed toward the commander's private quarters with all the enthusiasm of a criminal being marched to the gallows. Troy Fletcher's footsteps followed, and then the bedchamber door clicked shut.

Nerves quivering, she placed the goblet and bottle on a pine table, then straightened a stack of papers to give her fidgety fingers something to do. Flames snapped in the hearth, the only sound aside from the agitated fluttering of parchment. Firmly, she got a grip on her wits. There was no reason to feel so panicked. French officers occupied the chamber right next door; under the circumstances, even this Englishman wouldn't try anything.

Slowly Elise turned. Fletcher was lounging against the stone mantel, watching her. Shooting him a hostile look, she went to a rough-hewn armoire and withdrew a pair of the commander's breeches. Then she stepped over to the Englishman and silently held out the garment to him.

He ignored her offering. "I have a better idea, mam'selle."

He snatched up a cloth from a nearby washstand and made an exaggerated swipe at his breeches. Then he pushed the square of fabric into her hand, pantomiming that she should do the same.

He wanted her to clean his breeches while he had them on!

Her face flamed as she stared at the wine-soaked material below his waist. Although her knowledge of the more intimate aspects of the male anatomy was almost nonexistent, she was mortifyingly aware that beneath that fabric lay the most elemental proof of his masculinity. Her gaze skittered down his muscled thighs and polished black boots, and then she looked up—to spy a wicked grin on his face.

Outrage jolted her. He was teasing her again, the pig!

"Cochon!" she snapped, hurling the commander's breeches at him. Wheeling, she snatched up a ewer and marched indignantly toward a small portal that led directly outside, the deep sound of his laughter ringing in her ears.

Elise took great delight in slamming the door behind her. As she headed over the icy path to fetch water, the heat of her wrath helped ward off the bone-chilling bite of the wind. She jerked the shawl tighter around her shoulders. Satan take that infernal man! How was it that he could so easily destroy her composure?

By the time she returned to the commander's lodging, her temper was again under control. No more would he catch her off guard, she vowed grimly. She wouldn't let an Englishman provoke her into a display of anger that might result in her losing her precious position here at the fort. Taking a deep breath of frigid air, she lifted a hand to rap on the door that led into the private quarters.

Footsteps sounded inside and the door swung open to Troy Fletcher's tall form. Her eyes widened as shock drove all resolution from her mind.

Though a shirt still covered his broad chest, below the waist he wore only a rough linen towel. The skimpy cloth was loosely looped over his hips, extending down to the middle of two very bare, very masculine thighs.

Chapter Two

Troy Fletcher saw a pink flush steal over her cheeks, and sensed it was due to more than just the cold weather. He felt a moment of discomfort. Who would have imagined the sight of a man's naked legs could cause such obvious embarrassment to a woman accustomed to living in a fort filled with soldiers? The borrowed breeches had been too tight on his muscular frame, and he hadn't thought twice about draping a towel over himself instead.

Had he misjudged her? With those guileless brandy-hued eyes and that softly curving mouth, she appeared to be an innocent . . . but then, looks could be deceiving. He frowned, perplexed by his conflicting impressions of her. Earlier she had exhibited a defiance that had piqued his curiosity, yet now she brought to mind a frightened fawn. He detected a vulnerability in her that touched him deeply.

Suddenly an icy breeze raised goose bumps over his flesh. With the same caution he would have used to keep from startling a wild creature of the forest, Troy reached out and gently captured the girl's arm. His fingers registered the velvety press of her breast, but he resisted the impulse to enfold her in his arms. He drew her into the warmth of the bedchamber, then closed the door against the invading cold.

Releasing her, he walked over to brace his elbow on the fireplace mantel, surreptitiously watching the graceful sway of her hips as she hurried over to pick up his breeches. She sat down at a table, dipping a cloth into the ewer of water before vigorously scrubbing the wine stain. In the firelight, her hair glowed with the jeweled sheen of autumn leaves. His fingers itched to unpin the prim bun at the back of her head. In his mind he saw her naked, with copper curls cascading over her breasts, her body soft and yielding, her ivory skin flushed with passion. The fantasy sent hot blood pulsing through his veins, and it took several deep breaths to discipline his desire.

She glanced sideways at him. Long lashes fluttered down to conceal her eyes, but not before he had glimpsed the dislike burning there. He was both intrigued and frustrated by her hostility. Why did she hate him, a total stranger? Though it was true their countries were at odds over control of the frontier, even to the brink of war, he had a nagging suspicion that this woman's enmity extended beyond mere politics.

Perhaps, Troy reflected, he shouldn't have teased her so mercilessly. But who would have thought a little harmless flirting would have driven her to the point of dumping a glassful of wine in his lap?

Watching her work, he felt a strange stirring of emotion. What was it about her that roused such tenderness in him . . . such an urge to protect? He wanted to gather her to him and ease the disquiet he sensed in her soul.

Yet he had to tread carefully or risk scaring her off. Silently he cursed the language barrier that prevented him from discovering even her full name. For the first time in his life, Troy wished he'd paid closer attention to the French lessons that had been a part of his schooling. Back then, books had paled in comparison to the fascination of learning to run a tobacco plantation.

He had been fourteen when his father had died and left him a vast parcel of land bordering the James River in tidewater Virginia, upstream from the estate inherited by his elder brother, Jason. Over the ensuing years, Troy had transformed the wild acreage into a thriving plantation, reaping a profit through trade with England.

Yet ever since his business enterprises had grown so successful, he had been wrestling with a vague dissatisfaction. It was a tenuous, gut-level feeling, something he couldn't quite put a finger on. That was why, when he'd happened upon Major Washington in Fredericksburg a month earlier, he had jumped at the chance to accompany the expedition to the frontier, hoping a brief absence from the tedium of duty might help allay this restlessness in him.

Abruptly the girl rose from her chair. Though she eyed him with caution, her chin was tilted stubbornly as she marched to the side of the hearth opposite to where he stood. Still watching him suspiciously, she held his breeches over the flames to dry the damp, cleaned spot. As she leaned forward, her gown stretched taut over her full breasts and tiny waist. Through the acrid scent of the fire, Troy caught a whiff of her delicate feminine fragrance. Again he had to fight a surge of desire that was stronger than anything he had ever before felt. The need to communicate with her became a compulsion.

36

"Mam'selle d'Evereaux," he murmured.

A faint look of alarm clouded her luminous eyes. Troy resisted an urge to reach out and soothe her. Instead he stood still, his elbow resting on the mantelpiece. He hoped that the gentleness of his tone would convey what his foreign language could not.

"I mean you no harm, mam'selle," he went on quietly. "If you could understand me, I would but tell you how lovely you are . . . how your eyes are as rich and lustrous as brandy . . . how I long to see you smile."

Listening to him, Elise felt something warm and pleasant stir within her. His deep voice was strangely like a caress. She wished he would move away and yet she wanted him to come nearer. It was a struggle to keep a blank expression on her face when there was such a peculiar turmoil in her belly. The only betrayal of her inner agitation was the almost frantic way her hands waved his breeches over the fire, trying to dry them as swiftly as possible. It had been unnerving enough when she'd had to clean the garment, bringing to mind what the fabric had so recently covered, without now having to hear him say such provocative things. She tried to close her ears to him, but his husky words burned through her resolve.

"I wonder if you can guess how much I'd like to taste your lips, to see if they're as soft and sweet as they look? I'd like to see your bare skin glowing by the light of the fire . . . your hair spilling over your naked breasts. . . ."

Elise kept her gaze trained downward in pretended nonchalance, yet the intimate image he painted danced in the flames before her. Her heart fluttered wildly as the edge of her vision strayed irresistibly to the towel that covered his hips. She had seen a baby boy naked, but never a grown man. What secrets lay beneath that cloth?

Disconcerted, she tried to focus her attention on the task of drying the breeches. Yet her thoughts were a labyrinth of confusion. How could the words of this English stranger have such potent power over her when Yves's occasional kisses had failed to affect her so?

Fletcher's deep, drawling voice flowed over her like honey. "I wonder, lovely lady, have you ever lain with a man? Have you tasted the delights of lovemaking, or are you a virgin still? Your eyes speak of innocence, but surely with all the soldiers in this fort, at least one would have taken you to his bed by now."

Elise felt a rush of reality sweep away the weakness in her legs. How could she have forgotten, even for a moment, that Troy Fletcher thought her a woman of questionable morals? The nerve of him to condemn her without a scrap of evidence! She gritted her teeth in sudden rage, her fingers digging into the breeches as he continued to speak.

"I want you, mam'selle," he murmured. "I want to bury myself in you. No doubt our coupling would bring us both great pleasure, for if the passion of your body matches the fire of your temper, 'twould be a bedding neither of us would ever forget."

That did it. Wrath compelled Elise to spin toward him, the full force of her resentment tumbling from her tongue: "English pig! I would sooner lie with Satan himself!"

Fury seethed in her as she glared at the startled expression on his face. There, that would show him! Doubtless he was used to women leaping at the chance to share his bed.

"You little minx," Fletcher said with a soft laugh.

38

"You *do* speak English!"

Elise gasped, then clapped a hand over her mouth belatedly. *Sacré Dieu!* She had responded without thinking in the language he understood. Now this Virginian was privy to the secret she had guarded for so long!

"I-I know only a few words," she stammered. Pivoting, she scurried across the chamber to drop the breeches onto the table, her trembling fingers smoothing the fabric.

Her heightened senses warned Elise of Fletcher's closeness a split second before his hands descended to her shoulders. Sickness squeezed her stomach as he turned her to face him. She stared mutely at his white shirt, knowing even before he spoke that she had failed to deceive him.

His thumb and forefinger tilted her chin so that she met the green of his eyes, as calculating as a cat's. "Where did you learn to speak English so well?"

"That is no concern of yours," she uttered hoarsely, willing a steel into her voice that was at odds with the wobbly sensation in her knees.

"And not simply English," he mused thoughtfully, "but the refined speech of an aristocrat. What is your background?"

She stared at him in stubborn silence.

"Does St. Pierre know of your skill?" he persisted.

"But of course," she said, too quickly.

"Then you won't mind if I should happen to mention it to him?" he asked smoothly.

Fear sent her pride flying. "You wouldn't . . . please . . ." She swallowed hard at the dismaying knowledge that her future was in his hands. If he said anything to the commander, there would be questions she didn't want to answer . . . or more correctly, she reminded herself bitterly, questions she would be *ashamed* to answer.

A wicked humor hovered at the corners of Fletcher's mouth. "Perhaps," he murmured, lifting a hand to caress her silken cheek, "I might be persuaded to keep silent."

"What do you mean?"

He laughed. "Don't look so suspicious—I could demand a far higher price than I will. You need only fulfill two conditions, the first of which is telling me your full name."

She eyed him warily, then decided an honest answer could do little harm. "Elise Bernadette d'Evereaux."

"Elise," he repeated, his husky voice stroking her senses.

She was suddenly conscious of his nearness. His eyes held her mesmerized as his fingertips feathered over the delicate contours of her face. She was awash with his scent, a heady mixture of leather and sandalwood. Shivers spread across her skin wherever he touched her.

"The other condition," she demanded coldly. "What is it?"

Fletcher ran a thumb over her lips. "Grant me a kiss, and I'll not breathe a word to anyone of your skill with the English language."

The crackle of the fire was deafening in the stillness. A torrent of panic engulfed Elise, and her gaze strayed to his mouth, then shied away in chagrin. She hadn't really felt a fleeting curiosity; the bribe he proposed was disgusting! Yet if she failed to comply, and Troy Fletcher betrayed her to the commander, embarrassing questions would arise.

"What say you, Elise?" he pressed. "Is one kiss too steep a price to secure my silence?"

She hesitated, despising him for putting her in such an untenable position, and herself for so foolishly letting slip her secret. With sick resignation, she knew there was only one choice.

"I agree to your terms," she forced out.

Fletcher smiled, and the heat in his eyes sent a tremor down her spine. "'Tis a bargain, then," he murmured. "And now to collect my due."

The corded strength of his arms snared her securely against him. His breath was a warm whisper against her skin an instant before his lips touched hers. She held herself rigid, intent only on enduring his loathsome touch. But the gentleness of his kiss surprised her; it was not at all the crude display of lust she had expected of an Englishman.

Her lashes drifted shut, making her more acutely aware of her other senses. His tongue entered her mouth by degrees, tasting the sensitive inner surfaces of her lips before venturing farther to fully probe the sweetness within.

Feeling fluttered through her, a shameful vulnerability that she fought with all her might. But its powerful pull slowly melted her defenses. His lips demanded a response, and at last temptation exceeded the threshhold of her restraint. Her arms wreathed his neck as she touched her tongue to his. Against her breasts she felt the hardness of his chest and the deep thud of his heart. She was drunk on his warm wine taste, plunged into a pleasure that was instinctive and irresistible.

When his big hands slid down to her derriere to lift her to him, the knowledge of his partial nudity set her body aflame. Blood swirled swiftly through her veins and quivered between her thighs. A strange anticipation swelled within her as she felt his fingers circle her breast.

"Elise," he uttered huskily, trailing his fingers over her flushed cheek. "Anyone might discover us here. Is there somewhere we could go which would afford us more privacy?"

Dazed, she gathered her spinning senses. Her mind felt as if it had been scattered into a thousand fragments. Abruptly the pieces righted themselves and she was staring at the face of her enemy. Mortification flooded her. Fletcher thought she wanted more than just a kiss!

Elise wrested herself from his arms and backed up rather unsteadily until her palms met the rough stone of the hearth. "Our pact is fulfilled," she stated, trying to keep her voice from quavering. "Or do you seek to go back on your word and demand a different bargain?"

"I want only what you're willing to give," Troy countered. "A moment ago, 'twas you who wanted to make love with me."

Her mind reeled with shame and confusion and self-loathing. How was it that Troy Fletcher could coax a response from her when a handsome French officer like Yves had failed? What had happened to her sense of decency?

Seeing Fletcher's confident smile, she felt a hot rush of fury. The bastard! He had probably never intended to betray her to St. Pierre; all he had wanted was to use his discovery of her English fluency as a means to satisfy his lust.

She curled her fingers into fists. "Stupid English! Always wanting more than you're entitled to."

"If you refer to the frontier," he drawled, "'tis the

French who are taking more than their just due."

"The Treaty of Utrecht gave us this land!"

"That was never the intent. The French were granted the Mississippi River alone, not all the land that drains into it."

The interpretation of the treaty made some forty years earlier had long been a bone of contention between France and England. Smug in the certainty of her beliefs, Elise was determined to get in the last word.

"But as you can see, the French possess the land, and that is all that truly matters. Now, I gave you what we agreed upon, so go now and leave me in peace!"

Her tart words only appeared to amuse him. "As m'lady wishes," he said, sweeping her an exaggerated bow. "'Tisn't to my liking to end this pleasant interlude, but if it pleases you, then so be it. There is but one problem."

"What?" she ground out.

"I must don my breeches before leaving lest anyone suspect something unseemly has occurred here. Feel free to stay and watch; you'll find I have little modesty."

With a wicked smile, he put his hands to his waist and began to unloop the towel. It took but an instant for her to move. She sped to the door, silently cursing the blush that heated her cheeks.

"Elise, wait."

The soft drawl froze her fingers on the latch. She kept her eyes trained on the wooden panel before her, nervous that he might already have removed the towel. It vexed her to have to obey him, yet she was trapped by the fear that he knew her secret and might still bear witness against her should she anger him.

"There's something I wish to make clear," he went on.

"What I said earlier, when I thought you understood no English, were things no gentleman would say to a lady he'd just met. I apologize if my frankness caused you distress." Troy paused and when he spoke again, his voice was soft and disarming. "Yet never make the mistake of thinking I merely rambled falsehoods to pass the time; I meant every word."

Remembering his provocative statements all too well, Elise felt the blush on her cheeks grow hotter. "And you mustn't think I would share any stranger's bed," she retorted stiffly, not turning her head from the door.

The faint pad of his bare feet came closer. "I know that. I admit I thought differently at first, but I realize now I was mistaken." His hands came down gently on her shoulders. "Elise, I know not what I've done to earn your hatred, but I assure you, you can trust me."

The feel of his fingers was somehow comforting. Deep down, she felt an impulse to believe him, and it took an effort to regain control of her reason. Doubtless he meant only to put her off guard so that he might later continue his seduction.

"I could never trust a devil like you," she said bitterly.

She shook off his hand and threw open the door. As she stepped out into the icy air, his drawling voice followed her.

"Then prepare yourself, Elise. For so long as I'm here, I'll do my best to change your mind."

Chapter Three

Elise bent over the cauldron hanging above the flames in the fireplace, stirring bits of dried corn and peas into the vegetable soup she was preparing. Along with thick hunks of the bread she had baked earlier, the soup would serve as a hearty supper for the commander and the other officers. She hoped there would be leftovers; if not, she would be forced to beg an extra ration from the sergeant in charge of the storehouse so that she and Marc would not go to bed hungry. During the long winter months, scarcity of food was a fact of life at this frontier fort, since supplies had to be hauled from Montreal through hundreds of miles of wilderness.

Elise straightened, wiping her hands on her apron. Affection softened her face as her eyes strayed to her brother. Marc was perched on a stool beside the hearth, his dark head bent, his youthful brow furrowed with concentration as he read silently from a dog-eared Bible.

Suddenly he clapped the book shut. "I can't concentrate any longer," he grumbled. "Learning Latin is a waste of time when all I want is to be a soldier."

Elise stifled a smile. A typical twelve-year-old, Marc changed his ambitions at least once a week. Just the other day, his burning goal in life had been to become an explorer.

"Marc, you know Maman wanted you to have a good education. Don't you think you should respect that wish?"

The boy released a heavy sigh. *"Oui,* but can I not finish my lessons this evening? The afternoon is already half over, and I haven't had any free time at all."

His pleading expression made Elise relent. "All right—so long as you promise to complete your work by the time Father Rochon arrives tomorrow."

"Parbleu! You know I will!"

Marc sprang eagerly to his feet, tossing the book down on the stool. As he sprinted across the tiny one-room cabin to fetch his coat from the peg beside the door, Elise spotted something outlined against the back of his breeches.

"Marc Eduard d'Evereaux, what is that in your pocket?"

The boy flashed her a guilty look. "Uh, nothing," he mumbled, yanking on his coat. *"Au revoir,* Elise."

She caught his arm just as he was slipping out the door. Reaching into his pocket, she drew out a clay pipe and balanced it in her palm. "This is nothing? Marc, you haven't taken to smoking, have you?"

"Of course not! Yesterday, Little Bear showed me how to make a peace pipe, that's all."

"Well, then, now that you know how, there's no need to carry this around with you, *n'est-ce pas?"*

An expression of almost comical distress crossed her brother's face as he watched her slide the pipe in a pocket

46

of her apron. But he voiced no objection, muttering a farewell as he went outside.

For a moment, Elise stood in the doorway gazing after him with wry affection. If there were a way to get in trouble, Marc would find it. Snowflakes swirled from a pewter sky, dotting his black hair with pinpricks of white. Hunching his thin shoulders against the icy wind, he hurried across the compound, disappearing out the gate.

Undoubtedly her brother was headed in search of Little Bear, Elise guessed. Last summer, when they had moved to the fort, he had become friends with Little Bear, a boy from a nearby Indian village. Though Elise saw a certain value to the relationship—Marc had learned how to track animals and how to speak the language of the savages, both valuable skills in the wilderness—there had been a few near-disastrous escapades as well. Like the time Marc and Little Bear had "borrowed" canoes belonging to the fort, and had paddled down La Rivière au Boeuf, not returning until the following day. The commander had been so infuriated he had come close to sending her and her brother back to Montreal.

Shivering, Elise shut the door against the cold. Her homespun gray gown swished gently around her slim thighs as she crossed the room to the fireplace. Stirring the soup, she realized she had failed to remind Marc to stay clear of the party of Virginians. Not that he needed the warning, she reflected. Marc hated the English as much as she did, and for the same cause. The shared secret behind their animosity had made their relationship closer than that of most other siblings.

Elise tightened her lips. Three days had passed since her initial confrontation with Troy Fletcher, and in that time, the Englishman had not missed an opportunity to plague her. He was a most disturbing and exasperating man. He seemed to have an uncanny sixth sense regarding her whereabouts, for he appeared at the most unexpected moments.

To avoid him, she had made an effort to stay within the relative security of the cabin. Yet there were times when duty forced her to go out, such as now, when she could no longer postpone washing the commander's laundry.

To prevent the soup from burning while she was gone, Elise readjusted the hooks that held the cauldron over the fire. Then she threw a tattered cape over her shoulders and stepped outside, a large wooden bucket swinging from her hand.

Snow stung her cheeks as she trudged through the drifts toward the well in the center of the garrison. Although a wide creek surrounded the fort on three sides, fast-running even in this wintry weather, it was prudent to have a safe water source inside in case of an attack.

The walls of the small, square fort were constructed of piles driven into the ground and sharpened at the top to prevent any enemy from climbing over. Cannon were mounted on platforms at regular intervals, and soldiers could fire guns through slits cut in the logs. Each corner of the stronghold held a blockhouse, while along the sides were storerooms, a tiny chapel, the magazine, the infirmary, and the officers' quarters.

Elise felt a moment's sympathy for the men standing guard, muskets clenched in their numb fingers, blankets thrown over their shoulders to provide protection from the bitter cold. It was no wonder so many of them idled away their off-duty hours by warming their bellies with rum.

The small compound buzzed with activity. Troops drilled in one corner, their bayonets stabbing harmlessly into the snowy air. A bevy of ragged Indian women carted provisions out the main gate to several canoes that the commander had lent to the Virginians. Their packhorses had already been dispatched to Venango, a small settlement many miles downstream, where the delegation of Englishmen planned to catch up with the cavalcade.

The rest of the party must be leaving soon, Elise realized. A peculiar pang gripped her, but she was unwilling to examine its source. She peered out the opened gate, her bare fingers stiff around the cold bucket handle. She saw St. Pierre speaking to a group of Indian braves, while Major Washington stood nearby, directing the loading of the canoes. To her relief, Troy was nowhere to be seen.

A frigid gust of wind swirled her skirts as Elise scurried to the well. She attached the bucket to a long rope, lowering it until she felt it enter the water. Then she had to bend awkwardly over the low stone coping to haul out the bucket. It was heavy with liquid, and her slight muscles were straining as she slowly drew up the rope, hand over hand.

"Elise."

An unexpected touch on her shoulder caused her icy fingers to let loose of the rope. The bucket hurtled back down the well to strike the water with a muted splash.

In startled anger, Elise spun to face Troy. It didn't improve her temper to feel the involuntary cartwheeling in her stomach that occurred each time she saw him. No matter how much she loathed the man, she couldn't deny his effect on her. Swathed in his thick beaverskin coat, with snowflakes clinging to the lashes of his warm, jade eyes, he made her insides melt. She squashed a traitorous impulse to throw herself into his arms.

"*Bête!*" she hissed. "Must you always creep up behind me like a . . . a *sauvage?* Look at what you've done!"

Faced with the task of again lifting the cumbersome bucket, she felt exasperated tears prick her eyes.

"I apologize for frightening you. Allow me to make amends." Troy turned and effortlessly raised the filled bucket, setting it on top of the low stone wall that encircled the well.

"*Merci,*" Elise said sarcastically. She plucked at the rope to untie the knot, then grabbed the handle, anxious to escape him.

"Wait. I want to talk to you." His hand came down over hers, and his brow furrowed. "Good God, you're freezing!"

He covered her numb fingers with his large palms and began to rub them briskly. While his attention was occupied, she couldn't resist indulging a desire to study his ruggedly attractive features. Snowflakes melted on her upturned face. She felt hot and weak inside, but somehow found the strength to yank her hands free.

"That's enough," she said stiffly. "I'm about to return home and warm myself before the fire."

His eyes twinkled at her. "If you want the truth, I was looking for an excuse to touch you. Couldn't you at least try to humor me, sherry?"

He meant *chérie,* but even his clumsy pronunciation of the endearment made her heart skip a beat.

"I must go." Abruptly she reached for the bucket and swung it to her side, heedless of the droplets of cold water that spattered her cape. "Everyone will wonder why we're standing together when we do not speak the same language."

"Perhaps they'll think we're gazing into each other's eyes."

"*Quelle bêtise.* That is nonsense."

Troy grinned. "Is it? People won't think it odd that a man and woman are attracted to one another."

"I am *not* attracted to you," she huffed, and turned toward her cabin, lugging the heavy bucket.

He took it from her and fell into step beside her. Elise pursed her lips in frustration. She couldn't wrest the bucket from him without spilling its contents all over herself, which would only serve to draw attention to them.

She stewed in silence as they crossed the grounds to her cabin. There, she grabbed for the bucket, but Troy held it out of her reach.

"Won't you invite me inside?" he cajoled. "'Tis a cold day, and besides, I'd like to speak to you away from prying eyes."

"There is naught for us to say."

"You could tell me where you learned to speak English."

"No."

Again she lunged for the bucket, but he easily kept it from her.

"If you're too busy to talk now, then perhaps if I came by this evening—"

"No!"

"But I depart at dawn tomorrow. Tonight may be the last time we'll ever see each other."

The falling snow hissed softly all around them. Troy

51

lifted his hand to touch her cheek, the teasing gone from his face. They were standing so close their breaths mingled in tiny clouds. Elise felt a curious wrenching sensation in her heart. She hadn't thought of it before, but he was right. After all, what chance was there that fate would again bring them together?

Yet she couldn't succumb to this mad impulse to invite him in. They were enemies! The memory was as sobering as a blast of arctic air.

"*This* is the last time we will see each other, Monsieur Fletcher," she said, infusing frost into her voice. "You must not come back here, not ever."

She held out her hand, and after a moment Troy gave her the bucket. "Why do you hate me so?" he asked, eyeing her intently. "Is it that you're afraid of me?"

She whirled toward the door and fumbled with the latch. Her haste in entering the cabin caused the bucket to lurch clumsily against her thigh, soaking her skirts with icy water. She thumped the vessel to the floor and slammed the door. Troy's muffled voice growled her name once through the wood, then she heard the heavy tread of his departing footsteps.

Moving automatically, Elise stripped off her cloak, hanging it on a peg beside the door. She went to the fire to warm her icy fingers. The fact that Troy Fletcher was leaving her life was cause for rejoicing, she told herself. So why were her spirits so low?

Over the next few hours, she tried to purge the inexplicable melancholy with a vigorous bout of clothes scrubbing. But when a line of garments hung dripping across the tiny cabin, she was still plagued by a vague discontent. Intent on banishing the feeling, she turned her back on dinner preparations and left the cabin once more, heading through the lavender twilight toward the officers' quarters.

The long building was built of logs. Icicles hung from the eaves like bony fingers and smoke curled lazily from several chimneys. At the main portal, Elise hesitated. Only once before had she invaded this masculine domain, when the commander had dispatched her to summon one of the officers. The few bold females who dared enter the dwelling were camp followers and, Maman had always warned, not fit for the company of any virtuous woman.

Taking a deep breath, Elise scurried inside without pausing to stamp the snow from her boots. By some miracle, no one was in the narrow hall. She found the door she was looking for and rapped softly.

Boots thudded the wooden floor inside, then the door swung open. "Elise!" Yves Larousse exclaimed. "Does the commander wish to see me?" The French officer made a move as if to grab his greatcoat, but she stopped him with a touch of her hand.

"*Non,* Yves, I bring no message from St. Pierre." She brushed past him, shutting the door.

The lieutenant lifted his dark brows in puzzlement. "Oh? Why do you come here, then? Is something wrong?"

Elise was well aware of his brown eyes studying her as she slipped off her cloak and draped it over a bench before a small pine desk. This was the first time she had ventured into his quarters, but it didn't surprise her to see how neat the place was. Even the hearth was swept free of ashes and a fire burned merrily, warming the tiny chamber. In the few months she had known him, she had learned that Yves was a meticulous man, with an all-consuming ambition to advance in the military.

And although his features were average, he was a pleasant companion. He would be a loyal husband, Elise knew, for Yves would be as precise in the handling of his personal affairs as he was with his career. So why, then, when such a perfect image of manhood stood before her, did a pair of laughing green eyes rise to the surface of her mind?

Resolutely, Elise dismissed the trespassing vision. She, of all people, should know that any Frenchman was preferable to an Englishman.

"Naught is wrong, Yves. I only wished to see you."

"If there is no emergency, then why are you here in my quarters?" he chided. "You should know better than to behave so improperly."

"But I—"

"Unless the matter is urgent, you should have asked one of the soldiers to relay a message to me."

"Yet I'm here now and no one is the wiser," she soothed. "Can you not forget propriety for a moment? We have seen each other only at a distance these past few days, and I wanted to tell you how much I missed you."

Yves unbent a fraction. "I've missed you, too, *petite*. But I care also for your good name. It was foolhardy of you to take such a risk, *n'est-ce pas?*"

Elise felt a ripple of irritation. It struck her that Troy Fletcher would never have wasted time rebuking her; the Virginian would have already had her in his arms. She clenched her teeth at the traitorous thought and stepped toward Yves, placing a hand on the lapel of his uniform. Never before had she played the temptress, but now she was determined to prove to herself that Yves's kiss was more appealing than Troy's.

"Can you not forget your scolding?" she said, injecting a sultry note into her voice. "We are alone and naught else should matter."

She gazed up at him through the silky sweep of her lashes, curving her lips into a seductive smile. Feminine instinct alerted her to the appreciative gleam in his eyes, but just then the bark of a voice could be heard out in the hall, followed by the tramping of many boots.

Distracted, Yves shot a glance toward the door. "My troops are assembling for the evening roll call. I must go and review them."

"Oh, Yves," she pouted, "can someone else not handle it just this once?"

But he pulled away and drew on his coat. "I'm sorry, *petite,* but duty requires me outside. If you wait until all the men are gone, then you can slip away without anyone seeing you."

The door closed behind him and Elise let out a sigh that was more annoyance than disappointment. Why was it that even the prospect of kissing her could not keep Yves from his responsibilities? Though she understood his need to fulfill his obligations as second-in-command at the fort, there were times when his unceasing devotion to duty irked her. She couldn't help the nagging feeling that in his list of priorities, she came in a poor second to his career. Now, if Troy Fletcher cared for a woman. . . .

Elise stifled the half-formed thought. She snatched up her cape and sent it swirling over her shoulders, aware that she had accomplished little by this impulsive visit. If anything, her insides only roiled with confusion all the more.

Uttering a low cry of frustration, she swept out of the room.

Chapter Four

The wind howled its fury, flinging snow flurries that twisted and twirled against the night sky. The dwellings within the small garrison sat huddled like a flock of sheep caught in a bitter blast of winter. Icy air swooped down chimneys to send stinging smoke into the eyes of the fort's inhabitants. Only a few pinpricks of light, protected by sturdy log walls and scarce glass windows, dared to pierce the stygian shroud.

Snug within the warmth of her tiny cabin, Elise sat alone beside the hearth, a basket of mending lying forgotten on her lap. She frowned into the flames, unable to shake the nagging discontent that had plagued her since her encounter with Troy Fletcher that afternoon.

He would be departing come dawn, and she was glad, Elise told herself fiercely. The instant he left the fort for good, things would return to normal; she was marrying Yves, and that was all she really wanted. But for now, the mere knowledge of Troy Fletcher's presence somewhere outside made her nerve endings prickle.

Releasing an irritated sigh, she jabbed a needle and

thread into a pair of her brother's breeches, where a rip had rent the threadbare fabric. Yes, it was her animosity toward Troy that made her feel on edge tonight. A typical Englishman, he would use a woman and then abandon her without regard for the child he might have implanted in her belly. A sudden memory washed over Elise, inundating her in a pain that the passage of years had failed to dim. As if it were yesterday, she could feel the anguish of betrayal, the crushing hurt of a young heart torn asunder. . . .

Intent on her dark meditations, at first she failed to hear the rapping on the door. The sound was so soft it blended with the rattling of the shutters, until at last it penetrated her consciousness.

Rising from the stool, Elise realized the newcomer couldn't be Marc, for her brother would have entered without knocking. It must be Yves, then, wanting to apologize for his earlier abrupt departure in the officers' quarters.

But when she opened the door her welcoming smile vanished.

"You!" she cried.

Troy Fletcher filled the threshold, seeming taller and more powerful than ever in his lush beaverskin coat. The light from the fire behind her cast a golden sheen over his strong features and sparkled the snow crystals that scattered the tawny richness of his hair. His jade eyes studied her with a look of stern resolution.

"Elise, we must talk."

"Nay!"

She tried to slam the door, but his wide shoulder easily blocked the wooden panel. He clasped her around the waist and lifted her out of the way.

"Sauvage!" she hissed as he dumped her without ceremony in the middle of the cabin. "I did not invite you into my home, Monsieur Fletcher!"

With casual arrogance, he shucked his coat and draped it over a chair. Then he turned to face her, his hands astride his hips. "Call me Troy," he drawled. "Don't you think 'tis time you and I were on a first-name basis?"

"If you fail to leave at once, Monsieur Fletcher, I shall call for help."

"Take one step toward that door, and I'll detain you, using whatever means necessary."

His gaze raked her slender figure, leaving no question as to the methods he threatened. Elise drew herself up to the fullest extent of her petite height, vowing not to let him see how he had shaken her composure.

"My brother will soon be home," she bluffed. "I must warn you, he hates the English as much as I." In truth, she had no idea when Marc would return; he had wolfed down his supper, poring over his lessons as he ate, then had snuck out again while her back was turned.

Amusement quirked the corners of Troy's mouth. "Who, that pup I've seen you with? Do you think me so fainthearted as to quake with fear before a mere boy?"

How could she evict the man if he refused to go? "Stay if you must, then, m'sieur," Elise ground out in ungracious defeat. "But speak quickly, for I am anxious to see you gone."

"Call me Troy," he corrected.

When she pursed her lips in stony silence, he added, "I won't leave here until I hear you say my name."

"You have no right to tell me what to do—"

"Say it, Elise."

"Tiens!" she burst out. "Must you torment me so?"

She tossed her head back, hating the way he had maneuvered her, yet knowing she would do anything to rid herself of his disturbing presence. "Troy. There, will you now go?"

Troy was enchanted with her musical French pronunciation of his name. He only wished there was some way to erase the anger from her tone and hear her speak to him the soft words of a lover. But no hint of tender emotion could be detected in her expression. Her arms were clasped across the fullness of her breasts and defiance sparkled in her dark brandy eyes.

Still, her beauty was a feast to his starving senses. The firelight painted her complexion with a rosy glow and made her copper hair shine. God, how he ached to feel her naked and yielding beneath him! There was something rare and special about her, something that set her apart from all other women, something that made him wish she belonged to him alone. For the first time in his life, he felt the stirrings of a need for more than a casual night's toss.

But bitter reality returned to haunt him. Elise hated him, and until he knew why, he would have to hide his hunger. Troy clenched his fists in frustration. There was so little time—why was he bothering, anyway, when after tonight he would never again see her? Yet he couldn't help this compulsion to break through her armor. Though the effort might be futile, he felt a need to at least try to goad her into revealing the root of her resentment toward him.

He paced the length of the tiny cabin, girding himself for the battle. "I did say I'd go if you spoke my first name, but I did not say *when*. I'd like to talk to you, Elise."

"I do not care to listen."

Despite her brave words, Elise felt a prickle of apprehension. There *was* one topic he could use to capture her undivided attention—her knowledge of the English language. Would he again threaten to betray her to St. Pierre? She watched warily as Troy settled himself onto a stool beside the fire, stretching out his long legs and crossing his polished black boots at the ankles. There was something in his gaze that set her nerves to quivering.

But the soft words he uttered caught her by surprise: "Come with me."

Nonplussed, she tilted her head. "I do not understand."

"'Tis simple," he said with a shrug. "I leave tomorrow morning for my plantation on the James River. I want you to accompany me there."

For an instant she gaped at him in disbelief as an unexpected twinge of hurt rippled through her. So she had been right all along; he viewed her as no better than a whore. Then a tide of outrage drowned that brief moment of pain.

"*Cochon!*" she spat. "Never will I be mistress to an Englishman. If that is all you have to say to me, then leave my home."

Troy paid no heed to the finger she jabbed at the door. Clasping his hands behind his head, he settled into a more comfortable position on the stool. "You needn't decide so hastily, my sweet. Feel free to take the entire evening to contemplate my offer."

Elise trembled with fury. "Your offer sickens me. Indeed, the more I think on it, the more am I in danger of losing my dinner."

"Hmmm . . . to the best of my knowledge never have I

made a woman ill by the mere prospect of my touch." He stroked his jaw reflectively, humor dancing in his emerald eyes. "And suppose I were to say you are mistaken, that I propose you be not mistress, but wife?"

"I would sooner burn in hell for all eternity than spend my life shackled to an Englishman."

"Englishman, Englishman," he mocked. "Over and over you hold my heritage against me." He surged to his feet and prowled toward her. "And why, I wonder? What crime did an Englishman commit to rouse such malice in your heart?"

Elise presented her back to him, as if he might glimpse her past by gazing into her eyes. A lump lodged painfully in her throat as old memories burst forth to assault the wall protecting her emotions. Biting her lip, she banished the unwelcome images, but the inner battle left her defenseless, too weak to move away when she heard Troy approach from behind.

"Tell me what happened," he commanded softly.

"I don't know what you mean." Her voice sounded shaky and unconvincing even to her own ears.

"I want to know why you've hated me from the moment of our first meeting."

She attempted a shrug. "You are English and I, French. What more reason need there be?"

"'Tis more than mere politics."

"You are mistaken."

"Nay, I'm not," he pressed. "Tell me, Elise. Tell me what's bothering you."

"I don't know what it is you want me to say!" she choked out.

She buried her face in her palms, fighting an inexplicable rush of tears. *Sacré Dieu,* why did he have to

61

badger her so?

As if he understood her turmoil, his hands came down gently on her shoulders and began to massage the tension from her muscles. Elise felt a wave of vulnerability wash through her. Though logic warned her his touch was dangerous, she could not find the energy to move away. The heat of his body began to assuage the distress that chilled her spirit. She wanted to turn and hide her face against his chest, to let his strong arms keep her safe. It would be a relief to have someone else share the burden of shame that had shadowed her life for so long.

She felt his warm breath at her nape, then his mouth met her skin. A shiver whispered down her spine, and she closed her eyes as flickers of feeling stirred within her. His lips tasted the tender column of her neck; the slickness of his tongue left a trail of moist heat over her flesh. Light as a moth's wing, his fingers toyed with the baby-fine wisps of curls that had escaped the prim coil of copper at the back of her head. His touch stole her strength and diluted her reason. She uttered no protest when his arms encircled her waist, molding her spine to the firmness of his chest.

"I'm not your enemy, Elise," he murmured. "You mustn't judge me harshly because some other Englishman jilted you."

She stiffened. He thought her hatred for the English stemmed from some childish love affair!

Troy went on, "You may have been hurt once, but that doesn't mean it has to happen again. I know how angry and hurt you must feel, but you can trust me. I won't hurt you."

Angrily she jerked out of his arms and swung to face him. "You couldn't begin to understand my feelings," she said bitterly. "What do you know of my past? I've told you naught, yet you presume to give me advice."

"I seek only to help you in whatever way I can."

"Help!" she scorned. Long ago she had learned to depend on no man. Now this Englishman thought he could undermine her defenses with a few sweet words. He was a liar, just as her father had been. "How could you possibly help me? There is naught I want of you, Monsieur Fletcher, do you understand me? Naught but to see you leave here at once."

Troy gritted his teeth, wrestling with a strong urge to do exactly as she said. By the devil, she couldn't make her wishes any plainer! And yet . . . in those brief moments when he had held her against him, she had seemed so vulnerable. He couldn't slink out in defeat just because his masculine pride had suffered a blow.

Behind all that defensive anger, he sensed a sweetness that fascinated him. God, she was so soft and spirited! Somehow he had to get past the bees to the honey within. . . .

"Nay, I won't leave just yet," he murmured. "Not without first getting what I came here for this night."

"What do you mean?"

"I think you know."

The intensity in his eyes unraveled a knot of desire inside Elise. He took a step toward her, and she found herself retreating until the stones of the hearth were behind her, warm and smooth beneath her fingertips. Her heart pounded painfully in her chest. Paralyzed, she watched Troy come nearer until he stood right in front of her. It was mortifying to realize that in the deepest core of her, she wanted to surrender. . . .

"If you dare touch me, I'll scream."

"Will you?"

He was so close that she could feel the heat radiating from his body. His hand lifted to skim the delicate length of her jaw. The deep jade of his eyes held her mesmerized. She wanted to melt against him, to feel the hardness of his chest pressing into her breasts, to taste his lips one more time. Was this what Maman had warned her against so long ago, when she'd said to follow your head, not your heart?

Memories throbbed inside Elise like an ancient, aching wound and she jerked her face aside.

"Get away from me! You'll only use me just as Papa—" Her throat tightened, choking off her voice.

"Your father?" Troy's fingers seized her chin and brought her eyes back to his. "What has he to do with your hatred for the English?"

"Nothing . . . everything!"

Her insides seethed with emotion. No longer could she deny the memories that had plagued her these past few days. She was beyond restraint, past caring that no one but Marc knew her shameful secret. She craved release from the pain that racked her, a pain that had been buried deep inside her ever since her father had left for good, a pain that Troy Fletcher had resurrected with his prodding and prying.

Words poured from her lips like a dam overflowing. "Let me tell you why I despise the English—because my father was an Englishman!" Elise wrenched herself from Troy and walked away to clench her fingers around the back of a chair. "He used my mother and then cast her aside when he tired of her. It didn't matter to him that he left her with a seven-year-old daughter and another baby in her belly. It didn't matter that she would have to struggle to earn the money to put food into the mouths of his children. Nay, my father didn't care. He deserted his family when we became a burden to him.''

Troy's heart twisted. He could picture the helpless little girl she had been, could imagine the torment she must have suffered from her father's cruel betrayal. He wanted to pull her into his arms and comfort her, yet he was uncertain as to how she would react to his sympathy.

''How is it, then, that you bear a French surname?'' he asked gently. ''Did your mother remarry?''

''Nay, d'Evereaux was her maiden name. After my father left, she took it back, and I don't blame her. I didn't want any reminders of him, either.''

An inner agitation belied the coldness of her words. Elise hugged her arms over her breasts, unable to stop remembering that awful moment when she had realized her father hadn't even loved her enough to say good-bye.

Her righteous anger was submerged beneath the flood of a stronger, more perilous emotion. The stress of subduing the tears that pricked her eyes made her body rigid. She would not weep, she could not! *Sacré Dieu*, she was no longer a lonely, unhappy child who yearned desperately for the affection of a delinquent father.

Yet the moisture in her eyes seemed to have a mind of its own, and there was nothing she could do to halt the flow of hot tears down her cheeks. Pride made her hide the weakness by turning away to the wall.

Troy's arms enfolded her, swinging her back around to face him. Unable to help herself, she clung to him like a drowning person to driftwood, the power of her need for comfort blinding her to the fact that he was her enemy. His embrace held the warmth and solace she craved, and that was all that mattered.

Gradually the heart-rending sobs abated. Elise was conscious of a sense of cathartic relief, coupled with a growing mortification. Troy must have relished seeing her behave like a typical weak female!

But when she lifted her head, there was no mockery or amusement in his expression, only a concern that touched her heart. In an effort to regain her dignity, she swallowed the lump in her throat and wiped the tears away.

"Now do you see why I've told no one I speak English?" she asked bitterly. "'Twould raise questions about my past, questions I'd be ashamed to answer. How could I bear to tell anyone that I, a Frenchwoman, am half-English? Or that my own father didn't want me?"

"There's no need to feel shame," Troy murmured. "None of us can be held responsible for the circumstances of our birth, or for the actions of people around us. 'Tis what we make of ourselves that matters most." He ran a finger over her wet cheek. "There's no disgrace to your having English blood. You mustn't condemn all of my countrymen because of the misdeeds of one."

Gazing into his eyes, Elise could almost believe him to be speaking the truth. But the pain and hatred still festered within her, locked safely away within a secret niche of her heart. Mistrust of the English was too deeply ingrained in her to be forgotten so easily. So why, then, did she still want his arms around her?

Emptied of emotion, she stood weaponless against his masculine appeal. She had shown more of her inner self to Troy than she had to any other person in her life, and the effort had left her drained.

When she felt the slight pressure of his hand at the back of her head, Elise let him guide her face into the

66

crook of his neck. Her eyelids fluttered shut as she breathed in the faint essence of sandalwood and sweat that scented his skin. Warmth flooded her. She felt his lips touch her brow and his hand move along her spine, molding her tightly to his hard length. Desire began to spin its silken web around her senses as reason gave way to instinct.

Her fingers lifted to his chest and tracked lightly over the fine wool of his shirt, slipping inside his open collar to touch his bare skin. He inhaled sharply. When he lifted her chin, she saw passion blazing in his dark jade eyes. She was courting danger, a corner of her mind whispered. Yet she was too spellbound to end the seduction.

"Elise . . ."

The rasp of her name trailed over her nerves like a caress. His hands combed into her hair, loosening the chignon at the back of her head. Several of the wooden pins that held her curls in place fell to the floor with a tiny clatter.

The warmth of his breath bathed her skin an instant before their mouths merged. Her quivering lips parted to the invasion of his tongue, and his kiss was thorough and relentless, setting her veins on fire. Surrendering to the wild urges pulsing inside her, she pressed herself against him, conscious of the height and breadth of him, so commanding beside her petiteness.

A boundless yearning welled up in her. It seemed only natural for his hand to stray to her breast, his thumb stroking the nipple through the fabric of her gown. His lips left hers to lay moist kisses over the delicate bone structure of her face. She arched her neck as his mouth moved to the madly beating pulse in her throat.

Her hand sought his cheek, feeling the slight abrasion

of stubble. He turned his head and took her fingertip into his mouth, gently nipping and suckling it, then nuzzling her sensitive palm. Elise felt a rush of fluid warmth in her loins. Never before had she known the attraction between a man and a woman could be so overwhelming, so irresistible.

His mouth found hers again, and she felt his hands at her nape as he unfastened a hook at the back of her gown. Deep within the recesses of her mind, she knew the time to stop this seduction was long overdue. Yet the anticipation of his touch upon her bare flesh was a surging excitement inside her.

She was torn between sanity and pleasure, rationality and temptation. It made her draw back in confusion, clasping her hands around the hard muscles of his forearms.

"Troy, please. . . ."

She twisted against him and his hands tightened involuntarily around her shoulders. At the same instant she saw the comprehension of her resistance cross his face, the door to the cabin swung open.

A rush of frigid air struck Elise as Marc entered the room. He quietly closed the door, then brushed back the snow-covered hood of his coat. He turned, saw them, and stopped dead in his tracks.

In that moment of paralyzed shock, Elise felt her heart plummet. She was all too aware that Troy's arms were around her, that several hooks at the back of her gown were undone, that her hair was tumbled around her flushed face. How incriminating the scene must look to her brother!

Marc sprang toward them. "*Bâtard anglais!* Take your filthy hands off my sister!"

He launched himself at Troy with all the fledgling courage of a pup facing a full-grown wolf. He elbowed in front of Elise so that she went stumbling backward against a table. Pummeling the elder man's chest with his fists, he spouted fierce curses in French. Troy easily caught Marc by the shoulders and held him off so that he was of no more consequence than a buzzing mosquito.

"What in holy hell's his problem?" Troy snapped to Elise.

It was only then that she realized Marc spoke no English, and Troy, no French. Nervously she ran a hand over her tousled hair. "He thought . . . you were attacking me."

"Well, for God's sake, will you tell him he's wrong?"

Getting a grip on herself, she refastened her gown, addressing her brother in their native tongue: "Marc, calm yourself! I will not tolerate fighting in this house."

"He has no right to touch you, the *diable!*" Jerking ineffectively against Troy's iron grip, the boy screamed in French, "I'll kill him!"

"That's enough!" Elise ordered sharply. "Your defense of me is admirable, but unnecessary, do you understand?"

"But he was trying to rape you!"

"I prefer to handle this myself, Marc! Now, I will tell Monsieur Fletcher to let you go, but only if you promise to behave yourself."

"*Merde!*" Marc spat furiously. But after a moment he gave a sullen nod of agreement, though he flashed his captor a look of intense hatred.

"You may release him now," Elise informed Troy in English. "I have his word he'll control his temper."

"By the devil, he'd better, or he'll regret it."

Troy relaxed his hold on the youth, and Marc yanked his shoulders free and stepped back. Both males eyed each other warily. Elise swallowed a half-hysterical impulse to laugh aloud. They reminded her of two dogs, each sizing up the opponent to weigh the outcome of a potential fight.

"You cannot blame Marc for wanting to protect his own sister," she told Troy. "He knew only what he saw when he walked inside."

"Then tell him what really happened. Tell him you weren't unwilling."

At a loss for words, Elise stared at him. Confusion and humiliation warred within her as she faced the bitter truth: for a few impetuous moments, she had wanted this Englishman with a passion she had never before felt. Who could fault him for taking what she had so freely offered?

Then a rush of outrage swept her mortification. Why was she feeling so guilty? Troy had pressed his attentions upon her when she was at her most vulnerable. Only a cad would resort to such base trickery; he and her father were one of a kind.

"You took advantage of me," she retorted coldly. "My brother has every right to be angry at you."

"You mean you're going to let him think I was raping you? You know that isn't the truth, so admit it to him!"

"I will do no such thing."

"You little liar."

Frowning darkly, Troy took a step forward. Elise saw that Marc was observing the elder man with hostile eyes, his fingers balled into fists. The boy might not comprehend their words, but he did their actions. She had to do something quickly to defuse the situation

70

before it exploded into violence again.

Wheeling around, she snatched up Troy's coat from a chair and threw it at him. "'Tis best you leave now." She marched to the door and lifted the bar.

Troy donned the fur as he strode across the room after her. Frustration ate away at his insides, a feeling that came from more than the mere denial of any physical desire. Dammit, why had she thrown up those defenses again? Couldn't she see that he was not to blame for her father's mistakes?

He put his hand over hers before she could swing open the door. Their eyes met, cold copper clashing with warm jade. Before she could hurl any more scathing words at him, he spoke quickly, persuasively.

"Come with me tomorrow, please." Troy wasn't certain he'd meant the invitation earlier, but he did now. She had awakened a need in him that permeated every fiber of his being.

"No," she said haughtily.

Bleakness ran through him, though her response was what he'd expected. After tonight, they would never see each other again.

He felt tricked by a fate that had handed him his heart's fantasy, then had cruelly snatched it away. The facts could not be changed. He was obliged to leave at dawn with Major Washington's party; there was no excuse imaginable for an Englishman to remain here at this French fort. For an instant Troy felt a primitive impulse to take her with him forcibly. But reason told him it was insane even to think of carrying her off kicking and screaming, especially with that watchdog of a brother hovering nearby.

Staring down at her lovely features, he racked his

brain for a last-ditch scheme to get her to change her mind. There was nothing. Even the words of parting that sprang to his lips seemed trite, inadequate. In the end, he could only utter hoarsely, "Good-bye, Elise."

Troy touched her cheek, imprinting her image in his memory for the last time. Something flickered in her eyes, but it vanished into that icy stare of hers.

Turning sharply, he left the cabin. As the snowy darkness swallowed him, the cold finality of the door slamming behind him echoed in his head.

Chapter Five

A few fat snowflakes floated from the afternoon sky as Elise hurried across the grounds inside the fort, preoccupied by a nagging apprehension. Marc was missing. The last time she'd seen her brother had been at Mass in the chapel early that morning. Of course, it was nothing unusual for the boy to disappear all day, but never before had he been so bold as to skip his lesson with Father Rochon, the missionary who made the fifteen-mile trip from Fort Presque Isle once a week.

Elise had been angry at first, and it was only after she had made an excuse to the priest that worry had set in. The uneasy feeling had grown stronger, until at last she had grabbed her cloak and gone in search of her brother. The discreet inquiries she'd made at the stables and the smithy had been fruitless, for it appeared no one had seen Marc that day.

Her skirts dragged in the drifts of snow as she headed toward the main gate in hopes the guard on duty might have spotted Marc leaving the fort. She was almost there when a voice hailed her.

73

"Elise, wait!"

She turned to see Yves approaching from the direction of the officer's quarters, his boots crunching across the freshly fallen snow. Irritation nipped at her, but she subdued the feeling instantly. She was glad to see Yves! Her appalling weakness for Troy Fletcher was best forgotten; he had left with the other Englishmen early that morning and she would never encounter him again. The hollow sensation inside her would soon fade.

"Did you not see me waving to you?" asked Yves.

"*Pardonnez-moi*. My mind must have been wandering."

"No matter," he said with a shrug. "*Petite*, I wondered if I might call on you this evening. When you came to my room yesterday, we had so little time to talk, and then last night I was obliged to help the commander entertain our English visitors."

Had that been only yesterday? To Elise it seemed as if eons had passed since then. A sharp ache sliced through her heart as she remembered the longing in Troy's eyes just before he'd left her cabin. It had taken all of her willpower to ignore the tenderness of that last touch of his hand on her cheek.

"Elise?"

The sound of her name brought her back to the present. She blinked, surveying the man in front of her. His conventional features were a familiar sight to her, yet today she felt as if she were viewing him through new eyes. His gloved hands rested formally at the sides of the greatcoat he wore over his military uniform. The wind ruffling his brown hair, he stood ramrod-stiff despite the cold weather that made other men hunch their shoulders to help contain every bit of body warmth. A proper distance separated them, and she realized bitterly that he would never dream of taking her into his arms here, in full view of his soldiers. But Troy would have no such scruples. . . .

"Elise?" Yves repeated, sharper this time. "Is something wrong?"

"Nay, of course not." She almost mentioned Marc's absence, then thought better of it. Yves would feel duty-bound to inform St. Pierre, and that might only get her brother into trouble. "I-I'm just a little distracted today, that's all."

"Have I your permission to stop by tonight?"

"Of course, you—"

"Sir?" It was one of the junior officers, a husky man by the name of Douville. "Pardon me for interrupting, mam'selle," he said to Elise before returning his attention to Yves. "Sir, one of the canoes is missing. I noticed it just a few moments ago."

"You're certain?"

Douville nodded. "I made the count myself, twice. There were two lent to the English party, but we're short another also."

"Hmm . . . it must have been stolen. If it happens again, we may have to post a guard. For now, though, let's find out if there were any Indians seen around the area today."

Yves turned to Elise and gave her a formal bow. "*A bientôt, mademoiselle.*" The two men began walking out the gate toward the barracks.

Elise stared after them, stupefied by the thoughts racing through her head. A canoe was gone. So was Marc. Putting those two facts together could result in only one conclusion.

Her brother must have stolen a canoe and gone after Troy.

She tried to tell herself that she was mistaken, that even Marc would never be so reckless. But she couldn't stop remembering the words he had screamed last night, after he'd caught her struggling in Troy's arms: *"I'll kill him!"*

Elise swallowed hard as a sick sensation rose in her throat. It was all her fault. She should have admitted to Marc that she had been a willing participant in the scene he'd witnessed. But no, she'd been too buried in pride to act reasonably.

Now everything clicked into place. She recalled Marc's brooding behavior late last night, his distracted replies to her questions, the lack of his usual groaning and complaining when she'd told him to go to bed. At the time she had been too absorbed in her own meditations to pay much attention to the difference in his behavior.

But then why hadn't he simply snuck out in the middle of the night to attack Troy before the delegation had left the fort? She could only conclude that because Marc knew the commander had ordered the visitors be treated with respect, he had reasoned he was less likely to get into trouble with St. Pierre if he waited to act until the Virginians were far out in the wilderness.

Sacré Dieu! The commander would be blazingly angry when—if—he discovered Marc's absence, not to mention the reason behind it. She must do something before it was too late.

The knowledge spurred Elise to action. A desperate plan forming in her mind, she hurried out the main gate of the fort in a direction opposite to the one taken by Yves and Douville. Her boots sank into the deep drifts as

76

she bypassed the rows of canoes, half-buried by the snow, which the French forces would employ come spring to make their way downstream in an effort to gain control of the frontier.

The air was alive with the sound of water rushing over rocks. Afternoon was beginning to ease into evening; it was *l'heure bleue*, the blue hour, a time when daylight deepened to lilac, when harsh edges became soft silhouettes.

But Elise was too engrossed in worry to pay much heed to the beauty around her. Plunging into the forest, she hastened onward, relying on instinct to find the snow-covered trail that led through the trees. She felt a shudder of fear as she pictured her brother stalking the party of Virginians, waiting until they were asleep, then sliding a knife between Troy's ribs. Marc might be imprisoned or even executed in retaliation!

And what about Troy? Even now he might lie injured—or dead. Elise thrust aside the thought. Of course, she cared only for her brother's welfare, not for that bothersome Englishman.

She quickened her pace, lifting her skirts above the snow that concealed the path. Her eyes strained to see ahead in the growing darkness. Though frigid air stung her lungs and an ache stabbed her side, she refused to slow down. At long last, as she reached the top of a low rise, she spotted her destination. It was an Indian village, home to a small band of Erie.

Elise headed down the hill to the group of longhouses huddled in the clearing. Smoke curled up from holes in the roofs, evidence of the cookfires within. Each dwelling housed several families of one clan. She had been here only once before, looking for her brother last summer, but if her memory served her right, it was in the bark-covered hut to the left that Little Bear lived with his family.

As she drew nearer, several dogs raced up, growling and yapping. The cacophony served to alert the Indians to her presence, and a number of them emerged from the longhouses to silently observe her approach. Though she knew this particular tribe was neutral in the hostilities between the English and the French, she couldn't help a tiny ripple of apprehension. The Erie were a part of the vast Iroquoian nation, a group renowned for their torture of prisoners.

Ignoring the curious glances directed at her, Elise took a deep breath and marched toward Little Bear's hut. The hide flap over the entrance opened. A tall brave in a fringed buckskin shirt and leggings came out and stopped a few paces in front of her. Frowning at her, he uttered something in his own language.

"*Je ne comprends pas,*" Elise said, lifting her shoulders to express her lack of understanding. After a moment's hesitation, she added, "I've come to speak to Little Bear. Is he here?"

The man made a reply, but his foreign dialect told her nothing. She was wondering what to do when the boy stuck his head out the door to see who the visitor was.

Little Bear hurried toward her, his face alight with interest. Younger than Marc, he stood a few inches shy of Elise's petite height. The boy subdued his excitement when he caught sight of the Indian brave's stern look, but there was still a thread of enthusiasm in his voice as he spoke in broken French.

"*Mam'selle* come for brother? Marc not here."

If she'd harbored any faint hope that she was

mistaken, that information had destroyed it. "Did he tell you where he was going?"

"No, mam'selle." He vigorously shook his head. "Little Bear not see Marc this day. Little Bear wait at meeting place, but Marc not come."

"I think I know where he went. Last night Marc swore he'd kill one of the English visitors. After they left this morning, he stole a canoe from the fort and went after them. That's why I had to see you, Little Bear. I need your help in getting him back."

"*Oui*, Little Bear help sister of friend."

The elder Indian broke in, saying something in his strange tongue as he gestured a brown hand at the longhouse.

"Uncle say mam'selle come inside," Little Bear interpreted. "Sister of Marc come out of cold and eat."

For the first time, Elise noticed the mouth-watering scent of roasting venison that drifted through the air. But she stifled the tempting thought of warming herself before a fire.

"Tell your uncle his offer is most kind, but that I must return to the fort to prepare the evening meal. And please, tell him only that I've come here looking for Marc. I don't want anyone else to know I plan to go after him."

After the boy had translated her message, she went on rapidly, "Little Bear, I must find Marc before he ends up in terrible trouble. That's where you can help. I dare not risk being seen leaving the fort with everything I'll need for the trip. Could you lend me provisions and a pair of snowshoes?"

He bobbed his braided head up and down, and his dark eyes danced with eagerness. "*Oui, mam'selle*. Little Bear

79

go with sister of Marc. Go tonight."

"Nay, you're to stay here," Elise corrected. "There's enough for me to worry about without involving you, too." Remembering that Yves planned to see her later, she suppressed a groan of frustration. "And I fear 'tis necessary for me to wait until dawn to leave."

The boy regarded her intently. *"Oui, mam'selle,* it will be done."

Marc crouched beside his canoe, his eyes straining through the inky night at the Englishmen gathered around the distant campfire. A raw wind flung stinging shards of snow at the boy's face and threatened to tear off the woolen cap pulled down over his ears. He huddled into his buckskin jacket in an effort to conserve warmth. At least, he reflected with a shiver, there was little chance of being caught; the darkness combined with the splashing of the creek had masked his movements when he'd dragged the canoe up the rocky bank.

Peering through the thickly falling snowflakes, Marc tried to decide what to do. Thus far, he had focused all of his energy on catching up to the Virginians, and his mind had formed only a vague notion of what would happen when he found them. To keep from being captured, he knew it was necessary to confront Troy Fletcher alone. Yet how was he to accomplish that, with so many other men around?

Suddenly, Marc was filled with misgivings. What reckless impulse had made him think he could murder a man and get away with it? Inside his head, the commandment echoed: *Thou shalt not kill.* Did he have the right to take another man's life? Perhaps he should simply give up and go home. After all, Fletcher hadn't harmed Elise; the rape had been interrupted before any real damage had been done.

The momentary weakening vanished as Marc relived the memory of seeing his sister struggling in Fletcher's arms. *Merde!* No Englishman could take such liberties and get away with it. Though Marc had no firsthand knowledge of what transpired in the bedroom, he'd heard the soldiers boast of their experiences with whores often enough to realize the necessity of protecting his sister.

What had happened to their mother would not happen to Elise, Marc vowed fiercely. He could still recall the sick horror he'd felt when he'd discovered the truth about his father. It had been a rainy Saturday several summers ago in Montreal. Stealing a few hours of free time, he had curled up in a windowseat with a copy of *La Chanson de Roland*, and fantasized that his own sire had been a brave, handsome knight. Hoping to have the notion confirmed, he had tossed aside the leather-bound volume and gone in search of his mother.

She was in the kitchen, fixing dinner with Elise's help. In the past, Brigitte had sidestepped his questions, hinting only that his father was dead. Today he was determined to learn more. But no matter how much he pestered, his mother refused to say a word. Then, to his astonishment, her stony expression crumbled, and she darted out of the room in tears.

That had been when Elise had gently apprised him of the truth. His father was no knight in shining armor, but a scoundrel and a blackguard who had used his wife and then deserted her and their children. The crushing news had destroyed Marc's dreams. He would sooner have discovered he was a bastard than the son of a hated Englishman!

Marc shifted position as an icy blast of wind sent shivers over his thin body. Yes, Fletcher had sadly miscalculated to think he could force himself on Elise and escape without punishment. He would pay for that mistake with his life.

Grasping the rough bark of the canoe, the boy rose to his feet, his muscles stiff and aching. The hard day's journey had taken its toll on him. But he refused to let any physical discomfort distract him from his purpose.

Slowly he crept toward the campfire, his knee-high moccasins moving silently on the snow in the way Little Bear had taught him. When he was close enough to identify the men, he crouched down behind the shield of a tree trunk. Yes, there was Fletcher, a beaverskin coat covering his large frame, his tawny hair hidden by a fur hat. The Englishmen were sitting around the blaze finishing their supper. Somehow, Marc mused, he had to get Fletcher apart from the others. But how?

Briefly he noted that the Indians who had traveled with the English party were nowhere in sight. The savages must have stopped for the night farther downstream. At least that bit of luck was encouraging.

Marc's stomach grumbled as the scent of cooking food reached him. To distract himself, he studied the encampment, situated in a clearing beside the river. At the edge of the forest, the Virginians had erected a large tent to protect themselves from the elements. Marc wondered if he dared venture inside the canvas structure after everyone was asleep. The risky proposition made him swallow hard. If one of the other men were to awaken and catch him. . . .

Time dragged by, minute by slow minute. Snow

sprinkled silently to the ground. The cold seeped into Marc's bones until he feared he would be frozen in position like a marble statue. And still, the Englishmen dallied around the fire, only a few snatches of their conversation audible over the sound of the creek.

At long last, one man yawned and stretched before heading into the tent. A few moments later, three of the others did likewise. Only Fletcher now remained.

Heart pounding, Marc watched his enemy stroll away from the circle of light cast by the dying flames. Fletcher headed down to the bank, where the Englishmen's canoe was berthed for the night. At the edge of the water he stopped, gazing upstream in the direction of Fort LeBoeuf, some fifteen miles to the north.

Marc could hardly believe his good fortune. This was the chance he had been awaiting! Quietly he inched his way around behind the tall man.

He slipped off his gloves and stuffed them into a pocket. Then he drew the knife from the scabbard hanging from his belt. His palm was cold and sweaty around the wooden handle as he continued to creep forward, the rushing water masking any sound of his approach.

In the underbrush barely a yard away he paused, doubts crowding his mind once more. Could he really kill a man? Was it right to seek revenge by committing another wrong?

Or did he hesitate simply because he was afraid?

From close up, Fletcher looked more dangerous than a bear, his powerful body capable of crushing anyone who dared oppose him. Given the chance, he would have forced Elise to assuage his lust.

A surge of hot anger blinded Marc to caution. The

knife poised for striking, he lunged forward with a low cry.

But Fletcher whirled around. The boy caught a quick glimpse of the Englishman's look of startled disbelief as the blade flashed through the air, plunging toward the beaverskin coat that covered his chest.

Only a faint lifting of the darkness hinted at dawn as Elise stole out of her cabin the following morning. A careful scrutiny of the gloomy grounds assured her the place was deserted at this early hour; it appeared even the guard on duty had slunk off to some corner to warm his belly with rum. Murmuring a prayer that her luck would hold, she pulled the hood of her cloak tight around her head and started across the compound.

An icy wind tore at her as she hurried through the snow. She found a massive bar across the gate, but thankfully, there was a wicket to provide passage in and out of the fort. Elise glanced around cautiously, her heart thudding as she slipped out through the small door. At any moment, she half expected to hear a guard cry out in French, *Halt, who goes there?*

But the only sound was the ever-present splashing of French Creek, which curved around three sides of the slumbering garrison. Despite the frigid temperature, the swift-running water remained unfrozen, because of the constant snowfall that fed the creek. Bolstering her courage, Elise began to make her way toward the designated spot where Little Bear had promised to leave the supplies.

She kept close to the winding embankment to keep from getting lost. The forest was dark beyond the clearing near the fort, and the snow was slick and treacherous beneath her feet, hiding roots and other obstacles from her view. More than once she had to clutch at a tree trunk to keep from falling. She was grateful for the ease of movement afforded by an old pair of Marc's buckskin breeches, which she had worn beneath her cloak in lieu of dragging skirts.

The bitter cold penetrated her clothing, but Elise resisted the urge to return to her warm bed. She had to find Marc and stop him. If she reached him in time, there was a slim chance that something might be salvaged from this fiasco.

What she feared most was that the commander would discover her brother's absence. She had persuaded an Indian woman, the wife of one of the soldiers, to cook for St. Pierre while she was gone, hoping he would attribute her brief disappearance to illness. And the previous night, when Yves had come by to visit, she'd been in an agony of worry that the French officer would become suspicious of Marc's whereabouts. But he had accepted her explanation that the boy was out with Little Bear. For once, she hadn't even minded Yves's scolding words about keeping her brother under stricter control.

The dark outline of a boulder alongside the bank loomed ahead. With a sense of relief, Elise moved toward it, straining her eyes to find the pack of provisions Little Bear had left last night. But she could see only snow beside the massive rock. Circling the stone sentinel, she steadied herself by placing a gloved hand on its cold surface.

She froze as a black form rose from a murky crevice. Then her muscles relaxed as she identified the stranger.

"Little Bear!" she exclaimed. "You frightened me! I

85

didn't expect you to still be here."

"Little Bear bring food—and canoe." The Indian boy waved a hand at a long, dark shape lying on the embankment a short distance away.

"But I didn't ask you for . . ." Elise paused, then said sternly, "Did you steal that canoe from the fort?"

He shrugged, and in the faint light from the eastern sky, she could just barely discern the proud grin on his face.

She sighed. "I appreciate your effort, but you're going to have to take it back before the soldiers wake up and discover it gone."

"But canoe help mam'selle find Marc fast!" he protested.

"*Oui*, but I know naught of handling a canoe. I'm better off walking as I'd planned."

"Little Bear paddle."

"Oh, no," she said, shaking her head for emphasis. "I'm going by myself, and that's final."

"Little Bear take canoe to find Marc while mam'selle walk," the Indian boy said stubbornly.

Exasperated, Elise studied his young, determined face in the dim light of dawn. Perhaps he was right—the canoe *would* be a swifter way to track Marc. On foot, chances were she'd never locate her brother in time to prevent him from attacking Troy. And if Little Bear intended to go after Marc regardless of what she did, then it would serve no purpose to refuse the boy's help. Besides, she admitted silently, it was unnerving to think of venturing alone into the vast stretch of wilderness where dangerous animals and hostile Indians abounded.

"All right," Elise said reluctantly. "We'll go together."

Quickly they loaded the provisions into the canoe. Within minutes, the bark-covered craft was afloat in French Creek, the boy sitting in the front and Elise at the rear.

Mimicking Little Bear's smooth strokes, she soon acquired the knack of paddling the canoe through the treacherous rapids. Runoff from recent snowfalls had caused the creek to rise high up the embankment. The music of gurgling water filled the air as they maneuvered the small boat along a heart-stopping course of twists and turns. More than once, the canoe came close to being crushed by the rocks embedded in the river bottom.

The current was strong, swiftly propelling them downstream, where, many miles ahead, the water flowed into the Allegheny, and from there into La Belle Rivière, the mighty Ohio. It was by building forts along this vital network of waterways that the French hoped to gain control of the frontier.

Elise's breath condensed in the frigid air and her cheeks felt an occasional icy spray of water, yet the strenuous exertion of paddling kept her warm. As the morning sky brightened to pearl-gray, she caught sight of a deer watching from the tangled underbrush onshore. A portion of her tension lifted. At least she was doing *something* to rescue Marc from his impetuous act. She refused to let herself think of what would happen if she failed.

As morning became afternoon they made a brief stop to eat. Elise found the meal reviving, though her weary muscles protested when she again picked up the paddle. All that kept her going was the knowledge that she had to reach her brother.

A light snow began to fall, the flakes dissolving on

contact with the swift-flowing creek. Elise threw a worried glance up at the pewter sky, breathing a fervent prayer that the storm wouldn't worsen. A blizzard would slow their progress, perhaps even force them to halt.

It was midafternoon when they spotted the first sign that others had passed this way. Little Bear shouted to Elise over the rush of the water, pointing his paddle to an abandoned encampment in a clearing onshore. As the canoe sped past, she caught a quick glimpse of the site. The trampled area around the ashes of a fire was partially covered by fresh snow.

Her spirits rose briefly, then plummeted. They may have reached the place the Englishmen had camped the previous night, but there was still a full day's worth of catching up ahead. With only a few hours of light left, what chance was there of finding Marc before nightfall?

It took an effort to summon enough energy and willpower to go on. Dipping deeply into the reserves of her strength, Elise valiantly continued paddling, despite the mental and physical fatigue that threatened to swamp her.

Twilight soon spread a veil of misty shadows over the surrounding forest. Visibility was further impaired by the lightly falling snow. It became more and more difficult to avoid the perilous rocks that could dash their canoe into a thousand pieces. Elise hoped Little Bear would have the sense to stop when the darkness became so thick it would be suicidal to press onward.

Still, she couldn't help feeling depressed when at last he motioned to the shore. Carefully they maneuvered between the rocks, fighting the current that threatened to carry them away.

Elise hitched her cloak to the waistband of her

breeches, then stepped into icy water that lapped at the tops of her boots as she helped Little Bear haul the canoe out of the creek. Her spirits were lower than they'd been all day. She was cold, exhausted, and hungry. So much effort and they hadn't yet accomplished their goal.

"I suppose we'd better get a fire going—"

"Ssshhh." The Indian boy cut off her words with a quick, slicing movement of his hand. Then he jabbed a finger toward an area farther downstream.

Elise squinted into the snowy gloom, shivering as the chilly wind penetrated her cloak. Her tired eyes strained to discern the object of Little Bear's attention. Suddenly through the trees she saw a barely perceptible glimmer. A campfire!

"Do you suppose 'tis them?" she whispered, barely able to contain her excitement.

"Little Bear go," he replied in a low voice. "Mam'selle stay by canoe."

He took a step forward, but Elise grabbed his buckskin-covered arm. "I'm going with you," she hissed forcefully.

Little Bear opened his mouth as if to dissuade her, then he shrugged. He put a finger over his lips to indicate silence before turning to creep toward the pinprick of light.

Elise crouched low as she trailed him, gathering her cloak around her for concealment and warmth. The forest was still, except for an occasional soft squeak of her boots sinking into the snow. The Indian boy's moccasins made no sound.

Her heart was thudding against her breast as the glint ahead grew larger. Now she could see dark shapes moving around the campfire. Was it the Englishmen or not? Her physical discomforts were forgotten, and she struggled to contain an urge to run forward and satisfy her curiosity no matter what the consequences.

As they drew nearer, Little Bear slowed his pace and began gliding from the cover of one tree to the next. They snuck closer and closer until at last they could confirm it was indeed the party of Virginians who had halted downstream, along with the small group of Indians who had accompanied them to Fort LeBoeuf.

Hiding behind a huge fallen log, Elise strained to see through the veil of snowflakes. A jolt ran down her spine as she spotted Marc sitting against a tree trunk at the far end of the camp. His feet were tied and likely his hands also, for they were twisted behind his back. He must have attacked Troy and been captured!

And where was Troy? Her anxious eyes searched the camp, but she failed to spy his tall figure. *Sacré Dieu!* Had Marc really killed him? Her heart lurched in horror.

Despair welled inside her as she gazed at his small, helpless form. Now what were they to do?

Little Bear slithered up beside her and whispered in her ear, "They stop to hunt."

His words explained why it had been so easy to catch up to the party. Elise had been too intent on finding Marc to notice the smell of roasting meat that wafted through the air. Now, though, her stomach rumbled in response to the mouth-watering scent. Three bear hides hung from branches at the edge of the camp, identifying the substance of the meal. Bear wasn't her favorite dish, but at the moment she was so hungry she'd welcome even one bite of the greasy meat. It took a supreme effort to vanquish her physical wants and concentrate on Marc's dilemma.

"What are we going to do?" she hissed to the Indian boy at her side. The situation seemed hopeless. How could they free her brother when he was surrounded by so many men?

"Wait," came the low reply. "They sleep soon."

An upsurge of optimism bolstered her spirits. Of course! As soon as the others were sound asleep, she and Little Bear would sneak up to Marc and untie his bonds. The three of them would be far away from here by the time the Virginians woke at dawn to find their prisoner gone.

And what had happened to Troy? As quickly as the thought surfaced, Elise buried it. She vowed to not even think of him anymore. Only Marc mattered.

With the Indian boy beside her, she peered over the massive log, watching the activity around the campsite. After a while, the exertion of the day began to take its toll and her eyelids grew heavy. She huddled into her cloak for warmth, trying to ignore the emptiness in her belly and the aching of her muscles.

Snowflakes floated downward without cease, settling a pale shroud over her crouched form. Ice pricked her face. Her long lashes drooped and lifted, drooped and lifted; with each passing moment, it took more effort to keep them raised.

White flecks danced in the darkness before her, as soothing as a lullaby. She struggled to focus, but gradually the world dissolved to black.

Chapter Six

Strong fingers gripped her shoulders, jarring her from the depths of slumber. She whimpered a protest. Her dreams had been pleasant and cozy, but now consciousness intruded, threatening to thrust her into a teeth-chattering cold. Her tired body screamed in agony as she twisted in a feeble attempt to elude the awakening and return to painless oblivion.

A low voice spoke to her as if from a great distance: "Elise, can you hear me? Wake up!"

The implacable order overrode her resistance. She opened her eyes to see a hazy shape wavering before her, barely perceptible against the inky background. The apparition seemed to be that of a shaggy beast twice her size, imposing and broad of shoulder. Yet, oddly, she felt no fear.

"Are you all right?" the urgent whisper came again. "Answer me!"

Her vision sharpened, and a human face swam before her in the darkness. Abruptly she realized the creature was a crouching man. What she had mistaken for furry flesh was actually a beaverskin coat. Memory returned in a jolt of panic.

"Troy!" She tried to scramble up, but his powerful hands prevented her from rising higher than her knees. Heedless of her aching muscles, she fought frantically for freedom.

"Calm yourself!" he commanded softly in her ear. "You'll be in worse trouble if you awaken the rest of the camp."

A measure of reason penetrated her brain and she ceased struggling. An inexplicable gladness flooded her heart. "You're alive," she breathed, her voice a mere thread of sound.

"No thanks to you," Troy growled. "Was it your idea to send your brother to kill me? 'Tis a shame you had to be disappointed by his failure."

His harsh words crushed her momentary softening. Not bothering to correct his false impression, Elise glanced across the snowy log at the campfire, which smoldered in the distance. The blanketed forms of several Indians were huddled on the ground, while the Englishmen likely occupied the tent. Despair rippled through her as she realized she had lost the chance to secure Marc's release. Then another thought invaded, and she whipped her head around to search the gloomy forest. Where was Little Bear? Had he been able to free Marc? The hope was of short duration.

"If you're wondering what happened to your Indian friend, he's back there, tied up." Troy tilted his head toward the pitch-black underbrush. "When I caught him sneaking around outside of camp, I decided 'twould be wise to scout the area for an accomplice. That's how I found you."

He released her shoulders, and taking her gloved hand between his, began to rub briskly. "You ought to thank God you're alive," he hissed angrily. "What sort of damn-fool trick was that, falling asleep in the snow? You could have frozen to death!"

Feeling returned to her numb flesh like a thousand pricking ice needles. Blinking back tears of pain, Elise jerked her hand away and stumbled to her feet.

"And if I had, what concern would it be of yours?"

"Dammit, I told you to keep your voice down!" Troy said in a low hiss.

He sprang up, and she found herself retreating a step. Against the backdrop of the campfire, he seemed taller and tougher than ever. A sudden flame flickered deep within her, and the unexpected sensation enraged Elise. How could her body betray her with such a shameless response? All she wanted was to free Marc and return to the uncomplicated existence she had known before Troy Fletcher had come to wreak havoc with her life.

"I don't take orders from an Englishman." Only a glimmer of reason kept her tone subdued. She had no wish to awaken the others, either.

"Is that so? Those are brave words coming from a woman in your position."

"My position?" she whispered fiercely. "Do you plan to take me prisoner along with my brother? Just like any other Englishman, you enjoy preying on the helpless, don't you?"

He let out a quiet chuckle. "You're about as helpless as a rattler hiding in the underbrush."

His amusement fed her fury. "Laugh if you will. The fact remains that you have no right to hold either me or Marc captive!"

"Ah, but your brother relinquished his rights when he pulled a knife on me." Troy jerked open his coat and in the dim light a dark splotch was just barely visible against the paler buckskin of his shirt. "'Twas only my quick reflexes and the thickness of this beaverskin that saved my life."

Horror swept Elise as she realized the blemish just below his shoulder was blood. The slight bulge beneath it was likely a bandage. Troy might have been killed!

Slowly she lifted her eyes to the shadowy features of his face. It was difficult to read his expression through the gloom, but she sensed a strength of purpose emanating from him. Did he intend to make Marc stand trial for attempted murder?

She moistened her dry lips. "You forget you're in a foreign country. No matter what Marc has done, the commander will never permit you to take a French citizen prisoner."

"These lands belong to the English," Troy countered softly. "And besides, do you truly believe St. Pierre would bother sending out his troops after a boy and a woman?"

It galled her to admit it, but he was right about the commander. Elise felt as if the jaws of a trap were closing around her. Yet perhaps there was one slim hope. If she could save herself and then rescue Marc later. . . .

Haughtily she lifted her chin. "I've committed no crime. You must at least let *me* go free."

There was a long pause before his quiet reply broke the stillness: "I think not."

"But . . . why?"

"I have other plans for you."

A chill ran down her spine. "You daren't force me into

your bed."

"Force?" he murmured, a grim smile lurking in his tone. "You'll be there of your own accord."

"Never!"

"Is that a challenge?"

Elise felt her courage ebb as Troy narrowed the gap between them. The knowledge that she was at his mercy struck her in full force; the ebony forest was empty save for the enemy encampment in the distance and Little Bear helplessly tied up somewhere. Swallowing hard, she rapidly stepped backward before his relentless advance, her boots slipping and sliding in the snow.

Abruptly her spine struck the hard trunk of a tree. She could turn and run, but how far would she get? Her gloved fingers clutched at the rough bark behind her.

He put a hand on either side of her head, flat against the tree trunk. Silently he studied her in the faint light as the heat of his body enveloped her in its vibrant life.

"You were wrong about me," he murmured. "I never intended to make you my captive, not until you so charmingly put the notion into my head. Nevertheless, you may still have your freedom if you so desire it."

"I don't understand. . . ."

"It depends upon how much you love your brother. Would you strike a bargain to procure Marc's release? Or is your own liberty too precious to relinquish?"

Her lungs drew in gulps of frigid air, yet Elise felt as if she were suffocating. His meaning was all too plain. "You're saying you'll free him if I agree to be your mistress."

"My *willing* mistress," he qualified softly, letting the bare back of his hand caress her cold cheek. "You may either go now, leaving Marc in my custody—under close guard, mind you—or give me yourself in his stead. The choice is yours."

Snowflakes grazed her uptilted face. She could visualize herself lying naked in Troy's arms as he kissed her and fondled her breasts; beyond that, her knowledge of the act was hazy. The intimate image bathed her in a wanton heat that defied all logic.

In tortured misery, she stared up at him, trying to understand the stormy emotions he aroused in her. She wanted to pound on his chest with her fists, to curse him for forcing such a decision on her. Could she swallow her pride and self-respect, and submit to him to safeguard her brother's life?

"How can you be certain I'll come to you willingly once Marc is safely away?"

His soft laugh was laced with ironic humor. "Why, because I trust you, little love."

The more fool you, she wanted to retort. Yet somehow the knowledge that he would accept her pledge touched a chord deep inside her.

"I want your word of honor," he added, "that you'll stay with me for as long as I wish."

Elise gazed up at him through the darkness, her insides a turbulent mass of confusion, anger, and shame. She had to go with him; there was no other alternative.

The words came out half-choked: "All right, I agree."

She gritted her teeth, preparing herself for his triumph, but he only reached out and touched her face with a strange tenderness. His hands pushed off the hood to her cloak, baring her head to the frosty weather. Elise swallowed her pride, knowing he meant to seal their pact with a kiss—and that she must submit, for her brother's sake.

Rising on tiptoes, she met him halfway. Her cold lips warmed beneath his and parted to his tongue. The silken ministrations of his mouth were a winter's feast of roses and honey, the promise of spring and the glory of summer. The blood quickened through her body. Somehow her hands found their way inside his coat to wind around his lean waist. The tempting length of his body pressing her against the tree was bittersweet bondage, compelling captivity.

No matter how vehemently she denied it, she wanted him. There was no other explanation for the fire that swept through her veins and throbbed in her loins. *She wanted him.*

Abruptly Troy withdrew, holding her at arm's length. Elise shivered as the chill of the night pricked her heated skin. For a long moment he gazed at her without speaking. Then he grasped her hand and gave a gentle tug.

Numb with shame, she accompanied him through the darkened forest. They stopped and picked up his rifle, then found Little Bear and headed toward the flickering fire, to the camp of the enemy.

"This scheme of yours reeks of blackmail, Troy. The woman shouldn't pay for the mistakes of her brother."

Washington's deep voice held a ring of authority, though he was the younger of the two men. Troy braced a hand on a tree, conscious of a deep sense of guilt as he watched the tall major pace back and forth, the early morning sunlight glinting on his reddish-brown hair.

Washington was dead right. He *had* used unfair tactics to convince Elise to accompany him home.

With a self-derisive twist of his lips, Troy acknowledged that never in his life had he resorted to such base tricks. There had been no need to prey on virgins when he'd always had his pick of willing widows and high-bred whores. What in holy hell had gotten into him last night?

His hand rasped absently over the bristles covering his jaw as he looked across the clearing at Elise, where she sat huddled with her brother and his Indian friend. Even at a distance, with her delectable curves hidden beneath the enveloping folds of a cloak, he could still feel the impact of her attraction. What was it about her that intrigued him so, when many beautiful, more sophisticated women had tried and failed to win him?

No, he wasn't proud of the way he'd taunted her with Marc's freedom at the cost of denying her own. And yet deep in his heart he felt no regret for their devil's bargain. At the risk of intensifying her hatred, he'd felt compelled to grab his one and only chance to keep her at his side.

Pushing away from the tree, he lowered his arm, wincing at the pain in his shoulder. Damn that brat Marc! Although Troy had accused Elise of conspiracy, when his anger had cleared he'd realized the boy had acted alone. Her brother's action was ironic, Troy mused, for it had thrust Elise into the hands of her enemy.

"You're right, George," he said at last. "Elise shouldn't pay for his mistakes. But would it ease your objections were I to assure you my intentions toward her are honorable?"

Washington ceased pacing and sent him a startled look. "You can't mean to wed her."

"Yes, I can."

"For pity's sake, man, she's a penniless French-woman!"

Troy grinned, aware of a sudden lightening of his mood. For a wealthy landowner to marry beneath his class went against every dictate of Virginia society. But he didn't give a damn.

"I guess I'm in love," he explained with a shrug.

The major stared at him thoughtfully for a moment. "Make certain she doesn't slow us down, then," he said gruffly. "I'm duty-bound to deliver St. Pierre's reply to the governor as soon as possible."

A smile quirked Troy's mouth as he watched the lanky man stride away. It had been a shrewd guess that Washington would understand what it was to love a woman. The young major's *tendresse* for the married Sally Fairfax had been unmistakable when Troy had seen them together at a ball in Williamsburg the previous spring.

His attention returned to Elise. As if she sensed his scrutiny, she lifted her gaze to his. Even across the length of the clearing, it was impossible to miss the hatred burning in those brandy-hued eyes.

The jolting reminder of her antagonism was far more painful than the knife wound in his chest. Unable to face her any longer, he abruptly turned his back and headed over to the creek to check on the loading of the canoes.

It wasn't going to be easy to break through the shell to the warm, passionate woman he sensed within. But he was determined to make her love him if it took the rest of his life.

Elise observed Troy's departure from beneath the veil of her long lashes. Why was it, she wondered, that the mere sight of him could cause a pulse of excitement deep within her? The shadow of several days' growth covered his face, but instead of looking unkempt, he only appeared more ruggedly masculine than ever. The sinuous grace of his walk brought to mind a panther she had once seen prowling the wilderness. Soon she would feel the hard strength of his naked body covering hers. . . .

"Elise, you've got to untie me and Little Bear while no one's watching. I tell you, this is our only chance to get you away from here!"

Her brother's voice jerked her attention back to him. He was struggling against the rope that secured his hands behind his back. A wave of anger and frustration swept her. If only she could do as he requested!

"I dare not release you, Marc," she said, her voice low. "If we try to escape, the men would catch us quickly, and that would only make matters worse. Monsieur Fletcher might change his mind about freeing you."

"I'm not afraid to take the risk," he scoffed. "Are you, Little Bear?"

The Indian boy sat impassively beside him on the cold ground. His own tied hands remained still as he observed Marc's frantic wriggling. "Little Bear not afraid. But if mam'selle refuse to run, brother not force her."

"*Oui*, that is true," Elise said, speaking with as much conviction as she could muster. "You see, Marc, 'twould accomplish little to cut the rope. You'd have to drag me away from here, and you'd be captured before we went more than two steps."

"You're both cowards!" He yanked futilely at his bonds. "Elise, I'm not leaving you with that bastard, I swear it on our mother's grave!"

Suddenly Troy approached, flanked by two fierce-looking Indian braves. Elise felt her heart slam inside her chest. She rose from a crouching position, heedless of the soreness in her muscles. They were coming for Marc. It was time to say good-bye to her brother, the only person who mattered to her in the whole world.

One of the Indians knelt to unbind the boys' ankles. Glancing over at Troy, Elise was helpless to hide the despair that twisted her stomach. Instead of the gloating she'd expected, she saw only soft concern in his green eyes. A tiny flame of hope flickered inside her. Maybe he'd changed his mind. . . .

But she was grasping at straws.

"We must be on our way," Troy told her gently. " 'Tis time for the boys to return to the fort."

With a heavy heart, she looked at her brother, who had scrambled to his feet and was staring belligerently at Troy. She knew that given the chance Marc would fight to the death for her.

Elise darted forward to embrace him, painfully aware that this might be the last time she would ever see him. As she hugged him tightly, tears burned her eyes. She blinked them away, telling herself to be brave for his sake.

Then Troy's hands were on her shoulders, drawing her back. Marc fought like a madman as one of the Indians took him by the arm and tried to lead him away.

He spat at Troy, narrowly missing the Virginian's boot. "*Bâtard!*" he snarled in French.

Holding onto the struggling captive, the Indian pulled a clublike instrument from the sash at his waist and struck a light blow at the back of Marc's head. The boy slumped against him. Then the brave picked him up and slung him over his shoulder like a sack of flour.

Elise stared in horror. "No!" she screamed.

Troy's hands dug into her shoulders before she could run after Marc. She tried to struggle, but the futility of it washed over her and she slumped in Troy's arms. In sick despair, she watched the small party depart.

For many minutes she stood rooted in misery. One brave carried Marc, while the other prodded Little Bear along the snowy path that led through the trees. It would be a long, hard trek on foot, since the fort lay upstream and they could not paddle a canoe against the current.

In the grips of despair, she wondered what would happen to her brother; she could only hope Yves or perhaps the commander would watch after him. If worse came to worst, she told herself, Little Bear would take him in. Her only consolation was that at least Marc was free, at least he would not face charges of attempted murder.

When the figures could no longer be detected in the distance, Troy gently propelled her toward the creek. Tears blurred her eyes. Had it not been for his helping arm, she would have stumbled and fallen.

The icy water lapped at her boots as she clambered into the middle of the canoe. With the other Englishmen present, there was no need for her to paddle, and so with spine rigid, she sat on the hard wooden seat and gazed straight ahead, her hands clasped tightly in her lap.

Never in her life had she felt more alone.

Chapter Seven

Venango was a tiny settlement carved out of the wilderness at the point where French Creek emptied into the Allegheny River. Consisting of only a trading post and a few scattered log cabins, it was more a hamlet than the bustling town Elise had expected.

Wearily she trudged along with the party of Virginians as they approached the cluster of dwellings. For the last half-mile the creek had been frozen, the ice so solid that a channel could not be broken. Progress had been slow in the three days since she and Marc had parted. With no new snowfall to feed the creek, the water had become shallow and the current sluggish, easily susceptible to freezing. In many instances, they'd had to get out of the canoe and walk until they reached a section where a passage through the ice could be chopped.

The raw cold pricked at Elise's skin, yet more than her body was frozen; she was numb in spirit. Behind her was the familiar, everything she knew and loved; ahead lay the unknown and a life among the hated English. She wouldn't let herself think about it. Locking away her emotions, she kept her mind focused on surviving the rigorous journey.

At least Troy had made no move to assert his claim on her. He had kept his distance, though making it plain to the others that she belonged to him. She could only surmise he was awaiting a time when they were alone. Not even an Englishman would be so crude as to engage in the intimacy of lovemaking in a tent shared with four other men.

Now, as the party entered Venango, single-file, the late afternoon sunlight made the snow glisten like diamonds. Yet Elise paid little heed to the icy beauty. Gripped by a weariness of the soul, she could barely force one foot ahead of the other. The small leather pack of provisions she carried seemed to grow heavier with each step, until she doubted she could walk the short distance to the place where they would camp for the night. She started to lag behind Troy, whose long-legged stride carried him forward with tireless effort.

Some impulse made her lift her eyes to the building directly ahead. Fluttering from the roof of the log cabin was a flag—the fleur-de-lis, symbol of France.

A spark of spirit stiffened her spine. This was a French settlement and she would not disgrace her countrymen by collapsing like a weakling! She would show these Englishmen that she possessed every bit the stamina they did.

Tilting her chin, she caught up to Troy. The five hostlers who had brought the horses down from Fort LeBoeuf were camped in a clearing at the other side of the settlement, on the bank of the frozen Allegheny. The succulent aroma of roasting deer meat filled the air.

Captain Joincare, the head French officer at the

trading post, sent a message asking the Englishmen to sup with him. Elise and the servitors were not included in the invitation. With mixed feelings, she watched Troy and his comrades leave the camp. On the one hand, she was relieved to have a few hours away from his unnerving presence; on the other, she longed to go with him to have a chance to converse with someone in her native tongue.

She sat on her pack near the fire, nibbling half-heartedly at the tin plate of food in her lap. Briefly she toyed with the idea of escape. But night had fallen, and the woods looked dark and forbidding. The far-off howl of a wolf made her shiver. Besides, wasn't she honor-bound to keep her pledge to Troy?

A vow made to an enemy was invalid, a part of her mind argued. How could she be expected to abide by a promise extracted under duress, when she had been desperate to secure Marc's freedom?

And yet . . . Troy trusted her. He had accepted her word at face value, never questioning her sworn agreement. For the sake of her own self-respect, she couldn't run away. She had to stay and prove to this Englishman that a Frenchwoman could have a sense of honor, too.

A sudden prickling sped down her spine. Looking over at the group of servitors who were sprawled on the other side of the campfire, Elise saw one of them staring boldly at her. He was a brawny man with a shaggy black beard and a squat, misshapen nose. As she watched, he lifted a jug of rum, balancing it on his shoulder as he drank deeply, never once taking his coal-dark eyes from her.

There was something about his scrutiny that made her uneasy. She set down her plate and stood up, hoping a lack of interest would discourage him. Rummaging inside her leather pack, she found a withered apple and cut it into pieces. Then she headed across the moon-washed landscape to the perimeter of the camp.

The horses were tethered beside a clump of bushes, picking at the few blades of frozen grass that stuck out of the snow. Noting the weakened condition of the beasts, Elise clucked in sympathy; even in the shadows their feebleness was unmistakable. There was so little forage in the winter months.

The horses whinnied softly as they caught the scent of the apple. Quickly she fed them the meager rations, wishing there was more.

"*Je le regrette,*" she murmured apologetically, stroking the long neck of one animal as he nuzzled her empty palm.

"Ye're a Frenchie, ain't ye?"

The gritty male voice made Elise pivot sharply, her cloak swirling around her breeches. The burly servitor who had been watching her earlier was standing a short distance away, hands set on the hips of his fringed buckskin coat. His unkempt thatch of black hair was partially covered by a squirrel hat with a bushy tail dangling from the back.

"What do you want?" Elise asked warily.

"Why, I jist fancied talkin' to ye a spell. Me name's Jake Hubbell."

Having lived in a fort full of soldiers, she knew enough to doubt he was interested only in idle conversation. She trusted him about as far as she could throw a stick.

"Pray excuse my rudeness, Monsieur Hubbell, but I wish to be left alone."

"Aw, don't play shy with me, li'l lady," he cajoled. "Ain't ye at least gonna tell me yer name?"

The moonlight made his dark eyes glitter as he took a step nearer. Nervously, Elise glanced to the campfire beyond him. Could she seek refuge there, or were his comrades as shifty as he was?

"Come on now, gal, tell ol' Jake yer name." This time his gravelly voice had a harder, more threatening edge. And he was getting too close for comfort.

Acting on instinct, Elise turned abruptly and darted around behind the horses, hitching up her cloak to avoid tripping. She heard Jake Hubbell utter a startled curse, then heavy footsteps pounded the snow behind her.

Fear sent her hurtling along the path at a reckless speed. Skirting the edge of the clearing, she raced headlong toward the small cluster of buildings in Venango. The moon had gone behind a cloud and the woods were wrapped in shadows. But the darkness failed to slow her down.

Branches clutched at her like bony fingers and her boots slipped and slid on the snow. Her heart felt as if it were about to burst.

A log cabin loomed ahead through the murk. Gasping, Elise sprinted toward the building, her eyes straining to find the dim outline of a door. She ran around the corner and crashed into something solid.

It was a man. His hands were on her shoulders, steadying her. "Are you all right?" he demanded.

"He's chasing me!" she babbled, clinging to the lapels of his coat. "Don't let him touch me, please!"

"I won't," he promised. "You're safe. There's no one there."

She risked a glance over her shoulder toward the camp. Jake Hubbell was nowhere to be seen. The frosty air was silent except for her panting breaths. Her blood slowed its frantic surging.

It was then that Elise realized they had spoken in French, and she looked back at her rescuer. The moon came out from behind a cloud to illuminate his face in pale silver light. His features had the freshness of a man not much older than her own nineteen years. He was only an inch or two taller than she was, enabling her to gaze almost directly into his dark, concerned eyes.

Embarrassment washed over her, and she released her death grip on his coat. *Sacré Dieu!* Considering the way she had burst out of the darkness he must think her a madwoman!

"There really was a man," she explained lamely. "I ran away and I thought he was right behind me."

"Do you wish me to go after him? I can fetch my gun—"

"Nay, that isn't necessary," she interjected. It would accomplish little to stir up trouble between the French and the English. Henceforth, she would stay close to Troy for protection, although for now she was afraid to return to camp. "I-I need to sit down for a few moments. I feel weak. . . ."

"But of course! How stupid of me."

Instantly his arm came around her waist to offer assistance. Elise found her legs were indeed wobbly, and she was grateful for his support as they walked slowly toward the entrance to the log cabin.

"I'll get you some brandy, and when you feel better, you must tell me who you are," he said with a hint of flirtation. "I'm new here, and I had no idea there was such a pretty Frenchwoman living near Venango—"

Abruptly the door swung open, and a shaft of yellow light spilled out onto the snow. A man stood framed in the entryway, his hands astride his lean hips. Her heart skipped a beat as she felt the force of his aggressive virility.

"What the devil's going on here?" Troy growled.

Without waiting for a reply, he sprang forward and snatched Elise from her companion. His arm went around her shoulders in a distinct gesture of ownership. "Who the hell are you?" he demanded of the other man.

Though he spoke in English, the anger in his tone was plain. The Frenchman clenched his fingers into fists.

"Do you know him?" he asked Elise in her native tongue.

She bit her lip, fighting tears at the concern in his expression. If she were to give one indication of a need, he would defend her. But no matter how much she hungered for the company of a fellow countryman, she dared not antagonize Troy into fighting a man who had been so kind to her.

"*Oui*, I know him," she said slowly. "I'm traveling with him."

With a sick sensation in the pit of her stomach, Elise saw the cynical understanding dawn on the Frenchman's face. His gaze roamed the length of her slender figure as if he were viewing her through new eyes. "I see. Do not let me keep you any longer, then." After sketching a bow, he walked into the cabin, closing the door behind him.

Humiliation settled over her like a suffocating blanket. To be regarded by a compatriot as no better than a slut was almost more than she could bear. She wanted to shout after him that he was mistaken, but the words would not come. What did it matter, anyway? Elise thought bitterly. She might as well get used to such treatment, for she had given her solemn vow to be

110

mistress to an Englishman for as long as he wanted her.

"By the devil, I thought I could trust you to stay put! What are you doing away from camp?"

Troy's sharp voice sliced her like a sword. Resentment rose in her throat, half-choking her. "I thought you knew—I was selling my favors. Have you an objection to my earning a few extra coins in my free time?"

His grip on her tightened and for a moment he looked angry enough to strike her. She tilted her chin, daring him to do so. Let the English swine use force on her, she thought scornfully; it would be proof he was no better than an animal.

Unexpectedly he loosened his hands. His mouth relaxed into a familiar smile, moonlight gleaming on his white teeth.

"Out whoring, were you? And here I thought you might be running away."

"I gave you my word of honor I would not," she said stiffly.

"I know and I'm sorry for doubting you," he answered softly. "But can you blame me for fearing I might lose you?"

His mouth came down over hers, warm and demanding, swamping her with his taste and scent. The silken plunge of his tongue between her lips awakened a shameful hunger within Elise, but she resisted the sultry seduction with every fiber of her being. Did he think a few sweet words and a kiss could compensate for the loss of her good name?

She would abide by her vow to be willing, but her self-respect could be salvaged if she at least demonstrated no pleasure in his touch. It took a determined effort to remain passive. The growth of his beard prickled her skin in a way that was unbearably enticing, and there was no denying the wild erotic need that pulsed in her belly. But she refrained from yielding. Her fingers rested limply on his coat instead of winding into his hair; her body was rigid within his embrace rather than melting against him.

At last he raised his head to study her in the moonlight. The annoyance she'd expected was not there; he merely looked amused. Her triumph at winning the battle of wills vanished like a pricked bubble.

"You might take my body," she hissed, "but I'll never stop hating you."

"Is that so? Don't forget, I have the rest of our lives to wear down your resistance. You won't be able to keep up that pretense once I make love to you."

"You'll tire of me quickly."

"And if I don't?" he inquired softly. "Not all Englishmen are like your father, Elise. What if you were to fall in love with me?"

"Do you take me for a complete fool?"

In the grips of turbulent emotion, she pivoted sharply, marching down the path that led to the encampment. She crushed the peculiar pang in her heart. Love, indeed! That would be the ultimate humiliation for her and the final victory for him.

Behind her, she heard the crunch of his boots on the snow. A sudden thought occurred to her and, despite her seething insides, she felt a grudging relief at his presence. She had nearly forgotten about Jake Hubbell.

The hostlers were bedded down near the horses, and the sound of their snoring drifted through the night air. Elise headed over to the large canvas tent, then she hesitated, turning to see Troy crouched before the fire. He had picked up a stick and was poking at the smoldering

112

wood. Tiny orange flames shot up, licking at the charred logs with renewed life.

She should tell him about her encounter with Hubbell. But there was something in Troy's pensive expression that roused a strange weakness inside her. No, she had no wish to engage him in conversation again.

She entered the tent and flopped down on a bedroll in a dark corner. The ground was cold and hard beneath her; she told herself that was the cause of her restless tossing. She was still awake much later when the other Englishmen returned from the settlement. Feigning sleep, she heard them settle down for the night, Troy taking his usual place beside her. He lay so close she could feel his body heat. Slowly her tension seeped away, and she slept.

Elise trudged behind the cavalcade of horses moving through the woods. The borrowed canoes had been left in Venango two days ago, for the rest of the journey was overland. Gamely she kept pace with the others, not wanting to be accused of slowing down the party.

The walking wasn't so difficult now that the horses were tramping down a path through the snow. Just ahead of her, Troy strode along as easily as if they were on their way to a summer picnic. Elise scowled at his back. It was unfair that she should feel the force of his attraction despite the cold and exhaustion that weighed her down.

In her heart she admitted she was piqued that he had resumed a casual attitude toward her. They hadn't spoken more than a handful of words since that night at Venango. Consequently, she'd kept silent about her encounter with Jake Hubbell. A few times, she had

113

caught the hostler staring at her, but thankfully, he seemed to have figured out that she belonged to Troy.

Belonged. Sickness curdled her stomach at the thought. She was Troy's possession, his for as long as he wanted her. When would he assert his claim?

Resolutely, she thrust that thought aside. Her gaze moved to the string of pack animals winding through the icy wilderness. The cold had grown steadily worse, and the crust of ice covering the snow had cut the horses' legs. The previous day, Troy had tried to convince Elise to ride, but she had been reluctant to add weight to the burdened animals. If the Englishmen could walk, then so could she.

It was midafternoon when they halted beside the bank of a frozen stream. The tent was erected, a fire was built, then the men gathered up their rifles and began filtering out of the camp. Warming her hands by the fire, Elise watched as Troy walked over to her.

"We're going to hunt fresh meat for our holiday dinner," he said. "If we spread out in different directions, there'll be more chance of finding game."

"Holiday?" she said blankly.

Smiling, he touched her cold cheek. "'Tis Christmas Day, little love. Didn't you know?"

She shook her head in numb disbelief. Time had passed in a blur of long, drab hours marching along an endless trail.

"You're to stay at the camp while I'm gone, do you hear me? No venturing into the woods, not for any reason."

Elise was too caught up in memories to take offense at the order. As he headed off through the trees, scenes of past Christmases flashed through her head. Last year

Maman had been alive, and they had spent a festive holiday in Montreal. What was Marc doing today? she wondered wistfully. Did he miss her as much as she missed him? Guiltily she remembered Yves, realizing she hadn't thought of her fiance in days. What had been his reaction on hearing she had run off with an Englishman?

Elise crouched near the fire, wishing she were alone with her dismal meditations. Three of the hostlers were suffering from frostbite and had remained at the camp. She was thankful Jake Hubbell had been healthy enough to join the hunting party.

As one hour inched past and then another, she became aware of a steadily increasing physical discomfort. At last the need for relief could not be delayed. Despite Troy's admonition to remain at the camp, she had to slip away for a few moments' privacy.

She felt the impact of watchful eyes as she left the warmth of the fire. But the servitors made no move to stop her from walking into the woods. Dusk bathed the trees in shadows. Elise knew she could easily find a secluded spot close by, but a little devil of defiance made her venture farther than necessary. So what if Troy had told her to stay in camp? The short rest after the long day's journey had revived her, and now she relished the peace of the forest.

The snow crunching beneath her feet was the only sound in the stillness of the evening. Then suddenly she heard the far-off crack of a musket shot. The hunters must have finally found game.

The thought made her hurry, for she wanted to be back before the others returned. Hastening over a low rise, she found a clump of bushes that afforded a modicum of privacy, and attended to her needs.

She had just finished rebuttoning her breeches when the snap of brittle wood made her whirl around. Shock froze her in a half-turned position.

A few yards away stood a bearded man dressed in fringed buckskins. His leering dark eyes devoured her, as if he contemplated stripping her slender figure. Horror choked her throat.

It was Jake Hubbell.

Chapter Eight

Even as Elise gasped, her vulnerability struck her in full force. She was alone in the woods with this Englishman. And he meant her no good.

Fear clogged her chest. Then he laughed and the evil sound spurred her into motion. Spinning around, she raced off in the direction of the camp, her cloak flapping behind her like the wings of a terrified sparrow. Close behind her came the heavy thud of pursuing feet.

Her hood flew off, the chilly air streaming over her head. Icicles pierced her lungs with each breath. She strained to see through the deepening gloom. *Dieu,* how far had she ventured? Why couldn't she spot the light of the fire ahead?

With a sob of desperation, she glanced over her shoulder at her burly hunter. It was a mistake that cost her dearly.

As she whipped her head back around, her arm grazed a tree, throwing her off balance. She clutched at the trunk for support, but her boot slipped on a patch of ice and she landed bottom-first in a snowdrift. She was scrambling to her feet when Hubbell's bulky body slammed her back down.

"I got ye now, ye high-an'-mighty bitch!" he snarled.

His words filled her with renewed terror. Breathing hard, she fought for freedom with the fury of a wildcat. Her twisting and writhing strained the limits of her strength. With his brawny weight pinning her to the snow, she was as helpless as a bird fluttering against the steel bars of a cage.

Wrenching her hand free, she raked her fingernails across his face, but the thickness of his beard prevented her from inflicting much damage. Still, he let out a howl of pain and smacked her hard across the cheek.

Her head reeled from the force of the blow. As much as it hurt, it brought back to her a measure of sanity. Struggling was futile. All that might save her was her wits.

Suppressing the whimper of fear that threatened to bubble from her lips, Elise forced herself to go limp. Perhaps if Hubbell thought he had her cowed into submission, he might get careless. It was her only hope.

"Now that be more like it," he grunted, his breath smelling of sour rum. "Ye're goin' to give ol' Jake a li'l taste of what ye been passin' out free to that fancy-pants Fletcher. Ain't ye, gal?"

"Y-yes." The stammer was no act; she was quivering from the impact of her predicament.

His chuckle sent chills over her skin. "Aye, we're gonna have us some fun, an' ol' Fletcher won't never know what happened." Hubbell rubbed his swollen groin against her belly. "This'll be our li'l secret. Ye won't tell nobody, will ye, Frenchie?"

"N-no . . . of course not."

In the failing light, his eyes glittered with lust. He pawed at her breast, kneading the soft flesh through the buckskin of her shirt. Gritting her teeth in silent disgust, she endured the crude caress.

"Ain't never seen a female dressed like no boy before," he commented. "I kinda like yer tight britches. Ever time I look at them curvy legs, I get all hot an' sweaty."

Hubbell shifted position, partially sliding his large body off of her so his hand could move down to squeeze her thigh. It was the chance she had been awaiting. She put her palms against his shoulders and thrust hard. Caught by surprise, the brawny man toppled backward.

Elise sprang up, but before she was able to rise all the way to her feet, something choked her throat. Hubbell must be lying on her cloak!

Her fingers clawed recklessly at the tie, but she wasn't swift enough.

Roaring like an outraged bull, Hubbell clamped onto her legs and sent her tumbling facedown into the snowdrift. As she shifted her head to regain her breath, an icy wetness stung her cheek. She groped wildly for a weapon, anything that might be used to strike a blow in her defense. Her fingers grasped only handfuls of snow.

With a cry of despair, she tried to crawl out from beneath him. Futilely she bucked against him with every ounce of her strength.

"Ye damn bitch!" he hissed in her ear. "I ain't gonna give ye no chance to trick me again!"

Roughly he rolled her over. Again she went for his face with her nails, but he was ready for her this time, using one broad hand to snare her wrists above her head.

With his other hand, Hubbell fumbled with the buttons to her breeches. Her knee thrust instinctively

119

toward his groin to make firm contact. Hearing his yelp of pain, she felt a flash of primitive triumph.

Abruptly his substantial bulk lifted from her. For one dazed instant Elise thought she had driven him away. Then she blinked, her wide eyes focusing on the man who grasped Hubbell by the overshirt.

It was Troy. Through the dim light, she saw his fist meet Hubbell's jaw in a loud crack that sent the burly servant sprawling in the snow, his squirrel cap flying off his head. Hubbell surged to his feet, shaking his ragged hair as if dazed. He lurched forward drunkenly. Troy sidestepped him and planted a booted foot on Hubbell's broad behind so he went tumbling to the ground again.

Troy picked up his rifle from beside a tree and sighted down the long barrel at his adversary. "If by chance you're wondering, this is primed and ready to fire," he drawled coldly. "But because I'm a generous man, I'll allow you ten minutes to gather up your gear and clear out of camp."

"Ye ain't got no call to do that," Hubbell blustered. "Why, that li'l slut was askin' for it! Always wigglin' her tail afore me!"

"Nine minutes," Troy said with soft menace. His finger shifted slightly to caress the trigger.

Jake Hubbell scrambled up, snatching his hat from the ground and using it to brush the snow off his trousers. "Ye cain't do this an' git away with it," he muttered darkly. "'Tain't the las' ye'll hear of me." He gave the gun one final glare before he loped off toward the camp.

In numb relief, Elise watched his departure. *Mon Dieu, merci!* she prayed in thanksgiving. If Troy hadn't come along. . . .

Tremors ran through her at the thought of what might

have happened. She saw Troy set down his rifle and come toward her. Jumping up, she hurled herself at him, blindly seeking the safety of his warm embrace. She burrowed her face into his coat, her heart still thumping wildly. It was heaven to hear his voice murmuring words of reassurance, to feel his comforting arms clasping her to his hard length and to breathe his familiar male scent.

"What the devil are you doing out here?" Troy chided huskily. "You should have stayed in camp as I told you to!"

"I—"

She drew in a shuddering breath. It caught in her throat, emerging from her lips in a sob. The aftershock of Hubbell's malicious attack had left her weak and trembling, and hot tears cascaded down her cheeks. Troy was right. She should have listened to him rather than venturing so far from safety. By her own foolish defiance, she had placed herself in grave danger.

"Don't weep, little love," he murmured. He lifted her chin, putting his lips to the tears that dewed her face. "'Tis over . . . there's naught to fear now."

Gazing down at her forlorn expression, Troy felt a knot of emotion squeeze his chest. She was so small and defenseless within his embrace. How beautiful she was, with her brandy eyes glossed with tears and her soft breasts straining against him! His fingers combed into the silken strands of her hair, dislodging the wooden pins that held her chignon in place. The shining mass of curls tumbled over his hand and down her back in a cascade of copper.

His insides twisted with love and desire and possessiveness, mingled with a strong sense of self-reproach. My God, he had almost failed to keep her safe from harm!

121

How could he have been so remiss? The salt taste of her tears was in his mouth, tears that were a result of his own neglect.

The knowledge that another man had dared lay a hand on his woman filled him with a rage more acute than anything he had ever before felt. Several times over the past few days he had noticed Jake Hubbell watching Elise, but he had stupidly assumed his prior claim would deter the man. He should have killed the bastard! Only a thread of reason had kept him from pounding Hubbell's face into a bloody pulp.

"I should never have left your side!" His arms tightened fiercely around her slender body. "My God, you might have been hurt!"

He bent his head and took her mouth in a kiss so searing and sweet it stole her breath away. Parting her lips, she welcomed the solace of his familiar warmth. She needed his tenderness to help rinse away the terror of Hubbell's violation. Her body tingled with the reawakening of life. The feel of his tongue caressing the sensitive crevices of her mouth thawed the numbness that had gripped her limbs. Her hands slid over the lush fur of his coat, stretching up to loop around his neck.

Abruptly he reached inside her cloak and drew the shirt out of her breeches. His hand was beneath the soft buckskin before Elise could recover from the shock of his boldness. She stiffened as the memory of Hubbell pawing at her breasts flashed through her mind. When she recoiled and tried to draw away, Troy kept her pressed closely to his muscled form.

"I won't hurt you, love," he whispered. "I seek only to give you pleasure."

His fingers curled around her bare breast. The touch

of his calloused skin, cold from the frosty weather, made her nipples tighten in instantaneous reaction. A thrill of excitement shot through her. He flicked his thumb over the taut peak, cradling the rounded flesh in his large palm. She caught her breath as a growing exhilaration fluttered within her.

When she was limp and melting in his arms, he slid his hand down her warm belly to the front of her breeches, where he began twisting open the buttons. Through the deepening darkness, the desire on his face was unmistakable.

Elise felt her insides quiver with heat. It was shaming to realize he had the power to ignite such a response in her. She would not yield to him, she *could* not! Where was her pride, her sense of self-respect?

"Troy, nay," she moaned, wriggling in a feeble attempt to pull away. "We mustn't do this."

"Ssshhh," he murmured. "After what that bastard did to you, let me show you how good it can be. Let me give this much to you."

He wrested the last button from its hole and smoothed his palm over the satiny skin inside her breeches. Then his hand dipped lower still, to the triangular patch of silk at the top of her thighs. She gasped at the sudden intimacy. No man had ever touched her so! Though she held herself rigid, the feel of his fingers exploring her most private place was unbearably exquisite, undeniably exciting.

A molten surge of passion swept away the vestiges of resistance. Uttering a tiny whimper, she surrendered helplessly to the expertise of his caresses, leaning heavily into his surrounding arm for support. Intense pulses of arousal gripped her abdomen, and she could not keep herself from pressing more firmly against his hand in an effort to assuage the urgent need blossoming inside her.

His fingers moved in maddening strokes across her moist and sensitive secrets. She tilted her head back, unable to quiet the soft sounds of delight that rose from deep within her. Against her throat she felt the warmth of his lips and the brush of his whiskers. Shivers of bliss coursed through her. She was drowning in pure sensation, transported to a plane where nothing existed but the responses of the flesh.

A sudden, startling rapture burst forth, inundating her in waves of the most perfect pleasure she had ever felt. The ecstasy of release was stunning, and for long moments afterward, she leaned limply against Troy, her face buried in the soft fur of his coat.

But reality could not be eluded forever.

Even as her own respiration returned to normal, she heard the quickened rasp of Troy's breathing and the heavy thud of the heartbeat beneath her ear. Tension tightened the arm that held her close to him. He drew in a deep, shuddering gulp of air, then his fingers slid out of her breeches and began to fumble with the buttons.

Slowly she raised her head and opened her eyes to see that dusk still hung heavily all around them. The cold air struck her fevered skin. In mere minutes, her world had been shattered forever.

Elise wrenched herself from his embrace and backed away. She felt utterly humiliated. Though her flesh was sated, her spirit was sickened. He had made her body leap to life as if it were a puppet on a string. What a naive fool she had been to think she possessed the willpower to resist him!

From the ashes of her pride rose an overwhelming

need to relieve the shame and confusion that clawed at her insides.

"How dare you do that to me?" she accused in a hoarse whisper. "You're no better than Jake Hubbell."

Troy felt the force of her words like a blow to his gut. How could she make such an ugly comparison? Nothing could be further from the truth! Didn't she see that his body was taut with the strain of holding back his passion? He had known she wasn't ready to accept the final commitment of lovemaking, but he had wanted to give her a taste of pleasure, to prove to her that not all men were interested only in their own gratification. His motive had been completely unselfish.

Or had it?

Even as the protests rose to his mind, a mixture of remorse and guilt washed them away. The memory of her plea to stop resounded through his head. He had ignored her protest, his passion fired by endless nights spent lying beside her in feverish frustration. The fantasies that had sustained him since their first meeting were no longer enough. He had been hell-bent on touching her intimately, even if he could not yet relieve his own burning desire. Never in his life had he treated a woman so arrogantly, without the least regard for her wishes.

Reproach was written over Elise's lovely features. She had finished rebuttoning her breeches and stood with her cloak wrapped defensively around her slim form. The riot of curls framing her face gave her the appearance of a lost waif. A surge of protectiveness made him want to gather her in his arms, but the hatred burning in her eyes pierced him like a dagger. He had to make her understand that he was not another Jake Hubbell.

"Elise, let me explain—" Troy began.

"No." She cut him off with a cold sweep of her hand. "What is done is done, and there is naught more to say."

"You're wrong," he said urgently. "God knows I want to make love to you, but only if you're willing. I never meant to force you into anything."

She drew herself up stiffly, meeting his gaze with a valiant dignity. "I suppose you have the right to do whatsoever you please with me. After all, you own me, don't you?"

Pivoting, Elise set out blindly in the direction of the camp. Bitter tears tightened her throat, but she refused to give in to them. She had lost her pride once today, and, no matter what the cost, it would not happen again.

Close behind her, she heard the squeak of Troy's boots on the snow. He made no attempt to speak to her, apparently having realized that his paltry excuses had failed. No matter what he said to the contrary, she knew the real reason he had manipulated her.

Though her experience of lovemaking was limited, she suspected there was more to the act than what had gone on between them today. For men to want it so badly, it made sense that they too achieved a physical gratification similar to what she had felt. Yet she was certain Troy had not reached that exhilarating release. Desire had still glittered in his eyes afterward.

Thus, his goal must have been to humiliate her. There could be no other reason for him to deny his own pleasure. He had wanted to exercise his power over her, to demonstrate his ownership of her body.

And she had played into his hands like a spineless wanton.

Mortification washed over her anew. How could she have succumbed as easily as butter melting under a hot sun? Troy Fletcher was the enemy! And yet he was the only man who could arouse her to a fever pitch, her mind whispered. Why, *why?*

Recalling the gentleness of his touch, Elise felt a sudden, unfamiliar tenderness invade her heart. Her palms broke out in a cold sweat. Swiftly she squashed the budding emotion with the hard stone of hatred. It was unthinkable to regard an Englishman with any feeling other than the loathing that had guided her life for so many years.

One thing was certain, she decided, seeing the campfire glow through the darkness. She could not bear to be under Troy's control. Even now, the memory of his touch made her loins throb with renewed longing, and she knew if he touched her again, she would succumb. Surrendering to that traitorous desire would be far more damaging to her self-respect than the mere breaking of a pledge.

She had no choice but to forsake her vow to stay with him. At the first opportunity, she would run away.

Her chance came five days later.

At Venango, they had left the Allegheny to follow a more direct route overland through the wilderness. Now the small party had again reached the wide, curving river, several miles above the forks where it flowed into La Belle Rivière, the mighty Ohio.

Elise stood on the embankment, gazing at the swiftly moving current. They had expected to find the river frozen and easy to cross, but the solid portion extended out only about fifty feet from shore. Massive chunks of ice surged through the turbulent waters, bobbing their way downstream.

The journey to the opposite shore would have to be made on rafts. The men had spent the entire day felling trees and lashing the trunks together in preparation for the crossing. Now, as the gray afternoon sky began to darken slightly, the supplies were being secured onto the wooden platforms.

Turning to watch the loading procedures, Elise shivered, knowing it was from more than the biting cold. There would never be a better time to slip away. All day she had been planning her escape. A sick anticipation had upset her stomach, and she'd had to force down her food at noon in order to avoid arousing suspicion.

And now the moment had come to set the final part of her plan in motion.

She looked for Troy. He had tossed aside his beaver-skin coat during the course of the day, and his powerful muscles rippled beneath his buckskin shirt as he hefted a sack onto one of the three rafts that lined the riverbank. A tawny beard covered his face; he hadn't bothered to shave since they'd left the fort. The growth of hair lent a rakish cast to his handsome features.

She felt a twist of regret mingled with desire, but she crushed the sensation ruthlessly, taking in several deep breaths of frosty air as she walked toward him. When she reached his side, his eyes met hers, intense and probing. Despite the chilly weather, sweat beaded his forehead. Elise had to ball her fingers into fists to keep from reaching up to wipe the droplets away.

"I'm crossing on Monsieur Van Braam's raft," she said, her voice low so that no one else could hear.

His eyebrows settled into a frown. "The hell you are."

"I am. I've already made the arrangements." Her reply

128

bore the coolness that had marked their relationship since the encounter in the woods five days earlier. He had tried to repair the damage, but she had paid no heed to his offers of peace. Desperate to escape, she thrust in the knife that she knew would wound his pride the most. "I refuse to spend even a few moments near a man like you."

Something akin to pain flared in his jade eyes, then his lips thinned. "As you wish," he said coldly. Pivoting, he strode away.

Elise stifled a peculiar urge to run after him. *Sacré Dieu!* She should be glad he'd taken the bait so easily!

Assuring herself she was doing the right thing, she went over to stand near the Dutchman's raft. George Washington and his guide, Christopher Gist, had left the party several days earlier, hoping to make better time than the slow cavalcade of packhorses. The young major had been in a hurry to deliver St. Pierre's letter to the governor of Virginia.

Nervously, Elise folded her arms beneath her cloak. She had lied to Troy; Van Braam had no idea she was supposed to be crossing with him, and so each man would believe she was safely with the other. In the confusion of departure, she prayed there would be a chance to make her escape. By the time the party was across the river, darkness would have fallen, and it would be impossible for Troy to come after her until morning. The gray sky which foretold snow further tilted the odds in her favor. A storm would obliterate any tracks she would leave behind.

"Let's go!"

As Troy's voice split the air, the men began to slide the rafts across the short stretch of ice toward the open water beyond. Elise followed cautiously. Beneath her feet, the slippery ice groaned and creaked.

Once the rafts were poised near the edge, Troy directed the servitors, who had their hands full enticing the skittish, travel-weary horses into the frigid waters. Elise felt a moment's pity for the animals; their reluctance to swim to the other side was understandable.

Catching Troy's brooding glance, she stepped onto the Dutchman's raft, carefully keeping her balance on the rounded logs. She made a show of crouching down among the piles of supplies as if settling into a safe position, hoping all the while that Van Braam would stay busy with the horses and not question her presence on his raft.

Apparently satisfied that she was secure, Troy turned his attention back to the horses. Instantly Elise crept off the raft and scurried toward the shore. The few feet seemed to take forever to cross. At any moment she expected to hear someone yell after her.

Heart pounding, she scrambled up the bank and darted behind a boulder, hunching herself down as low as possible. She closed her eyes and tried to catch her breath. In the distance the cacophony of shouted orders and neighing horses continued without pause. With trembling hands, she picked up the pack of provisions that she had hidden in a crevice earlier, and secured the leather strap over one shoulder, beneath her cloak. As soon as the others were out of sight, she was ready to start the long trek back to Fort LeBoeuf.

Cautiously she peeked around the edge of the rock. Two of the rafts were in the river now, bucking against the angry current. An ice floe wobbled past them and nearly collided with the flimsy wooden boats.

Troy's was the only raft remaining on shore. As she

watched, it slipped into the dark waters, propelled by a thrust of the long pole in his hands.

Her fingers dug into the pockmarked surface before her. The knowledge that she would never see him again struck Elise like a blow to her heart. Her throat tightened and, without thinking, she rose to her feet, hefting up the heavy pack that hung from her shoulder. A desire to keep Troy in her sight until the last possible moment overrode her sense of caution.

In that instant she saw him glance at the bank. He saw her and froze for a split second, then he whipped around and peered toward Van Braam's raft before digging his pole into the river bottom in a reckless attempt to return to shore.

Elise spotted a huge chunk of ice shooting toward him, moving more swiftly than the heavily laden craft. Apparently Troy was too preoccupied to notice. Horrified, she raced toward the river, waving her arm and shouting a warning.

He was almost to shore when the ice floe struck. The raft broke apart, spewing logs in every direction.

Paralyzed with shock, she watched him plunge into the frigid waters.

Chapter Nine

Elise stared aghast at the spot where he had vanished beneath the churning surface. Floating logs littered the area, but there was no sign of Troy.

Her fingers tightened convulsively around the leather pack that hung from her shoulder. It seemed an eon passed, in which she stood gripped by a hideous panic. The blood hammered wildly in her ears. He couldn't be dead, he couldn't be! It was because of her that he had turned back, because of her that he had fallen in!

Her eye was caught by a flash of movement in the water. Troy had risen to the surface! Her heart lodged in her throat. *Sacré Dieu!* He was alive, but at any instant he would be struck by one of the chunks of ice that crowded the river.

Then to her relief he managed to latch on to a passing log. At the same moment, she saw a man on one of the surviving rafts point to Troy, hollering something that was lost to her over the roar of the river. Wielding their long poles, the others tried to turn around, but the profusion of ice floes impeded them.

They were too far away to be of any help.

The knowledge galvanized Elise, and she went scrambling down the embankment without giving even a thought to the fact that Troy was her enemy.

Slipping and sliding on the snow-covered ice, she raced to catch up with him. She could see him ahead, a distant form clinging to the log as it careened downstream.

A litany repeated in her head. *Please, please, please* . . .

Panting breaths of cold air froze her lungs. The current carried Troy more swiftly than she could run, and soon he was so far in front of her that she could no longer see him through the darkening dusk. Sobbing with effort, she hurried onward, refusing to give up.

It seemed an eternity had passed when she caught sight of him again. The log had come to a stop against a jam of ice floes that rimmed the shore, and Troy was struggling unsuccessfully to crawl out of the freezing water.

She started to dart toward him, then realized she still held her pack. Dropping it, she ran out over the short stretch of ice, halting almost at the edge. Instinct made her flatten down on her belly and extend an arm to him. His wet fingers closed over hers, as stiff and cold as marble.

She pulled with the strength of desperation, but she couldn't draw out his moisture-soaked body. The ice beneath her gave an ominous groan. Biting her lip so hard it bled, she tried again, and again she failed. All she was doing was sliding over that slick surface, coming closer each time to falling into the river herself.

Hot tears of frustration coursed down her chilled cheeks. It was plain that he couldn't last much longer in the frigid water. Ice crystals coated his hair and beard, and his grip on her hand was weakening. There had to be a way to rescue him!

Glancing around wildly, she saw a branch poking out of the snow on shore. She released Troy's hand and scrambled up the embankment to snatch the tree limb and drag it onto the ice.

He was still hanging valiantly to the edge when she returned. She lay down again, grasping one end of the branch and stretching it out so that he could grab the other. To keep from being dragged in, she hooked the toes of her boots over an exposed root that stuck out of the snowy bank.

Her fingers tightened over the rough bark as Elise felt the heaviness of his water-logged body tugging on the branch. Her arms cried out in pain, feeling as if they were being pulled from their sockets. Exerting every ounce of her strength, she hung on doggedly, driven by a primitive determination.

Gradually, he managed to haul himself halfway out. Then he collapsed, his upper body sprawled over the edge, his grip slackening on the branch. With a heart-stopping jolt of horror, she thought he had lost consciousness.

"Fight, damn you! I won't let you die, do you hear me?"

She screamed the words with the combined fierceness of rage and panic. She never knew if it was her voice or his own willpower, but slowly he lifted his head, and to her intense relief she again felt the pressure of his weight on the tree limb.

At last he crawled all the way out of the river. She scrambled to her feet and rushed forward to help him up. He clutched at her with hands that felt colder than death. The ice beneath them creaked a warning. Praying they wouldn't be plunged into the freezing waters below, she let him lean heavily on her as they moved to the shore.

He seemed dazed and disoriented. His body was so chilled he was beyond shivering. Already his wet clothing was sheeted in ice. Elise knew she would have to get him warm quickly or he would not survive long in the bitter cold.

She needed to build a fire in a place that would provide them shelter from the impending storm. Snowflakes already were beginning to swirl from the darkening sky, and the wind was gusting. There was no time to squander.

She snatched up her pack and heaved it over her shoulder, supporting Troy on her other side. Under the crushing weight of the dual burden, she headed into the shadowed woods, searching desperately for a place to camp.

"Sit . . . down," he gasped.

Feeling him start to sag to the ground, Elise pushed him upright with a thrust of her shoulder. "No!" she snapped sharply. "Keep walking. We can't stop here."

Apparently her tone got through to him, for he let her lead him on like a child. The light was fading fast. She was beginning to think they would have to take their chances camping out in the open when she spotted the dim outline of a cabin up ahead.

It seemed to take forever to cover the short distance to the clearing. Elise's heart fell as they drew nearer. No smoke rose from the chimney, and that meant the place must be deserted. Her vision of a crackling fire, hot food, and the succor of a welcoming frontier family faded into oblivion.

She buoyed her sagging spirits. It was miracle enough that they would have a roof over their heads.

The door creaked open at a push of her hand. The darkness inside was thick; the air had a musty odor that assured her the place hadn't been occupied in a while.

She prayed there were no wild animals within, for she had once heard a tale of a bear that had lumbered into an empty cabin and had inadvertently shut the door, not knowing how to get back out. The cornered beast had spent his rage by killing the unfortunate fur trapper who'd entered the cabin several weeks later.

But Troy's growing lethargy was more frightening than any folk story of her youth. He would die if she didn't act quickly. Half-dragging him, she got him through the doorway and eased him to the dirt floor beside the hearth.

A fire. She had to start a fire and get him warm before it was too late. Dropping her pack, Elise sped out the door to find wood. Her luck held. Beside the cabin lay the remains of a stack of split logs left by the previous occupant.

Snatching up as much wood as she could carry, she went back inside and dumped the pile in the hearth. The darkness forced her to take her pack outside to locate the tinderbox.

Kneeling before the cold stone hearth, she fumbled with the flint and steel. Her hands were trembling, and it took several frustrated tries before the wood shavings caught the spark. Bending over, she blew carefully on the tiny flames until the kindling started to burn in earnest.

The blessed heat of blazing logs began to radiate throughout the cabin. The light of the fire illuminated the man who sat nearby. Ice crusted his beard and clothing. His head was tilted back against the stones of the hearth, and his eyelids fluttered, as if he were fighting to stay awake.

Get him warm. The frantic message throbbed through her brain. There was a bedstead built into the corner at the opposite wall of the cabin, but it was too far away

136

from the fire. The deerhide padding that covered the hard wooden platform, though, would help insulate Troy from the cold floor.

The filling of dried leaves and moss rustled as Elise hurriedly dragged the thin mattress over to the hearth. She rummaged in her pack and located a blanket and a small flask. Then she dropped to her knees beside Troy.

Uncorking the bottle, she sniffed at it to assure herself the fumes smelled of brandy. She raised the flask to his blue lips. Droplets of dark liquid trickled from the corners of his mouth and into his beard, but she saw his throat work convulsively as he managed to swallow most of the spirits.

Quickly she set the flask aside. The warmth of the fire was melting the thin sheet of ice that covered his clothing, the water plopping into puddles on the dirt floor. He couldn't remain in those wet garments.

Her trembling fingers untied the belt at his waist with its bullet pouch and powder horn, then tugged urgently at the stiffened leather thong that laced the neck of his buckskin shirt. She breathed a prayer of thanks that he hadn't been wearing his beaver coat, for the fur might have weighed him down and caused him to drown.

His breathing was alarmingly shallow. She knew a lapse into unconsciousness would be dangerous. She grasped his shoulders and gave him a rough shake.

"Troy! Stay awake, do you hear me?"

He stirred restlessly, mumbling something incoherent. Then his eyes opened and he seemed to focus on her.

Tipping his heavy body against her, she yanked at the back of his shirt, somehow managing to wrest the cold, clammy garment up and over his head. Firelight gleamed across the contours of his bare chest. His shoulders were broad and muscled, and between his male nipples there was a thatch of tawny hair that narrowed to a thin line, leading her eyes down his hard belly to his breeches.

Fiercely Elise squelched the involuntary leap of her senses, concentrating her attention on the task of removing his boots. After no more than an instant's hesitation, she applied her fingers to the buttons below his waist. This was no time for maidenly shyness.

It proved to be impossible to peel off the water-logged breeches while he was sitting. "Troy," she said urgently, jerking on his arm. "Come, you must move."

Tugging insistently, she managed to get him up and over to the mattress, where he collapsed on his back. Quickly she stripped the trousers off his long legs until the only thing keeping him from total nudity was the breechclout over his privates. She drew the line there. Wet or not, that scrap of cloth was staying put.

Elise snatched up the blanket, briskly rubbing him dry as she studied him with worried eyes. Despite the heat of the fire, he looked only half-conscious, and there was a rigid set to his muscles that frightened her. A wave of panic swept her. He couldn't die, he just couldn't!

Without further consideration, she whipped the cloak from her shoulders and hastily began to peel away the apparel beneath. Her clothing was saturated on the side where Troy had leaned against her. Clad in a thin woolen chemise, underdrawers and stockings, she slipped beneath the blanket, putting Troy between her and the fire. She molded herself to his lean length and tried to ignore the shivers that coursed through her. His skin was no longer like ice, but it was still dreadfully cold.

She smoothed her palms over the carved strength of his muscles in the hopes of restoring warmth to his blood. At last she felt deep tremors begin to shake him; it was a sign that his body was fighting for survival.

Elise wound her arms around his bare chest, hugging him close for the long time it took his trembling to cease. Now his flesh felt much warmer to the touch. His limbs were relaxed and his eyes were closed in slumber.

The knowledge that he would live brought tears of gladness to her eyes. She put her lips to the blessed heat of his throat and kissed him, relishing the brush of his beard against her skin. The awful tension slid out of her, leaving her boneless and empty. She was drifting off to sleep when a memory of the fire entered her mind. Troy must be kept warm.

Only that compelling thought could pull her from the depths of exhaustion and push her out from beneath the covers, into the coolness of the cabin. Wearily she dragged on her boots and cloak, not bothering with shirt or breeches. A fierce wind flung stinging snowflakes at her as she ventured outside to fetch an armload of logs. After stoking the fire, she undressed again and slipped gratefully beneath the blanket, arranging her cloak over them for added warmth.

Troy murmured drowsily, his arms reaching out to draw her close. Elise snuggled into the heated curve of his body and within seconds she was asleep.

A pale pearl gray painted the room when she awoke the next morning. For one hazy moment she fancied she was back in her own bed at the fort. She yawned lazily, indulging herself in a delicious stretch that brushed her skin against the warm body lying beside her. Reality returned with a jolt.

Turning, she found her head was pillowed on Troy's shoulder, her copper hair spilling in a glorious tangle over his bare torso. One breast was crushed into his chest, and her hand lay casually at the lean indentation of his waist. Against her hip she felt the heated pressure of his fingers. It struck her that they were virtually naked. All that separated their bodies was the thin wool of her undergarments, and his breechclout.

Her nipples tightened in a flash of erotic awareness. Elise knew she ought to get up and don her clothing before he awoke, but she couldn't move. She wanted to stay.

An infinitesimal stirring of his muscles drew her gaze to his face. He was watching her, his jade eyes still hazy with slumber. His warm breath feathered her hair. Slowly his hand moved upward from her hip, smoothing over her chemise, and coming to a halt tantalizingly close to her breast.

"I must have died and gone to heaven," he murmured, "and you're my very own little angel."

He shifted position, his hard body pressing into her as he brought his mouth down over hers, searing her lips with a seductive hunger. The hot flick of his tongue tasted her inner sweetness, finding each moist and vulnerable crevice. A flame of excitement uncurled within her. She was acutely aware of the nakedness of his chest beneath her fingertips, the crisp texture of hair, the warm expanse of skin, the corded strength of muscle. The need to touch him, to be touched by him, flooded her being.

His hand brushed the blanket to her waist, and his lips left hers to trail a path of fire down the delicate arch of her throat and to her breasts. Through her thin chemise, his tongue caressed first one taut peak and then the other. Her long lashes quivered shut as the scorching heat of his mouth melted her insides. She gloried in the feel of his body, so warm and alive. When he lifted his head, shivers ran over her skin as the cool air struck the dampened spots of fabric.

He took her face in his large palms, his thumbs stroking over her silken cheeks. "I want to make love to you, little angel," he whispered. "Will you let me?"

Through the passion that veiled her reason came an awareness that he was giving her a choice. A simple "no" and he would honor her wishes by ceasing his seduction. A "yes" and he would plumb the depths of her chastity until their lovemaking achieved the stunning conclusion she had experienced only once before. In her heart she knew that this time, when it was over, she would be a virgin no more.

His muscles felt tense to her touch, and she realized he curbed his own needs, awaiting her reply. Could she surrender herself to his control, in essence, acknowledge his ownership of her? Or was it already too late to abolish his power over her? After all, she had saved his life in spite of the fact that he was her enemy. Didn't that prove the existence of a bond between them that could not be broken no matter how many times she denied him her body?

His jade eyes studied her with a tender watchfulness. Even with his tawny hair tousled from the dunking in the river, he was the most rakishly handsome man she had ever met. There was something about him, something beyond the mere physical that tugged at her insides. With every fiber of her being, she wanted him to make her a woman . . . his woman.

"Yes . . . yes, I want you. . . ."

With a soft sigh of surrender, she moved her hips instinctively, wreathing her arms around his powerful shoulders. Troy's rigid constraint vanished in a sharp exhalation of breath. Then his mouth was on hers and he

141

was pressing her against the mattress with a passion so fierce it ignited a throbbing fire in her veins. She kissed him back with all the turbulent emotion in her heart.

His lips left hers to nibble a hot trail along her jaw. A fluid warmth filled her loins as his tongue delved into the intricate whorls of her ear.

"Elise . . . Elise, how many nights I've dreamed of this . . . to feel you yielding beneath me . . . to know your need is as great as my own."

She shifted slightly to aid him in sliding her chemise up and over her head. Pausing only long enough to kiss the tip of each breast, his tongue flicking out in teasing temptation, he peeled away the rest of her undergarments. Then he knelt over her, straddling her bare hips. The pulsing in her lower body quickened as his gaze roamed over the creamy beauty of her breasts, and down her belly to the soft mound of dark copper at the top of her thighs. Cool air whispered over her skin, but that was not what made her shiver. It was the raw desire that shadowed the jade of his eyes.

His hands went to the breechclout that hung from his narrow waist and the scrap of deerskin dropped off to render him naked. Elise glanced away in sudden shyness.

"Look at me," he murmured, grasping her chin to turn her face back. "Don't be afraid."

Blushing, she satisfied her curiosity. Her breath caught at her first sight of a mature man in full arousal. His physique had a rugged beauty all its own, hard and strong and undeniably virile.

He lowered himself to her, his mouth branding her with a kiss that was sweet and full of promise. A calloused thumb flicked across her nipple, sending flashes of pleasure to her abdomen, as if transmitted by a taut

142

thread. His lips burned downward to sample the softness of her breasts. He buried his face in the warm valley there before turning his attention to the rounded swells. Circling a honey-pink tip with his tongue, he enclosed it in a moist, suckling warmth that coaxed a moan from the depths of her throat.

Elise arched her hips to him in reckless abandon. Against her thigh she felt the heat and hardness of him, but there was no fear, only a need building inside her, a yearning made all the more desperate by the touch of his hand. As he probed the delicate folds of flesh to find her moist center, her legs parted instinctively to his intimate exploration. Gently he stroked her virginal passage in preparation for his entry. Then he came down over her, pressing deep within her, ending her innocence.

There was an instant of pain that was quickly soothed by the delicious sensation of him, big and throbbing, filling her completely. She was awash in a sense of oneness, an indescribable vulnerability.

"You're mine," he said fiercely. "No other man can claim you so."

She felt the force of his whispered words in every fiber of her being. The imprint of his body was indeed seared into hers for all time, yet she felt no distaste at the knowledge. Instead a sense of exultation swelled her heart.

"Oh, Troy . . . yes . . . yes . . ."

He began to move again, and the erotic rhythm of his thrusts drove all conscious thought from her mind. She abandoned herself to the purity of pleasure, clinging deliriously to him. Her body seemed to glow with heat despite the cold of the air. Eyes closed, she heard the rasp of his breath, felt the heavy thud of his heartbeat against her breasts. The need that pulsed inside her gathered force until it encompassed every part of her. And when the white-hot explosion came, she cried out at its cleansing release. At some dim level of awareness, she felt the shudder of Troy's body as he emptied his seed inside her.

Clasped together, they drifted in the ebbing ripples of spent passion. A gust of wind rattled the shutters that covered the single oil-papered window. Elise was drowsily conscious of a mellow peace that she had never before felt. Her face was buried in the moist scent of his neck, the softness of his whiskers against her cheek. The heaviness of him was sprawled atop her, and their bodies were still joined.

After a time Troy shifted his weight. Chilly air scooted across her skin, gooseflesh rising on her shivering body even as he drew the blanket over their nakedness. He propped himself on his elbow and regarded her, the softness in his eyes overlaid with the merest hint of something deeper.

"Will you teach me to speak French?" he asked.

The unexpected question startled her into a smile. *"Oui, m'sieur.* Where shall we begin? With *bonjour* or perhaps *comment allez-vous?"*

Quietly, he said, "What are the words that mean 'I love you'?"

Her heart stopped in midbeat.

He couldn't mean . . . no, it was impossible. She was unfamiliar with the aftermath of loveplay; to an experienced man like Troy this was undoubtedly all a part of the sport of seduction. Still, her voice emerged as a mere thread of sound. *"Je t'aime."*

"Je t'aime," he echoed softly.

There was such a vivid tenderness in his eyes that she turned her gaze to his naked chest, a whirl of strange emotions beating inside her. Never before had any man spoken those words to her. But he didn't mean them, *couldn't* mean them, she told herself furiously. This was all a game to him.

His hand angled her chin up, forcing her to meet his gaze, warm and searching. "Elise, what I said is true. I'm in love with you."

Uncertainty engulfed her. She was caught in the snare of his eyes, and all she could manage was to move her head back and forth in soundless denial. He was lying. This was a trick. He thought he could worm his way into her heart and destroy her.

"Nay!" she whispered sharply. "I don't . . . I *can't* believe you."

Jerking back the blanket, she rolled out from under him before he could stop her. She snatched up her cloak from where it lay in a heap on the floor, wrapping it around her more as a shield over her vulnerable nakedness than as protection against the icy air.

Although Troy was silent, she was intensely aware of his eyes following her every move. Elise grabbed her breeches, and as she slid on the garment, she caught sight of a rusty brown smear on her thigh.

A tumult of anger and confusion roiled inside her. Disregarding the teachings of a lifetime, she had handed the gift of her innocence to a deceitful Englishman. She had given him the chasteness of body that should have been her offering to her husband on the night of their wedding. What was the worse, she still wanted him, even now.

Chased by demons of bewilderment, Elise carelessly

145

stuffed her bare feet into her boots and sped to the door. As her fingers fumbled with the wooden latch, she heard the sound of footsteps behind her and then Troy's hand came down over hers.

"Where are you going?"

"We need wood for the fire," she mumbled.

"That can wait. Elise, look at me."

"No."

"Please."

Unwillingly, she half twisted toward him. He was so close that his warmth enveloped her, though only their hands touched. The naked splendor of his body brought her senses leaping to vibrant life in defiance of all logic. The taste of him lingered in her mouth, and she ached to stroke her fingers across that broad chest. How could she still want him so?

"You should put something on," she said curtly. "Your fall in the river can have ill effects if you don't take care."

"Mmmm," he agreed with the suspicion of a smile. "Does that mean you care whether I live or die?"

"I wouldn't want to have your death on my conscience," she snapped.

"I see. Have you happened to notice any symptoms of a physical impairment today?"

His gentle teasing brought a blush to her cheeks. Quickly she tried to lift the doorlatch, but his hand held her immobile. "Please," she grated, hating herself for begging. "I—I must fetch some firewood."

"You needn't bother. I'll get it as soon as I've dressed."

"No!" Desperate to be alone with her churning thoughts, she searched for a way to dissuade him. "Your clothing is still too wet for you to venture out."

"And neither should you go out clad so scantily." His hand slipped inside her cloak, curling around her bare breast.

She caught her breath at the sweet rush of desire that coursed through her. They couldn't make love again, at least not until she'd had a chance to sort through the confusion in her mind.

"Please, Troy, don't," she said, her voice low. "I'll put on the shirt, but at least grant me a few moments alone."

His green eyes were soft with a tenderness she couldn't allow herself to believe in. "All right," he conceded. "But when you return, you and I are going to have a talk."

He stepped back, and she ducked past him to snatch up the shirt that had once belonged to her brother. With her back to Troy, she let the cloak drop from her bare shoulders long enough to yank the garment over her head.

Keeping her eyes averted from him, she grabbed her cloak and scurried out the door like a scared rabbit, heedless of the gusting snow that lashed her burning cheeks.

Chapter Ten

Elise delayed their talk for as long as possible. Though chastising herself for being a coward, she couldn't keep from dawdling over the fire, then over the preparation of a meal. A search of the cabin yielded a small, rusty skillet, which she rubbed clean with snow. Using a bit of cornmeal from her pack, she cooked johnnycakes to supplement the strips of jerky that had been the mainstay of their journey.

Troy seemed to understand her need for silence, for he made little attempt at conversation. He sat amiably beside the hearth, wolfing down his food with a healthy appetite that annoyed Elise. The flat cornmeal cakes stuck like sawdust in her own throat. Perched stiffly on a stool near the fireplace, she tried to remain aloof to Troy, but through the corner of her eye she was conscious of his long, bare legs stretching out of the blanket he had draped over his nakedness. While she had been outside gathering wood, he had spread his wet clothing close to the fire so the garments could dry.

She wished he were fully dressed. The thought of what

148

lay beneath his inadequate covering filled her belly with a hot, heavy sensation. Nervous and on edge, she picked at her food without eating it until her tin plate held a pile of crumbs. *Sacré Dieu,* if only she were anywhere but alone in this cabin with him, so many miles from civilization!

A jumble of unanswered questions crowded her mind. Why had she given herself to Troy, of all men? What made her so foolish as to still want him, even now? And how could she bear it if he continued to speak his lies of love?

She jumped to her feet and flung the remains of her meal into the flames. Cleaning up would occupy a few more minutes. As she reached for the skillet, Troy leaned over to wrap his fingers around her wrist.

"No more stalling," he said firmly. "Sit down."

Elise complied with all the eagerness of a child anticipating a well-deserved scolding. She shifted on the hard stool, staring at the fingers clenched in her lap. It was useless to postpone the inevitable. She was stuck here with him, and there was nowhere to run and hide.

"Elise, look at me."

Reluctantly she obeyed the quiet command. Averting her gaze from the tempting length of his body, she forced herself to meet his eyes.

"Why did you save my life?" he asked softly. "Why did you throw away the perfect opportunity to be free of me once and for all?"

It was a question she had been unable to answer herself, but she had to say *something.* "You needed help," she mumbled. "I would have done the same for anyone."

"Even for a sworn enemy? The man you despised so much you would break your vow not to run away?" Troy shook his head. "Nay, I cannot accept that, Elise. You acted as you did because you no longer hate me."

With a flash of dismay, she realized he was right. What had become of the animosity he deserved as an Englishman? She was suddenly, uncomfortably aware of a sense of vulnerability. Malice had been her protective shield, but that feeling was gone forever. It was the only explanation for why she had been unable to let him die and why she had surrendered her body to him. Her nails dug painfully into the tender skin of her palms. What would fill the void in her emotions now that hatred had vanished?

Troy extended a hand to her. "Come sit with me."

She hesitated. In his eyes she saw a gentleness and an understanding that melted the barrier around her heart. Though common sense warned her of the peril in trusting him, the warmth he radiated bore an irresistible appeal.

Elise rose from the stool and put her hand in his. The fingers that curled around hers were firm and strong, drawing her down into his lap. His arms enfolded her to nestle her securely against his chest. Tucking her face into his neck, she absorbed the comfort he offered.

He lifted her chin. "Elise, I love you," he said huskily. "I want you to be my wife."

The notion was unthinkable . . . yet why did his proposal cause a liquid sensation deep inside of her? It was a feeling she had never experienced with Yves.

Yves. She clutched desperately at the excuse. "Nay, I could never wed you—I'm promised to another."

Troy's arms stiffened. "Another? Who are you talking about?"

"Yves Larousse. We were to be wed until you came along."

Troy heard the censure in her voice, and felt a flash of

guilt mingled with fear. Was she in love with Larousse? No, he decided an instant later, it was impossible. A woman of her integrity couldn't have given her virginity to him so unreservedly unless she had felt no bond to any other man.

A rush of fierce possessiveness engulfed him. By God, she was his now. Whatever hold Larousse had once had on her, it was gone forever, it *had* to be. Troy shook off a small quiver of apprehension. He had fixed his claim on her and he would let no man come between them. No man. He was taking her far away from any link with her past.

"You're mine now," he said. "I love you and I want to marry you."

Elise thrilled to the quiet vehemence in his tone, yet logic made her stifle the unsettling sensation. "Nay, Troy, you ask the impossible—"

His fingers came down on her lips to silence the protest. "I promise I won't pressure you to wed me," he murmured. "All I ask is that you come home with me of your own free will. Perhaps in time you'll see I could never abandon you as your father did."

She was torn between common sense and wild impulse. "I don't know. . . ."

"You must come, for your own sake as well as mine," he urged. "There is a bond between us, Elise. You feel it, too, or you wouldn't have saved my life . . . and you wouldn't have let me make love to you."

A burning log shifted, showering sparks over the hearth. She could not deny his words, for she had felt the reality of that link as strongly as if the solidness of a rope joined them. Yet surely he mistook lust for love. For some mysterious reason, their bodies responded to each other with a depth of passion that was rare and beautiful . . . and bound to burn out in time.

Follow your head and not your heart. The long-ago words of her mother echoed through Elise's brain, yet she brushed them aside. Her need for Troy was not emotional but physical. He lacked the power to hurt her because she knew better than to fall in love with him. And it seemed logical that the more they indulged their passions, the sooner he would tire of her. When the fierceness of their desire waned, then she could break this hold he had on her.

The decision left her cleansed with relief. Yes, it was impossible for him to destroy her if she granted him access only to her body and not her heart. And right now, her flesh was responding to his nearness with an unquenchable need.

Elise slid her hands inside the blanket, taking pleasure in the hardness of his bare chest beneath her palms. "I'll stay with you, Troy," she whispered, stirring sinuously in his lap. "But only if you make love to me again."

"As often as you like, little angel."

His iridescent jade eyes echoed the husky promise in his voice. Their mouths met with a mutual hunger. She needed no coaxing to part her lips; the slide of his tongue was an erotic delight that made her senses spin.

His hand burrowed into the soft strands of hair that curled down her back, while the other glided over her thigh, pressing her more firmly to him, so that she could feel the hardness of his arousal. The knowledge that she had the power to affect him so ran through her veins like sweet fire. Her fingers sought the lean indentation of his waist, her thumbs caressing his lower belly.

"Please, Troy. . . ."

He sucked in his breath. "There's no need to rush," he murmured against her lips. "We have all day." Yet the ragged quality in his deep voice told her his desire was as great as her own.

He dragged the shirt over her head and tossed it aside. His palm cupped her bare breast as his lips circled the honeyed tip, his whiskers brushing against her sensitive skin, sending throbbing darts of pleasure straight to her loins. The sound of his harsh breathing enthralled her, and she put her lips to his neck, tasting the salt of his skin.

When his hand flattened over the silken flesh just below her breasts, her muscles contracted with pleasure. He inserted a fingertip into her waistband, moving it back and forth across her abdomen, tantalizing her until Elise could bear no more. Hands shaking, she reached down and began to unfasten her breeches.

"Allow me," he said, brushing her efforts aside.

With infinite patience, he opened each button, one by one, until at last the triangle of dark copper at the joining of her thighs was visible to his gaze. Without bothering to remove the garment, he slipped his hand inside. She gasped with pleasure as he caressed her most sensitive place. His skillful fingers teased and aroused until she could no longer bear the sweet, heavy pulses that gripped her loins.

"Troy, please . . . I want to feel you inside me."

"Sweet angel," he rasped, "I want you, too."

He lifted her in his arms, and the blanket that was his only covering dropped to the floor as he carried her over to the pallet in front of the hearth and laid her down. Lovingly he stripped away the remainder of her clothing, pausing to plant kisses over every inch of her body.

She felt the heated hardness of him against her soft thigh as he positioned himself over her. Her fingers threaded into his hair, reveling in its texture, like raw silk. He was so warm and vital that to even think he might have died made her throat tighten.

"Je t'aime, Elise . . . I love you."

The words whispered against her temple made her heart swell with some indefinable emotion. His chest hairs grazed her sensitive nipples as she pressed herself to him, needing him as she had never needed any other man. She opened her legs in wanton abandon, craving the sense of wholeness he alone could give her.

When at last he entered her velvet depths, she moaned from the beauty of their mating, her perceptions so heightened that she fancied she could feel his responses as acutely as her own. Together they surged and strained, seeking release from the sweet torment that held them captive. Limbs entwined, they plunged into a pulsating pleasure so powerful it blotted out all else.

Awareness crept back by degrees. Drifting in drowsy fulfillment, Elise felt the slowing thrum of his heart against her breasts. The taste of his skin lingered in her mouth. When Troy shifted his weight off her body, the heat of the fire kept her bathed in warmth.

Her lashes lifted and she looked up to see him studying her tenderly. He raised a hand to her cheek, caressing her with infinite gentleness before trailing his fingertips downward, tracing first the fragility of her jaw and then the silken contour of her shoulder.

"This is heaven," he murmured, "and I'd love to stay here forever . . . kissing you . . . touching you."

She was loath to face the real world beyond the

confines of this cozy cabin. "Why don't we?" she asked wistfully.

"You tempt me, little angel." Troy bent his head to nuzzle her throat, his beard tickling her skin. "At least we can't leave right away; we'll have to stay until my clothing dries."

Elise propped up on her elbow, stretching out a hand to test the dampness of the shirt that was draped over a nearby bench. It was stiffening from the water and would have to be kneaded before it was wearable.

"That might not be until tomorrow . . . late tomorrow."

"Then I suppose we'll have to stay here until the following day." He heaved an irritated sigh though his eyes danced with devilish humor. "Whatever do you suppose we can do to occupy all those long hours?"

She stretched like a contented cat, exulting in the pure pleasure of his presence. "Stare at each other in boredom?" she suggested drolly.

He chuckled. "As soon as I get my strength back, I'll show you just how boring I find you." Abruptly his expression grew serious, and he put an arm around her, nestling her head on his hard shoulder. "I could never tire of you, and yet we must not linger here overlong, for 'twill be reported I perished in the river. I cannot let my family think me dead."

"Your family?" Elise stiffened, stunned by a sudden, searing nausea. Did Troy have a wife? As swiftly as the notion had struck, logic banished it. Surely he wouldn't have asked *her* to wed him if that were the case . . . would he?

"I have an elder brother, Jason, who'll be worried

155

about me," he explained. "He and his wife, Mirella, have a small son and daughter. And then, of course, there's my younger sister, Pandora. She's about your age, and as pretty as can be."

As they cuddled together before the fire, he entertained her with stories of his family, speaking of them with such warmth and affection that they became real people to Elise, people she felt as if she had known all her life. When he told her about his plantation, she pictured a cozy homestead nestled in a thicket of shade trees and surrounded by rich fields, much like the small farms she had seen near Montreal. The image appealed to her heart, and a yearning to be a part of that scenario startled her with its intensity.

With Troy's every word and gesture, she had the impression that he viewed her as a firm fixture in his future. Could it be possible that he truly loved her? Or was she only spinning fanciful thoughts, sparked by the illusion of security she felt in his arms . . . a mood that was enhanced by the laziness of the day and the warm aftermath of lovemaking?

Encouraged by Troy, she spoke shyly of her own background, even dipping far into the recesses of memory to tell him of her life during the time when her parents had still been together. She concentrated on the happy times, skirting around the painful topic of her father's desertion.

For Elise, their conversation was a baring of the soul, the gift of her innermost thoughts and experiences, which she had never given to any other man. It set the tone for the next few days. By circumstance and by choice they spent every moment together, both waking and sleeping. It was an interlude in which they were simply man and woman, without political identity or diverse backgrounds.

By the following afternoon, Troy's clothing had dried, and he dressed, informing her that he was assuming the duty of gathering wood for the fire. She trailed him outside on the excuse that she wanted to escape the cabin for a moment; deep in her heart, she admitted an unwillingness to let him out of her sight.

The sun angled through winter-bare trees to spread lacy patterns over the pristine landscape. Not a cloud marred the sapphire sky; the blizzard had ended early that morning. The crisp cold air made her breath condense like fog.

Troy was crouched by the side of the cabin, brushing away the drift that covered the woodpile. A devilish impulse made Elise bend down to scoop up a handful of snow. She formed it into a ball and threw it straight at him.

She hit him square in the middle of the back. He leaped to his feet and advanced on her with a growl of counterfeit fury. Laughter bubbled from her throat as she backed away, wildly tossing snowballs at him in an effort to keep him at bay. He joined in the mock battle with a few well-aimed missiles that sent icy particles sifting down her collar.

Troy circled her, coming dangerously close to nabbing her. With a gasping giggle, she tried to stay out of his clutches by darting behind a tree. In turning, she stepped on the edge of her cloak and stumbled, and he pushed her down into a snowbank, his powerful body entrapping her.

"You little minx!" he said with a grin. "Cry truce, or I

vow you'll be sorry you ever started this!"

She gave a breathless laugh, thrusting her hands against his shoulders as she twisted in a halfhearted attempt to wriggle free. Her action only served to enhance her awareness of his masculine form. Looking into his green eyes, she saw the mirror of her own dawning desire.

"Do you know this is the first time I've ever heard you laugh, little angel?" Troy said softly. "You have two of the loveliest dimples, one here,"—he kissed a spot beside her mouth—"and one over here." His tongue flicked out to taste the matching place on her other cheek.

Warmth uncurled inside Elise despite the coldness of the snow beneath her. The breath left her lungs in a sigh as he nuzzled kisses over the delicate contours of her face. His mouth found hers, moving with such honeyed persuasion that her limbs felt as if they were melting. His hard arousal was unmistakable despite the barrier of their clothing. Entranced, she touched her tongue to his, willingly submitting to the spell he had cast over her.

"Sweet, sweet love," he whispered huskily. "I need you . . . I need your warmth and your laughter and your fire."

His words touched her heart, and she was bewildered by his power over her. "Oh, Troy . . . what are you doing to me?"

He smiled. "I'm making love to you."

"That's not what I meant."

"I know. But I'm still going to make love to you."

Swiftly he scooped her up into his arms. Carrying her toward the cabin, he shouldered the door open and laid her down before the fire. They discarded their clothing in haste, coming together in a coupling that was intense and tumultuous, so dazzling in its wild beauty that it left them gasping.

Much later, Troy lay awake, staring at the fire shadows that danced on the cabin walls. Elise had long since fallen asleep, her small body cuddled against him. Bending his head, he pressed a soft kiss into her tousled hair. Tenderness washed through him as he gazed at her lovely features, so angelic in slumber. It was no wonder she was exhausted. Never in his life had he seen such a capacity for lovemaking in a woman . . . or in himself. Always before, he had been content to satisfy his physical needs with the occasional bedding of some willing widow or tavern wench.

If love was at the root of his insatiable desire, then what explained the depth of Elise's passion? Had he merely awakened lust in her virginal body?

Doubt and uncertainty returned to haunt him. Though he was confident she no longer hated him, he was almost afraid to hope she might someday develop an affection for him. Troy now understood the dissatisfaction that had plagued him over the past few years. He wanted to experience for himself the happiness his brother Jason had found with Mirella. He wanted Elise to share his life and to bear his children.

His arms tightened around her slender form. By God, if there were only some way to bind her to him forever! Perhaps if his seed bore fruit within her womb, then he could induce her to wed him for the child's sake. . . .

He released a deep sigh. Love was not something that could be forced upon a person; it had to originate within the heart. All he could do was exercise patience. Silently he cursed her father for causing such mistrust in her.

Troy's thoughts turned to the long journey ahead. Though he was anxious to reach home, he was aware of a strange reluctance to depart this cabin where they had first made love. It was almost as if there were some sort of magic here that they might lose forever by leaving.

He shook off his misgivings, closing his eyes in a determined effort to sleep. Elise was at his side now, and that was all that mattered.

Chapter Eleven

"Look, we're almost there," Troy said over his shoulder, pointing toward the trees ahead. Without slowing his pace, he forged onward through the deep drifts.

Elise strained to see past the light snow that had begun to fall earlier in the afternoon. With a surge of relief she spotted smoke curling from a distant chimney, charcoal against a pewter sky. After tramping through wooded hills since dawn, they were at last approaching their destination, the trading post operated by John Frazier.

It was located near where Turtle Creek emptied into the Monongahela River, some ten miles southeast of the cabin where they'd spent two idyllic days. Elise had felt a wistful reluctance to leave their cozy haven. Small and crude as the accommodations were, it was the place where she had learned the joys of physical intimacy, the place where she had become a woman.

They had set out early that morning, discovering it was now unnecessary to build a raft to cross the Allegheny. The bitter-cold weather had frozen the river, making it simple to walk over the ice to the other side. Troy stayed in the lead so he could blaze a trail through the snow.

They would be arriving none too soon, she thought, wrapping her cloak more tightly around her. It would be heaven to have a warm spot to sleep, a hot meal, and a chance to rest her weary bones. Troy must be feeling the effects of the cold, too, she thought, for with his coat lost he had only the blanket to protect him from it.

As they neared the trading post, Elise saw two log cabins, one larger than the other, with several barns in the clearing behind. The door of the smaller cabin opened and a man stepped out to stare at them, a rifle tucked under his arm. His rangy form was clad in fringed buckskins, and a shock of ill-cut brown hair brushed his shoulders. The frontiersman raised a hand in greeting as they approached.

"Why, Troy Fletcher, I heard you was drowned! I shoulda known a mean old devil like you couldn't get hisself kilt so easy."

"I would have died if it hadn't been for a certain lady pulling me out of the river." Troy drew Elise forward, putting an arm around her shoulders. "This is my savior, Mademoiselle Elise d'Evereaux. Elise, allow me to introduce you to John Frazier, a fine trader I met on the journey to Fort LeBoeuf."

The frontiersman gave her a nod of approval. "Pleased to meet you, mam'selle. Why is't Troy Fletcher gets a pretty lady like you to rescue him? Only time I ever got saved by anybody 'twas by an old coot uglier'n meself."

"Oh, but you're not ugly," Elise disagreed, charmed by his easy smile. "I'm sure you've made a few female hearts flutter in your time."

"Why, that's right nice of you to say so." Flashing

162

Troy a broad wink, Frazier added, "I might just steal this gal away from you if'n you don't watch out."

"Don't let that lovely face fool you," Troy cautioned. "She's ornery, willful, greedy, stubborn . . . not at all the sort of woman you're looking for."

Elise gasped, then saw his eyes were twinkling.

"Guess you may's well keep this pretty pack o' trouble for yourself, then," Frazier said with mock dejection.

Seriously, Troy said, "So the rest of the party must have passed through recently. They still here?"

"No, siree. They headed on out yesterday mornin', bright an' early. Come on in out o' the cold, and I'll tell you all about it."

They entered the smaller log cabin, which was crammed with everything from blankets to food to firearms. Bundles of muskrat and beaver pelts were stacked at one end of the room. The musky scent of raw animal hides hung heavy in the air. A clerk looked up as they came inside, then returned to his task of counting the furs, using a quill pen to record the numbers in a leather-bound ledger.

Squatting near the hearth was an Indian brave of indeterminate age, his obsidian eyes revealing no hint of his thoughts. Elise stayed close behind Troy and Frazier. The presence of the savage didn't seem to bother the two Englishmen, who wended their way past the piles of supplies to the hard benches in a corner.

On a nearby table a gun lay in pieces—lock, barrel, and hammer, and a beautifully carved stock of black walnut. Frazier explained to Elise that he repaired rifles for anyone who had the goods or coin to pay him, including the redskin who waited by the fire.

After they sat down, the frontiersman lit a pipe,

163

gesturing with it as he related the story he'd heard from Van Braam, that Troy had fallen into the icy river and they'd been unable to turn their rafts around to rescue him or the French girl they'd assumed was traveling on his raft.

As the warmth of the room seeped into her bones, Elise removed her gloves and pushed back the hood of her cloak. She tried to stave off drowsiness and concentrate politely on the conversation, but the effect proved futile. A yawn escaped before she could stifle it.

"Forgive me, Elise," Troy exclaimed. "You must be dead tired after walking so far." He turned to Frazier and asked, "Can we send her next door?"

"Why, sure. You just run along an' knock on the door; my cook, Large Betty, 'll fix you up with some vittles and a place to rest your head."

The prospect of food made her mouth water. As she rose from the bench, Troy took her hand. "I won't be much longer," he murmured, his thumb stroking the sensitive skin of her palm.

The gleam in his green eyes made her heart race. His wicked grin told her he knew precisely his effect on her. Feeling a blush suffuse her body, she pulled her hand free and glanced over at Frazier to find him watching the exchange with amused curiosity. Embarrassed, she mumbled a good-bye and headed toward the door.

Outside, Elise paused for a moment, letting the frigid air cool her hot cheeks. Dusk cloaked the landscape in gray shadows and chilly gusts of wind sent snowflakes swirling all around her. Would Troy sleep beside her tonight?

The question popped into her mind without warning. She didn't relish the idea of flaunting their intimate relationship in front of other people. Even here in the wilderness, rules of convention surely must prevail. Yet the prospect of spending the night in a lonely bed held little appeal. The physical hunger Troy had awakened in her was far from satisfied. How long would it take to destroy the bond that linked them?

Lost in thought, Elise walked through the snow toward the larger log cabin. Suddenly a man rounded the corner, his furtive eyes shifting back and forth. Seeing her, he stopped dead in his tracks.

A gasp choked her throat. That brawny build and shaggy black beard belonged to Jake Hubbell! What was he doing here?

Uttering a grunt of surprise, Hubbell came barreling toward her. The shock that gripped her limbs vanished in a rush of fear. Only a few feet separated her from the cabin, and she ran for it blindly.

He was swifter. His meaty hands clamped painfully around her shoulders and thrust her up against the wall just as she was lifting her fist to pound on the door.

"Well, well," he drawled, his breath reeking of stale liquor. "If 'tain't me li'l Frenchie. I knowed I'd run into ye again sometime; I jest didn't reckon it'd be so soon."

"Let me go," Elise ordered bravely, her heart thumping. "Troy is nearby. If you dare hurt me, he'll kill you."

"I ain't gonna hurt ye—I'm gonna show ye how a honest-to-God man kin pleasure ye. I got the biggest one ye ever done seen."

To substantiate his crude bragging, he rubbed his groin against her lower belly so that she couldn't help but feel his hardness. Her skin crawled at the thought of his touching her intimately.

"Get away from me!" Frantically, Elise tried to twist free, kicking at his legs and pounding the filthy buckskin that covered his chest. But she was trapped securely between his broad body and the rough logs behind her. When she opened her mouth to scream, his large paw clapped over her lips so she could scarcely draw a breath.

"Ye ain't gettin' away from me this time," he snarled.

After stuffing a dirty rag in her mouth, Hubbell dragged her toward the corner of the cabin. Elise struggled futilely against his bulk. The barns were situated to the rear of the compound, and beyond them was nothing but a vast stretch of wilderness. *Sacré Dieu!* No one would ever find her!

There was a sudden creak of hinges, and a bar of light spilled out onto the snow. A giant of a woman filled the doorframe, the wind whipping her homespun skirt.

"Thought I heared voices out here," she said, aiming her long rifle with the competence of a seasoned hunter. "Less'n ya want buckshot in yer britches, mister, ya'd best let 'er loose."

Instantly Elise felt Hubbell's grip slacken. She backed away, yanking off the filthy cloth that choked her.

"Now, Betty, I ain't done nothin'," he whined.

A shot exploded from the rifle. Hubbell leaped back with a howl as the bullet struck the snow beside him, spraying Elise with a shower of ice particles.

"Mister, ya ain't got no call to use me Christian name. Now git on out o' here afore ya makes me madder."

Hubbell hesitated only a split second before taking off running toward the stables. The door to the other cabin burst open and Troy came hurrying out with John Frazier and the clerk. Each man carried a rifle.

"We heard the shootin'," Frazier said to the woman in

the doorway. "What's goin' on?"

She lifted her broad shoulders in a casual shrug. "Jist scarin' off a varmint."

Troy drew Elise close, studying her searchingly in the pale light from the open door. "Are you all right?"

She nodded, burying her face in the familiar warmth of his chest. Her body trembled from the aftermath of terror. After a moment, she lifted her head, knowing she had to warn Troy. "'Twas Jake Hubbell," she told him.

"That bastard is here?" he asked, incredulous. "Did he touch you again?"

"Yes, but—"

"Which way did he go?"

"Toward the barns."

"By the devil, I'll kill him this time!"

"Troy, wait!" She caught at his arm, fearing Hubbell might have gone for his own rifle. Troy could be murdered. "Just let him go. He didn't hurt me. Can we not forget it happened?"

The sudden, muffled thunder of hoofbeats on the snow drew their attention to the stables. A horse galloped across the clearing, its mahogany coat barely visible in the deep shadows of twilight. Hubbell's burly form crouched low on the animal's back.

"God damn, that's my stallion!" Frazier roared.

"Let's get him," Troy said grimly.

The men sprinted toward the stables. Within moments, they were mounted and riding off in the direction Hubbell had vanished. Elise watched them leave, her heart in her throat. If anything happened to Troy. . . .

"Ain't no use in us freezin' our tails off. Them boys could be gone fer hours. Come on in an' I'll give ya a nip of me best home brew."

Elise let the tall woman lead her inside and seat her on a stool near the fire. Numbly she took the pewter mug the woman offered and put it to her lips. The whiskey burned down her throat, making her gag, but after a minute its restorative powers took effect.

Her hostess sat down on a bench opposite Elise, tilting her head back to drink from a mug with a daintiness that belied her Amazon appearance. She was over six feet tall. It wasn't that the woman was overweight, Elise decided; she simply had magnificent proportions. Man-sized feet shod in beaded moccasins peeked out from beneath her brown homespun skirt, and her bosom was ample but firm. She had leathery skin and black hair wound into a bun, while her eyes were a startling bright blue.

"Me pap was an Injun," she said, explaining her dark coloring matter-of-factly. "Most folks 'round these parts call me Large Betty. So, ya be Troy Fletcher's woman?"

The question caught Elise by surprise. *Troy Fletcher's woman.* Well, it was true, at least for the time being, wasn't it?

She gave a small nod. "My name is Elise d'Evereaux."

"French, hmm?" Large Betty scowled. "Word is they be plannin' t' push us off our land. Buildin' forts all up and down th' rivers, an' tellin' us English we ain't got no right t' be here."

"The French were granted this territory by treaty," Elise felt obliged to argue.

"Don't go spoutin' no fancy words to me. Fact is, them French plan t' steal us blind."

"I'm sure everyone will be treated fairly!"

The Englishwoman snorted. "Fair! Why, they already pushed Frazier out o' Venango last May. Stepped right in and took over th' land he been livin' on fer more'n twelve years. We was all lucky to get out alive."

"I-I didn't know." Elise was taken aback. That cluster of cabins in Venango had once belonged to John Frazier? For the first time, she felt a glimmer of insight into the English cause. Could there be any justification for driving a man out of his home?

Large Betty shrugged. "Well, guess I ain't got no call t' blame ya when ya ain't th' one doin' th' fightin. Kin I fetch ya some vittles?"

Without waiting for a reply, the woman rose and dipped a ladle into the cooking pot that hung over the fire. She filled a wooden trencher with a heaping portion of delicious-smelling venison stew and handed it to Elise.

"Ya be wantin' t' take a bath?"

"Why, yes, thank you." Elise felt a flash of surprise that the woman could be so generous to an enemy.

Large Betty lifted a pot from beside the fire, then tucked a rifle under her arm before going outside. Reentering the cabin a few minutes later, she hung the potful of snow over the fire to melt, then replaced the bar over the door.

She sat down before a little spinning wheel and began to manipulate the foot pedal, twisting glossy flax fibers into yarn that would be used to make linen. Her movements were deft and graceful despite her size. After a while, Large Betty said, "Lordy, we all thought Fletcher'd drowned. What happened?"

Elise related the story, though skimming over her escape attempt. There was no need to tell anyone else about that part; she had little wish to discuss the nature of her and Troy's private relationship.

When Elise was through eating, Large Betty dragged a wooden washtub in front of the fire, and then filled the vessel with steaming water. A couple of chairs with blankets thrown over the backs screened the bathing area. Large Betty said she'd fetch some clean clothing, and she left the cabin.

Elise stripped off her buckskins and sank into the heated liquid with a sigh of pure sensual delight. It had been days—weeks—since she'd enjoyed the luxury of anything more than a sponge bath. The warmth soothed the slight tenderness that lingered between her thighs, and she blushed to remember her wanton lovemaking with Troy.

Troy. Silently she admitted she felt closer to him than to any other man on earth. Back in the deserted cabin, they'd spent long hours cuddled before the fireplace, sharing their lives and their dreams. The fact that he was English continued to trouble her. Was she a fool for beginning to trust him?

Worry nagged at her as she thought of Jake Hubbell's evil face. What if he had ambushed the men? What if Troy were hurt . . . or killed?

Her anxiety forced her to face the truth. Deep in her heart, she felt the stirrings of an emotion that went beyond mere physical desire. It was only affection, she told herself, the sort of feeling one might have for a friend. Love was unthinkable. . . .

She dunked her coppery hair beneath the water and vigorously scrubbed it clean with a bar of lye soap. The harsh cleanser abraded her tender skin, but diligently she washed away every bit of grime. Elise got out of the tub and wrapped a coarse blanket around her nakedness just as the door opened and Large Betty came back into the cabin, frigid air invading the warmth.

"I fetched ya some things from the storehouse." The

woman draped a honey-colored gown over a chair, along with undergarments, linen petticoats, and a pretty lace-and-wool nightgown.

"Oh, but I don't need all that," Elise exclaimed.

"Mr. Fletcher'd be wantin' ya to have 'em."

Elise refused to ask Troy for anything, let alone such finery. "I'll just wear my other clothing."

"Nope." Large Betty stubbornly snatched up the heap of soiled buckskins. "I ain't gonna be accused o' treatin' ya like some riff-raff."

With a sigh, Elise gave up the battle. She'd explain to Troy later and return the garments. Sitting down by the fire, she began to comb her fingers through her tangled, wet hair.

"What do you suppose could be taking the men so long?" she asked.

"They be back when they be back," was the only answer Large Betty offered.

She began talking about her husband, a groom at the trading post, and the quarters they shared over the stables. The soft pump of the spinning wheel pedal mingled with the cracking of the fire. Elise's eyelids began to droop again, and Large Betty looked sharply at her.

"'Tain't needful for ya to stay up with me. Come along, I'll show ya to a bed."

Elise trailed the woman into a small chamber off the main room. Large Betty insisted that John Frazier would want her to have his own quarters. The furnishings were sparse but comfortable-looking—a bedstead with a feather mattress, a simple pine wardrobe, a wingback chair by the hearth.

Having nothing else to wear, Elise donned the

nightgown. Though tired, she paced restlessly in front of the fireplace, at last sinking down on the coarse fur of the bearskin rug that lay before the hearth. Worry kept her on edge and she realized sleep was impossible until she knew Troy was safe.

Distant hoofbeats sounded outside. A short time later, she heard booted feet stamp into the cabin. There was the low murmur of voices and then a muted scrape, which she guessed was the ladle against the cooking pot. The men were eating dinner.

Elise struggled to contain her impatience. If Troy were sleeping elsewhere, that meant she wouldn't know until morning if they'd captured Jake Hubbell. At last she snatched the quilt off the bed, intending to wrap it around herself before going into the main room to satisfy her curiosity.

Suddenly the door opened and Troy walked inside. Elise dropped the quilt and rushed over to him. "Did you find him?"

"Too dark," he announced in disgust as he threw a bundle of clothing onto a chair. "Frazier'll try again tomorrow—if the snow hasn't covered Hubbell's tracks by then."

"Oh." The single word conveyed her disappointment. Then, as Troy sat down on the edge of the bed to tug off his boots, realization struck. "Are you sleeping in here with me?"

"Where else?" he asked, a smile touching his mouth.

"But what—" She faltered and fell silent.

"But what will people think?"

Elise felt her cheeks grow hot. "Well, yes. I'm not a . . . a whore, as everyone seems to think I am."

"Angel, no one thinks you're a whore," he scoffed

172

gently, tossing one of his boots aside.

"Well, Large Betty asked me if I was your woman."

"She didn't mean anything derogatory by it. Believe me, she would never have put us in here together if she didn't approve."

"Do you really think so?" Elise asked doubtfully.

"Absolutely." He dropped the other boot to the floor, then looked up, his eyes intent. "So, what did you tell her?"

"What do you mean?" she stalled.

"Are you my woman?"

Somehow, it was harder to admit the truth aloud to him than it had been to Large Betty. Elise crossed her arms across her breasts, mumbling, "For the moment."

"Forever," he corrected. Warm with possessiveness, his gaze roamed over the nightgown that clung to her slender form. He reached out for her, pulling her over to the bed and sliding an arm around her hips. "You're my woman and I'm your man. We belong to each other."

His hand flattened over her belly, causing molten desire to spread through her loins. "I still don't feel right flaunting our relationship in front of others," she felt compelled to argue.

"Frazier won't condemn you for spending the night with me. He knows I intend to marry you."

"You told him that?"

Troy nodded, a mischievous smile playing at the corners of his mouth. "And so now you can't turn down my proposal without ruining your reputation."

Tempted to laugh, Elise pulled away and paced over to the hearth. "A very neat trick," she said coolly.

"Ah, little angel," he groaned, his expression half-frustrated, half-amused. "I don't mean to trick you. I

173

want you to marry me of your own free choice."

Her spine stiffened. "That will never—"

"Let's not discuss it now," Troy interrupted. "We'll be forced to adhere to convention once we reach home, but until then, I've no intention of sleeping apart from you." He rose, sending her a look that made her blood quicken. "I'm taking a bath now, then I'm taking my woman to bed."

He left the chamber and returned shortly with the washtub she'd used earlier, kicking aside the bear rug and setting the tub before the fire. After filling it with several buckets of steaming water, he began to strip off his clothing.

Elise sat on the edge of the bed, pretending to stare at her hands, but watching him from beneath the veil of her lashes. There was such casual intimacy about his undressing in front of her that she was suddenly shy. She felt almost like a voyeur peeping through a window.

As he shucked his shirt, the hard contours of his chest gleamed in the firelight. Nonchalantly, he began unbuttoning his breeches. Soon he would come to bed. Warmth raced through her in a rapture of anticipation. She shouldn't be such a wanton, she told herself sternly. Surely a lady wouldn't feel such base desires.

Still, she couldn't keep from sneaking a sidelong glance as his trousers hit the floor. Only a breechclout preserved his magnificent body from total nudity. His fingers went to his waist—but he made no move to untie the strings that held the scrap of pliant buckskin in place.

His soft chuckle drew her eyes up to his impudent grin. He'd caught her watching him! Blushing, Elise averted her face. She heard the breechclout drop, then a splash of water told her he'd entered the tub.

"'Tis safe to look now," he said, his voice brimming with amusement.

His teasing made her color deepen. Vexed with herself, she slid off the bed and, with a show of indifference, gathered up his scattered clothing. When she went to put the garments on the chair, she found the bundle he'd left there. On top was an elk-skin shirt, as pure white as milk, the front embroidered with intricate Indian beadwork. Admiring its beauty, she stroked a hand over the soft leather.

"I hope you like it," Troy said. "'Tis yours."

"Mine?" Elise threw him a questioning glance. He was lounging lazily in the small tub, his knees sticking out of the water, his arms propped along the rim. She turned and picked up the shirt; it looked to be about her size. Beneath it on the chair was a matching pair of breeches.

"I figured you'd be more comfortable dressing like a boy until we reach more civilized country," he said. "When we arrive at Will's Creek, you can start wearing the gown Large Betty picked out for you."

Taken aback, Elise clutched the shirt to her breasts. "This is much too fine. You needn't buy it for me."

He flashed her a wicked grin. "Would you rather go naked? I wouldn't mind the view, but it can get mighty cold out there in the snow."

"I can wear my old things."

"Don't be stubborn. I bought you a fur-lined cape, too. I left it out in the other chamber."

She was appalled yet strangely pleased. "Troy! I can't accept such expensive gifts."

"'Tis too late, I've already paid Frazier."

"Didn't you lose your money when you fell off the raft?"

175

"I had some tobacco notes stashed in my bullet pouch. When we get home, I want you to order a complete wardrobe—silks, satins, whatever you like."

Though touched, she had no desire to take advantage of his good nature. He was only a farmer and couldn't have much money to spare. "Troy, you really needn't—"

"Have I ever told you how much I love the way you say my name?" he interrupted. "You have such a musical French accent."

She stared at him in exasperation. It was plain Troy was in no mood to discuss his personal finances. For now, she would accept the elk-skin garments and fur-lined cape; surviving the trip would require warm clothing. But once they reached his home, she would allow him to buy her only the bare necessities. Her pride dictated that as much as her concern for his spending habits.

"Stop frowning and come over here," he ordered softly, motioning to her with a large hand that glistened wetly in the firelight.

The affectionate amusement of his smile made her heart leap. Though his body was half-hidden by the tub, Elise was intensely aware of his nakedness. Curls of steam rose from the water, beading on his bare chest and beard. She longed for the willpower to resist his charm, but the bond between them was too strong to be broken. She dropped the shirt and walked slowly toward the tub.

He plucked a cloth from the water and held it out to her. "If I asked you very nicely, would you scrub my back?"

Elise hesitated for a moment, then pushed up the long sleeves of her nightgown and took the dripping square of fabric. "Lean forward," she ordered, hoping her crisp tone would hide the quiver in her hands.

Troy flashed her a grin before bending over obediently. Using a bar of soap, she began to cleanse the contours of his broad shoulders. The feel of his rippling muscles beneath the cloth touched off a flush of heat throughout her body. Desire battled with pride; it was difficult to keep from throwing her arms around him. Anxious to distract herself, she said the first thing that popped into her head.

"Large Betty told me John Frazier used to live in Venango."

"Aye, until the French claimed the land belonged to them—even though Frazier had been operating a trading post there for twelve years."

"But if he'd taken property that wasn't his in the first place—"

"He hadn't," Troy interrupted brusquely. "You forget, the English own the Ohio Valley. And Frazier's not the only one who's been driven out. Many English settlers have been forced to abandon their homesteads or risk retribution from French forces."

His hard tone stung Elise into arguing, "The land belongs to whoever is strong enough to defend it. If neither the Indians nor the English can hold it, then it rightfully belongs to the French."

He slanted her a look from under his brows. "A noteworthy point, yet the question of who is the stronger is still to be determined."

The washrag slipped from her hand and fell into the water with a muted plop. He meant war. The thought drove the anger from her mind. Would the conflict between their two countries come to bloodshed?

Lost in thought, she cupped her hands and dribbled water over the broad expanse of his back, rinsing away

177

the slick film of soap. Today was the first time she had seen that there might be another side to the issue. In the past it had only seemed right and proper that the French take what was theirs. But now she wondered. What would happen to the settlers who were pushed off the land they had cultivated? What of the lives that would be lost on both sides?

Elise fished the washcloth from the water and began scrubbing Troy's shoulder. It wasn't that she was doubting the French cause, she told herself. But now that she had met a few of the English and discovered they were people who wanted only to live in peace, she could sympathize with their viewpoint.

"Hey, there!" Troy admonished. "Careful how you're wielding that rag . . . we aren't at war yet."

She dropped the cloth, seeing the reddened patch of flesh where she had rubbed him too hard. *"Pardon . . . I* didn't mean to hurt you!"

"You could kiss it and make it feel better."

His devilish half-grin sent heat curling down to her toes. On impulse, Elise bent and planted a quick, chaste peck on his bare shoulder. "There, how was that?" she asked demurely.

"You little tease."

Quick as lightning, he grabbed her by the waist, his dripping hands saturating her thin nightgown as he pulled her down toward him, capturing her mouth in a long, delicious kiss. His lips crushed hers, his tongue plunging inside to stake his claim. Her loose hair cascaded around them in a veil of shining copper. When at last he freed her mouth, her senses were spinning and her heart was pounding.

"Now look what you've done—you've gotten me all

wet," she said breathlessly, aware of his warm fingers around her slender waist. "This gown doesn't even belong to me."

"Stubborn wench," he said, chuckling. "There you go again, harping about spending my money. I'll buy you a thousand nightgowns if it so pleases you."

"It doesn't please me," she said tartly.

"And what does, pray tell? Perhaps this?"

His hands tightened, lifting her up and over the edge before she could guess his intent. She gasped as he set her down into the heated water, liquid sloshing over the sides of the tub. Breast-deep in bathwater, she sat startled, bare legs splayed wide on either side of his knees, the hem of the gown twisted to the top of her thighs.

"Troy! You . . . you *cochon!*" she sputtered.

"*Cochon*—you've called me that before," he said with a grin. "What does it mean?"

"Pig," Elise retorted indignantly.

He groaned. "I had a suspicion 'twas something like that."

"You deserve that and much more. How dare you act so overbearing." But she had trouble containing her laughter.

"I just had to find out if you were naked beneath this damn nun's robe."

His hands slid along the silken length of her thighs, bypassing the throbbing center of her to glide over her bare hips, pushing the drenched nightgown up to her waist.

"So, I guessed right," he said, his voice ripe with male satisfaction. "Little minx . . . you know just how to inflame a man, don't you?"

"I don't know what you mean," she breathed, unable

to think of anything but the pattern his thumbs were tracing over her abdomen.

"Like hell you don't."

Again he lifted her, this time up and over his knees, settling her dripping body against his thighs, her legs spread to encompass his hips. Against the cradle of her womanhood she felt the hot press of his masculinity. She was too enthralled with the intimacy of their position to utter a protest. Waves of primitive passion radiated over her raw nerves. The blood surged through her veins, gravitating to her lower belly in a heavy, pulsating coil.

Troy held her gaze for a long moment, then his eyes lowered to her bosom, where the full glory of her breasts was outlined against the saturated cloth. He bent his head and took one taut tip into his mouth, his tongue flicking out to circle the sensitive nipple through the thin fabric. Slowly he plucked open the buttons that held together the bodice, then he dragged the sodden nightgown over her head. His mouth descended to bathe her naked flesh in scorching kisses.

Elise exhaled in a soft sound of exhilaration. Her fingers dug into the symmetry of his shoulder muscles, and she curved her spine toward him, her pelvis twisting against him in a compulsive expression of need.

"Have you any more complaints about the way I'm treating you?" he asked raggedly.

"You're too slow," she whispered, rubbing her bare breasts across the damp thatch of tawny hair that covered his chest. "I want you inside me . . . now."

Troy drew in a sharp breath. "As m'lady wishes."

His large hands surrounded her waist, raising her slightly, easing her down onto his hardened shaft until he filled her completely. A wash of intense pleasure rippled over her skin and she moved her hips in an instinctive search for fulfillment.

Though the tub was cramped, her position gave Elise a sense of freedom she had never before experienced in lovemaking. She took full advantage of that fact, teasing his ear with her tongue and threading her fingers into his damp hair. His powerful chest gleamed in the firelight, his flat nipples tempting the exploration of her lips, rewarding her with the salty taste of his skin.

"I love you, little angel."

There was such heart-stopping tenderness in his green eyes that she felt a bittersweet burst of answering emotion, washing away any last prickling doubts. "I need you, *mon chéri*," she whispered. "I need you more than you can imagine."

With a deep groan, he stole the reins of control from her in a kiss so savagely intense it plumbed the depths of her being. Water lapped at their bodies, enveloping them in a sensual cocoon. His hand came between them to stroke the soft folds of her flesh at the point of their joining.

Her belly tightened with an unbearable rush of sweet tension. She arched her throat to his lips, her copper hair tumbling over her shoulders to trail in the water. Her body exulted in the torturous delight of his touch. They surged against each other until the shattering climax plunged them both into ecstasy.

Chapter Twelve

It was the following afternoon when Elise first felt the uneasy sensation that someone—or something—was stalking them.

They had departed the trading post in the pale light of dawn. Discovering she'd had only limited experience in riding, Troy had insisted she mount behind him, on the chestnut gelding he had purchased from John Frazier. Frazier traveled with them for a time, tracing the snow-covered tracks of the horse Jake Hubbell had stolen. After an hour, the barely visible depressions had led the fur trader off on a divergent path into the wilderness.

Elise's arms were wrapped around Troy's waist. His large form blocked the icy wind, while the new muskrat-lined cape she wore helped keep her toasty warm. A packhorse trotted along after them carrying supplies: blankets, food, an extra rifle. Troy had also bought a compass, which would aid them in finding their way home.

Home. It was strange how she had begun to think of Troy's plantation in that way. Her mind had embellished the mental image of a cozy farmhouse until it was so appealing she felt impatient to reach there. A thought stole into her head. Perhaps her eagerness was due to a desire to become so necessary to him that he would never send her away.

That was ridiculous, Elise assured herself. She knew from her own mother's experience the impossibility of ever trusting an Englishman. Even after eight years of marriage, her father had abandoned his family with callous disregard for their welfare.

So why was it that last night, in the throes of passion, she'd called Troy *chéri* . . . darling? Was she falling in love with him?

In the cold light of day that notion seemed ludicrous. She and Troy were linked only by feelings of the flesh. Once the feverish excitement wore off, their relationship would fizzle to nothing. Troy said he loved her, but then her father had uttered the same false words. Englishmen were fickle creatures who never followed through on their promises.

Yet Elise found herself tightening her arms around Troy's lean waist, laying her head against his back. His strong muscles shifted beneath her cheek as he guided the horse through the drifts. In spite of all logic, she felt a sense of security in his presence. For now at least, he was her man and she was his woman.

They rode for long hours, making only a brief stop at noon. The sunlight sparkled across the snow and dazzled her eyes. After a time, it made Elise drowsy. She was dozing in the saddle, clinging to Troy, when he reined the gelding to a halt.

"Let me help you down," he said.

There was a tension in his voice that made her obey

without question. Taking hold of his proffered hand, she slid off the horse, Troy following.

"Stay here," he ordered. When he thrust out the reins, her fingers closed around the leather ribbons automatically.

Without a word of explanation, he grabbed his rifle, which was slung across his chest by a strap, and strode toward a cabin nestled in a clearing up ahead. It was the only sign of civilization they had seen since the trading post.

The place was eerily silent, with no smoke rising from the chimney and the door swinging wide open. Elise felt a strange prickling down her spine, as if there were some unidentifiable evil in the air.

She saw Troy pause in the middle of the clearing, bending down on one knee for a moment to look at something. Then he rose and disappeared through the open door.

After an instant's hesitation, Elise tied the reins to a nearby bush. She couldn't just stand here; she had to find out what was wrong.

As she neared the cabin, she spied something sticking out of a snowdrift. Shock clutched at her. It was a dead man, half-buried beneath brown-tinged snow. Morbid curiosity forced her to move closer, and her stomach churned when she saw his body had been torn apart by wild animals. His hair was gone, the top of his head a frozen mass of congealed blood.

Indians. He had been scalped.

Blindly Elise stumbled toward the cabin, driven by a sick horror. The hideous sight that met her eyes stopped her in the doorway, her gloved fingers grasping desperately at the wooden jamb, her flesh crawling.

Bright sunlight poured into the gloomy interior to illuminate the scene within. The stench of death hung heavy in the cold air. Troy was draping a quilt over a woman who was sprawled on the dirt floor, her mouth agape in a thwarted scream. Before the covering settled into place, Elise saw the tiny form clutched to the woman's torn bodice. A baby. And all around the mother lay the bodies of several more children. Every scalp was gone.

Troy looked up, his face grim. "Get the hell out of here!" he snapped.

Stupefied, Elise couldn't react for a moment. Then she pivoted and fled from the grisly sight, not stopping until she reached the horses. Leaning weakly against a tree, she watched in a daze as Troy emerged from the cabin to drag the dead man inside. Dimly she realized that with the ground frozen, he wouldn't be able to bury the bodies.

She wasn't sure how much time had passed when Troy closed the door behind him and came toward her. His expression reflected the dreadfulness of the atrocity he had just witnessed. His lips were tightened into a thin line, his eyebrows drawn together in a frown. Stopping near her, he peeled off his gloves and flung them aside. He flattened his bare palms on a tree trunk and stared off into the distance. The harsh rasp of his breathing was audible in the stillness.

Then, with an abruptness that made Elise step back involuntarily, he slammed his fist against the tree, so hard that a shower of snow dislodged from the branches above.

"God damn the French to hell," he snarled.

The unexpected words bewildered her. She cocked her

185

head, stammering, "But . . . Indians. . . ."

His look paralyzed her voice. "Rumor has it the French pay the Indians for every scalp they bring in," he said coldly. "'Tis a simple but effective method of ridding this territory of English settlers."

Disbelief enveloped her like a suffocating blanket. What he said was impossible! Bile rose in her throat as the vivid image of the dead mother and children flashed through her head. That her countrymen could authorize such a gruesome, barbaric act was beyond comprehension.

"Nay," she whispered, shaking her head. "You're lying. How dare you even suggest such a thing?"

Wide-eyed, she backed away from him, her trembling fingers touching her cold cheeks. Suddenly it was all too much to bear . . . the horror of the discovering the massacred family and now the shock of Troy's cruel words.

Spinning around, Elise plunged blindly through the snow. Icy air stabbed her lungs. The wind rushed past her as she fled from him, and her cape billowed behind, its tie choking her throat. The hood flew back, the long plaited length of copper hair bouncing against her back. Yet no matter how hard and fast she ran, she could not escape the haunting picture of the dead or the sting of Troy's merciless damnation of everything she had ever known.

She fell sobbing to the ground, her fists pounding the snow in a frenzy. Anguished tears poured down her cheeks; her breath came in ragged gasps. *No, no, no!* None of it was true; it was all a bad dream. Coiled tightly in the ball of her pain was the certainty that Troy despised her. There had been such hardness on his face, such hatred in his eyes! She couldn't bear it!

Comforting arms encircled her and gathered her close. Instinctively she leaned into the hard warmth, grasping at the solace offered. The wild weeping subsided until there were no more tears left. Gradually she became aware that it was Troy who rocked her in his arms, his tormented voice filtering through the shroud of her despair.

"Hush, little angel, don't cry. I'm sorry, so sorry . . . I never meant to hurt you."

She lifted her head to look at him, her fingers digging convulsively into his coat. "Tell me—" Her voice broke and she had to swallow hard before continuing. "Tell me you lied to me. Tell me it isn't true."

Troy stared at her for a long moment, his eyes dark with pain. "I shouldn't have been so blunt," he said heavily. "I was angry and bitter, but that was no excuse for me to take it out on you. Please, forgive me."

Sickness washed through Elise as she saw he was not going to give her the assurance she so desperately needed. *He believed he had spoken the truth.* The realization pierced her soul and his staunch conviction lit a tiny flicker of doubt inside her. Was there even a chance that he was right, that the French sanctioned the murder of innocent settlers? That they rewarded the Indians for each bloodied English scalp?

The horror of it sent a shudder of revulsion over her flesh. She buried her face in Troy's chest, crying, "I cannot believe it . . . I cannot!"

But the weed of uncertainty had taken root in her heart and nothing could rip it out. A fresh wave of weeping overtook her. Troy stroked her hair, murmuring to her and holding her until the tears ran out.

"We must go," he said at last. "Dusk will soon be upon us."

He drew her up, placing a supportive arm around her shoulders as they returned to the horses. The thought of being trapped here for the night gave Elise the strength to move. She was driven by a desire to get as far away as possible from this awful setting.

Keeping her eyes averted from the cabin, she took Troy's helping hand to mount the chestnut gelding. As they cantered off, she looped her arms around his waist and stared fiercely at the passing woods. The slant of the late afternoon sun cast deep shadows in the underbrush. Though she took a certain comfort in Troy's closeness, there was an anxiety in her that hadn't been present earlier. It prickled across her skin like the touch of ghostly fingers. . . .

Suddenly she was swept by the vivid impression that someone was out there stalking them.

Quickly she glanced over her shoulder, but saw only the crimson sunset glowing through the bare trees. Who would be following them? she scoffed to herself. The Indians who had committed that barbaric act must be long since gone.

And what of Jake Hubbell? her mind whispered. She pushed the thought away. It was absurd. In so vast a wilderness, the chance of their paths crossing again was slim indeed.

Resolutely Elise shook off her uneasiness. She was on edge, imagining things because of the shock she'd suffered. Granted, there were the usual dangers of wild animals and renegade Indians, but little could be accomplished by giving in to the debilitating lure of fear.

The shadows spread slowly, growing deeper and denser until blackness began to swallow the forest. The moon had not yet risen. When it was too dark to see, Troy reined the gelding to a halt and they set up camp for the night in a small hollow, their fire partially concealed by a surrounding thicket of evergreen bushes.

Warming themselves before the blaze, they ate the corn pone and slices of ham that Large Betty had packed for them that morning. Elise could only pick at her food. Somewhere far off, a wolf howled. Accustomed to such sounds, the horses munched placidly from their feed bags.

But Elise again felt the clutching fingers of apprehension, aware of a vulnerable sensation that someone—or something—was out there in the darkness, watching them. Determined to control her nerves, she set aside the remains of her meal and scrambled to her feet.

"Will you teach me to use that?" she asked, pointing at the rifle that lay beside Troy.

A faint grin curved his lips for the first time since they had come upon the murdered family. "Only if you promise never to shoot me."

Moving with a limber grace, he rose and brought her the gun. It was heavier than she'd thought it would be, and felt cold and deadly in her small hands. She was impatient to get the firing of it over and done with, but Troy took his time explaining to her the purpose of each individual part, from lock to stock to barrel. They practiced loading the rifle, ramming in the powder and bullet with a long rod. Then he showed her how to hold the gun and sight down the barrel at the target.

"All you need is practice," he said at last, and took the rifle from her.

"Can't I shoot it?"

"Perhaps tomorrow—'tis too dark now to see a target. Besides, the sound of a shot carries far and we'd best not attract the attention of any Indians in the area."

He was right, Elise admitted, swallowing her disappointment. Yet she felt a little better now, knowing they carried an extra gun in their supplies. In a pinch, she at least knew the rudiments of using the weapon and could help Troy defend them against any dangers.

She sat down near the fire, staring intently into the orange flames. The image of the murdered settlers continued to haunt her. *Sacré Dieu!* If the French really *had* made a pact with the Indians, then any Englishman out here in the wilderness, including Troy himself, was a potential victim. . . .

Elise shivered. When Troy came over to sit beside her, she lay her head on his shoulder. "Those poor, poor people."

"I know," he said softly. "I didn't want you to see—that's why I told you to stay away."

He got up, then returned a moment later with a flask of brandy. "Here, if you drink some of this, you'll feel better."

Taking the flask from him, she swallowed a gulp of the liquid, feeling it burn all the way down her throat to warm her insides. "When do you think it happened?"

He shrugged. "Perhaps a couple of days ago. Most of the families stick together near a settlement for protection's sake, but there're always a few stubborn enough to try to make it on their own."

"Will the Indians come back?"

"Who knows? There usually aren't many war parties out during the winter. Still, I'd like for us to press on and try to catch up to the pack train. 'Twould be safer to travel with a group."

Thoughtfully she took another sip from the flask, then set it aside. "How much farther is it to civilization?"

"We ought to arrive at Gist's settlement sometime tomorrow, then 'twill be another three or four days through mountainous country to Will's Creek and after that, perhaps five or six more days to Winchester, which is the outskirts of civilized Virginia."

"Is that where your home is?"

"Nay, I'm afraid we'll be few more days on the road to reach there." He took her hand and stroked the back of it. "Elise, I want you to think of my home as yours, too."

She averted her eyes from his face, aware of a hollow feeling inside her. "How can you not hate me?" she asked, her voice low. "I'm French, and if you truly believe my people could be so cruel. . . ."

Troy tightened his arms around her. "Little angel, long before today I'd heard the French were encouraging such atrocities, yet that didn't stop me from falling in love with you."

"Then . . . you don't blame me?"

"Blame you?" he repeated in amazement. "How could I? You haven't done anything wrong." He took her face in his broad palms, his eyes dark and serious in the light from the campfire. "Elise, one of these days, you'll trust me enough to become my wife. And then we'll spend the rest of our lives together."

The urge to believe him burned strong in her. A trembling of soft emotion flowed inside her and melted the ice around her heart. Something hot and savage beat in her blood. What would it be like to accept his love, to meet it with the fierceness of her own feelings, to bear his children and to share his bed each night?

A wave of intense yearning swept her. She pressed herself to him, inviting his kiss—

A twig snapped in the darkness beyond. Troy's arms tensed around her. Elise whipped her head toward the noise, her eyes widening in disbelief as a familiar figure stepped into the circle of firelight. The blood drained from her face, leaving her pale with shock.

She was staring up the long barrel of a rifle aimed directly at them.

Chapter Thirteen

"Marc!" Elise exclaimed.

Involuntarily she surged to her feet, her mind whirling with bewilderment. What was her brother doing so many miles from the fort?

Troy rose, shoving her behind him protectively. "What the devil's going on here?" he growled.

"Elise, move away from the bastard so I can kill him," Marc snapped in French.

The significance of the gun struck her with icy horror. *Marc had come to murder Troy!* He still believed Troy was holding her captive, forcing her to be his whore.

Disobeying her brother's command, she stepped around to Troy's side, reasoning that so long as she stayed close to him, Marc dared not shoot for fear of hitting her. Desperately, she sought for the words that would defuse the situation.

"Marc, you don't understand," she argued in rapid French. "Give me the gun and then we'll talk."

The boy's aim never faltered. "What is there to say?" he scoffed harshly. "The *bâtard anglais* thinks he can use you and get away with it. Well, he won't . . . I swear it on our mother's grave!"

"Marc, he's not using me. I'm here of my own free will."

"That's not true."

"You don't see me tied up, do you? Don't you think I could have found an opportunity to escape if I'd really wanted to?"

"He's stronger. He would have stopped you."

But the barrel of his firearm wavered just a fraction, and Elise knew she had shaken him. "He hasn't forced me into anything," she said urgently. "If I were so eager to seek revenge for his rape, why would I now be defending his life?"

In silence Marc stared at her, and she could sense the confusion emanating from his wiry body. *Sacré Dieu,* please make him see logic!

"What the devil are you two talking about?" Troy demanded. "By God, if that little pup intends to steal you away at gunpoint, I'll break his puny neck!"

Elise knew it must be frustrating for him to stand by helplessly, unable to understand French, but there was no time to waste. "I'll explain later," she said. "Let me deal with this first."

She took a step forward, extending a hand to her brother. "Give the gun to me, Marc. I refuse to discuss this matter any further so long as there's a rifle staring me in the face."

The boy shifted from one moccasined foot to the other. "Elise, you can't expect me to—"

"Give me the gun," she repeated, her voice low but firm. "If you don't, I'll come get it from you. You don't want me to get shot by mistake, do you?"

194

"Merde," he muttered fiercely. But after a moment he lowered the rifle. Casting a hateful look at the man standing behind his sister, he stepped toward her slowly and surrendered the weapon into her hands.

"Bon," Elise said. "Now we can talk."

Despite her calm exterior, her legs were shaky, and she was grateful for the excuse to sink down near the campfire, balancing the rifle in her lap. After an instant's hesitation, Marc joined her on the hard-packed snow.

Only Troy remained standing. "Are you going to sit there like you're at some damn tea party?" he accused Elise. "By the devil, I ought to take that half-grown brat over my knee and thrash him good!"

Marc balled his fingers into fists. *"Cochon anglais,"* he spat.

Though the boy knew no English, Elise realized he had caught Troy's angry tone. She had to grab his arm to keep him from springing up to fight. "Behave yourself!"

When she was assured he would obey, she glared up at Troy. "Can you not trust me to handle this my own way?"

"My God, Elise, he threatened you with a gun! Are you going to act as if he just strolled in for a neighborly visit?"

"I can deal with him," she retorted. "I got the rifle away from him, didn't I? He's my brother, and I will not tolerate your interference."

Troy regarded her with frosty eyes. "Have it your own way, then," he bit out. Wheeling around, he strode to the edge of the encampment, where he leaned a stiff shoulder against a tree trunk, gazing into the darkness beyond.

Elise felt a pang of remorse. His fury stemmed only from concern for her. Why couldn't she have shown more sympathy for his feelings?

Sighing, she turned back to her brother and addressed him in their native tongue. "Marc, why are you here? You were supposed to stay at the fort."

The youth glowered. "How could I, when you'd given up your own freedom for me? I had to come and save you."

"How did you get away without being caught?"

"The commander thinks I'm a troublemaker—he was probably happy to see me go," Marc said with a shrug. "He was furious when he discovered you'd left without any explanations. Yves Larousse wanted to go find you and bring you back, but the commander forbade him to."

Yves. Guiltily, Elise realized she hadn't thought about the French officer in days. She knew without even asking that he had obeyed St. Pierre's order. Yves was too much a military man to defy the directive of his superior.

"So you came by yourself and tracked me through the wilderness," she stated, torn between admiration and anger. "Marc, you shouldn't have done that. It can serve no purpose."

"I'm taking you back to the fort with me," he said, his youthful jaw set stubbornly.

She shook her head. "You don't understand."

"What don't I understand?" he demanded. "Are you saying you enjoy having the hands of that *bâtard* all over you each night?"

Elise stared down at the rifle in her lap, unable to bear the accusation in his eyes. How could she explain to a twelve-year-old boy about the lure of physical intimacy between a man and a woman?

"I'm bound to Troy," she said awkwardly.

"Why? Because you promised to stay with him in

exchange for my release? Elise, he blackmailed you into that so he could use you as a whore. No man can do that to my sister and get away with it!"

"He isn't using me," she blurted. "Troy loves me . . . he wants to marry me."

Marc stared in open-mouthed disbelief. "But you're not going to do it! My sister wouldn't shackle herself to an Englishman."

"I haven't yet decided," Elise said defensively.

"Then you're really considering it." His young voice was filled with disgust.

Shame and confusion twisted inside her. She buried her face in her hands for a moment before finding the courage to look at him again. "I don't know what I want to do," Elise whispered, her copper eyes pleading for understanding. "I need time to think."

Marc's expression was stony. "While you're thinking, *ma soeur*, remember this: If you go with that bastard, you can be sure I'll never come near you again."

The boy leaped nimbly to his feet and stalked off to stand at the opposite end of the encampment from where Troy still leaned against the tree.

Despair wrenching her heart, Elise looked from one male to the other. Now both of them were angry at her. What was she to do? If she chose to go with Troy, she would never see Marc again. On the other hand, if she returned to the fort with her brother, she would lose Troy.

Who was more important to her?

Less than a week ago, there would have been no need even to think twice. Now Troy had awakened her to a woman's passion . . . yet how could she select him over the brother she loved with all her heart?

An unbearable weariness weighed her down. No longer did she want to face the awful choice; she would make her decision in the morning.

Setting aside Marc's rifle, Elise prepared a pallet near the flames, deeming it wise to sleep apart from Troy. She was conscious of his brooding stare as she slipped beneath the blankets. Resolutely she closed her eyes, aching for his warmth to thaw the cold misery in her heart.

Elise awoke to a frosty dawn. For a moment she lay there, still caught in the cobwebs of sleep. Then memory came rushing back to her and she sat straight up.

Troy was kneeling on the other side of the fire. He held a skillet over the flames, from which emanated the hiss and spit of frying ham. Marc stood at the edge of the encampment, sliding a feed bag over the head of a bay stallion. Slowly she got up and huddled in her fur-lined cloak for warmth.

Breakfast was a silent meal. It was plain that Marc and Troy were steering clear of each other, though once Elise caught them exchanging a look of mutual distrust. Were it not for the two sets of rumpled blankets at either end of the fire, she would have thought neither male had even slept the night.

When they were through eating, Troy began to pack up their belongings. Tension clawed at her stomach; the moment of decision was at hand. Should she go with her brother or her lover? Even in the cold light of morning, the answer seemed no clearer, no less painful.

Mustering all of her courage, she walked over to Troy, who was crouched near the fire, gathering up his bedroll.

She clasped her damp, icy palms together.

"Troy, couldn't we stay here a while longer?"

He looked up at her, his eyes cool. "Why?"

"Well, because Marc won't go with us."

"So?"

"He . . . he's asking me to choose between the two of you."

"And?"

His monosyllabic replies were disheartening. He seemed more interested in the blankets he was folding than in her. Racked by an agony of anxiety, she blurted, "Doesn't it matter to you what I decide:?"

"I didn't realize there was a decision to make," he countered, shooting her an impatient glance. "'Twas my impression you'd vowed to stay with me."

"Aye, but that was before my brother came."

"Damn your brother," he growled. "You're actually considering going with him, aren't you?"

"I—I don't know what to do."

Troy stood up, the bedroll in his arms. "And I thought you were beginning to care for me," he said with bitter self-derision. "Shows you what a fool I am, doesn't it?" Pivoting, he strode off toward the horses.

Elise stared after him, wretched distress knotting her stomach. There had been pain in his eyes and it was all her fault. How could she do this to him?

And yet how could she choose him over her brother?

Suddenly she noticed that Troy was saddling the chestnut gelding. He was departing without her! Panic flashed through her and she went scurrying across the clearing to him.

"Where are you going?" she demanded breathlessly.

"Does it matter?"

"Of course it matters!" She gripped his arm, beyond caring that she was begging. "Troy, please, don't leave like this. Can you not at least allow me time to think?"

He checked the adjustment of the girth before looking at her. Brushing his fingers across her silken cheek, he said gruffly, "That's what I was intending, little angel. I'll be back in a couple of hours. All I ask is that if you decide on Marc, you be gone when I return."

He swung lithely into the saddle, cantering off without a backward glance. Absently she rubbed her arms beneath her cloak as horse and rider disappeared over a low rise. Her relief at the reprieve was only momentary; unhappiness formed a tight ball inside her. Yes, he was coming back, but would she still be here to greet him?

"*Tiens!* I see you'll be returning to the fort with me."

Marc's pleased voice came from behind, and Elise wheeled around to see an expression of satisfaction on her brother's face.

"I haven't decided anything yet," she admitted. "Troy has agreed only to give me time alone to make my choice."

The boy scowled, jamming his hands into the pockets of his breeches. "Then maybe you should have gone with him," he said resentfully. "If that Englishman means more to you than I do, maybe I'll just go and leave you to him."

"Marc, please try to understand," Elise begged. "I love you. You're the only family I have left."

"Then why won't you come with me?"

"Because—" She hesitated, feeling as if her heart were being ripped in two. She couldn't bring herself to leave Troy . . . or her brother. "Marc, perhaps you could go with us," she ventured. "I—I could talk to Troy about making a place for you in his home—"

"As a stableboy to an English swine?" Marc scoffed coldly. "How can you even think of living with an Englishman after what our father did to Maman? Didn't you learn anything from her experience?"

"Of course," Elise defended herself. "But I must also live my own life as I see fit. I have . . . certain feelings for Troy, feelings I hope you'll understand someday."

"You mean you like what he does to you in bed," Marc jeered. "Stay with your lover, then; see if I care."

Before he turned away, Elise caught the glitter of tears in his eyes. The sight made her throat tighten, and she forgave him his cruel words. He stalked over to saddle his horse, surreptitiously wiping his face on his sleeve. *Sacré Dieu*, he was her brother! How could she hurt him like this?

It struck her then how much Marc needed her. Being the only male in the family, he tried to act like a man. It was easy to forget sometimes that he was only twelve years old and not yet ready to face the world alone. Perhaps she could try one last time to reason with him before she was forced into a decision that would make her give up Troy. . . .

As she started toward her brother, a flash of movement in the bushes caught her eye. She stopped, paralyzed. In open-mouthed horror, she watched as an Indian rose from behind the screen of underbrush, his face painted in hideous patterns of red and black. A single strip of hair ran back from his forehead; the rest of his skull was shaved clean.

Another savage appeared beside the first, then another and another. Each brandished a wicked-looking tomahawk.

A scream of terror tore from her numb throat. "Marc, watch out!"

Simultaneously a wild whooping rent the air. Two of the Indians leaped nimbly over the bush, heading straight at her, the others darting toward Marc.

Elise dove instinctively for her brother's rifle, which lay beside her rumpled bedroll. Heart pounding, she had no more than an instant to sight down the barrel.

She pulled the trigger and a shot exploded in a puff of smoke. The recoil sent her stumbling backward.

But inexperience made her aim wild, and the bullet ripped harmlessly through the air. Uttering a primitive war cry, the savages knocked the gun from her hands and wrenched her wrists behind her back.

Heedless of the pain that lanced her arms, she twisted and fought. They couldn't do this! She had to fight for her life!

One of the warriors slapped her hard across her cheek. The blow dazed Elise and black spots danced before her eyes. She swayed on her feet; only the cruel grip on her wrists kept her from falling.

The other Indian wrenched the cloak from her shoulders and fingered the soft fur with a look of satisfaction. Then he donned the cloak himself, and Elise was helpless to stop him.

As she was hauled toward the horses, she saw that Marc had been taken prisoner also. He struggled, and his fierce captor struck the boy senseless with a blow from the edge of a tomahawk. A scream of outrage mingled with terror tore from her lips.

An Indian leaped onto each mount, then Elise was lifted behind one of the savages, her hands jerked around his waist and tied. In the same manner, Marc secured on the other horse, behind one of the Indians. The two remaining braves grabbed up the belongings, trotting along on foot as the party headed away from the camp.

Numb with aftershock, Elise sat rigid, the musky scent of her captor enveloping her. Soon they reached a place where there were four horses concealed in a thicket of trees. The men who had walked loaded the pilfered provisions on the spare horses, then each jumped astride an animal.

They pressed onward through the snowy woods, up and over the hills. Elise noted from the slant of the sun that they were heading north. Her cheek still throbbed with pain; the skin felt puffy and hot. Without her cloak, the icy wind made her shiver. In a haze of despair she wondered how Marc was faring. Caught tightly against the Indian's broad back, she could not see her brother.

By chance she looked down and saw the two bundles dangling from the leather belt at her captor's waist. A mass of blonde hair, another of brown. *Scalps.*

Bile rose in her throat. She closed her eyes, drawing in great gulps of cold air until the sickness passed. Logic told her if the Indians had intended such a fate for her and Marc, they wouldn't have bothered to imprison them.

In the faint hope that these were Indians who sided with the French, she spoke loudly, *"Parlez-vous français?"*

Her stiff-backed captor made no reply.

She tried once more. "Do you speak English?"

Again, he made no answer. Elise blinked back the sting of tears. It was imperative that she not give in to weakness.

Ignoring her bodily discomforts, she focused feverishly on escape. She prayed the jolting ride had roused Marc to consciousness; they'd have to be prepared for any opportunity. She must stay alert and watch where they were going in case a fresh snowfall covered their tracks. When they ran away from the Indians, it was imperative that she be able to find her way back to Troy.

Troy. Hopelessness washed over her in waves of agony. How hurt and angry he would be when he returned to the camp to discover her gone! Would he think she had left with Marc? No, she told herself fiercely, he would see the signs of a struggle, see the footsteps of Indians. He would track them down. She clung to that shining thread of hope.

In the meantime, her wits might save them. At some point when the party stopped, she would be untied. Then she would watch for her chance.

Chapter Fourteen

Troy spurred his mount to a gallop, wanting only to get as far away as possible from the camp. The breakneck pace caused tiny clods of white to fly out from beneath the horse's hooves. In the morning sunshine, the snow glittered with the blinding brilliance of diamonds. The land had become hillier these past few days, and the barren stretch of wilderness matched the desolation in his soul.

Elise would go with her brother; he feared it in every fiber of his being.

Chased by the demons of despair, Troy rode hard, crouching close to the horse's neck to avoid low-hanging branches. Gradually the cold rushing air restored his sense, and he slowed the gelding to a walk near the bank of a frozen creek. It was the Youghiogheny, which he and Elise would cross to reach the next settlement. Or rather, he amended bitterly, which he alone would cross.

The memory of her father's desertion still ruled Elise's mind. Troy was certain that, if fate hadn't intervened, in time he could have convinced her to trust him. Damn that interfering brat, Marc!

Frustration ate at Troy as he guided the horse along a path that paralleled the creek. Rationally, he knew his resentment of Marc stemmed from jealousy—and fear. Under any other circumstances, he would have admired the boy's courage in tracking down his sister through miles of uncharted wilderness.

But logic failed to erase the dark emotions that squeezed Troy's chest. Deep down, he felt a nagging dread that he would lose Elise for good. Frantically he searched his brain for reassurance. Before Marc had arrived, she had agreed to go home with him, hadn't she? Didn't that prove she felt something for him?

Fool, he chastised himself. There was no escaping the brutal truth: She didn't love him. It was absurd to hope that her feelings toward him might be softening, that she might forsake brother for lover. How could mere physical desire triumph over the ties of flesh and blood?

Morosely Troy squinted into the early morning sun. The snow-covered path ahead led toward his home on the James River, a sprawling plantation in the tidewater region of Virginia. He told himself he ought to press onward instead of returning to camp to confirm the inevitable.

But in defiance of all logic a fierce yearning gripped him. How he wanted to marry Elise, to keep her by his side forever! He couldn't leave if there were even the remotest chance that she might choose him.

Suddenly a distant gunshot echoed through the hills. Troy stiffened, his heart giving a sickening lurch inside his chest. The sound had come from behind . . . from the direction of the camp!

Fear chilled his blood. Swiftly he jerked on the reins

and turned the horse, cursing himself for straying so far. By God, if something happened to Elise, he would never forgive himself.

Throwing caution to the wind, he jabbed his heels into the sides of his mount. The gelding sped down the path at a furious gallop. Twigs tore at Troy's clothing, yet he slapped the reins and urged the animal to an even more reckless pace.

Nightmares of wild animals and Indians darted through his mind. *Elise*. He must reach her before it was too late!

As the horse thundered up and over a low rise, Troy strained to see through the thick screen of trees. Surely the camp could not be much farther.

Intent on the hilly landscape in the distance, he failed to watch the path ahead. His mount stepped into a depression in the snow and stumbled. Even as Troy grabbed wildly at the pommel, he felt the reins yank out of his fingers and momentum jolted him from the saddle.

He saw a fleeting image of branches against the blue sky. Then a hard impact jarred his body. Ice stung his cheek, the only sensation in the moment before a burning agony clawed at his gut.

A thought pierced his scrambled senses. *Elise*.

He couldn't remember why, but he had to reach her. Groaning, he raised his head. The world swam giddily, and he struggled to focus, prodded by a primitive urgency. *He must reach Elise.*

He tried to lift himself up, but a sudden, unbearable spasm of pain gripped his body.

Everything went black.

*   *   *

Elise slouched wearily against the broad back of her captor. Each hoofbeat sent relentless quivers of soreness throughout her muscles. It was night; they had ridden hard all day, making only a brief stop at sunset. There, her wrists had been untied so she could slide to the ground. Tired as she had been, she had kept alert for a chance to slip away. But the Indian had fastened her to his waist by a rope, forcing her to stumble after him wherever he went. At least she'd had a chance to see Marc, though they had been too far apart to speak. The look they'd exchanged assured her he was as anxious as she was to escape.

The rhythmic trot of the horse lulled her into a haze of fatigue. The darkness did not seem to matter to the Indians, for they maintained their swift pace through the black forest. Elise drifted in and out of sleep, too exhausted to care that her head rested against the broad shoulders of a savage. No longer did she even notice the musky scent of bear grease and sweat that clung to him.

It was daybreak when they halted again. The warriors gave a whoop that jolted her awake. Half-dazed, she saw they had entered an Indian village. Smoke spiraled from holes in the roofs of the longhouses, and the smell of cooking filled the air. There were women with cradle-boards strapped to their backs, children giggling and chattering, a brave with a buck slung over his shoulders. Yapping dogs raced in circles around the new arrivals.

When Elise was untied and let down, her legs nearly collapsed; only sheer force of willpower kept her standing upright. Her bottom throbbed and her thighs felt painfully chafed from the long hours in the saddle. But stubborn pride refused to let her show any weakness in front of these savages.

Marc sidled up to her. "Are you all right?" he hissed.

At the sight of his familiar face, relief washed through Elise, and she nodded. Horrible tales churned through her head, stories of the tortures and cruelties that certain Indian tribes practiced. "Marc, what will they do to us?"

"They might make us slaves or adopt us into the tribe," he whispered. "But first we'll have to prove we're worthy by getting through that."

He nodded toward the villagers, who were organizing into two lines opposite one another. Confusion furrowed Elise's brow. Everyone, even old men, women, and children, carried a club or stick.

"You mustn't fall or they'll kill you," Marc warned.

One of the warriors came over and gave him a push. Comprehension hit her in a rush of horror as Marc was forced to run between the two lines, the Indians gleefully raining blows over his slight body.

Elise gasped. They couldn't do that to her brother! She made a lunge toward him, but one of the braves grabbed her arm and yanked her back, forcing her to watch from the sidelines. When Marc stumbled, her heart beat frantically in her throat until he made it through to the end.

The brave shoved her toward the line of villagers. Talons of dread dug into her chest. If she took one step, surely her knees would buckle. Yet if she fell, she would die. And the instinct to live was strong in her.

When the Indian gave her another thrust, she started forward on shaky legs. A cacophony of jeers and taunts greeted her approach. She reminded herself that the more swiftly she ran, the fewer strikes she would have to endure.

Gritting her teeth, she darted between the two rows of

Indians. Sticks swatted and jabbed at her. Pain gnawed at her flesh like a hundred stinging bees, and she bit her lip to keep from crying out. A stone struck her shoulder, but she blinked back the tears in her eyes. *Sacré Dieu*, she wouldn't give these savages the satisfaction of seeing her defeated.

At last the harrowing nightmare was over. She stood half bent over, her arms wrapped tightly around her middle, her breath coming in lung-searing gasps. Every inch of her skin smarted, every muscle screamed in agony. Only a deep-seated pride kept her from sinking to the ground.

Helplessly she watched as two warriors prodded Marc into one of the longhouses. Her brother's clothing was torn and spattered with blood, but at least he was alive. Fiercely she clung to thoughts of escape. She would survive, she had to! Someday she would be in Troy's arms again.

The Indian brave who had captured her approached with a woman at his side. She was slim, with pretty, copper-skinned features, and wore a long dress of ornately beaded doeskin. A small boy peeped shyly from behind her skirt, his black eyes round with curiosity. The warrior said something to the woman. As he waved a hand at Elise, his bearing was stiff with pride.

Gall choked Elise's throat. So she was to be handed over to this Indian woman like a slave, a piece of property. Resolutely she reminded herself to be grateful that her scalp wasn't hanging from some savage's belt.

It was obvious that the squaw was pleased with her husband's gift. Her dark eyes sparkled in the sunlight, and she reached out and fingered Elise's tangled copper hair, uttering a phrase in her strange language. The

Indian woman gave her a gentle shove in the direction opposite to the one Marc had taken.

Elise trudged through the village beside the woman and her small son. As the hopelessness of her situation struck her in full force, her spirit no longer seemed capable of fighting. Later, she told herself wearily, she would plan for escape. Later . . . when there weren't scores of savages around to watch her every move.

They neared one of the longhouses, made of elm bark laid on like clapboards. The woman lifted a flap over the entrance and waved Elise inside. The interior was dim and smoky, with a row of fires down the middle and rooms on either side.

She followed the squaw to the second blaze, thankful that at least it was warmer in here than outside. Evidently this lodge housed several families, for there were other women busy at tasks around the fires, one scraping a hide, another grinding corn with a mortar and pestle. All stopped what they were doing to stare at her.

The fragrance of cooking meat made Elisa's mouth water, but fatigue overrode even hunger. In a haze of misery, she sank to the hard dirt floor, sitting with knees drawn up, her body throbbing with soreness. Her cheek was still puffy and her shoulder ached where the stone had struck it. It felt as if there were bruises over every inch of her flesh.

The Indian woman thrust a clay bowl and wooden ladle at her. Automatically Elise reached out, but her fingers were stiff and the spoon fell to the ground. The squaw clucked her tongue in disapproval as she picked up the utensil and returned it to Elise.

Heat from the bowl warmed Elise's hands. After more than twenty-four hours without nourishment, the corn mush inside tasted like ambrosia. She managed to eat only half of the food when exhaustion overcame her. Intending to rest for just a moment, she set aside the bowl and lay her forehead on her knees.

The next thing she knew she was curled up on something firm. A soothing warmth enveloped her. Lifting her fingers from beneath the heavy covering, she felt the coarseness of bear fur. Elise blinked the sleep from her eyes, realizing she was lying on a narrow platform built into a wall.

The memory of her capture by the Indians made her sit straight up in bed. The bearskin fell to her waist, and her aching body screamed a protest. The physical discomfort failed to distract her. How many hours had passed? From the glint of light through the smokehole in the roof, it was evident that the day was not yet over.

The Indian woman was sewing near the fire, speaking softly to the small boy crouched at her feet. Noticing Elise was awake, she rose and took a bowl from beside the flames, then walked gracefully across the small chamber.

A hint of friendliness softened her dark eyes. "Eat," she said, thrusting a bowl of venison stew into Elise's hands.

"You speak English!" The words tumbled from Elise's mouth in a rush of excitement. "Can you tell me where my brother is—the boy who was captured with me?"

The woman frowned, then shook her head in puzzlement.

Elise repeated her request, speaking more slowly.

A light of comprehension flashed over the squaw's lovely face. "Ah . . . boy join People. Grow to big warrior man."

Elise was content with the reassurance; at least Marc

212

was safe for the time being. "What is your name?" she asked.

"Me Morning Star, wife to Dark Wolf."

"My name is Elise." She deemed it wise to withhold her surname until she discovered if these Indians were friendly to the French or the English.

Morning Star nodded. "Soon have true name, at time of New Moon. Then be sister to Morning Star."

"Sister?" Elise repeated, amazed.

Sadness touched the Indian woman's face. "True sister to Morning Star die three moons ago."

She returned to her sewing by the fire. Pensively, Elise stared into the bowl that warmed her hands. So she was to be adopted into the tribe as a replacement for Morning Star's dead sister. At least that had to be better than being a slave.

This time, Elise managed to consume every morsel of food. When she was finished, Morning Star handed her a long doeskin dress with warm leggings to wear underneath. After Elise changed clothing, the Indian woman led her outside.

The sun hung low in the afternoon sky; there was perhaps an hour of daylight left. Elise was conscious of the villagers staring at her. It took a determined effort to keep her eyes focused straight ahead. Weakness trembled in her legs, but she forced herself to walk normally.

They headed over to some furs stretched out on a rack to dry, then gathered them up and carried them inside the longhouse. Morning Star showed her how to scrape the inner skin; it brought bittersweet memories to Elise's mind, of a time long ago when she had sat by the fire watching her father perform the same task.

The activity loosened up the stiffness in her muscles,

213

though the soreness remained. As she worked, thoughts of escape crowded her mind. Was there a chance she could play on Morning Star's sympathies?

"Morning Star," she ventured. "My brother and I will be mourned as dead if we don't return home soon. Will you not let us go?"

The friendliness vanished from the Indian woman's eyes. "White woman stay," she said stonily. "Be sister to Morning Star."

Frustrated, Elise dropped the subject. It was plain that Morning Star would never even consider releasing a valuable captive.

Resolutely she scraped at the fur with a stone awl, her thoughts turning to Troy. Perhaps it was best to be patient until he had a chance to reach her. But where was he? her heart cried out. By now he would have returned to camp and discovered the evidence of her capture. She calmed herself with the thought that at this very moment he probably was tracking them down.

The hope sustained her over the next few weeks, and she found herself watching the wilderness around the village, keeping her eyes alert for some sign of his presence, some signal that he was out there, waiting to guide her and Marc to safety. But slowly a dread crept into the forefront of her mind. What if Troy never rescued them?

Elise tried to push the doubt away, but it nagged at her like a buzzing mosquito. The weather had been good, so he should have had little trouble trailing the party of Indians. Painfully she reminded herself that he was an Englishman and therefore couldn't be trusted.

The more she thought about it, the more her uncertainty grew. Perhaps Troy didn't want to risk his own life to save her. What if he had grown tired of her and saw her capture as a convenient way to end their relationship? That meant his words of love had been lies.

It was a bitter pill to swallow. Her heart resisted the notion, but as the days passed logic forced her to accept the truth. No longer could she count on anyone but herself—and Marc. Ruthlessly she buried the tender emotions that brought tears to her eyes and an ache to her chest.

The urge to escape remained strong. Everyone in the village watched suspiciously wherever she went, and never was she allowed near the perimeter of the forest. The only plan she could come up with was to act the dutiful slave until an opportunity presented itself. Perhaps if the Indians believed she had accepted her fate, they eventually would let down their guard.

As adopted sister of Morning Star, Elise was treated with a guarded respect. Her fears of rape never came true; though several young braves eyed her openly, none forced their attentions on her. And Dark Wolf seemed satisfied with Morning Star. In the evenings, Elise would often see them slip off together into the woods to make love, in accordance with the Indian custom.

A relationship of equals developed between Elise and her Indian sister. Morning Star was quick to smile and spent many hours laughing and playing with her young son. The little English she knew had been learned from a captive white man who had died the previous summer. Elise began to teach her more English words, while Morning Star reciprocated by coaching her in the Indian language.

One morning Elise was squatting just outside the longhouse, grinding corn. It was cold even in the sunshine, but she preferred working out here rather than cooped up inside. Morning Star was a short distance away, supervising the gutting and roasting of a buck that had been brought in earlier.

Bored with her monotonous task, Elise glanced around idly. Today the village was a beehive of activity. Preparations were in full swing for the midwinter New Year's festival, which would begin tonight, the time of the second moon after the winter solstice. The women were busy cooking a feast, and many of the braves were out hunting fresh game after long months of eating only dried meat.

A sudden tension tightened Elise's muscles. Across the village, Marc stood in the center of a group of boys younger than himself. Several braves were teaching them the skills of archery. In the few weeks since her capture, she had seen her brother only from a distance. Eagerly she observed him from beneath the veil of her lashes. Marc seemed in good health, obediently imitating his Indian instructor, though there was a hint of sullenness on his face.

Emotion twisted her heart. It wasn't fair that Marc was forced to accept the life of a savage. She yearned to talk to him, to reassure him they would escape. The feeling grew until she could think of nothing else.

Glancing around, she saw that Morning Star was nowhere in sight. Decisively Elise put down the mortar and pestle. If she were quick about it, she could have a word with her brother and return here before the Indian woman discovered her absence. There might never be a better chance.

She walked through the village, keeping an air of purpose about her in the hopes that anyone watching would think she had been sent on a legitimate errand. The ploy worked. More than one pair of vigilant eyes observed her passage, but no one challenged her.

Elise paused in the shadow of a lodge that stood nearest to the gathering of men and boys practicing with their bows and arrows. Her heart pounded and her palms were cold and damp. Long minutes dragged by as she tried to catch Marc's attention. She was near despair when at last he turned and saw her.

She made a small, beckoning motion with her hand. Marc gave an almost imperceptible nod and began to edge out of the group, clutching the long bow to his thin frame. When no one was looking, he darted over to her.

Elise hugged him close, then drew back, anxiously searching his pale face. "How are you? Have they hurt you?" she asked quickly, her voice low.

"They're treating me well enough," he whispered. "What of you?"

"I'm fine. Oh, Marc, we must make plans for escape. We can't stay here forever."

"*Oui*." His hand tightened on the long bow that was almost as tall as he was. "And what I wouldn't give to kill every one of these heathen bastards before we go!"

"Marc, we must make them think we're happy here. If we learn more of their habits and get them to trust us, then we might have a chance."

"How long do you think that will take?"

Elise shrugged helplessly, wishing she knew. "We'll just have to bide our time—"

Her voice died and her muscles tensed. Morning Star was rounding the corner of the longhouse, a look of grim anger on her lovely, copper-skinned face. The Indian woman stalked up to Elise and grabbed her by the arm.

217

"No run away."

"But I wasn't running away," Elise protested. "I wish only to talk to my brother."

"No talk," Morning Star said firmly.

She called out to one of the braves nearby. He ran up and gave Mare a cuff on the side of the head, then dragged him back over to the group of boys. Morning Star nudged Elise toward the longhouse and set her to work again.

For the remainder of the day, the Indian woman watched her like a hawk. Elise knew it would take time to allay the squaw's suspicions, time in which she would have to play the submissive captive and wait patiently for a chance to escape.

After sunset, the ceremony of the New Year began. The old fires that had burned for the past year were doused and new ones started. There were cleansing rituals and prayers to help overcome the forces of evil and encourage the new growth of spring.

Elise sat cross-legged beside Morning Star and the other women, who huddled around a huge bonfire in the middle of the village. Cold seeped through her doeskin dress from the cold ground beneath her. A full moon inched upward from the tangle of black trees beyond the perimeter of the settlement.

A group of braves gathered beneath the only tree in the clearing, a tall oak with a platform built around it. The men were preparing for a ritual dance, and some carried masks, which identified them as members of the False Face Society. These masks were caricatures of human faces, with grotesquely distorted features and long, stringy wigs made of horsehair. Morning Star had told her that the members of the False Face Society participated in a ceremony to drive away evil spirits.

Suddenly a whoop split the air. The men took off running in the direction of the sound, the women and children trailing after them. Since no one brandished weapons, Elise concluded the newcomers were friends, rather than foes. With Morning Star prodding her along, she made her way through the throng to a place near the front. She looked for Marc and caught a glimpse of him in the company of a watchful brave.

Two returning warriors leaped nimbly from the backs of their horses. Dark Wolf strode forward to engage them in conversation. Their speech was unintelligible to Elise, who had only a limited understanding of the Indian language, but the people around her murmured their approval of what was said.

Then one of the braves untied a rope attached to his horse. He yanked on the lead, and a captive stumbled into view, a pitiful, hunched-over figure.

Elise caught her breath. It was a white man, and when he lifted his head, she saw that his face was shadowed by a dark beard, his eyes darting around fearfully. In that same instant, she recognized him.

Jake Hubbell.

She blinked, sure her eyes were playing tricks on her. But it was he, there could be no doubt about it. Though his usual arrogance had vanished, he had the same burly build and misshapen nose that she remembered so well.

Elise's heart pounded. Another captive might mean a lessening of vigilance toward her and Marc. Perhaps Hubbell himself would join them in an escape attempt; though the villain was untrustworthy under other circumstances, here he would surely see the practicality of joining together against a common enemy.

The crowd began to move away. Morning Star seized

Elise's hand and pulled her toward their longhouse, where she swooped up a heavy stick. Still hanging tightly on to Elise, the Indian woman rejoined the others near the blazing bonfire.

Seeing the two long rows of Indians forming, Elise realized it must be Jake Hubbell's turn to run the gauntlet. She couldn't help but shudder; the memory of her own ordeal was still fresh in her mind. Morning Star yanked her into line, wielding the cudgel in her small, copper-skinned hand.

Several braves gave Jake Hubbell a push. The big man staggered between the rows of savages, covering his head as the first blows struck him. Suddenly he stopped and bellowed like an enraged bear. Blinking dazedly, he stood wobbling on his feet, his ham fists flailing at the sticks that pummeled him.

Someone gave him a thrust and he fell to his hands and knees. Jeers filled the night. An Indian boy leaped forward and struck him hard on the back. Morning Star surged toward the prisoner along with the rest of the Indians, dragging Elise along behind.

Elise strained to see through the crush. The strange feeling that rippled through the crowd was unlike anything she had ever before felt. It was a savage excitement, a blood lust that sent cold shivers down her spine.

Two of the braves hauled Hubbell to his feet, half-dragging him over to the tree near the center of the village. They forced him to mount the scaffold, tore the buckskin shirt from his body, then tied him loosely to the tree trunk.

Several men holding burning brands climbed onto the platform above the crowd. When Hubbell caught sight of the flaming sticks, he came out of his stupor and began struggling against his bonds, the sound of his petrified voice piercing the air. "Oh, please don't, please . . . sweet Jesus, save me!"

Even from a distance, the fear on his face was illuminated starkly by the huge bonfire. His massive chest heaved visibly, his dark eyes scuttling back and forth at the approaching Indians. Taut with shock, Elise watched them begin to torment the Englishman. They thrust their brands at his torso, searing his bare flesh. Hubbell screamed, yanking at the rope that tied him, but the Indians continued their relentless punishment.

The breath left Elise's lungs in a gasp of horror. Morning Star turned to her and said scornfully, "White man show no bravery. Cry like baby."

Elise was taken aback by the cold words. Was this the same warm-hearted woman who had laughed with her son and showed Elise many small kindnesses? How could Morning Star approve of such cruelty?

"If you intend to kill him, then why not do it quickly?" Elise burst out. "There is no need to make him suffer."

"Is way of People," Morning Star said stonily. "Fail test and die, pass test and join People."

It was a simple yet savage means of culling the weak from the prisoners taken. Revulsion churned in Elise's stomach, and the sound of Hubbell's agonized screams made her forget all caution.

"Well, I refuse to stand here and watch while a man is tortured to death." Pivoting, she started to walk away.

Morning Star grabbed her by the arm. "Stay," she ordered.

Angrily Elise tried to twist free, but another woman sprang to Morning Star's aid. They dragged Elise over to

221

one of the longhouses. There, Morning Star used a strip of deerskin to secure Elise's wrists to the pole that formed the corner of the lodge.

"Watch," Morning Star said firmly. "See what happen if you run away."

She pointed to Jake Hubbell, who writhed in torment on the platform above the jeering crowd. Sickness rose in Elise's throat. Death by torture would be her fate, then, if she were caught in an escape attempt.

Morning Star left with the other woman, blending into the spectators surrounding Hubbell. Elise yanked and twisted in an attempt to loosen the thong that imprisoned her hands. But the knot held and finally she ceased trying, leaning numbly against the corner of the lodge.

Horror formed a tight lump in the pit of her stomach. She closed her eyes, trying to block out the nightmarish scene, but Hubbell's whimpering cries continued without cease. The faint stench of burning flesh drifted across the compound. As if drawn by a magnet, she opened her eyes again and looked across the clearing.

No part of Hubbell's body was immune to the punishment. If he tried to crouch down, someone would thrust up a burning torch from beneath the platform. They applied flames to his face, his hair, even his privates. The torture went on for hours, the Indians pouring water into their victim's mouth whenever he fainted, to keep him alive for as long as possible.

Elise felt a deep-rooted pity for Jake Hubbell. Her own discomforts in being tied up seemed negligible compared to his suffering. No matter what sins the man had committed, he didn't deserve to die in such a painful manner. Fervently she wished there was some way to end the cruelty.

As she averted her face, a sudden flash of motion to the side caught her eye. Whipping her head around, she saw a tall Indian brave creeping toward her from the deep shadows behind the longhouse. His features were hidden in the gloom and his stealthy movements hinted of danger.

Elise's heart began to race wildly. He was heading straight for her!

Closer and closer he came until he reached out and grabbed her arm. As he did so, the faint light from the bonfire fell upon his face.

She stiffened in shock. Bulging eyes leered at her from beneath a stringy mop of hair and thick lips grimaced in an evil smile. It was the grotesque visage of a monster.

Chapter Fifteen

A scream rose in Elise's throat, but the Indian swiftly clapped a hand over her mouth. In a frenzy of panic, she fought wildly, her tied wrists hindering her escape. Her foot lashed out to kick his shin. With a muffled oath, he slammed his lean body against her.

"Elise, for God's sake, stop it!" he hissed into her ear. "'Tis me, Troy!"

His urgent voice penetrated the terror that gripped her brain. She went limp, unable to stop staring up at his gruesome features. Of course . . . that was only a mask, similar to those worn by the members of the False Face Society. A flicker of joyous hope uncurled inside her.

"Troy?" she ventured breathlessly. "Can it truly be you?"

"Aye," he whispered back. "I've got to get you out of here before someone sees us together."

He let go of her, crouching low to untie the thong that snared her wrists. As the tight fastening fell to the ground, her numb fingers tingled to life. Troy threw a swift glance at the crowd of Indians intent on the torture of their victim, then he drew Elise into the shadows behind the lodge.

He pulled off the ugly mask and dropped it. "Forgive me for frightening you like that, but I had to have some way to disguise myself."

She could just barely make out his face through the gloom. Familiar green eyes twinkled down at her from above his tawny beard. The sight of his handsome features filled her with an overwhelming rush of emotion.

Hot tears spilled down her cheeks. "Oh, Troy, I thought you weren't coming," she babbled, clutching at his buckskin shirt. "I was so afraid . . . I thought you'd forgotten me."

He put his arms around her, hugging her tightly, smoothing a finger over her wet cheek. "Little angel," he murmured, his voice full of warm affection. "How could I ever leave you behind? You're more important to me than my own life. But are you all right?" he added roughly. "They didn't hurt you, rape you?"

"Nay, I'm fine . . . now that you're here."

The feel of his hard body made her heart swell with happiness. She could scarcely believe he was real. Troy hadn't forsaken her, after all; he was here, and he still loved her.

Elise lifted her face for his kiss, arching to him on tiptoe. His lips came down on hers with a fierce but gentle hunger that set her world to spinning. The silken sweep of his tongue sent a dizzying desire burning through her veins. Her strength dissolved and she leaned into his warm embrace, threading her fingers into his hair, feeling more joyously alive than she had in weeks.

After a moment, Troy drew back, his hands moving

hungrily over her as if he couldn't get enough of her. "We mustn't delay any longer. I've got to find your brother so we can get out of here while the Indians are too busy to notice."

Recalling their danger, she felt a cold shiver. "The last time I saw Marc, he was in the crowd with one of the braves. I'll go with you—"

"No." He pointed toward the dark forest beyond. "I left three horses tethered back there. You head straight over the next rise and you can't miss them."

"But you don't speak French," she argued. "With that mask on, how will Marc know who you are?"

"I'm going to give him a lock of your hair and pray he has the sense to figure things out." Troy took a knife from his belt and held it against the end of her braid. "You don't mind if I cut this, do you?"

"Of course not, but—"

"Stubborn wench," he teased. "You're supposed to be tied up, remember? Don't you think 'twould look suspicious if someone sees you walking around free? All three of us might be killed, like that poor bastard they're torturing."

The sound of Hubbell's weak cries still drifted through the cold night air. Troy was right, Elise admitted. She couldn't jeopardize their chances of escaping.

"All right." She caught at his arm as he was replacing the knife in his belt. "But Troy, I think you should know . . . that man up there is Jake Hubbell."

Troy frowned and stepped away to peer around the corner of the lodge. "Damn if you're not right," he muttered. "I'm afraid there's naught we can do for him without dooming ourselves to the same fate."

"You'll be careful, won't you?" Elise asked anxiously.

He flashed her a cocky grin. "I have a powerful incentive—I want to live to make love to you again. Now get moving."

He picked up the hideous mask and pulled it over his face and hair, then strode away, looking every inch the powerful Indian warrior. Where had he gotten that mask and clothing? she wondered with a shiver. He must have killed a brave who had strayed too far from the village.

Crouching by the corner of the lodge, she watched as he walked casually to the perimeter of the throng. Her pulse throbbed in her throat. What if one of the Indians challenged him, pulled off his mask? He would die.

Fear made her palms clammy. She longed to be at his side, to share in whatever fate befell him. But he was right, the risks were too great. She mustn't endanger him because of her foolish stubbornness.

Resolutely, Elise turned her back on the jeering crowd and headed into the cold, dark forest.

Standing at the edge of the gathering, Troy peered up at the platform through the eyeholes of his mask. He felt a sick disgust rise in his throat. The hoots and taunts of the spectators mingled with Hubbell's croaking pleas for mercy.

It was hard for Troy to believe that people could derive such enjoyment out of torturing another human being. Even the women and children joined in the blood lust, taking turns poking and prodding Hubbell with their burning sticks. Hubbell writhed against the tree trunk, the exposed flesh on his massive chest and arms reddened with burns.

Poor bastard, Troy thought. He'd heard tales that the

Iroquois thrived on such gruesome entertainment, and were careful to keep their victim alive for as long as twenty-four hours. This was the first time he had witnessed it himself.

His fingers tightened around the lock of soft hair that curled in his sweating palm, and a sense of urgency gripped him. While the Indians were still engrossed in their macabre entertainment, he must find Marc and spirit him away.

With an outward show of nonchalance, Troy strolled through the milling horde, keeping his eyes alert for the boy. His vision was restricted by the narrow slits of the mask; he was forced to move his head back and forth in a slow sweep to make certain he didn't miss the object of his search.

A huge bonfire burned in the center of the clearing, making it easy to discern the features of each Indian. Men and women alike yelled insults to their hapless victim. The elders were gathered in a group off to one side, observing the proceedings with stoic faces.

Troy concentrated his attention on the boys scattered throughout the assemblage. He noticed a few curious glances turn his way, and realized uneasily that none of the other braves wore their masks. For whatever ceremony the Indians used this grotesque facial disguise, apparently now was not it. God help him if someone became suspicious enough to challenge him and discovered just how little he knew of the Iroquoian language.

Then he saw Marc. The boy was hunkered down at the edge of the crowd, an expression of tired dejection on his youthful features. His dark hair was mussed, his face smudged with dirt. He showed no interest in the torture that gripped the attention of the Indians.

Taking a cautious glance around, Troy walked to him and got down on his haunches. The boy glanced over and stiffened slightly.

"Marc, I've come to get you out of here," Troy murmured, so that no one around them could hear. "I know you don't understand English, but for God's sake I hope you can guess what I'm saying. I've come for you and your sister—*Elise.*"

Troy pressed the curl of hair into Marc's palm. The youth sat up straight, frowning down at the coppery strands. After a moment, he closed his fingers tightly around the lock of hair and lifted his eyes to study the man beside him.

Ever so slightly, Troy inclined his head toward the night-darkened forest where Elise waited. Casually he rose and sauntered off, praying the boy had the sense to slip away as soon as it was safe. He didn't look back, for fear someone might be watching them.

Feigning an interest in the proceedings, Troy strolled around the perimeter of the throng. A prickling sixth sense warned him he had stretched his luck far enough.

He moved to the side of the crowd farthest from the bonfire, edging away until the shadows swallowed him. Once out of sight, he rapidly made his way toward the boundary of the woods, his moccasins skimming over the snow with the silence of an Indian. He found a vantage point behind a tree trunk and stood close to the rough bark.

Removing the mask, he concealed it in the underbrush. Nervous impatience made him want to pace back and forth, but he quelled the impulse. It was more prudent to stay hidden.

The minutes dragged by. The night was quiet, except

229

for the jeering of the crowd in the distance. A cloud passed over the moon, deepening the gloom in the forest. At last, just as Troy was debating the risks of going to look for the boy, Marc rounded the corner of a longhouse at the edge of the village.

He paused and looked around, then walked swiftly toward the trees. Troy was about to wave to him when the moon came out from behind the cloud, its pale light glimmering off something metallic in the shadow of the lodge. *A knife.*

Cold tension tightened his gut. There was an Indian brave following Marc!

Quietly Troy drew a hunting knife from the scabbard that hung from his belt. He began to inch away from the place where Marc was heading, taking care not to make a sound.

The moonlight vanished again; the Indian was the merest rippling of movement in the gloom. Troy found a hiding spot behind a fallen log. Muscles taut, the blood surging heavily through his veins, he crouched down to wait.

Marc paused at the edge of the forest, looking around uncertainly. He took a few tentative steps into the woods, coming so close that Troy could almost reach out and touch him.

Keep walking, Troy urged silently. To his relief, the boy ventured farther into the dark maze of trees.

"Elise?" Marc whispered.

Troy's eyes were trained on the Indian creeping into the woods behind Marc. The pale light of the moon spilled through the tangle of bare branches overhead.

Despite the cold, there was a prickling of sweat down his spine. The handle of the knife fit into his palm like an extension of his arm. He had one chance to silence the man without risking a sound that might attract the attention of the other villagers.

Troy waited until the brave was just past the fallen log. Then he sprang up and onto the man's back, his arms snaking around his neck. The Indian tried to throw him off, but the sharp blade had already sliced into his throat.

It was over in seconds. Troy felt the spurt of warm blood on his hands, and the Indian dropped lifelessly to the ground.

The knife slipped out of Troy's fingers. He stood still, torn between relief and sickness as the adrenaline ebbed from his body. He despised killing, even now, when there had been no other choice.

The soft squeak of a footstep on the snow startled him. He swooped up the knife and spun toward the sound.

It was only Marc. The boy approached cautiously, gazing wide-eyed at the crumpled figure of the Indian brave, then back at Troy. He said something in French, his voice small and shaky.

Troy knew the danger was far from over. Time was of the essence if they were to make good their escape before someone noticed the two captives were gone.

He crouched down and used snow to cleanse the blood from his hands and knife. Then he motioned to Marc. The boy obediently fell into step behind him.

Swiftly they traversed the darkened forest, with only an occasional moonbeam to light the way. Within moments they reached the thicket of trees where Troy had hidden the horses.

Elise came hurrying out of the shadows. "Troy . . . Marc!" she whispered. "*Mon Dieu, merci* . . . you're both safe!"

She gave her brother a brief hug before turning to Troy. "I was afraid . . . you were gone so long."

Troy pulled her close and kissed her brow. "I'm sorry we worried you," he murmured. "We need to get out of here fast, little angel. I hope you're prepared to ride like the wind."

She nodded, gazing up at him trustingly. A knot of fierce love tightened his chest. By God, he would keep her safe from this moment forward, even if it cost him his own life.

Quickly he hoisted her into the saddle. Her skirt was hiked up to her thighs, revealing the doeskin leggings beneath. The moon emerged from behind a cloud, highlighting the determination on her face. Except for the gleam of copper in her braids, she might have been an Indian princess.

Troy swung onto his own horse. Marc had already mounted, and the three of them trotted off into the darkness, Troy leading the way. He rode as fast as he dared through the black wilderness. Apprehension dogged his heels; time was their best bet against the expert tracking skills of the Indians.

Never in his wildest dreams had he thought there would come a moment when he'd feel grateful to Jake Hubbell. But he did now.

Chapter Sixteen

Slowly Elise drifted from the depths of a dreamless sleep. One by one her senses returned to life, registering the distant hum of voices, the faint aroma of cooking, the snug warmth enveloping her body. As she stretched, soreness wrenched her muscles.

Memory came flashing back to her. They had escaped from the Indians, spending long hours in the saddle until she had been ready to drop with fatigue, feeling fear coupled with the fierce joy of freedom. Then, finally, they had arrived here at Gist's settlement.

Elise opened her eyes to see the angled timbers of the roofline. She was in the tiny loft of a log cabin. The wind wailed outside, reminding her of the previous day's blizzard, which had wiped away their tracks from any pursuing Indians.

The feather pillow next to her bore the impression of someone's head, but now she was alone in the tiny chamber. Had Troy slept here with her?

Shaking the cobwebs from her mind, Elise threw back the quilt and swung out of bed. The crude plank floor was cold beneath her bare feet. She dressed hurriedly, donning the Indian garb for lack of other clothing.

Careful of her aching muscles, she descended the peg ladder to the main room of the cabin, where a gray-haired woman was bending over the fire, stirring a kettle of stew and dumplings. She looked over her shoulder at Elise, then set down the spoon and turned, wiping her hands on the apron that covered her ample girth.

"Mornin'. You done almost missed the noon meal, lazin' abed so late." The woman's merry smile turned the words into teasing. "I'm Mrs. Gist, 'case you don't recall meetin' me last night."

The memory was a blur. "I'm afraid not," Elise apologized.

"Well, you were plumb tuckered out, dead on yore feet. That man of your'n had to half-carry you up to bed. You must be hungry. Lemme call the boys an' we'll eat."

Mrs. Gist opened the door and let out a loud "yoo-hoo." Then she came back inside and waved at a bench. "Pull up a cheer. I'll have the vittles on the table in no time flat."

Elise sat down, listening in bemusement as the woman chattered nonstop. The "boys" ambled in, shaking the snow from their clothing—Christopher Gist, his full-grown son, and Troy and Marc.

As Christopher said grace, Elise bowed her head in thanks. Gratitude swelled her heart. Praise be that Troy had managed to find her and Marc! His leg pressed warmly against hers, his familiar scent of horses and leather filling her senses. She was overjoyed to have this chance to share his life again.

And yet . . .

Troubled, she looked at Marc, who sat across from her

234

and Troy. The issue of her choice between them had never been resolved. Soon her brother would be anxious to return to Fort LeBoeuf. Even now he was studying Troy with an absorbed expression, as if he were pondering some inner problem. Would she go with him? The dilemma cast a pall upon her happiness.

When they were through eating, Elise helped Mrs. Gist clear away the wooden trenchers. The men left the cabin to return to their chores, but when she turned around, she saw Marc still standing there, fidgeting with his fur cap.

"Elise," he said, beckoning to her. "I'd like to speak to you."

He must be anxious to make plans to go back to the fort. Suddenly she felt unprepared to face the future. "*Plus tard*, Marc. I'm too tired now."

"But I think you'll want to hear what I have to say," he argued. "Come here."

Resigned, she complied. "*Oui?*"

Marc hesitated, shifting the fur cap from hand to hand. Then his words tumbled out in a rush. "I've decided not to return to Fort LeBoeuf. I'm going with you and Troy. I want to learn to speak English, too."

Elise stared at him in astonishment. "But . . . why?"

"Because I was wrong about Troy. He isn't like our father. You should have seen the way he walked into that Indian village, as if he weren't a bit scared! And then when that warrior came after me, Troy jumped him and killed him, as cool as can be."

"Killed—?" she choked out.

Marc nodded. "Slit his throat with a knife," he said with youthful relish, lifting a hand to make a slicing motion across his own throat. "If he hadn't been so brave, we might never have escaped. That's why I've decided I was wrong to hate him and all the other English. I think you should marry him, Elise. He's much better than that stuffy old Yves Larousse. *A bientôt.*"

Marc lifted his cap in a jaunty wave and walked out the door.

Elise gazed after him in stunned disbelief. How could her brother switch from hatred to hero worship so quickly? Despite Troy's daring rescue, she herself couldn't shake off a deep-seated mistrust of the English.

Frowning, she decided their father's desertion must not have made as big an impact on Marc as it had on her. After all, that betrayal had occurred before Marc had even been born. Since her brother hadn't witnessed the heartache their mother had suffered, it must be easier for him to forgive and forget.

But not for her. There was no denying her hunger for Troy's lips, for the touch of his hands on her body. Lust was the only thing holding them together . . . wasn't it?

Distressed, she mumbled a good-bye to Mrs. Gist and left the cabin. Outside, the sky was gray and a few snowflakes pricked her cheeks. Gusts of wind whipped her long coppery braids against the doeskin of her dress. She shivered violently, the cold tempting her to turn back, but an inner restlessness impelled her toward a cluster of outbuildings.

She followed a trampled path over the snow leading to a large structure made of logs. Slipping through one of the double doors, Elise ventured into the dim interior. It was warmer here, and the air smelled of hay and horses.

The murmur of voices caught her attention. She walked down a wide corridor with stalls on either side, her moccasined feet moving soundlessly over the dirt floor. Looking over the half-door to a stall, she found Troy and Marc inside.

The two were crouched beside a chestnut mare, her brother watching raptly as Troy applied salve to a cut on the animal's leg. Although the boy couldn't understand English, Troy was speaking of the purpose of the medication. When Troy glanced up and saw her, he handed the jar of ointment to the boy, pantomiming that Marc was to finish the task.

Somehow the change in their relationship was disturbing to Elise. Why did it bother her so? she fretted. She should be glad her brother had made friends with Troy and was now willing to go with them.

Smiling warmly, Troy walked over to her, wiping his fingers on a scrap of tow linen. "I'm glad you came by, angel," he said in an intimate undertone. "I didn't want to wait until tonight to see you again, either."

Desire stirred in her belly, but something compelled her to deny the sensation. "I was just out for a walk, that's all."

"Then walk with me."

Troy threw aside the square of cloth and came out the door to grab her hand, drawing her into an empty stall nearby. There, he pulled her into his arms. "I've been wanting this all day," he murmured, lowering his mouth to hers.

It was the first time he had kissed her since they'd left the Indian village. At first she held back, but the feel of his hands moving down to cup her derriere, his tongue probing the sweet depths of her mouth, was too much to bear. Her vague resistance vanished beneath a tidal wave of need. She pressed herself to his hard chest, her bones melting from the heat of his embrace. Her hands stole around his neck to thread into the thickness of his hair. She couldn't get enough of him; the taste and scent of him were like drugs to her senses.

Her lips moved to the pulse beating wildly in her throat. She arched her head back, her fingers digging into his shoulders for support. He stroked her breast through the pliant doeskin of her bodice.

"By God, I wish we were alone," Troy swore softly. His fingers caressed her cheek, his jade eyes staring intently into hers. "I love you, Elise, and tonight I intend to show you how much."

"Yes," she agreed shakily. When he touched her like that, she was helpless to resist him. He roused in her a compulsive desire to surrender her entire self, body and soul. But through the shimmering magic, she was conscious of a hollow note of distress. More and more she was coming to realize that her need for him was a flame that burned eternally in her heart. He possessed the power to destroy her.

She pulled out of his arms and walked to the other side of the stall, grasping for a change of subject. "You never did tell me why it took you so many weeks to find the Indian village. Did you have trouble following our tracks?"

"Nay, I heard a gunshot when the Indians captured you, but when I came galloping to your rescue, I fell off my trusty steed and impaled myself on a branch lying on the ground."

Elise caught her breath. "Were you hurt?"

"Not so badly that I couldn't make it back to John Frazier's." A wicked grin stole over his face. "Would you like to see my scar?"

He lifted his shirt and unbuttoned his breeches,

showing her the jagged pink line that ran from his waist down to his hip. His action also displayed the breechclout that concealed his privates.

Flustered, she wavered between concern and embarrassment. "Troy, cover yourself—Marc could walk in."

His expression was the picture of innocence. "So? I'm sure he's seen a naked man before."

"I don't care," she hissed. "You cover yourself this instant!"

Blushing furiously, she glanced out the door of the stall, then looked back, unable to keep her eyes from returning to his bare flesh.

"All right, all right," Troy relented, his eyes twinkling.

After rearranging his clothing, he strolled over to her and caught her trim waist in his big hands. "You know, Elise, I think Marc has changed his opinion of me. Ever since I rescued you two from the Indians, he's been following me around like a puppy."

She stiffened slightly, the vague feeling of resentment sweeping over her again. "You seem to have made quite an impression on him," she forced out. "He told me earlier that he's willing to go with us."

Troy looked pleased. "Well, then, all of our problems are solved. Maybe he won't even object to your marrying me."

"I've never agreed to marry you."

"You will."

"You're full of confidence, aren't you?"

He grinned. "One of us has to be."

"What is that supposed to mean?"

"I mean, if I didn't keep pursuing you, little angel, we might lose this rare and beautiful thing between us," he said softly. "We have a lifetime of happiness ahead of us, and I won't rest until you realize that, too."

His hands were firm about her waist. He looked so positive and steadfast that for a fleeting moment Elise was tempted to forget her mistrust of the English. But mere words could not bury the hard lessons of experience.

She wrenched herself from him, backing away until her hands met the rough wood side of the stall. "I'm sure my father spoke such lovely words to my mother, too," she said coldly.

Troy's face took on a hint of irritation. "Elise, I'm not like your father. Can't you judge me for myself, instead of forever comparing me to someone else?"

"I'm only trying to learn by the mistakes of the past," she defended herself.

"Tell me," he said with a hint of sarcasm, "have I really made life such a hell for you?"

"No . . . yes! You forced me to be your mistress in exchange for my brother's freedom."

"I don't recall ever forcing you to sleep with me."

Hot color flooded her cheeks, and the truth of his statement filled her with an irrational rage. "You pressure me to go home with you . . . to marry you. I want only to be left alone, do you understand?"

"So that's what this is all about. What you're trying to say is that you'd rather return to the French than stay with me, aren't you?"

The hurt in his eyes deflated her anger. How had the conversation gotten so out of control? "I—I don't know," Elise stammered.

"I see," he said bitterly. "Well, be forewarned that I've no intention of cooling my heels around here, waiting for you to make up your mind. I'm leaving in the morning, with or without you."

"All I ask for is a little understanding—"

"I've tried to understand you, Elise," he cut in. "The trouble is, you refuse to see the truth—you're afraid to let down that wall around your heart. You're afraid to take a risk because you think you might get hurt."

"I don't know what you're talking about."

"I think you do." Grimly he stalked out of the stall, then wheeled back around. "And don't feel obligated to stay with me just because I saved your skin. You saved me once, too, so now we're even."

Pivoting, he strode away, his hard footsteps heading out the door.

Elise squeezed her eyes shut, tilting the back of her head against the stable wall. Confusion clouded her brain. How had she gotten herself into such a miserable mess? She didn't want to leave Troy. What had induced her to imply that she did?

Oh, *Dieu*, love was so cruel, so painful. Her palms turned ice-cold and she opened her eyes wide. *Love?* It couldn't be true, it just couldn't be.

But it was . . . somehow she had fallen in love with Troy.

She stood there in stunned paralysis, wild joy warring with dark despair. He was an Englishman, he was her enemy, yet he had captured her heart and soul. For so long, she had been deluding herself that their relationship was merely physical, but now she could see her feelings went far deeper. That explained why she had argued with Troy; it had been a blind attempt to protect herself from hurt by putting more distance between them.

It also explained why she had been so irritated by

Marc's hero worship of Troy. She was jealous of the ease with which her brother had forgotten his prejudices, and angry with herself for being incapable of doing the same.

Her insides ached with vulnerability. Now Troy really did possess the power to destroy her. She told herself it would be best to leave him now, rather than risk even worse pain later. Yet she couldn't do it. She wanted to be at his side when he rode away in the morning.

In the meantime, Elise realized, she had to repair the damage wrought by her own foolish words. As difficult as it might be, she must put aside her pride and apologize to Troy, and pray he wouldn't leave her behind.

But when she went in search of him, he was with Christopher Gist, and he ignored her attempts to draw him aside. Again and again that day he turned curtly away from her, his eyes cold and brooding.

Heartsore, Elise sat alone in the loft late that night, her bare legs curled beneath her, a thick goosedown quilt wrapped around her nakedness. A single candle burned on a bedside table, throwing flickering shadows in the corners of the tiny room. She had bathed that afternoon; her clean coppery curls cascaded past her shoulders in artful disarray.

Mrs. Gist had informed her earlier that Marc would be sleeping in the cabin of a neighboring settler. A blush heated Elise's cheeks as she recalled Mrs. Gist's knowing wink. She herself could not get used to the casual attitude these English frontierspeople had toward lovemaking.

The rise and fall of male voices drifted from the main room below, though the conversation was too low for her to distinguish words. She had come up to bed more than an hour ago, hoping that Troy would take a hint and follow.

Elise yawned, drawing in a lungful of cold air. Determined to stay awake, she punched the feather pillow into a shape that cushioned her spine against the hard log wall. Then she leaned back to wait.

She must have dozed. Time passed in a blur, then suddenly she came awake with a jolt. For a moment she struggled to recall why she was sitting up, her legs cramped beneath her. The candle flame guttered in a pool of molten wax, and silvery threads of moonlight crept through the cracks in the shutters.

In the silence of the cabin her ears discerned a faint creak and a brushing sound like fabric against wood. She clutched the quilt closely around her . . . then Troy's head and broad shoulders appeared through the opening to the loft.

Coming up into the small room, he hunched his tall frame to avoid hitting his head on the rafters. His eyes were as cold as emeralds.

"Why aren't you asleep?"

"I—I was waiting up for you," Elise said tentatively.

"You've wasted your time. I'm in no mood for more arguments."

Turning away, he began to strip off his clothing. Elise swallowed the hurt that welled in her throat. He couldn't hate her too much, she told herself, or he'd have gone to sleep in the stables.

Fingers digging into the patchwork quilt, she watched him undress. The candlelight cast a golden sheen over the contours of his back. His physique was that of a Roman athlete, bronze-skinned and tautly muscled. He removed his breeches and tossed them aside. As he swiveled toward her, she caught a glimpse of the jagged scar along his hip.

Without giving her so much as a glance, Troy slid into bed, presenting his back to her as he drew a corner of the quilt over his nudity.

"Troy, I'd like to speak to you," she ventured.

"I told you, I didn't want to argue anymore."

"I don't want to argue, either. I only wanted to tell you . . ." Pride choked her voice, but she forced the humble words to her lips. "I wanted to tell you I'm sorry."

"For what?"

"For saying the things I did and . . . for hurting you."

"You needn't apologize for being honest."

"But you don't understand," Elise said miserably. "I didn't mean some of the things I said."

He rolled onto his back to look at her, casually folding his arms behind his head. "Such as?"

His cool gaze revealed nothing of his thoughts, and her fingers plucked nervously at the quilt. What if Troy had changed his mind about taking her to his home? The mere prospect made her chest tighten.

"I want to stay with you," she whispered. "I never really wanted to return to Fort LeBoeuf."

"Because you desire me," he stated flatly.

She shifted uneasily on the mattress. "Well, yes—"

"And you believe I'm using this attraction between us to force you into a relationship you don't really want."

"Nay, that isn't true," she protested. "I don't think that at all."

Troy propped himself up on an elbow, the quilt slipping to his lean waist. "Listen, Elise, I'm tired of being punished for the crime of loving you. I must have your promise that from now on, you'll at least try to judge me for myself."

"I will," she whispered.

"I don't want to be used any more than you do," he added. "I need to know there's more between us than the passions of the flesh, do you understand?"

Elise stared at him in dismay. How could she respond to that? She dare not bare her heart, not when her love for him was still a new and fragile bloom. She needed time to accept her feelings and decide what to do about them.

"Troy, I—I wish I could say what you want to hear. . . ."

Troy felt a rush of painful disappointment, though she'd said only what he'd expected. Perhaps he was deluding himself to hope that she could ever care for him with the same gut-wrenching power of his own love for her. He knew he ought to end their relationship right now rather than risk being hurt even worse.

But his senses reeled with the closeness of her, the scent of her, the softness of her hair tumbling over her bare shoulders. His pride melted like mist before the morning sun. God help him, he could no more leave her behind than cut off his own arm. He'd settle for anything she was willing to give.

He drew her down into his embrace, adjusting the folds of the quilt around them. "Don't fret, little angel," he murmured into the fragrant cloud of her hair. "I know how difficult it must be for you to forget the past."

Elise didn't correct his mistaken reading of her distress. It was a joy to be with him again, to feel his strong body pressed against hers. Nothing else mattered. She put her lips to his neck, relishing the faint saltiness of his skin. She heard Troy suck in his breath, and his arms tightened around her.

"So many weeks without you," he whispered.

"Sometimes I thought I'd go crazy with worry."

She raised her head to look at him in the glow of the candle. The torment he'd suffered showed in the faint, new lines radiating from his eyes. She lifted a hand to stroke his bearded jaw.

"The Indians treated me well enough," she said softly. "One of the women even adopted me as a sister."

"And the men—?"

"They didn't touch me," she reassured him. "They viewed me with the same respect as one of their own tribe."

"Praise God for that," Troy growled fervently. "I don't think I could bear knowing that I'd failed to protect you from harm."

His hands glided down her bare back, molding her hips to his heated flesh. Arousal swept over her. Yet she remained still, hypnotized by the naked emotion shining in his jade eyes. It was a moment of revelation for her; at last she could accept in the depths of her heart the love he had voiced to her so many times. He was not an Englishman but a man, both strong and gentle, and she was his woman.

Mere words were inadequate to convey the depths of her joy. "Oh, Troy, I'm so happy to be back with you."

"My own little angel," he muttered hoarsely. "How I love you."

He pressed her against the pillows, his mouth capturing hers with a hunger that stole her breath away. Their bodies strained against each other, each moving restlessly under the onslaught of a desire too long denied. Elise moaned softly as his practiced hands explored her curves, seeking out each gentle slope and valley, tarrying on her breasts and luring her ever deeper into the magic

246

of his spell.

A trace of the masculine aroma of horses and leather clung to his skin. Her arms circled him tightly, her fingers digging into the steely muscles of his shoulders, holding him as if he might vanish if she were foolish enough to let loose of him. The knowledge of their love made her respond with a giddy and wild abandon; if only she dared tell him how much he meant to her.

Against her soft thigh, she felt his hardness, and she opened herself to him, catching her breath as the heat of him filled the very depths of her body. He paused above her, and their eyes met in the rapture of the moment. Illuminated by the glow of candlelight, his features reflected the intense excitement that gripped his flesh, along with a tender emotion that touched Elise's heart. She knew there was no other closeness on earth that could match the perfection of this joining.

She lifted her mouth to him, her kiss feminine and inviting, her small tongue slipping between his lips to inflame their passion. A tremor gripped Troy, and he groaned deep in his throat. He began to move inside her, arousing her to a storm of passion. The need to share her entire self with him burned stronger and stronger within her until it became a conflagration that exceeded the bounds of reason.

"Troy . . . je t'aime . . . je t'aime. . . ."

The sighing sound of her voice was dim to her ears, muffled by the sudden, shimmering cloud of pleasure that dazzled her senses. The unbearable bliss throbbed through her body in a golden surge of fulfillment that was echoed in Troy's hoarse cry of triumph.

For long moments afterward, she lazed in a sea of contentment. The outside world seemed distant and hazy; her only reality was the feel of his arms wrapped around her. Against her breasts she was conscious of the slowing beat of their hearts.

Then Troy propped himself up on his elbow. He surveyed her tumbled hair and softly flushed face with an expression of profound satisfaction mingled with a hint of elation.

"You do love me, don't you?" he asked huskily.

Her euphoria vanished. "I—I don't know what you mean," she said, although the French phrase she'd murmured to him in the throes of passion echoed through her mind.

"You said the words yourself," Troy persisted. "Can you deny it?"

Jolted, Elise looked away, locked in chains of fear. What had she done? It was too late for a retraction; now her heart was in his hands.

"You know I cannot," she whispered.

Gently he grasped her chin and drew her eyes back to his. "Elise, 'tis naught to be ashamed of. To know you return my feelings is cause for rejoicing, not sorrow."

"You don't understand—"

"I understand more than you think I do. 'Tis hard for you to accept the fact that you can fall in love with your enemy, is it not?"

Tormented, she gave a jerky nod. "Oh, Troy, you're right. I *am* afraid . . . that someday you'll leave me."

"Never," he said firmly. "Trust in me, Elise. I want to wed you, to pledge my life to you."

"You ask too much," she murmured. "You know I cannot make such a promise."

He looked as if he were about to argue, then abruptly he released a heavy sigh. "All right, I won't press you;

248

we'll speak of this another time."

Troy tucked her face into the crook of his neck, fighting the frustration that threatened to engulf him. Damn that father of hers for giving her such a rotten image of the English! There were times when he'd cheerfully give up his entire fortune for the chance to wring that bastard's neck.

He tightened his arms around Elise, forcing himself to accept the fact that at the moment her mind was made up; it would be futile to continue to push her. But it was so hard to be patient when he wanted desperately to proclaim to the world that she was his. And by God, he vowed, someday he would have his wish!

He looked down at her, emotion beating fiercely within him. When his hand stroked the softness of her hair, she moved slightly, cuddling her slender form more closely to him. Her breathing was soft and relaxed, so trusting in slumber.

An exquisite joy rushed through him at the feel of her in his arms. The memory of her voice murmuring sweet words of love filled him with a strength of purpose. Once they arrived home and things settled into a routine, she would come to believe in his loyalty and faithfulness. And then she would agree to marry him.

For now, though, he would have to content himself with the exhilarating miracle of her love.

Chapter Seventeen

"This is your brother's home?" Elise asked Troy, trying to conceal the dismay that swept through her.

Uneasily, she shifted in the sidesaddle, her gloved fingers gripping the reins as she held the gray mare quiet. They had paused at the end of a long drive lined by poplars that led to a three-story brick house in the distance. It was a mansion, Elise corrected herself silently, again feeling that combination of awe and distress. Never in her wildest dreams had she thought Troy came from such a wealthy family.

"This is it," he replied, apparently too excited to notice her air of restraint. "Let's go."

He cantered down the hard-packed drive. Marc slapped his reins and joined Troy, but Elise lagged behind. Numbly she stared straight ahead, the house looming larger and more imposing the closer they drew. It was built of red brick, with white pillars supporting the porch and balcony above. Smoke curled from several chimneys, charcoal against the clear afternoon sky.

Once they'd passed a tall hedge of boxwood, other

buildings came into view. Glancing around in bewildered awe, Elise saw a complex similar to a small village, with barns and stables, a kitchen separate from the house, a laundry, and other structures she couldn't identify. Dark-skinned servants paused in their duties to stare at the arrivals.

A formal garden stretched off to one side, where crocuses thrust their gaily colored heads against the crisp breezes of late February. Beyond the house, a spacious lawn sloped down toward the winding James, the river's frozen edge glinting in the sunshine. Clusters of bare-branched trees framed the magnificent view.

Elise's misgivings grew stronger. All day they'd ridden past many such homes, separated by long stretches of winter-barren fields. But only now were her suspicions confirmed; Troy did not live in the cozy farmhouse she had anticipated. How would she, a servant all of her life, fit into such a grand setting?

As they rode up to the house, a tall man strode around the corner. He stopped dead in his tracks and stared at the arriving party, hands on his lean hips. His wide shoulders were covered by a tan frock coat worn over an open-necked white shirt, and his legs were long and muscular. Elise was struck by his resemblance to Troy—both had the same tawny-brown hair drawn back into a queue, the same square jaw and strong cheekbones, though unlike Troy, this man was clean-shaven.

"Jase!" Troy hailed him with a wave of the hand, then dismounted.

His brother broke into a run, reaching the party just as Troy was handing the reins to a waiting servant. The two men threw their arms around each other in a quick embrace.

"Troy!" There was a suspicious glint in Jason's golden eyes as he gripped his younger brother by the shoulders. "By damn, they told us you'd drowned! What happened?" Without giving Troy a chance to reply, he turned and bellowed toward the house, "Mirella! Come out here at once!"

A petite, ebony-haired beauty slipped out the double doors and onto the porch. She stopped and stared, her smoky-blue eyes wide with shock, a small hand lifting to the bodice of her lavender gown. Then she flew down the steps to hug Troy. "Oh, thank heavens, you're safe," she cried out, tears coursing down her cheeks.

A moment later, another young woman came out of the house and darted eagerly toward the others, the petticoats rustling beneath her shell-pink gown. She was tall and willowy, with honey-blond hair, her pretty features a delicate version of the two men's. Uttering a sob of happiness, she threw herself into Troy's arms.

Feeling awkward, Elise accepted Marc's hand as he helped her down from the gray mare. A black man came and took the reins from her to lead the animal away. She stood off to one side, watching the happy family reunion, drawing her cloak tightly around her slim form in an instinctively defensive gesture.

Beside the elegance of the two women, she felt like a country bumpkin. The blue wool gown that Troy had purchased for her at Will's Creek, which she had thought the most beautiful garment in the world, now seemed drab in comparison to these ladies of the *haute volè*. And her hair, she moaned silently. Braids had been practical for the journey, but now Elise wished she had wound her bedraggled curls into a less tomboyish style.

She didn't fit in here, she reflected miserably. If this

was the world to which Troy was accustomed, how had he ever been attracted to *her?*

Her heart thudded painfully when he turned toward her with that familiar warm smile. Stepping toward her, he slipped an arm around her waist and drew her to the hard length of his side.

"Elise, I want you to meet my brother, Jason, his wife, Mirella, and my sister, Pandora. Everyone, this is Elise d'Evereaux and her brother, Marc."

"We're pleased to make the acquaintance of both of you," Mirella said, dipping into a gracious curtsey.

"Thank you," Elise murmured. She bit her lip, unsure of what else to say to such a lady so *chic.*

Suddenly Mirella shivered, and Jason put his arm around her shoulders. "'Tis a trifle cold to be standing out here with no cloak," he chided gently. "What say you to inviting our guests into the house?"

"Forgive me!" his wife exclaimed. "You must be tired after your long journey. Please come in and take some refreshment."

The party mounted the steps to the wide porch. Pandora clutched at Troy's arm, her silver-green eyes shining. "We knew you had to be alive," she chattered excitedly. "Why, Jason even forbade us to wear mourning. He said 'twould be bad luck."

Elise followed close behind. Her feeling of apprehension grew as they went through the double doors and into a spacious entrance hall. A graceful staircase with a carved walnut balustrade wound upward to the third story. Her boots clicked softly over the polished wooden floor as she trailed along with the others, past gilt-framed family portraits on the white walls, into an elegant drawing room.

She hesitated at the edge of the large Persian carpet that covered the middle of the floor. There were chairs upholstered in fine brocades, silver candlesticks on mahogany tables, porcelain figurines on the mantel. Damask drapes of a rich forest-green hung at the windows, drawn back by swags of thick gold cord. The air smelled faintly of beeswax mingled with smoke from the fire that snapped in the hearth.

"Come, Elise," Troy said, drawing her over to a settee covered in exquisite needlework. "Let me take your cloak."

She surrendered the garment to him. Gingerly she perched on the edge of the cushions, laying her gloves beside her and folding her work-roughened hands in her lap. In comparison to the blond-haired young woman who had seated herself nearby, she felt clumsy and drab.

"So, you're French?" Pandora asked Elise. "For many years I've been taking lessons in your language, but I fear I would embarrass myself were I to speak it to someone as fluent as you must be."

"Oh . . . I'm sure you're better than you think," Elise ventured.

Pandora laughed. "You haven't yet heard my atrocious pronunciation. Tell me, where did you learn to speak such perfect English?"

Elise threw a desperate glance at Troy, but he was busy pouring drinks from several decanters on a sideboard against the wall. She was saved from answering the awkward question as a childish voice resounded through the chamber.

"Unc' Troy!"

A small boy of no more than three years of age tore into the drawing room, running as fast as his chubby legs could move. A ponderous old black woman carrying a baby followed him.

Troy bent and swooped the youngster up in the air. "Well, well. If it isn't Alex, my favorite nephew!"

The boy squealed with laughter as Troy pretended to drop him, catching him in the nick of time.

"More, Unc' Troy!" Alex complained as the older man set him down.

"Later. Right now I've got to say hello to your baby sister."

Troy went over to the slave woman who held the baby. "You miss me, Ophelia?" he teased.

"Massah Troy, Ah sure be glad you be back. Yore ol' mammy done thought you was lost forever." Cradling the infant against her massive shoulder, she used her other hand to wipe her eyes with the corner of her apron.

Troy embraced the aging woman. "Ophelia, you should know you can't get rid of a devil like me so easily. How's little Becky?"

He took the baby from her. "My, you're getting to be a big girl, aren't you? Last time I saw you, you were only a couple of months old, weren't you, peanut?" Becky gurgled and smiled, grabbing at his hair with her tiny hand.

"Yeeouch! Time for you to go to mama." Quickly he disengaged the minuscule fingers tugging on his hair, then handed her to Mirella, who sat down, clucking softly to the child cuddled against her breast.

Troy took a seat on the settee beside Elise, and Jason brought them both glasses. "How long are you planning to hold us in suspense," he asked Troy. "How did you manage to save yourself from that fall in the river we heard about?"

255

Distractedly, Elise sipped her fine Madeira as Troy began to relate the tale of her rescue of him. It was impossible for her to stop staring at the wealthy surroundings. So this was his home. And he wanted her to be his wife, to live in a place so *magnifique?* She didn't know anything about being a fine lady!

Nervously she twisted the crystal goblet in her hands. She couldn't help but feel like a servant pretending to be one of her betters. In all of her life, she had never even *worked* for a family so rich, let alone been treated as their equal.

Marc seemed to have no such problem adjusting to his new home. The boy was sitting on a stool beside the fireplace, intent on following the English conversation. During the final weeks of their trip, she had begun teaching him the rudiments of the language. He had been a quick learner, and was now able to speak English in halting sentences.

"Would you like to freshen up before dinner?"

Troy's question intruded on Elise's thoughts. "Oh, yes, I would." She leaped to her feet, eager to be alone even if only for a few moments.

"Ophelia will take you upstairs and show you into one of the guest chambers. You, too, scamp," Troy added, gesturing to Marc.

The boy grumbled as he got up to follow his sister over to the old black woman standing in the doorway. With her charges in tow, Ophelia waddled out of the room like a hen with two chicks.

The rest of the group sat watching in silence. Once the guests were out of sight, Jason flashed Troy a wicked grin. "Well, now, is mam'selle d'Evereaux to share your chamber or shall we give her one of her own?"

"Do tell us, Troy," Pandora chimed in, her silver-green eyes sparkling with mischief.

"You two!" Mirella chided. "Don't you know better than to say such things in front of little ears?"

"What, Mama?" Alex had been stretched out on the rug, playing with a set of blocks, but now he sat up straight, tugging on his mother's skirt. "What did Papa say?"

"Nothing, imp." Jason swung the boy up on his knee. "We're just having an adult conversation. Quite dull and boring, I assure you."

He released his son, and the youngster returned to his game. "Well, little brother?" Jason prompted.

Nonchalantly, Troy slouched on the settee. "I don't know what you're talking about," he demurred, though his grin said otherwise.

"Don't you, now?" Jason drawled.

"As I told you all, she saved my life, so I brought her home with me," Troy said, his broad shoulders lifting in a careless shrug.

"And what exactly is the nature of your relationship with her?" his brother persisted.

"Jason, don't pry," Mirella scolded, rocking the sleepy Becky in her arms.

Troy chuckled. "Don't fret, Mirella, I don't mind answering my big brother's rude question. Elise and I are getting married."

"How wonderful!" Pandora broke in, the others exclaiming likewise.

"There's only one hitch," Troy continued. "She hasn't yet agreed to my proposal."

"Why not?" Jason asked.

"Oh . . . we have a few problems to iron out." Though

he spoke lightly, there was a hint of anxiety on his face.

"Well, I'm certain everything will work out for you and Elise," Mirella assured him. "Remember the troubles Jason and I went through?"

"Aye, we fought like cats and dogs, but we're truly happy now," Jason spoke softly, gazing into his wife's eyes.

Troy felt a rush of yearning as he looked at the two of them. That sort of loving relationship was precisely what he wanted with Elise. Someday it would come true, he thought fiercely. He only hoped he wasn't deluding himself.

Elise sat immersed in a tub of hot water in front of the fireplace, eyes closed, her head tilted back in languorous abandon. The faint scent of roses wafted from the steaming liquid that enveloped her naked body. The bath was a luxury she hadn't experienced in several weeks. For once, she felt squeaky clean all over, from the top of her freshly washed hair to the tips of her toes. The only sounds were the crackling of the fire and the soft tick of the clock on the white marble mantelpiece.

For a few precious moments she indulged in a fantasy, imagining herself married to Troy, with a family of their own. Troy would share her bed each night. Warmth began to pulse between her thighs at the thought of him touching her intimately. . . .

There was a knock on the door, and Ophelia bustled into the bedchamber. Returned to reality with a jolt, Elise sat straight up in the tub, then immediately sank down again in embarrassment to conceal her bare breasts beneath the water.

"Ah brung you somethin' to wear," the black woman said. She laid out the clothing on the bed, then walked around it, her broad body swaying as she walked over to pick up a thick towel. "You come out now, and Ah'll help dry you off and git you dressed."

"Oh, but there's no need—"

"Don't you argue none. Stand up now, child."

Meekly Elise complied, too intimidated to disobey the old black woman. Water rolled off her pink flesh as she stepped from the tub to stand shivering in front of the marble hearth.

Briskly Ophelia rubbed her down until every last drop had vanished. Waddling to the bed, she brought back a thin chemise which she drew over Elise's head. Then Elise perched on a stool near the fire as the old black woman toweled the moisture from her hair.

"Them curls shine like copper," Ophelia admired. "Massah Troy, he gonna be proud as a peacock when he see how purdy Ah'm gonna fix you."

Shyly Elise submitted to the slave's ministrations. Her hair soon dried with the heat of the fire and Ophelia's combing. The woman deftly arranged the natural curls into an elegant style. It felt strange but pleasant to Elise to have someone wait on her hand and foot, when she herself had once been a maid.

Ophelia dressed her in drawers and hooped petticoats, sewn of fine linen, then fitted her into a corset that felt stiff and confining. Over all that went a gown of moss-green silk with tight sleeves that ended at the elbow in a triple ruffle of creamy Belgian lace. The bodice dipped low over her breasts, revealing the shadowed valley between the swells.

Critically, Ophelia pinched a bit of fabric at the

waistline. "You be a mite bit skinnier than Miz Mirella, but there ain't no time now to fix your gown. Massah Jason, he be roarin' for his dinner soon, so Ah'll get Miz Colby, our seamstress, to take in these sides in the mornin'."

"But the gown belongs to Mrs. Fletcher," Elise protested. "I won't be keeping it."

"Miz Mirella done told me to give it to you. Now see, ain't you purdy?"

She swung Elise toward a looking glass in a corner of the bedchamber. Elise stared at the strange woman she saw reflected in the mirror. With her upswept hair and elaborate gown, she was every bit as fashionable as Mirella and Pandora. And yet she felt weighted down, constricted.

Nervously she fingered the shimmering green folds of her skirt, so much finer than anything she had ever worn. Could she maintain the illusion of elegance, or would everyone see through it to the awkward country girl underneath?

Her small chin lifted. Why was she letting herself be intimidated? She would prove to these English that she was as good as they were. Armed with Gallic pride, Elise swept out of the chamber and marched—very carefully—down the wide staircase.

The hum of voices came from the drawing room. Catching sight of Troy speaking to Jason, she faltered in the doorway, again assaulted by uncertainty.

Troy had also changed clothing. His face was clean-shaven, his broad shoulders covered by a chocolate-brown frock coat with waistcoat beneath, his muscled thighs clad in buff-colored breeches. He was the very image of a gentleman, rather than the rugged frontiersman she had grown to know. Now that he was back in his own social element, would his feelings toward her change as well?

His smile was reassuring as he came over to greet her. "You look ravishing, little angel," he murmured, his gaze frankly admiring.

His words helped restore her confidence, and Elise let him lead her into the room, where he seated her on a chair and fetched her a glass of wine. Yet she felt a trifle self-conscious when Jason's wife sat down near her.

"We all want to thank you from the bottom of our hearts for saving Troy's life," Mirella said.

"'Twas nothing."

"Oh, but you showed more courage than even many a man would have done. Believe me, we are so very grateful to you."

Elise shifted awkwardly, casting about for a change of subject. "'Twas kind of you to lend me this gown."

"Lend? Why, you must keep it."

"Oh, but I couldn't accept such a gift!"

"Nonsense," Mirella countered. "Tomorrow, we'll visit our seamstress and see what other gowns of mine or Pandora's can be altered to fit you. I'm certain Troy would want you to be properly attired until you have the leisure to select a wardrobe for yourself."

Elise was flattered by Mirella's kindness, yet she couldn't help feeling overwhelmed. Back at Fort LeBoeuf, she'd had a total of two gowns, one for everyday and one for church and other special occasions. It seemed these wealthy Virginia ladies were accustomed to having scores of dresses. There were so many things different in Troy's world—would she ever learn them all?

The party filed into the dining room. Jason and Mirella sat at either end of the long mahogany table, with Troy and Elise on one side and Marc and Pandora on the other. Elise stared at the magnificence of the room, with its pale green Chinese wallpaper and glass-fronted cabinet filled with silver. Overhead, a crystal chandelier blazed with candles.

When two young black girls began to serve the food, Elise automatically jumped up to help. Troy caught her arm as she placed a platter of sliced turkey on the table. "Sit down," he said gently. "The servants will do that."

Elise looked around to see that neither Pandora nor Mirella had gotten up to help. Realizing her mistake, she felt hot color rise to her cheeks. How *gauche* of her to forget that ladies didn't lift a finger when there were servants around! She longed to slink out of the room in shame, but a stubborn pride forced her back into her chair.

Fearful of embarrassing Troy again, Elise carefully observed what everyone else did before daring to do the same herself—which piece of silverware to use, how much wine to drink, how large a portion to put on her plate. Consequently, by the time dinner was over, her stomach was churning and her head was throbbing.

Murmuring an excuse about the tiring day, she fled to the sanctuary of her bedchamber. Although the plush surroundings were a reminder of Troy's wealthy lifestyle, at least here she could be alone.

Elise kicked off her slippers and paced the soft rug in front of the four-poster bed. Had she made a mistake by coming to Troy's home instead of staying in the familiar world of French Canada? She loved him—she had come to accept that now—yet how could she wed a man whose upbringing had been so very different from her own? Surely such a marriage could never work.

There was a knock on the door, and a shy black girl came in to help Elise disrobe. Despite her misgivings, Elise found she enjoyed the luxury of having someone wait on her. It made removing the gown with its myriad hooks a much less complicated task. The servant even passed a brass bedwarmer between the sheets, so that Elise felt no icy shock when she slipped beneath the quilt. Before leaving the room, the girl blew out the candles, and the scent of bayberries lingered in the air.

Elise plumped the feather pillow and settled onto her stomach. With worries still racing through her brain, she expected to toss and turn, but the exhaustion of the day quickly lulled her to sleep.

Delicious sensations coursed over her flesh; excitement throbbed deep inside her belly. A warm suckling tugged on her breasts, and she moaned softly, moving restlessly against the linen sheets in response to the growing turmoil within. The heat of calloused hands smoothed over her satiny skin until every part of her body quivered with arousal. Instinctively she parted her thighs, seeking the rapturous joining that would release her from this torment.

A drowsy awareness told her this was no dream. Her arms were wrapped around a male form, her fingers identifying each familiar contour of his muscled body. A rush of emotion flooded her. Mindless with need, she lifted her hips to him, catching her breath as his rigid heat plunged into her liquid depths. The magic of the moment swept her into a world of pure sensation, the feelings swirling and soaring inside her until they shattered into dazzling ecstasy.

The fire burned low in the hearth. Flickering shadows played on the richly-paneled walls, and the faint light from the dying blaze illuminated the figures entwined in the four-poster bed. Elise lay wrapped in Troy's embrace, the pillow cushioning her head, contentment relaxing her limbs.

"You shouldn't have come in here," she said softly. "What if Jason or Mirella should catch you leaving?"

He chuckled. "Of all people, they'd understand. After all, Alex was born a scant seven months after their wedding."

"Oh," Elise murmured in surprise. So these gently bred Virginia ladies did sometimes ignore propriety and succumb to the lure of the flesh.

Lazily Troy traced a finger over the delicate bone structure of her face. "Little angel, each time we make love, it gets better. I've never known such joy as that which you've given me."

She smiled at him with love. "What joy I've given you, you've returned a hundredfold. Would that we could lie here like this forever."

"We could, if you would but agree to marry me."

His gentle reminder cast a pall over her happiness. "Oh, Troy, I wish that were possible, but it simply isn't."

"Say no more," he replied softly, placing a finger over her lips. "Things will seem different soon. In a day or so, we'll leave for my home, and once you settle in there, you'll see how good our life together will be."

"Your home?" Elise questioned blankly. "Don't you live here, with your brother?"

"Nay, I have my own plantation, farther upstream. Haven't I told you so?"

She shook her head numbly, her eyes wide with dismay. If she were to wed Troy, that meant she would be expected to run a household as large as this one! The very thought made her weak with apprehension. She had no knowledge of those skills in which Mirella and Pandora had doubtless been trained since birth. As Troy's wife, she could only bring shame upon him.

He chuckled. "Don't look so alarmed. 'Tis no shack in the wilderness I'm taking you to. My home is every bit as fine as Jase's."

Elise didn't correct his mistaken reading of her distress. She buried her face against his shoulder, breathing in the faint saltiness of his skin. *Sacré Dieu*, she would never fit into his world! A sudden homesickness engulfed her, the desire to return to the freedom of the frontier was so fierce it was like a physical pain clawing her insides.

It was a pain equal only to the prospect of leaving Troy.

Chapter Eighteen

Elise fiddled with the tasseled cord of the venetian blind, staring absently through the open wooden slats at the blustery March morning. Troy's stately brick mansion stood at the top of a terraced hill overlooking the twists and turns of the James River. The scenery was breathtaking, but she was too preoccupied to take more than cursory notice.

Two days had passed since they had arrived here after visiting with Jason and Mirella. Elise had been sorry to leave, for Troy's relations had made her feel so welcome. And yet she was still plagued by the uneasy conviction that she didn't belong in this upper stratum of Virginia society.

The tinkle of the harpsichord drifted from the drawing room. Pandora was in there with her music master, who had arrived earlier that morning. Elise had discovered that instructors of skills such as music and dancing traveled from family to family, staying for a few days at a time.

Troy's sister had come for an extended visit at

Mirella's insistence. Conventions had to be observed to guard against gossip. It was improper for an unmarried man and woman to live together, Mirella had proclaimed, no matter that Marc would be staying in the same house, too. A twelve-year-old boy was not a suitable chaperone by the standards of polite society.

There were so many rules to remember, Elise reflected with a sigh. Wistfully she listened to the lilting tune emanating from the next chamber. Pandora was well versed in the accomplishments of a refined lady. How could she herself learn to be the sort of woman to whom Troy was accustomed?

There was a sudden rapping on the front door. Automatically Elise left the library to answer the summons, walking carefully across the polished parquet floor in her unfamiliar heeled slippers, the starched petticoats beneath her jonquil gown rustling.

The knocking again echoed through the spacious hall. Just as Elise reached for the brass knob on the front door, a voice made her whirl around.

"Miss d'Evereaux!"

A woman stood at the top of the winding staircase that led to the second floor. She was tall and gaunt, with a mobcap perched on her gray hair, her serviceable gray gown covered by a stark white apron.

"I will answer that, if you please, miss." Her bony hand on the mahogany balustrade, she swept majestically down the steps.

"Oh . . . *madame.* I—I forgot."

Elise felt a sinking sensation in the pit of her stomach. *Tiens,* she had done it again. She had committed yet another blunder in front of Mrs. MacGuire, Troy's formidable housekeeper. Ladies weren't supposed to open the door to visitors; that was the role of servants. The list of mistakes had begun the moment of her arrival here, when she had attempted to carry upstairs the small trunk of clothing Mirella had given her, only to have Mrs. MacGuire sternly direct one of the slaves to take the luggage from her.

The housekeeper reached the door and stared down her long nose at Elise. "Since Miss Pandora is at her lessons, you may wait in the library. I'll announce the callers to you there."

"Thank you."

Meekly Elise retreated to the book-lined chamber, taking a seat in a wingback chair beside the fireplace. Troy had told her not to worry about Mrs. MacGuire's brusqueness, and Elise was awed by the easy way he teased the housekeeper. She shouldn't allow a servant to intimidate her so, Elise chided herself. Wasn't a lady supposed to control her subordinates, rather than vice versa?

Determined to redeem herself, she sat up straight, folding her hands demurely in her lap. She would welcome Troy's guests as the lady of fashion she was supposed to be.

Mrs. MacGuire's spare frame came into the doorway. "Miss Caroline Whitman and Mr. Zachary Birmingham are here," she said in a formal tone.

The housekeeper stepped aside to let a young couple enter the library. Elise couldn't help staring at them. The woman was as dainty as a doll, with a porcelain complexion and midnight blue eyes. Her upswept hair was powdered white in the latest style, the cluster of ribbons that nestled in the curls matching the primrose hue of her gown.

The man at her side was the perfect foil to her delicate beauty. He had dark hair and eyes, and wore a charcoal-gray frock coat that emphasized the broadness of his shoulders. His handsome face bore a friendly smile.

"You're Miss d'Evereaux?" he inquired politely. "I'm sure I speak for Caroline when I say what a pleasure it is to make your acquaintance."

"Thank you. Please, sit down. Mrs. MacGuire, won't you bring us some tea?" The housekeeper raised her eyebrows haughtily, but left the room to do Elise's bidding. As the newcomers settled themselves in chairs, Elise frantically wished that Pandora would cease her harpsicord playing and come help entertain the guests. What was she to talk about with two such elegant personages?

"Have you come to see Troy?" she ventured.

"Yes, but Mrs. MacGuire informed us he's out riding the fields," Caroline said in a soft drawl.

"I'm afraid he left early this morning."

"You simply cannot imagine how disappointed I am," Caroline pouted. "Why, I haven't seen him for *months*, and I was so looking forward to this visit. He and I are very close, you know."

"No, I—I didn't know." Elise felt like a child playing grown-up beside this woman's graceful femininity. A sudden jolt of jealousy struck her. What was Caroline Whitman's relationship with Troy?

"You're probably wondering who we are," Zach Birmingham observed. "Caro and Troy and I have been neighbors for many years, Caro's father owns Thousand Oaks, the plantation adjoining this one, whilst I own Hearthstone, on the other side of Thousand Oaks."

"Will you be staying here long, Miss d'Evereaux?"

Caroline asked delicately.

"I—I'm not certain."

At that moment, Mrs. MacGuire entered the library carrying a silver tea tray, which she set down on a low table in front of the fireplace. Elise breathed a sigh of relief at the timely interruption.

To cover her nervousness, she reached for the silver pot and poured herself a cup of tea. As she took a sip of the steaming brew, she noticed her guests staring at her.

"Allow me to pour you some tea, Zach," Caroline said, extending a dainty white hand toward the silver tray.

With a hot blush of distress, Elise realized belatedly that as hostess it was her duty to serve the visitors. Now Troy's friends would see through her ladylike facade. Only by sheer stubborn pride was she able to keep her chin tilted high.

"I must confess, it's been a long time since I've made the acquaintance of any French person," Caroline commented, handing a porcelain teacup to Zach. "Some years ago, my father was English ambassador to France."

"Have you lived in France, then?" Elise asked politely.

"For a short time, but do not expect me to converse well in the language," Caroline admitted with a tinkling laugh. "I can recall only a few words . . . *bonjour*, *au revoir*, and *souillon*."

The blood drained from Elise's face. The last word Caroline had spoken was French for slut, and without a doubt it was meant as a subtle reference to her opinion of Elise. It confirmed Elise's suspicions that Caroline had designs on Troy and resented anyone who dared stand in her way.

"I must say, Miss d'Evereaux, you do have a most charming accent," Zach said, flashing her a warm smile.

Displeasure crossed Caroline's face for an instant. So the spoiled female wanted Zach's attention as well as Troy's, did she? Elise thought.

"Why, thank you, Mr. Birmingham," she said sweetly.

"You must call me Zach, if we're to be neighbors. Caroline doesn't go by formalities with friends, either, do you, Caro?"

"By all means, no," the petite woman said with the merest hint of sulkiness.

"Then you both must call me by my Christian name," Elise offered graciously.

"So, *Elise,*" Caroline said with pointed emphasis, "did you live in one of those forts the French are daring to build on Virginia's frontier?"

"Caro!" Zach chided. "That's hardly a question that concerns you."

"It concerns me as a Virginian. Why, the French are pushing us toward war! I should think you'd care about that."

"A social visit is not the time to discuss such matters."

Caroline lifted her chin stubbornly. "Really, Zach, this matter is of grave import and cannot be ignored. Why, just last week my father received word that someone had broken into the governor's mansion and rifled through Dinwiddie's papers. They think 'twas someone spying for the French." She turned to Elise and queried, "You passed through Williamsburg about that time, didn't you?"

"Caroline!" Zach warned.

Taken aback, Elise put her cup down on the table. The woman was hinting that *she* might be the spy! "I . . . how did you know I was there?"

"My father is a member of the governor's council.

Naturally he's informed of everything important that happens in this colony, including Troy's return."

"Which I understand we have you to thank for, Elise," Zach broke in, flashing Caroline a heated glance. "Rumor has it you saved Troy from certain death when he fell into a river out in the wilderness."

"'Twas nothing," Elise demurred.

"Don't be so modest," he teased gently. "You're a true heroine and you deserve your due."

A frown creased Caroline's brow. "Really, Zach, she only did what any of us would have done."

"You mean you'd have saved the life of a man who was supposed to be your enemy?" he drawled.

Caroline looked as if she were about to speak, then she pursed her lips, glowering at her handsome companion. At that moment, Troy strolled into the library, and Elise's pulse began to race. He looked devastatingly attractive in supple buckskin breeches, his tawny hair tousled from the wind. The white shirt beneath his burgundy frock coat was unbuttoned at the neck, affording a glimpse of his bare chest.

"Caro and Zach!" he exclaimed with a grin. "What a pleasant surprise!"

Caroline set down her teacup and flung herself into his arms. "Why, Troy, dearest, I've missed you so!"

Watching them embrace, Elise felt a dagger of jealousy twist in her heart. That little hussy made no attempt to hide her infatuation with Troy. She pressed her breasts against him, whispering something in his ear before uttering that feminine tinkle of a laugh. It was small consolation that Troy didn't bend his head and kiss the woman even though she lifted her lips invitingly.

Unhappiness flooded Elise. Caroline was the sort of

woman he belonged with, a poised, perfect lady who suited his station in life, someone who wouldn't shame him with her ineptness.

If she truly loved him, she would leave him for his own good.

That halfhearted resolve fled from Elise's mind as Troy disengaged himself and walked over to take her hands. "You look lovely today, little angel," he said in an intimate undertone. "I hope you've enjoyed meeting my friends."

"Of course," she said softly.

"I'm glad—I want them to be your friends, too."

He dropped a kiss on her forehead before turning back to the others, apparently not noticing the peevish pout on Caroline's pretty face.

"Well, Zach," he said, striding forward to shake the man's hand. "How have you fared these past months?"

"That's a question I should be asking you," Zach retorted. "You were the one fighting the dangers of the wilderness whilst I was snug in the comfort of my house, drinking brandy before a roaring fire."

Troy grinned. "And chasing women every now and again, no doubt."

"One might say so," Zach agreed dryly, casting an oblique glance at Caroline.

"Can you both stay for dinner?" Troy invited. "'Twill give us the leisure in which to trade stories."

Zach and Caroline agreed, and Troy gave instructions to Mrs. MacGuire.

"You did know, didn't you, that the Assembly is meeting in Williamsburg earlier than usual?" Zach said.

Troy nodded. "Elise and I stopped briefly in town. I plan to return as soon as I get a few things cleared up here

273

at the plantation."

The men discussed politics and, after a time, Pandora finished her lessons and joined the small party. Marc was nowhere to be found, and Elise assumed he had elected to eat in the kitchen, where he felt more comfortable. She envied him that freedom.

When the housekeeper entered the library to announce dinner, Caroline swiftly maneuvered herself beside Troy and took his arm, looking up at him with a girlish flutter of her long lashes.

"You wouldn't mind escorting little ol' me, would you?"

"Of course not," he said gallantly.

They strolled off in the direction of the dining room, Caroline murmuring to Troy so that he was forced to bend his head to hear her. Elise frowned at the attractive picture they made, Caroline so diminutive beside Troy's tall, masculine form. Her blood pulsed with resentment and she had to suppress an urge to claw the woman's perfect face.

Zach extended his elbows to Elise and Pandora. "'Twould seem I have the double pleasure of escorting both of you lovely ladies. Shall we go?"

The meal was an accomplishment of culinary delights, but it might as well have been dirt for all Elise noticed. She toyed with her food as Caroline directed the flow of conversation and used her feminine wiles to monopolize the attention of the men, especially Troy. It was plain that she had set her sights on winning him as a husband.

Elise stewed in silence, her insides a churning mixture of anger, jealousy, and misery. What if Troy regretted his proposal of marriage to her and decided he preferred to wed someone more suited to his station . . . a lady like Caroline?

At long last dinner was over and the party adjourned to the drawing room. Soon thereafter, Zach rose to his feet. "Come, Caro, we must not overstay our welcome."

"Oh, but we've only just gotten here," she sulked.

"We'll return another time. Troy and Elise will be in Williamsburg soon, and we'll see them at all the parties."

Caroline scowled at his coupling of the names, but Zach was adamant in his efforts to leave. The ill humor vanished from her face only when she stood before Troy to whisper a coy good-bye.

Elise watched in relief as Zach helped the petite woman into the carriage out front. The liveried driver slapped the reins and the horses started down the long drive that led to the main road. Good riddance, Elise thought fervently. Though the warm security of Troy's arm held her close, she couldn't help feeling the tentacles of fear squeeze her heart.

Was Troy even now comparing her to the charming beauty who had just departed?

"You should be ashamed of yourself," Zach said, frowning at the petite woman who sat on the opposite side of the gently rocking carriage.

"Why, I don't know what you're talking about," she demurred.

"Aye, you do. You behaved abominably toward Elise, when you should have been welcoming her to the neighborhood."

Caroline wrinkled her small nose. "That bit of French fluff? Why should I bother making friends with her? She won't be around long."

"You sound confident," he mocked.

"I am. Troy will soon tire of her, you'll see."

"If you weren't so blindly self-centered, you'd have realized he's in love with her."

Caroline wiggled impatiently on the leather cushion. "That's absurd. Troy would never fall for such a strumpet."

"You want him for yourself, don't you?"

She stared at him in the calculating fashion he knew so well, then abruptly she rose and came over to sit beside him, lifting a finger to trace his smooth-shaven jaw. "Why, Zach Birmingham, I do believe you're jealous," she drawled, fluttering her lashes at him.

Unwittingly, she had hit right on target. A powerful rush of a desire long repressed swept over Zach. He was intensely aware of her scent and the soft press of her breast against his arm.

Damn her for being such a tease! By God, he'd give her a taste of her own medicine!

He grabbed her arms and hauled her close. "And I think you're acting like a spoiled little girl who's lost a piece of candy," he taunted. "When will you learn there's sweetness to be had elsewhere?"

Deliberately he crushed his mouth to hers, thrusting his tongue between the softness of her lips. He wasn't sure if it was a result of shock or of desire, but she didn't resist. The taste of her inflamed his mind until his entire being throbbed with the supreme joy of kissing the woman he had loved for so long.

When at last he lifted his head, his breath was harsh and rasping. Fire burned through his veins. God, how tempted he was to take her right here on the floor of the carriage, and damn the consequences! Her lips were reddened and moist, her dark blue eyes wide and startled. Her gaze flitted over his face, as if she were seeing him for the first time.

Hope rose in him, hope that she might at last be ready to forsake her girlish infatuation for the love of a mature man.

"Let me go, Zach," Caroline whispered. "You're hurting me."

The fever fled his senses. With a rush of remorse, he loosened his fingers, and she scuttled across the carriage to the safety of her own seat.

"I'm sorry, Caro," he said gruffly. "I don't know what came over me. I didn't mean to frighten you."

She only bit her lip and turned to stare out the window of the carriage. Though she acted the worldly flirt, Zach knew that deep down she was an innocent. All of her life Caroline had been pampered by an indulgent father, given everything she asked for. Now she wanted Troy, and there was nothing that could be done to remedy the situation. He could only pray that in time she would grow up and recognize the folly of her ways.

She had to know he was attracted to her, Zach mused, yet he was certain she had little inkling of just how deep his feelings ran. Frustration ate away at him. He wanted her as his wife, but he knew she was not yet ready. That was why he must be more careful to hide his emotions in the future.

Were he ever to give full vent to his passion, he might ruin their friendship, and he couldn't take that risk. The pleasure of seeing her almost every day was too precious to lose.

* * *

Night covered the land in an ebony veil, the only illumination shed by a sliver of moon against a smattering of stars. The pale light sifted through the bare branches to the forest floor below, where the damp aroma of decaying leaves perfumed the air. A sleepy bird fluttered its wings, then silence settled over the woods again.

Suddenly the muffled clip-clop of hooves broke the stillness. From out of the gloom came a swiftly moving shape. It was a figure on horseback riding through the black maze of trees as if driven by unerring instinct.

Reaching a stream, the dark-cloaked rider swung out of the saddle and hunkered down to thrust a small packet into the hollow interior of a log, then rose quickly to remount the beast.

For a moment, the black forms of horse and rider were silhouetted in the silver moonlight . . . until the shadows swallowed them once more.

Chapter Nineteen

"Comment allez-vous, mademoiselle?" The dapper old gentleman bent over Elise's hand and kissed it with a flourish.

"Je vais très bien, merci."

Her dark copper eyes sparkling, Elise launched into a conversation with Will Granger, the French tutor. The familiar words spilled rapidly from her lips as she leaned forward in her chair, fingers curling into the blue silk of her skirt.

"Slow down, you two!" Pandora complained. "You're going too fast for me to understand."

Elise stopped guiltily, remembering the blonde sitting in the drawing room with them. It had been such a delight to speak her native language after all these long weeks that she had forgotten where she was.

"I'm sorry, Pandora," she apologized. "I didn't mean to leave you out."

Will Granger wagged a disapproving finger at Troy's sister. "If Mademoiselle Fletcher had been more diligent in her studies these past few years, she would have had no trouble following what we said."

Pandora grinned unabashedly. "Monsieur Granger, you're always scolding. Will you not tell me in plain English what you two were discussing?"

"The mademoiselle wanted to know where a man with a name like Will Granger learned to speak French."

"Flawless French," Elise qualified. "He told me his maternal grandmother was from France, and that for a year when he was a young man he lived in Paris with her."

"You never told me that," Pandora chided her tutor.

"You never asked." The gray-wigged man picked up the cane that lay beside his chair. "And now, ladies, I must be on my way and ride to the Websters' before the afternoon light fails. Mademoiselle Fletcher, we shall have our final lesson together in Williamsburg one week hence, is that not so?"

"*Oui*, our final lesson," Pandora repeated with a heartfelt sigh of relief.

"Then I will bid you both *adieu*." Gracing them with a courtly bow, Granger turned and strolled out of the room.

"You're stopping your French lessons?" Elise asked.

"Jason promised I could after my eighteenth birthday, which is next week," Pandora explained. "'Twill be great fun—we're all going to Williamsburg since the House of Burgesses is in session." Her brow puckered in worry. "Much as I despised my lessons, in a way I dislike having to end *Monsieur* Granger's services. He's getting old and I doubt he has much money saved."

The French tutor's garb *had* been shabby, Elise reflected. What would the man do if he could no longer work to earn his living? Unless he found another way to obtain gold. . . .

When Caroline had visited several days ago, she had made mention of a French spy rifling through the governor's papers. What if that secret agent had been Will Granger?

The notion was so far-fetched that Elise thrust it from her head. Although Granger might harbor a certain sympathy toward the French, that in itself was no proof that he would betray the English cause.

"Will you come for a walk with me?" Pandora asked. "After a morning of lessons, I vow I'll stifle if I spend another moment cooped up in this house."

"Of course."

The two women fetched their cloaks and headed out the river side of the mansion. The mid-March day was sunny, but a chill breeze blowing up the terraced slope from the river below made Elise glad for the enveloping warmth of her cape.

She and Pandora strolled toward a tangle of trees that edged the lawn.. Spring was in the air. Passing the formal gardens, Elise saw periwinkles and pansies blooming alongside hyacinths and narcissus. Clumps of jonquils and the season's first poppy anemones added more bright color to the dreary winter landscape. In the woods, tiny buds sprouted along the bare branches. A shrill whistle sounded as a cardinal swooped by in a tiny blaze of scarlet.

Silently Elise walked down a path that led deeper into the stand of timber. Even after several weeks, she couldn't help feeling a trifle tongue-tied around Troy's sister, who always looked so poised and perfect. Pandora's natural willowy grace only made Elise feel gawky.

281

"Look!" the blond girl cried suddenly.

To Elise's astonishment, Pandora kicked off her shoes and discarded her cloak, then hiked up her skirts and clambered up a tree. Precariously stretching out on a scrawny limb, she plucked something and then maneuvered herself around to perch in the fork between two branches, her silk-stockinged feet dangling from beneath her turquoise gown.

"See what I found," she announced in triumph, waving a cluster of tiny purplish flowers. "'Tis the very first redbud blooms of the spring."

Mouth agape, Elise stared up at her. Then the humor of the scene sank in and she began to laugh, leaning weakly against a nearby tree. All along she had thought of Pandora as the epitome of a lady. Now that image of perfection had been shattered by one totally unexpected, totally outrageous act.

"Oh, Pandora, I can't believe you! Aren't you afraid you'll fall?"

"Gracious, no. I've been climbing trees ever since I was old enough to walk."

Pandora stuck the sprig of redbud blooms into the side of her honey-blond chignon. With tomboyish grace, she climbed down from the tree and then tried to slap away the dirt smears that marred her turquoise gown. She abandoned the futile effort after a moment and lifted her skirts to slip her feet back into her shoes.

"Oh, dear, I've torn my stockings," she sighed, without a trace of regret. "'Tis a good thing Ophelia isn't here or she'd tan my hide."

Elise couldn't stop smiling. "Well, don't worry—I won't tell anyone."

Pandora grinned back. *"Merci, mademoiselle."* She

swooped up her sky-blue cloak from the ground and swirled it over her shoulders.

They resumed their walk, following the winding path through the woods. "I'm glad you climbed that tree," Elise ventured. "I was beginning to think you Virginia ladies never did anything improper."

Pandora laughed. "Jason would tell you I'm far from being the typical female. I used to be quite the hoyden only a few years ago—all I wanted to do was to go fishing and wear boy's clothing. Poor Jason had his hands full keeping me out of trouble."

"Truly?" Elise glanced sideways at her companion. "I don't mean to disbelieve you, but now you're so polished and elegant."

It was Pandora's turn to look surprised. "Me, elegant? Why, I wouldn't describe myself that way at all."

"Oh, but you are! And you're so pretty, I'm sure the men must fall all over themselves to court you."

Pandora sighed. "'Tis sweet of you to say so, but I'm too tall and clumsy, and when I'm around men other than my brothers I always seem to say the wrong things. Mirella taught me how to act like a lady, but sometimes I just don't feel like one inside. Maybe I was a tomboy for too long."

"Oh, Pandora, be glad you're the way you are," Elise exclaimed. "It makes you so much more interesting than other ladies, like Caroline."

Pandora sent her a crafty look. "Caroline, you say?"

"Oh, I didn't mean her necessarily. . . ." Elise stammered. *Sacré Dieu,* she'd blundered again! What if Pandora admired Caroline?

"There's no need to cover up your true feelings," Pandora said. "Caroline can be nice when she wants to

283

be, but I don't blame you a bit for disliking her."

"You don't?"

"Of course not." The blond girl stopped to pluck a daffodil, idly twirling the flower between her fingers. "I have eyes—I can see who she's after."

"You mean Troy." Jealous resentment gnawed at Elise, and she stopped walking, unable to hold in her fears any longer. "Oh, Pandora, he and I come from such different backgrounds. Caroline is so much more suited to him than I."

"Let Troy be the judge of that."

"But she's such a fine lady—"

"Surely you don't want to be the same as all the other boring ladies. Remember what you just got through telling me?"

Elise laughed sheepishly. *"Oui,* you're right. But still, I know naught of being a lady—not running a large household nor even how to dance and play music, all those skills you and Mirella seem to take for granted."

"You can learn. I'd be happy to teach you everything Mirella taught me."

"Would you?" Elise asked with a spark of hope. "You've been so kind to me—especially since our countries are enemies."

"Oh, posh, I don't care a whit for politics," Pandora said with an airy flutter of her fingers. Her silver-green eyes sparkled as she thrust the daffodil into Elise's hand. "But I do admit to an ulterior motive—I'd far prefer to have you for a sister-in-law than Caroline."

In the days that followed, a close friendship began to develop between Elise and Pandora. Elise was glad to have someone to confide in, for Troy was busy with the spring planting and Marc was forever tagging along with him. This comfortable life among the wealthy social class of Virginia was a far cry from the rugged conditions she had encountered on the Canadian frontier. It felt strange to Elise to oversee servants when she had once been the one who'd had to perform the strenuous tasks they were doing—such as making soap and candles, churning butter, and weaving cloth.

Quickly she grew to respect the role of lady of the manor, for duty required her to work hard yet maintain the appearance of leisure. Her responsibilities included supervising scores of activities all over the plantation. She had to watch the maids so that nothing was broken carelessly, the laundress to be sure the master's shirts were starched properly, the cook so that meals were prepared on time, using the freshest ingredients. When circumstances demanded it, she pitched in to help, even with such jobs as cleaning fish and feeding the poultry.

There were times when Elise wished fervently that she were back at the fort. Things might have been more primitive there, but at least it was a life familiar to her. She couldn't quite accustom herself to being the superior rather than the servant.

And then there was the problem of Mrs. MacGuire to contend with. Since Troy had no wife, the dour Scotswoman had come to the colonies many years ago to be his housekeeper and had elected to stay on when her period of indenture was over. She seemed to resent Elise's presence and remained aloof to every friendly overture Elise made to her.

Elise suspected that Mrs. MacGuire was appalled at the possibility of her beloved master's being enticed into wedlock by a scheming Frenchwoman. Little did the housekeeper know that it was Elise herself who balked at the marriage.

Late one night Elise lay in bed, wide awake. The tangled sheets gave evidence of her tossing and turning, for sleep had eluded her for several hours. Three days had passed since Troy had last come to her chamber, and her need for him had grown to the point where she couldn't rest.

He's lost interest in you, a voice taunted in her head. *He wants a woman like Caroline.*

Nonsense, argued another. It was simply that he was exhausted from the duties of the plantation, which kept him riding his lands from dawn until dusk. And yet . . . judging from his withdrawn attitude toward her over the past few days, there was something else troubling him, something he had as yet not spoken of to her.

It was foolish to lie here and wonder. If Troy would not come to her, then she would go to him.

Resolutely, Elise slipped out of bed and drew a thin silk wrapper over her nightgown. The rug was soft beneath her bare feet as she padded over to the hearth to light a candle from the flames that burned low.

She crept out into the darkened hall, moving quietly so as not to awaken Marc or Pandora. As was the custom in tidewater Virginia, the master's bedchamber was on the first floor. Elise descended the wide stairway, one hand clutching the lighted taper, the other holding up the hem of her gown.

The entrance hall was silent and gloomy. As she hurried across the icy floor, the clock on the drawing room mantel chimed twice, then stillness settled over the house once more.

What if Troy really *had* grown tired of her? The thought was so disturbing that Elise almost turned back. Taking a deep breath, she pushed open his door and stepped inside.

The darkened room was lit only by the embers glowing in the fireplace. She tiptoed toward the canopied four-poster that dominated the chamber, but the gleam from the candle in her hand revealed only rumpled sheets.

Where was Troy?

A sudden stirring near the window made Elise whirl around to see Troy step out of the shadows. His tawny hair was tousled, as if he had run his fingers through it innumerable times. He wore only a short robe tied at the waist, and his legs were long and bare below the hem at midthigh. A quiver ran through her as she caught a glimpse of his naked chest.

He said nothing, and Elise sensed he was waiting for her to make the first move. She felt paralyzed by a peculiar shyness, but a need to discover what was troubling him gave her strength. Hesitantly she walked in his direction, stopping in front of him.

"Troy, I've missed you these past nights," she said softly.

She put down the candle on a nearby table and spread her palms against the velvet robe that covered his shoulders. Shock jolted through her as he stepped away from her and over to the fireplace to prop his elbow on the mantel.

"'Tis late," he said curtly. "You should be in bed."

"I couldn't sleep. Troy, is something wrong?"

"What makes you think that?"

The chill in his voice made her blood run cold with

dread. Elise swallowed hard, forcing herself to go on with dogged determination. "You haven't come to me of late. There must be a reason why."

He stared at her for a moment, then combed his hand through his hair and muttered, "Aye, I suppose there is at that."

Elise hurried to him, catching hold of his sleeve. "Tell me what it is. Don't you . . ." Her voice broke and she continued in a strangled whisper, "Don't you want me anymore?"

"God, yes, I want you!" he burst out, focusing the full intensity of his gaze on her. "I want you so bad it twists my insides. But dammit, all that holds us together is physical desire, and I'm finding I need more than just that."

"We love each other—"

"If you really loved me, Elise, you'd marry me. I've been patient long enough."

The soft fabric of his sleeve slipped from her fingers. "What are you saying?" she asked faintly.

"I'm saying there'll be no more sharing of beds until you're willing to commit your life to me. In the meantime, I think it best we stay as far away from each other as possible."

The grim look in his eyes assured her he meant every word. A hard knot of pain burned in her abdomen as the fragile trust in her heart shattered into a thousand fragments. He was rejecting her; the nightmare had finally happened.

She pivoted and stumbled blindly to the door, driven by an urgent need to be alone.

"Elise!"

The harsh sound of his voice froze her hand on the

knob. His footsteps came across the rug and stopped behind her. "For God's sake, haven't you anything to say?"

Numbly she shook her head, unable to speak for fear of sparking the flow of moisture that stung her eyes. She felt the pressure of his hands on her shoulders, then he was turning her around. He studied her face for a long moment, his fingers flexing into the thin material of her wrapper.

"Are you certain you understand what I'm trying to do?"

The unexpected gentleness in his tone almost did her in. Elise looked away, blinking hard. "Of course," she choked out. "You want me gone . . . I'll leave here in the morning."

"No!" The word exploded from him as he pulled her close, burying his lips in her hair. "No, angel, that's not what I meant," he said, his voice raw with emotion. "Don't you dare even think of leaving me."

Tears trickled down her cheeks and into the velvet of his robe. "B-But you j-just told me to stay away," she cried brokenly.

"I meant we should live together in the same house but keep our distance. Don't you see? You need time alone to make up your mind about us." His arms tightened. "You thought I was turning my back on you as your father did, didn't you? I swear I'll never do that . . . never."

She heard the impassioned truth in his voice, and the awful heaviness inside her began to unravel, allowing her to draw in shaky lungfuls of air. Relief poured through her. Troy did still love her; he wasn't sending her away. She clung to the warm security of him, needing his strength to mend the rift in her heart.

He lifted her chin and wiped away her tears with his fingers. "Elise, I want you to be the mother of my children, but I can no longer take the risk of getting you pregnant if you refuse to marry me. When you're ready to set our wedding date, rest assured I'll be waiting here for you."

Troy left her standing there for a moment, then came back to press the pewter candlestick into her hand. Opening the door, he gave her a gentle push out of his chamber. "Now hie you to your own bed before I succumb to temptation and take you into mine."

The door closed with a quiet click, and she was alone in the shadowed entrance hall, her slender form bathed in a halo of candlelight.

Chapter Twenty

Pandora's eighteenth birthday fell on the day after they arrived in Williamsburg. The entire Fletcher clan, along with a few selected guests, gathered to celebrate the occasion in the rambling clapboard house Jason owned in town, facing the Palace Green.

Elise stood beside a mahogany bookcase in the drawing room, pretending an interest in a volume of Molière's plays as the sounds of talk and laughter swirled around her. She herself felt little inclination toward merriment.

For the umpteenth time, her gaze drifted to the foursome playing cards at the opposite end of the parlor. A soft sigh left her lips as she stared at the tall man sprawled in one of the chairs around the gaming table. Troy and Pandora were paired against Caroline and Zach.

Several days had passed since Troy had issued his ultimatum, and in that time he had been true to his word. He had kept his distance from her, indeed had barely given her a second glance. Despite his assurances of that night, Elise couldn't help but wonder if he really did still love her. He acted polite but remote, and sometimes she felt like one of the servants for all the attention he paid her. His cool indifference was beginning to grate on her nerves.

Restlessly, she flipped through the book pages. The memory of his touch burned in her blood and seemed to grow stronger every day. Yet it was unthinkable that she agree to his condition. Though she loved him, a gut-level feeling made her balk at the idea of marrying an Englishman. Was it simply her pride as a Frenchwoman, or was there some other cause?

"Elise!" She looked up to see Pandora standing beside her. "They need you to take my place in the foursome while I talk to some of the other guests."

"But I don't know how to play whist."

"Of course, you do," Pandora argued. "I taught you the rudiments of the game just yesterday—you'll quickly pick up the skill of strategy. Come now, this is my party and I mustn't neglect my duties as hostess."

With a resigned sigh, Elise set down the book. It would do little good to argue so long as Pandora wore that expression of Fletcher stubbornness. Slowly she crossed the room, dreading the prospect of being so close to Troy . . . and craving it at the same time.

Caroline looked none too pleased as Elise sat down at the small table across from Zach. Troy lounged in the seat to her right, and Elise nodded a cool hello. If he could act nonchalant, then so could she.

"I vow I'm surprised a Frenchwoman would know much of an English card game," Caroline commented. "If you'd rather not join in with us, we'll certainly understand."

Elise looked her square in the eye. "Afraid I'll best you?"

Zach chuckled. "That's the spirit, Elise! By the way, you're to be my partner, unless you've an objection to the arrangement?"

"Of course not."

"Troy and I are a pair," Caroline said, fluttering her lashes at him. "'Twill be like old times—remember all the fun we had playing together when we were growing up?"

Troy grinned. "We did at that, didn't we?"

Elise pursed her lips. The sight of his smile made her chest tighten with longing, but she willed away the sensation. So what if he had ignored her for weeks? Those two could have each other for all she cared!

Caroline dealt the cards, laying the last on the table before her to identify spades as the trump suit. Elise picked up her cards and examined them by the glow of the candles that burned at each corner of the table. Determined not to make a fool of herself, she carefully reviewed the rules of the game in her mind.

Then Troy's knee brushed her apricot skirts, and a shock of awareness surged through her. She darted a glance at him, but he was studying his cards as if he hadn't noticed the brief contact. It took an effort to force her eyes back to her own hand and regain her concentration.

"My lead, but I'm afraid I have a pile of nothing," Zach said, tossing down a card.

"Ah, hearts, my favorite suit," Caroline purred as Troy took the trick with the ace. "Will you be attending the governor's ball two weeks hence, Troy?"

"Naturally."

"And will you save a dance for me?" she teased, leaning forward and holding her cards low so that her

293

breasts swelled against the decolletage of her pink-flowered gown.

He smiled. "You know I will—providing you'll have time for me, what with all of your other beaus."

"I'll always have time for you, Troy."

Elise stared fiercely at her cards, itching to jump up and wipe that simpering expression off Caroline's face. And Troy had eyed that woman's breasts, the *cochon!* She felt an urge to give him a swift kick under the table, but thought better of it. Under no circumstances would she grant him cause to think she was jealous!

"Elise?" Zach prompted.

"Oh." She came out of her reverie to realize it was her turn. "I'm sorry, what was led?"

"Really, if you're not going to pay attention to the game—" Caroline began.

"Knave of diamonds, Elise," Zach broke in, sending Caroline a quelling glance.

A little flustered, Elise studied the cards on the table before taking one from her hand and laying it down. "Trump. 'Tis our trick, Zach."

"So it is," he said, gathering up the cards. "Your lead, dear partner."

Elise put down the king of diamonds.

"Why, that's a revoke!" Caroline said huffily. "You can't trump my knave when you had a diamond in your hand all the time! Whoever taught you to play whist?"

"First game is only practice," said Zach with a grin. Reaching across the table, he placed a reassuring hand over Elise's. "You're doing fine, partner, and don't let anyone tell you differently."

Troy kept the casual expression on his face only through sheer force of willpower. Inside, he was a seething mass of angry jealousy. Damn, but he wanted to punch Zach senseless for daring to touch Elise! Gritting his teeth, he watched in helpless rage as his friend stroked the back of her hand. His temper grew hotter as Zach's eyes roamed to the bodice of her apricot gown, where the tempting swell of her breasts spilled over the lace-edged fabric.

By God, had he made a mistake in denying Elise his bed? He'd meant only to force her to a decision, but thus far his plan had been a complete failure. Cold threads of fear snaked around Troy's heart. What if she lost interest in him and sought out another man to satisfy her newly awakened needs? It was a possibility he hadn't considered until this moment.

Absently he ran his fingers over the sharp edges of his cards. No, he reassured himself, he couldn't believe she would do such a thing. It would mean those long nights of frustration alone in his bed had been wasted. Only in his dreams had he felt her naked body curled against his, tasted the sweetness of her mouth, smelled the subtle rose-petal scent of her skin and hair. Troy swallowed a groan, deeming it a blessing the table hid the evidence of desire that pressed against his breeches.

Mechanically he dealt the cards when his turn to do so came. God in heaven, he had to be patient; it was the only way. He couldn't go on in the relationship without the commitment of marriage, yet his pride kept him from pressuring her. The decision to wed must arise from her own free choice.

He forced his gaze away from Elise and looked at the woman sitting opposite him, seeing not her china-doll beauty but an old friend he could depend on. She wouldn't mind if he used her to distract himself.

"Caro, why wasn't your father able to come tonight?" he asked.

"He has an important meeting tomorrow with Governor Dinwiddie and needed the time to prepare." Caroline's lips curved into a pretty smile. "By the way, he sends his congratulations on your appointment as a special advisor to the governor's council. We're all proud of you, Troy."

Elise stared at him, feeling a stab of pain. Why hadn't he told *her* about that appointment? Sick jealousy coursed through her, and her hands gripped the cards so tight that her nails left half-moon impressions in the pasteboard. Obviously, he had preferred to share his news with Caroline. If she had wondered how close he was to that woman, now she had her answer.

Zach reached over and clapped Troy on the back. "My compliments to you. When did this come about?"

"A few days ago," Troy replied, laying down a card. "Dinwiddie thought I might be of some use, since I've seen the French fortifications to the west."

"Don't be so modest," chided Caroline. "Why, you're an expert after accompanying Major Washington on that mission into the wilderness."

"The major is now a lieutenant-colonel," Zach said. "Dinwiddie's just appointed him head of our militia."

"Whatever," Caroline dismissed with a wave of her hand. "All that matters is that with Troy's expertise we can drive the French back into Canada in no time."

"The first rule of war is never to underestimate the enemy," Troy said.

Caroline wrinkled her nose. "The French are lily-livered cowards. They'll run the moment they see our troops."

"If we can muster sufficient manpower," Troy said dryly. "I understand Washington has had problems finding soldiers for the militia."

"Careful what you reveal," Caroline hissed. "Do recall we have one of *them* sitting in our midst."

"Caro!" admonished Zach with a frown. "Don't insult Elise by implying she can't be trusted."

Caroline narrowed her dark blue eyes. "Of course, Mr. Birmingham, whatever you say. Now, shall we get on with the game?"

Her mocking tone cut through Zach like a knife. Lately it seemed all they had done was quarrel. He was furious with Caroline for her childish treatment of Elise—and frustrated by her constant flirting with Troy. Though he knew his friend was not at fault, at times he had to restrain an urge to slam his fist into Troy's gut.

Automatically Zach laid down a card at his turn. He wondered what had gone wrong between Elise and Troy. Tonight those two were avoiding each other like the plague.

What a farce the four of them were embroiled in, Zach reflected with wry amusement. He and Elise were paired off, as were Caroline and Troy. Each yearned for another—with the exception of Caroline. And she didn't know better, Zach tried to console himself. If only there were some way to shake her up, to make her see the truth. . . .

"Nine of clubs takes the odd trick," Elise said, placing the last card on the table.

Zach sent her a smile of warm approval. "Well done, partner. We're quite the team."

"Don't gloat too soon," Caroline warned. "The night is not yet over. You've won two, as have we. The next game will decide the overall victor."

Zach's dark eyes studied her thoughtfully. "What say you to a wager on the outcome?"

"How much?" Troy drawled. "The last time you and I played, you dealt my finances a sore blow."

"Not money this time," Zach replied. "I was thinking more on the lines of a more interesting reward—the man on the prevailing team gets a kiss from one of these lovely ladies . . . the lady of his choice."

A provocative smile lit Caroline's face as she looked across the table at Troy. "A splendid idea, Zach. I do believe it has my approval."

Elise felt a stab of sickness. Caroline obviously thought Troy would choose *her.*

The wager was settled upon and the cards were dealt. Elise was so distracted she had a hard time paying attention to the game. What if Troy's team won? Who would he choose? She bit her lip, staring at the blur of colored pasteboard in her hand. Though tension stole her concentration, somehow she managed to lay down the proper card at the proper time.

"We did it, partner."

Startled, Elise looked up to see Zach grinning at her as he picked up the final round of cards. The knowledge of their victory sank in, and she felt a rush of relief. Troy couldn't pick Caroline over her; that was Zach's prerogative.

Relaxing, she leaned back in her chair as Zach rose to claim his kiss. Zach was enamored of Caroline; she had surmised that earlier. Though he kept his feelings well veiled, more than once Elise had glimpsed something deep and soft in his dark eyes when he gazed at Caroline. It was a shame Caroline didn't—

Her thoughts screeched to a halt. Zach was standing over *her*, bending over *her!* Determination was etched all over his handsome features. He meant to collect his kiss from her!

Elise gripped the chair arms with frozen fingers. Glancing wildly at Troy, she saw an odd expression on his face, but there was no time to analyze it. She heard Caroline gasp, then her own startled exclamation was swallowed by the gentle press of Zach's lips on hers.

Caroline glared at Zach's broad back as he bent over Elise. Anger and humiliation coursed through her; she wasn't sure which emotion was the stronger. Zach should have chosen *her*, not that copper-haired hussy! She should have seen this coming; all evening he had fawned over Elise, leaping to her defense at the slightest provocation. Why, *why?* The memory of his kiss that day in the carriage was so intense Caroline could almost taste it. The moment he had lain down the winning card, her heart had begun to pound with anticipation. Instead he had gone to Elise.

Suddenly Caroline realized she was reacting as if she were jealous. Confusion swept through her, but she brushed it away. That was absurd, she scoffed silently. It was Troy she wanted. The feelings churning inside her were a result of her disappointment that Troy had not won the right to kiss her.

She looked across the table at him, but he was watching Zach and Elise with the full force of his attention. His cold fury was obvious in his clenched fists and in the tic of a muscle in his jaw. *He was in love with Elise.*

As swiftly as that painful thought struck, Caroline rejected it. Tonight she had seen evidence that all was not right between Troy and Elise. Without a doubt, *she* loved him more than that interfering Frenchwoman ever could. Confidence flowed back into her. She would win him over, why of course, she would! It was only a matter of time.

"Thank you, partner." Zach's dark eyes were dancing with a hint of laughter as he bent over Elise.

She stared up at him, her hands still tight around the chair arms. Why was Zach looking so secretly amused? She had sat stiffly through his kiss, aware of the pressure of his lips but unable to feel any answering arousal. Why would he find that humorous?

Zach returned to his seat. "So, Elise," he drawled, "it occurs to me that you now have the choice of kissing either Troy or me, since you were also on the winning team."

"That wasn't part of the bargain," Caroline snapped.

"But 'tis only fair," Zach countered softly. "Go ahead, Elise, take your pick of us two charming gentlemen."

Elise glanced at Troy to find him looking at her, his gaze enigmatic. How she longed to feel the world blur under the assault of his kiss, to let her fingers caress the steely heat of his body. Dare she indulge that whim? Her heart thudded against her rib cage as she saw his jade eyes dip briefly to her lips . . . then abruptly he turned his head away, sending a smile to the woman sitting across from him.

Mortification enveloped Elise like a suffocating blanket. Troy didn't want her to kiss him; he was too besotted with Caroline!

A combination of anger and pride made her lift her chin high. "I appreciate your consideration, Zach," she said with biting sweetness. "But I've already kissed the man of my choice."

The April sun warmed the Palace Green, slanting through white picket fences to lay patterns of shade across the walkways. The stately avenue was bordered by budding catalpa trees. Bright splashes of color had banished the brown of winter, from white daisies and scarlet tulips to blue phlox and yellow buttercups. Robins and cardinals sang in the blooming redbud and dogwood trees whose branches swayed in the gentle spring breeze.

Elise strolled along the grass, reveling in the balmy weather. The hood of her cape was flung back so that sunlight shimmered on her coppery chignon. Unlike the cramped byways and medieval stone buildings she had known in Montreal, Williamsburg was a town of wide streets and elegant homes. Each house stood on a lot of half an acre, with gardens and fruit trees abounding. The result was a charming community pleasing to the eye.

Passing the brick church, Elise started down Duke of Gloucester Street, a spacious avenue that contained many shops, from the apothecary to the wigmaker. The brick walks were crowded with people on this late morning. It was the spring Public Time, when everyone left their plantations on the rivers to flock into town while the House of Burgesses met. Besides the political activities, the social calendar was packed with balls and banquets, fairs and horse races. Every available inn, tavern, and house was crammed to capacity.

Yesterday Pandora had broken the chain to her locket, and Elise had offered to take it to the silversmith to be repaired. As much as she liked Troy's family, she welcomed an excuse to escape the Fletcher household for a few moments.

In the week that had passed since the card game, she had been plagued by the fear that Troy no longer wanted her. He continued to avoid her as he had done for the past weeks. Had her inability to come to a decision about their marriage turned him against her?

Lost in thought, Elise hurried through the bustling crowd and almost bumped into a man who stopped in front of her.

"Mademoiselle d'Evereaux! Did you not hear me calling to you?"

"Oh, Monsieur Granger . . ."

Eyes wide with surprise, Elise stared at the French tutor. Gone was the shabby garb he had worn before, and in its place were a frock coat, waistcoat, and breeches sewn of the finest fabric and embroidered in gold thread. With a silver-topped cane in his hand and a white powdered wig on his head, Will Granger looked more like a wealthy planter than the humble teacher she knew he was.

"Well, mademoiselle, what do you think of my new image?"

"Why, you look *très magnifique*. But how could you—" She swallowed the impulsive query, remembering that a lady was not supposed to pry.

Granger's eyes twinkled. "Do you mean, how could I afford such fancy clothing? There is no need to be shy—I have naught to hide. You see, I came into a small inheritance from a distant relation, which enabled me to indulge in a few creature comforts."

"Will you continue teaching, then?"

"No, mademoiselle," he said proudly. "You are now

looking at a man of leisure."

As the elderly gentleman doffed his hat and walked on, Elise gazed after him, her brow furrowed in thought. According to gossip, there was a spy in their midst who was passing information to the French. Now Will Granger was garbed in finery he couldn't have afforded just a few weeks ago. Was it merely a coincidence?

A person should not be condemned on circumstantial evidence, Elise reminded herself as she continued down the street. After all, that was what Caroline had done to *her*, implying she was a spy solely because of her French heritage.

The silversmith shop was located in a charming two story building of pale blue clapboard with dark blue shutters. As Elise pushed open the door, a tiny bell tinkled overhead. The interior was dim after the bright sunshine outside. Glass-fronted cabinets lined the walls, displaying samples of teapots and tankards, candlesticks and snuff boxes, all fashioned of gleaming silver.

A tow-haired apprentice came out of the back room. "Be there somethin' I can help you with, ma'am?"

"Yes, I have a chain that wants repairing."

Elise dug into the pocket of her cranberry silk gown, drawing forth the locket. She was about to give it to the apprentice when a movement in the doorway to the rear caught her eye.

An older man was standing in the back room, holding up an ornate silver ewer to the sunlight streaming through an unseen window. But it was not the beauty of the object he turned slowly in his big hands that captured Elise's attention.

She stood as if caught in a nightmare, staring at the man in open-mouthed shock. A white apron covered his tall, husky frame. His hair was mostly gray, with only a few strands remaining of the dark red it had once been. There was something about his strong features that was impossibly familiar. . . .

The man pivoted and strode out of sight. For long moments she gazed numbly at the empty doorway, incapable of forming a coherent thought.

"Ma'am?"

Elise realized the apprentice was gazing at her curiously. Some automatic reflex made her fingers curl around the silver locket that lay in her palm. "I-I've changed my mind. Please forgive me."

The words seemed to thaw her frozen limbs. Spinning around, she ran out of the shop, the door banging shut behind her as she plunged blindly into the crowd. Oblivious of the stares of passersby, she elbowed her way through the throng. It was only when she reached the doorstep of the Fletcher home that Elise paused to lean against one of the white columns that supported the porch, her breath coming in deep, hurting gulps of air.

She squeezed her eyes shut. *No, no, it couldn't be true!* The refrain spun through her head, and she willed herself to believe it. But the image of the man's face kept flashing in her mind.

Panic washed over her anew. She pushed open the door and stumbled into the house in a desperate attempt to escape the truth. Troy was coming down the stairs, and his masculine form was a welcome sight. Heedless of the estrangement between them, she darted forward to throw herself into the security of his arms.

"Troy . . . oh, Troy . . ." she gasped, burying her face against the smooth linen of his shirt.

"Elise, what is it?" he demanded. "What's wrong?"

Wordlessly, she shook her head, too overwrought to explain. He didn't press her, instead drawing her into the library and closing the door, gently pushing her into a wingback chair near the fire. When he started to walk away, she grabbed frantically at his hand.

"I'm only going for some brandy," he said softly. "I'll be right back."

Troy returned in a moment to kneel before her, lifting a glass to her lips. The amber liquid burned down her throat and made her cough. He held her against him until the spell passed, then made her take another sip before placing the glass on a nearby table.

"Now tell me what happened," he commanded.

The brandy had softened the edges of her panic and a measure of courage fortified her. No matter how dismaying, she had to know for certain. She took a deep breath.

"The silversmith in the shop beside the printer's," she managed weakly. "How long has he been in Williamsburg?"

"For God's sake, Elise! I don't want to discuss the local tradesmen—I want to know what's put you in such a state!"

"Just tell me, Troy, please!" Her fingers dug into his shirtsleeve in an effort to convey the urgency of her request.

He stared at her for a moment before speaking. "All right. Let me think. . . . 'Twas shortly after my parents died, perhaps twelve or thirteen years ago, I can't say for certain. Why?"

Dread washed through her, but she forced herself to go on. "And his name—what is the silversmith's name?"

"Northrup Kingsley, I believe."

Elise tilted her head back to gaze sightlessly at the ceiling. Northrup Kingsley was alive and well and living here in Williamsburg. She felt no surprise, only a heaviness inside her, as if a leaden weight had crushed into the core of her. Somehow she had known it was he from the moment she'd seen him. She hadn't been mistaken, even after all these years.

"Elise, what is it?"

Troy's anxious words penetrated her stupor. She looked at him, running her tongue over her dry lips. When she spoke, her voice sounded strange to her ears, as if it belonged to someone else.

"Northrup Kingsley is my father."

Chapter Twenty-one

The ballroom at the governor's palace was an oblong chamber of commodious proportions. Chandeliers and wall sconces blazed with candlelight, casting a golden glow over the elegant assemblage of guests. Brocaded draperies at the windows stirred gently with the cool night breezes. The wood floor gleamed with polish, and mahogany chairs were scattered along the walls for those weary of dancing to the lilting tunes played by a quartet of musicians.

Elise stood on the threshold of the ballroom, her hand tucked in the crook of Troy's arm. She alone knew her serene exterior was a sham; inside, her heart was pounding with tension. She subdued a nervous impulse to smooth the sea-green silk of her skirt and check the stylish arrangement of curls atop her head. Even after all these weeks, the fashionable gown with its tiers of rustling petticoats felt strange. Would anyone here see that she was a simple country girl beneath all these trappings?

The majordomo stepped forth to announce their

arrival. "Miss Elise d'Evereaux and Mr. Troy Fletcher."

The chatter of voices and laughter died down as many a curious eye turned toward the doorway to observe the new arrivals. Elise lifted her small chin in stubborn pride. This was her first appearance at a public function, and she was determined to prove herself a lady. Instinct told her these aristocratic Virginians were less interested in the handsome man at her side than in viewing the Frenchwoman who had come to live in his household under somewhat suspicious circumstances. Undoubtedly they saw her as a fortune hunter out to steal one of society's most eligible bachelors.

The servant's voice rang out again, announcing Pandora, Jason, and Mirella, who followed them into the ballroom. Marc had stayed home, being too young as yet to join in such a formal occasion.

The sounds of merriment again filled the air as the guests turned to one another to gossip and dance. No sooner had Elise and Troy walked inside than Caroline came hurrying up, the baby-blue satin of her gown whispering. Like many of the other men and women present, her hair was powdered white. The rosebud perfection of her mouth formed a welcoming smile.

"Why, Troy, dear, I was beginning to fear you weren't coming." Somewhat less warmly, she added, "Hello, Elise," before returning her attention to Troy.

"I wouldn't dream of disappointing an old friend," he said, bending to bestow a gallant kiss upon her extended hand.

"Dare you call *me* old?" Caroline chided teasingly. "Why, you're at least seven years my senior, so what does that make you?"

"A doddering fool far too ancient for such a lovely

308

young lady."

She uttered a tinkling laugh, tapping his arm with her fan. "Sir, you are overly harsh on yourself. I see standing before me a gentleman so handsome I am the envy of all the other women present."

Elise listened to their banter with a jaundiced ear. Stubbornness caused her to keep her fingers wrapped around the hard muscles of Troy's arm. The moments when she had an excuse to be close to him were few and far between, and she would not allow Caroline to drive her away. The last time she had been so near him was three days ago, the day she had seen Northrup Kingsley.

Her father. A silent groan rippled through her at the thought of that selfish bastard. All those long years her mother had struggled to raise two children, and Kingsley had been living a comfortable life here in Williamsburg as proprietor of a thriving business. The least he could have done was to send them money!

Now that the initial shock had passed, Elise felt a hate so acute it made her quiver. Still, she had been unable to resist walking past his shop several times, her hood drawn around to conceal her face. She had longed to march inside and spew out the rage that festered within her, but something had held her back.

"Troy, why don't you come and say hello to my father?" Caroline suggested. "He's standing over there with the governor."

Elise knew it was a ploy to get him away from her. Pretending innocence, she clung to Troy's elbow. Caroline's lips tightened as she reached for his other arm to draw him through the throng of guests to the two men positioned near an opened window.

One was a plain-featured man of about sixty years,

with a double chin that obscured his jawline. He wore a curly wig, and his sober brown frock coat was buttoned across a stout chest. Speaking earnestly to him was a distinguished gentleman of shorter, more wiry stature, clad in fashionable tan breeches and a forest-green coat with large gold buttons.

Caroline glided up to the smaller man and laid a hand on his arm. "Father, look who I've brought to see you."

"Well, now, Troy, how are you?" the man asked, shaking Troy's hand. "And who is this lovely lady with you?"

"Miss Elise d'Evereaux," Troy replied.

"Ah, the little French girl everyone's been talking about. I'm Richard Whitman."

Elise didn't care for his faint air of condescension, but she curtseyed nonetheless, as Pandora had taught her a lady must do.

"Elise, might I have the honor of presenting to you Robert Dinwiddie, royal governor of Virginia colony," Troy then said.

The stout man inclined his bewigged head in a grave nod.

"What a coincidence," remarked Richard Whitman. "We were just discussing the French fortresses on His Majesty's dominions. Did you not reside at Fort LeBoeuf, Miss d'Evereaux?"

She stiffened slightly but managed to answer coolly, "Yes, I've lived there."

"Then perchance you might be able to help us out," Whitman said in an oily-smooth tone. "Undoubtedly you have inside information about the fortifications that could be of use to us."

"Sir, I know little of military matters," Elise protested.

"Nevertheless," Whitman continued sternly, "'twould be wise to prove your loyalty to this colony by telling us anything you know of the fort's weak points."

Elise stared at him, unsure of what to say. How could she betray secrets that might result in the death of soldiers she had known at the fort?

Troy slipped a protective arm around her waist. "Elise is not obliged to prove a thing to you, Whitman." His voice was hard and uncompromising as he frowned at Caroline's father.

"I concur," said Dinwiddie. "This is not a topic in which to embroil a lady."

At the mild rebuke, something dark flashed across Whitman's face, but he recovered quickly. "My abject apologies, Miss d'Evereaux," he murmured. "I fear I was so intent on defending Virginia's possessions that I overlooked my manners."

"Must we talk dreary politics?" Caroline pouted prettily. "Father, have you told the governor about the new carriage you ordered from England?"

Dinwiddie smiled. "Oho, now there is a subject of interest to the ladies. The purchase of clothing and gewgaws never fails to promote domestic felicity, I say."

"Whatsoever my daughter wants, she gets," Whitman said, gazing at her fondly. "Caroline has been such a comfort to me since the passing of her mother."

After a few more minutes of conversation, the governor and Richard Whitman excused themselves, leaving Elise alone with Caroline and Troy.

"Troy, you haven't forgotten your promise to dance

with me, have you?" asked Caroline.

"Of course not." He looked at Elise, stating formally, "Would you excuse us?"

She had no choice but to nod her head in gracious agreement. A tight knot of unhappiness formed in her stomach as she watched the two of them walk off. For that brief moment when he had defended her to Richard Whitman, she'd felt a glow of joy. But now she realized the incident had meant nothing; Troy had only been playing the gallant gentleman.

Aching with misery, Elise admitted silently that she missed the attention he had once lavished upon her. Would she ever again see that devilish grin of his turned on her?

"Careful, your jealousy is showing," came a low masculine voice from behind her.

Elise whirled around to see Zach lounging against a nearby wall. Tall and darkly handsome in a fawn-colored frock coat, he looked the type to have scores of women vying for his notice, yet he was alone.

"Have you been standing there all this time?" she asked.

"Long enough to see that unhappy expression on your pretty face."

Elise felt a flush of embarrassment. Were her feelings so very blatant? Then she noticed that Zach's eyes, too, turned brooding as he gazed through the milling crowd at the attractive couple dancing the minuet.

"Might I venture to guess you're the only one here who can fully appreciate how I feel?" she replied softly.

Zach made no attempt to deny her observation. "Mayhap we should console each other. Come, sit with me and talk."

Glad for the distraction, Elise sat down, carefully arranging her hooped skirts, as Zach seated himself beside her.

"This must be your first visit to the governor's palace," he commented. "Does the place meet with your approval?"

"Oh, yes," Elise said eagerly. "I've never seen anything like it before. It truly is a palace."

Zach smiled. "'Twas dubbed so due to the public funds lavished on its construction. 'Tis quite a magnificent structure for our humble colony, though it nowhere near matches the palaces of Europe."

Her gaze widened in awe. "Have you traveled to Europe, then?"

"I attended school in England," he said with a casual shrug. "Many parents around here send their children over there to be educated."

"This life is so very different from what I'm used to—" Elise blurted. Instantly she regretted her words, as the inevitable question came.

"And what are you used to?"

"It isn't important."

"Of course, it is," he countered, gently patting her hand. "Elise, I'll not judge you. You needn't be afraid to tell me anything."

She hesitated, twisting her fingers in her lap, but his sympathetic eyes encouraged her. Yes, he deserved to hear the truth.

"I—I'm not really a lady, you see. I was a servant before Troy brought me to Virginia. I don't really belong in a place like this."

Pride kept her chin high as she searched Zach's face for a sign of rejection.

"You're more a lady than a lot of women I've known," he drawled wryly. For a moment he studied her delicate features, then he lifted a finger to lightly touch her jaw. "What a winsome little creature you are, with those big copper eyes and that charming naiveté. 'Tis no wonder Troy is besotted with you."

"You're mistaken." Her wistful gaze strayed to the tawny-haired man who danced with Caroline. "I don't think he cares for me anymore."

"He does," Zach countered without a trace of doubt.

"How can you be so certain?"

"Because Troy is not a man to fall out of love so easily."

"I wish I could believe that."

"Look, I don't know what went wrong between you two, but pining won't help matters. Come, dance with me; you've been a wallflower long enough."

His warm smile raised her spirits. Zach was right. Why should she sit here moping?

"I warn you, I've not had much practice at dancing," she teased. "I may step on your toes and cripple you for life."

"Step away; I doubt those dainty slippers of yours could do me much damage." Zach extended an elbow to her. "Shall we, mam'selle?"

"I'd be delighted."

Taking his arm, she rose and walked with him to join the throng of dancers. The musicians were beginning to play a country tune, and at first Elise had to concentrate on the proper steps, not wanting to disgrace herself. But Zach's lead was flawless and she soon found herself relaxing.

Troy and Caroline had left the dance floor, though

they stood together at the fringe of the crowd, engrossed in conversation. Jealous anger rose in Elise as she caught a glimpse of Caroline leaning against him, brushing her fingers across his chest as if by mistake. How dare that woman touch him!

"Why don't you do something about it?"

Zach's whispered words startled Elise. "What do you mean?"

"Why don't you fight to get him back?"

"How? I stick to him like a burr whenever I can, but it doesn't seem to make any difference."

"Perhaps nearness is not enough . . . perhaps you need to seduce him."

A hot blush swept over Elise's cheeks. Luckily, she was forced to wait a moment to reply until the movements of the dance brought them close enough together that no one could hear their conversation.

"Sir, I hardly think that an appropriate suggestion to make," she said to cover her embarrassment.

Zach chuckled softly. "Come, Elise, set aside that stiff pride. If a woman wants to win a man, she must take drastic measures." He paused a moment, then added, "And think of it this way: You'll be doing me a favor as well by taking him away from Caroline."

Elise looked over at the couple in question, considering Zach's words. Resplendent in silver-gray frock coat, Troy was the most handsome man present. Could she be so bold as to seduce him and win him back? What if he rejected her?

Zach did have a point; a man had physical urges that could be manipulated by a knowing woman. She felt a sudden impulse to laugh aloud. Yes, she would do it; why hadn't she thought of it before? She would taunt and tease Troy until he was seething with frustration. . . .

Until he was so torn by desire he would take her back into his bed without any more of this disturbing talk of marriage.

"I wish you would forget about that Frenchwoman," Caroline complained. "'Tis plain to see she isn't worthy of you."

Knowing her words stemmed from the loyalty of a long friendship, Troy couldn't take offense. "True love cannot be forgotten so easily," he mused, unable to tear his eyes from the couple dancing a short distance away.

"True love!" exclaimed Caroline. "Why, she doesn't love you; she wants your money, your power. And now that you're an advisor to the governor's council, she also has a means of obtaining government papers that she can pass to the French."

Troy flashed her an angry scowl. "Caro, you press my patience! Elise is no spy."

"I'm sorry," she said hastily, placing a conciliatory hand on his sleeve. "Forgive me, but 'tis only that I care about what happens to you. I don't want to see you hurt."

Somewhat mollified, he relaxed. "You should mind your own fences before mine. If you're not careful, you could lose Zach."

"Lose Zach? Whatever are you talking about?"

"I think you know," Troy said softly. "He'd make a good husband, but he's not going to wait forever."

Caroline stared at him for a long moment, then tossed her chin up. "Zach is just an old friend. Why, he'll always be around, you'll see."

"Don't say I didn't warn you."

She pursed her lips into an appealing pout. "Let's not talk about him anymore. There are more important things I want—"

"Hello, Troy."

The sultry sound of Elise's voice made him pivot sharply to see her standing beside him. There was an alluring quality to her soft smile that he hadn't seen in weeks. The mere sight of it made Troy's blood begin to pound.

With innate grace, she glided up to him, coming so close that her breasts brushed against his arm. The brief contact sizzled through his system like a lightning bolt. His gaze flashed to those ripe swells straining against the decolletage of her sea-green gown, and he couldn't help but recall the enticing curves beneath her garments . . . curves he wasn't supposed to be thinking about. Swallowing hard, he forced his attention back to her face.

"Whatever have you two been talking about for so long?" Elise asked. "I must say, my curiosity is aroused."

The seductive look in her dark copper eyes seemed to hint that far more than her inquisitiveness was aroused. No, he must be mistaken, Troy decided an instant later; his lust for her was causing him to imagine a hidden meaning. Elise had too much pride to chase after him.

". . . weren't we, Troy?"

"Excuse me?" He glanced at Caroline, realizing that she was addressing him.

"Elise asked what we were conversing about, and I told her we had been speaking of love." She tapped the sleeve of his silver-gray frock coat with her fan, gazing at him with a smile that in another woman he would have

317

thought provocative.

"Ah, love," Elise said, touching his other arm. "Now there is a subject of interest to men and women alike."

Bemused, Troy gazed from one woman to the other. He wasn't sure if the subtle movement of Elise's fingers on his arm was intentional or accidental. Was he wrong to read a suggestive undertone to her words? He didn't know what to reply, and luckily Zach's arrival saved him from that dilemma.

"I've brought you some punch," Zach said, handing Elise a pewter cup.

"Why, thank you," she said with a sweet smile. "I'm ever so parched and weary after dancing."

Troy felt the slight pressure of her weight against his body. Without conscious intent, he found himself sliding an arm around her slim waist to lend her support. Her feminine fragrance intoxicated him. He couldn't keep from watching as she drank from the pewter cup. Desire knotted his loins as the tip of her tongue licked a droplet of punch from her lower lip. The memory of the sweet taste of her mouth nearly caused him to groan aloud. Despite the cool night breeze from a nearby window, Troy felt as though he were on fire. It was unseemly to keep his arm around her here in public, and with the utmost reluctance, he withdrew his fingers from her waist.

"You're not used to a life of such leisurely pursuits, are you, Elise?" Caroline asked.

"And yet she fits in here so well," Zach commented quickly, before Elise could speak. "Might I add, she is also a superb dancer."

Her copper eyes sparkled at him. "Sir, you are quite gallant to say so after I stepped upon your toes most ungracefully!"

318

Zach grinned. "You exaggerate. I was the envy of every man present here."

"Any gentleman would have said the same."

"I swear 'tis the truth," he avowed, placing a hand over his heart. "Methinks the purpose of the governor's ball is to give the men a chance to vie for the prettiest ladies." Zach turned his attention to Caroline. "And speaking of pretty ladies, you haven't yet danced with me this night."

"Oh, but we mustn't be rude and leave Troy and Elise all alone here," Caroline protested.

"You two won't mind, will you?" Without awaiting a reply, Zach took hold of her arm and towed her toward the dance floor.

Troy was not sorry to see them go. The way Zach flirted with Elise made him grind his teeth in helpless jealousy. Perhaps what he'd said earlier was true. Perhaps Zach already was losing interest in Caroline . . . and intended to pursue a new relationship with Elise. Obligation might be why he'd taken Caroline to dance.

"Are you enjoying yourself this evening?" Elise asked. "You look so grim of a sudden."

"Of course, I'm fine," Troy said quickly. By the devil, he couldn't let her think he was mooning over her! Searching for an excuse, he caught a glimpse of the governor through the crowd. "If you must know, my mind is still on the enemy agent loose here in Williamsburg."

There was a small silence, then she asked softly, "You do not believe I am the spy . . . do you?"

The unexpected worry on her face twisted his heart, and he couldn't keep from touching her cheek reassuringly. "That prospect had never even occurred to me."

"Are you certain?" she asked with a trace of anxiety. "Mr. Whitman seemed to think—"

"Mr. Whitman doesn't know you as well as I do."

The corners of her mouth curved provocatively. "Aye, we do know each other quite well, don't we?"

There she was again, that siren temptress who had teased him earlier. Elise leaned forward so that her breasts brushed lightly against his arm. Troy felt a rush of hot passion, then realized the momentary contact was no accident. His eyes narrowed as the beginnings of anger stirred within him. By God, she really *was* trying to lure him back into her bed. She must have decided her own physical desires were more important than his feelings on the matter.

"Elise, this game you're playing won't—"

Her sudden gasp interrupted him. She was staring beyond him as if frozen.

"What is it?" he asked.

When she didn't answer, Troy turned his eyes in the direction she was looking, and for a moment saw nothing that could have elicited such a strong response in her. Then, through a shifting of the crowd, he caught sight of the man and woman standing in the entrance to the ballroom.

A grim expression settled over Troy's face as the majordomo stepped forth to announce the late arrivals:

"Mrs. Abigail Banks and Mr. Northrup Kingsley."

Chapter Twenty=two

"Are you certain I'm presentable?" Abigail asked with a trace of anxiety.

As they strolled through the crowd, North smiled fondly at the woman beside him, relishing the feel of her small hand tucked into the crook of his arm. It was hard to believe Abigail was forty-six. Though her once black hair had silvered early, she was still as fine-boned and graceful as a girl. The russet gown set off her slim figure to perfection, and only a faint tracery of wrinkles marred the smooth skin of her face. Beneath her gentle beauty was a heart of gold and a nature as steadfast and strong as a rock.

"If you didn't look delectable," he murmured, bending low so that no one around them could hear, "we wouldn't have been so late arriving at this affair."

Abigail blushed becomingly. "Hush, North, someone might hear you."

"Are you ashamed of the feelings we have for each other?" he couldn't resist teasing. "Do you abhor the fact that I find you so desirable I cannot resist taking you to bed?"

The pink on her cheeks deepened to rose. "You know I'm not," she whispered. "'Tis only that . . . well, if we'd waited until after the ball, I wouldn't have had to redo my hair and clothing in such a rush."

"But we hadn't seen each other for nearly three days. Abby, my love, have you any idea what an ordeal it is to live apart from you?"

"Oh, North, if only we could be married!"

The moment the impassioned words left her lips, Abigail knew she'd said the wrong thing. The twinkle fled from North's dark brown eyes, and his mouth lost its endearing half-grin. Distressed, she gazed at her tall companion. This was always how one of his black moods started, with a reference to their impossible situation. Oh, gracious, why did she have to spoil things by reminding him they could not wed?

"We've gone over this before, Abby, and there's naught I can do. I cannot take you to wife so long as there's a chance Brigitte may still be alive somewhere."

"I realize that," Abigail said, valiantly covering her despair with a bright smile. "I don't know what made me bring that up—I am truly happy just being with you."

To her relief, North's expression softened and he lifted his finger to her cheek. "You're always so understanding. I don't know what I would do without you."

"I feel the same way about you," she murmured.

A hint of torment flashed over the rugged planes of his face. "Oh, Abby, you've been widowed for so long now. You deserve a husband, a fine man who could offer to share his life with you, free and clear. I tell myself to let you go, but I simply cannot bring myself to do it."

Impulsively she kissed the work-calloused palm of his

322

hand, uncaring of whever might be watching. "I don't want anyone else," she said fiercely. "I love *you*."

"Abby . . ."

A rush of emotion flooded North's heart. For a long, eloquent moment he gazed into her topaz eyes, conscious of a throbbing urge to drag her off to a dark, deserted corner where he could make sweet love to her until they were both gasping with pleasure. It never failed to astonish him, this pulse-pounding desire she could arouse in him. She made him feel more like a randy youth of seventeen than a mature man of forty-seven.

Someone jostled his elbow and the magical mood was broken by a reminder of the other people present. North took two goblets of wine from the silver tray carried by a passing servant and handed one to Abigail.

"To your health, m'lady," he said, lifting the goblet in a mock salute.

Her lips curved into a familiar, delightful smile. "And to yours, as well."

They strolled through the crowd, arm in arm, sipping at the wine. As Abigail paused to speak to some friends, North was aware of a deep-seated contentment. He had almost everything he had ever wanted out of life—a thriving silversmith shop, a loving woman to share his hopes and dreams. . . .

Everything but the privilege of claiming Abigail as his wife. Everything but children to brighten the nights when he rattled around alone in the big house behind the silversmith shop . . . the house he had built so long ago for his wife and daughter. . . .

Of course, Abigail had three married sons and several grandchildren, North reminded himself guiltily. Yet no matter how fond he had grown of her family, it wasn't quite the same as his own flesh and blood. Painful memories stirred inside him, but he firmly slammed the door on them. The past was over and done with. Nothing could be accomplished by raking over the mistakes he'd made many years ago.

Idly, his gaze swept the assemblage. He knew most of the guests, and more than once he raised a hand in friendly greeting to someone. Though many a man here was richer than himself, only rarely had he been slighted by any of the Virginia aristocracy. Back in England, where he'd been born and raised, a mere tradesman would never have been invited to attend a ball such as this one. Aye, this adopted land of his was a place where a man could be free. No one here knew of his background, and that was the way he preferred it.

Suddenly North froze, his large hand arrested in the act of lifting the goblet to his lips. His heart skipped a beat as he stared at a woman on the dance floor. She was slender and young, with rich copper hair that glinted in the candlelight. When she turned, there was something about her profile that brought an aching reminder of Brigitte. . . .

Nay, that was impossible, North told himself. He took a sip of wine to calm his nerves. Likely she was the daughter of one of the plantation owners. His fancy was running wild tonight because those old memories had surfaced earlier. That was all there was to it.

Still, he couldn't keep from watching the woman covertly. A spasm of pain gripped his gut. If she'd had sable hair, the resemblance to Brigitte would have been uncanny. . . .

His gaze strayed to her handsome partner in the minuet. That was one of the Fletcher brothers, wasn't it?

Troy Fletcher, he identified, owner of a vast plantation on the James River and member of one of the wealthiest families in the colony.

North frowned. What was it he'd heard about the man not so long ago? Fletcher had accompanied the Washington lad on a mission to one of the forts the French were building in the wilderness. And there was something else nagging at his memory. . . .

His eyes narrowed as he stared at the dancing couple with renewed interest. Rumor had it that Fletcher had brought a French girl back with him. Was that her? God in heaven, she looked about nineteen, the age Elise would be now. . . .

"What is it, North?"

The sound of Abigail's voice, soft with concern, drew his eyes away from the dancers. North took a deep breath in an effort to quell his growing agitation. God, he must be getting senile even to imagine such a preposterous thing. Yet the suspicions swirling inside his head refused to quit, and he knew he would not rest until he proved them wrong.

"Abby, are you acquainted with the lady who's dancing with Troy Fletcher?"

Abigail peered through the crowd for a moment, then looked back at North and shook her head. "Nay, I've never seen her before. Why?"

"I must find out her name."

Abigail saw North's big hand clenching the goblet so tight his knuckles turned white. What had put him into such a state? she wondered. She swallowed her curiosity, sensing that for now he needed her help more than her questions. When he was ready, then he would tell her everything.

"Stay here," she murmured, gently squeezing his arm. "I'll ask some of the ladies if they know."

Elise concentrated on the minuet in an attempt to keep from staring at the husky man with graying red hair who stood near the wall. Yet her eyes were drawn to him time and time again with almost morbid fascination. Every now and then the crowd would shift, affording her a clear view of him. Occasionally he turned his head to speak to someone, but then he would look her way again. She fancied he was gazing straight at her.

"Troy, he's watching me," she hissed nervously, when the formal dance steps brought them together.

"Try not to worry so," Troy replied softly. "I'm here with you. I won't let him come near you."

Despite his assurances, her palms were damp and her stomach was churning. Why hadn't she anticipated the chance that her father would come to the ball tonight? Her father. Elise stifled a half-hysterical laugh. Northrup Kingsley didn't deserve a title of such respect. What true parent could be so callous as to desert his own child?

Again, she tried to take her mind off her jittery nerves by gazing at the people around her. There was Pandora, being squired in a dance by the dapper old French tutor, Will Granger. Mirella and Jason stood together in a group at the edge of the throng.

Elise noticed some of the matrons whispering behind their fans as they stared at her and Troy. She tilted her chin in automatic defiance. The old biddies probably didn't think she was good enough for him.

And Northrup Kingsley was gazing at her, too, she was sure of it. Even from a distance she could discern the intent look in those dark brown eyes.

A wave of dizziness washed over her at the same moment the music ended. *Sacré Dieu*, she should never have let Troy convince her to dance. Her own instincts told her to get as far away from here as possible.

"Elise, are you all right?" Troy asked, frowning at her in concern.

"Please, I—I just need some air."

Pivoting, she plunged into the milling crowd, paying no heed to the murmurs of conversation all around. An open doorway at the rear of the ballroom led to a supper room, where liveried servants were laying out a light repast on several long walnut tables. Elise hurried through the chamber, too agitated to be tempted by the delectable aromas of food.

By luck, the back portal provided an escape. She stepped out into a deserted garden, breathing in great gulps of cool evening air. Troy was right behind her. He seemed to understand her need for silence, for he put his arm around her waist and guided her down a path leading away from the house.

The scents of flowers and freshly turned earth pervaded the night. The glow of lanterns dotted the garden pathways, and the light from a three-quarter moon spilled onto the formal arrangement of boxwoods and yaupons. Elise felt her dizzying panic begin to subside.

Troy led her into an arbor of beech trees. The branches overhead were woven together, making the interior like a long, shadowed tunnel. There was a stone bench, and he drew her down beside him, taking her hands in his.

"Little angel, there's no need to run," he said gently. "The chances of Kingsley recognizing you are nil."

"He was looking at me, I know he was."

"He was looking at an uncommonly pretty lady, as all men are wont to do."

"But Troy—"

"How old were you when he left?"

"Seven," she admitted.

"And you believe that he'd still recognize you now?" Troy shook his head emphatically. "Besides, you must remember that he deserted his responsibilities long ago. Even should he learn of your identity, 'tis unlikely that a man like him would want to have anything to do with his family."

Elise nibbled her lip thoughtfully. Perhaps Troy was right. Perhaps she was exaggerating Northrup Kingsley's interest in her. And, anyway, why should she feel cold terror at the prospect of confronting him? The man was lower than a worm and ill-deserving even of her hatred.

She drew in a shaky breath. "I suppose you think I acted like a fool in there."

Troy squeezed her hands gently. "I think you behaved admirably considering what that louse did to you. 'Tis strange, though," he mused, "on brief acquaintance, I wouldn't have thought Kingsley was such a scoundrel. It just goes to prove one shouldn't rely upon first impressions."

Elise found Troy's reaction gratifying. That he could so staunchly take her side must mean that he still loved her, and the knowledge filled her with joy.

She was suddenly aware of a sensual magic in the night. From a distance came the muted sound of music playing. Moonbeams penetrated the bare intertwined branches overhead, shedding a dappled light over Troy's familiar features. Her blood began to beat faster as she

328

studied the mature angles of his face. His warm thigh was pressed against hers, and his fingers gripped her hands securely. She felt an urge to curl up against the hard heat of his chest and put her mouth to the smooth, salty skin of his throat.

And why shouldn't she take advantage of his relaxed mood to tempt him back into her bed?

"Troy, *chéri*." Elise pulled her hands free and looped her arms around his neck, kissing the strong line of his jaw.

He drew in a sharp breath and stiffened. Before he could object, she moved her mouth to his, her tongue tracing the corners of his lips. After a moment, his arms came around her as if he could not resist what she so freely offered. The brief tension in his body fled, and then he was kissing her with a hunger that matched her own fierce need.

Exultant, Elise melted into Troy, her heart pounding. It was like an enchantment, feeling the firmness of his muscles against her breasts, breathing in his masculine scent. He was so virile, so powerful, and she craved him with every fiber of her being. Too many weeks had passed since they had last indulged their passion for each other.

His finger slipped inside her bodice to stroke the taut nipple of her breast. Trembles ran through her, and she arched against him, so full of wanting she was willing to let him take her right then and there, without a thought for the chance that one of the other guests might happen upon them.

In the glorious joy, she arched against him. "I knew you still wanted me," she murmured. "I knew it. . . ."

Abruptly his whole body tensed, and then he put his hands on her shoulders and thrust her away. Elise made a small whimper of protest. She tried to wriggle free, but his fingers dug into her tender flesh. His green eyes glittered darkly in the pale moonlight.

"What are you doing?" she gasped. "You're hurting me!"

His hands loosened a fraction without letting her go. "This is another trick of yours, isn't it?"

His furious tone made her swallow hard. "I—I don't know what you mean."

"The devil you don't." He threw back his head and gave a harsh laugh. "What a damn fool I am. You played on my sympathies and enticed me out here, all because you planned to seduce me."

"That's not true!"

"Don't think I didn't see through that game you were playing back there in the ballroom," he taunted, his jaw set hard. "Rubbing against my arm, teasing me with your little innuendoes. You were so eager to satisfy your own selfish wants that you couldn't give a damn for my feelings in the matter."

"I do care for you!"

"Then why won't you respect my wishes? I told you, there'd be no more sharing of beds until you're ready to commit your life to me."

"But I love you, Troy."

"Then prove it. Marry me."

She stared at his inflexible expression, her mind seething with confusion. A part of her was dying to say yes, while another part recoiled at pledging her life to an Englishman. If only there were an easy solution without having to take such a drastic step.

After a long moment of silence, Troy stood up. "I thought as much," he said bitterly.

Pivoting, he stalked out of the arbor and down the path that led to the governor's palace.

Elise heaved a deep sigh, leaning back against the narrow trunk of a beech tree. She stared up through the interwoven branches at the velvet-black sky. How had the evening turned into such a fiasco? First Caroline had to hang all over Troy, then Northrup Kingsley had appeared unexpectedly, and now this. She would have had a better time if she'd stayed home with her head buried beneath a pillow.

Frustration ate away at her. Why did Troy insist on complicating matters with marriage? Why couldn't he simply accept her love unconditionally? Most men would be thrilled to have a mistress who wanted nothing of them but the pleasures of the flesh! Why did she have to fall in love with the one man who demanded marriage?

The slight scrape of a footstep on the gravel path made Elise sit up straight. There was a man standing in the shadows at the entrance to the arbor. Her breath caught sharply. No, not here! Not when there was no one else around!

It was her father . . . Northrup Kingsley!

"Elise?" he uttered hoarsely.

Panic froze her to the stone bench. She couldn't have spoken if her life had depended upon it.

"Elise?" he asked again. He took a few hesitant steps forward. "Is it truly you?"

That deep, rusty voice was an echo of a memory. A memory still raw and hurting like an open wound. The thought that he might get close enough to touch her thawed her limbs. She surged up in a rustle of starched petticoats.

"Don't you come near me!"

331

Kingsley stopped dead. "Elise," he muttered brokenly, as if he couldn't trust his senses. "My daughter . . . my *daughter.*"

"You bastard," she spat. "Don't you dare call me that."

"But . . . don't you recognize me? I'm your father—"

"I don't have a father! He died over twelve years ago."

Silence stretched between them like a taut wire. Elise breathed unevenly as a tumult of rage and distress clouded her senses. How dare he even speak to her! She wanted to scream and sob and pound his chest with her fists, but that would only give him cause to think she still cared. And she didn't . . . she didn't!

"I see," he said. "Do you despise me so much, then?"

His voice was heavy with an emotion Elise might have called pain had she not been so sure of his insensitivity.

"If you must know, I don't consider you worthy even of my hatred."

Bolstered by icy anger, she stalked past him, intending to return to the ballroom. But his large hand shot out to grip her arm.

"Don't go," Kingsley pleaded. "I need to talk to you."

Elise glared at the fingers wrapped around her sleeve. An unexpected pang jolted her. That was the hand that had once stroked her forehead when she had a fever, the hand that had tucked her into bed at night.

Something snapped inside of her. After the way he'd rejected her, what right had he to make any demands?

"Talk!" she cried. "The time for talk was twelve years ago, when you deserted us without looking back. Without even saying good-bye, for that matter! Maman was forced to work like a slave just to put food on the table. But you didn't care! You never cared!" Elise's body

332

trembled with fury. "So tell me, why should I speak to you? You're the most sorry excuse for a father that ever walked this earth. Now let me go or I'll scream!"

Kingsley made no move to loosen his fingers. "I wrote to you and Brigitte," he protested. "I sent your mother money, but the letters were returned—"

"A likely tale," she sneered. "What is it you want of me now? Did you see me with Troy Fletcher and think to use my relationship with him to worm some money out of him?"

Kingsley ignored the innuendo. His eyes were dark and stormy in the shifting shadows. "What exactly is your relationship with Fletcher?"

"I'm whoring for him," she spat coldly, in a blind attempt to shock this man who sought to claim his rights as father. "So how does that make you feel, dear *Papa?* To know your only daughter has no morals? To know that growing up without the guidance of a father has had such a poor influence on me?"

"Stop it," he ordered through gritted teeth, giving her a shake.

"Don't try to tell me what to do! You gave up that right a long time ago!"

She saw him tighten his lips, and his breathing was audible in the quiet night air. Even the sound of distant music had ceased. The knowledge that she had finally driven this man to the brink of anger gave her great pleasure.

"I can see there's no getting through to you tonight," he said at last. "We'll speak of this another time."

"There will be no next time. I don't intend ever to see you again. Now release me!" She yanked ineffectively against his iron grip.

"I'll let you go if you answer one last question."

"I don't have to tell you anything."

Kingsley went on as if she hadn't spoken. "Your mother," he said in an odd, gutteral voice. "Is . . . is she here in Williamsburg with you?"

Elise felt a moment's softening. He didn't know her mother had died last summer. Abruptly she stiffened. The bastard, he was trying to play on her sympathies with that phony air of concern.

"Oh, I see," she scoffed. "You want to marry that woman I saw you with in the ballroom. Or have you found it convenient to have a wife somewhere so that no other woman could trick you to the altar?"

Her father's fingers tightened spasmodically. "Elise, for pity's sake, just answer my question!"

Inexplicably, tears sprang to her eyes. "Maman is dead," she cried out. "She worked herself to death and it's all your fault!"

Elise jerked against his grasp, and this time, his fingers let her go. She stumbled out of the arbor, scurrying down the path that led to the house, to the security of the crowd.

Watching her go, North Kingsley leaned weakly against a beech tree. His entire body felt numb with shock. After all these years, he finally knew. His daughter was alive. And Brigitte was dead. For an instant he thought he was going mad as the moonlit garden blurred before his eyes. Then he realized he was crying.

He sank down on a nearby bench and put his hands over his face, tears running down his fingers to soak the sleeves of his shirt and frock coat. Pain washed through him in agonizing waves. He had no idea how much time had passed when light footsteps sounded on the path and

334

feminine arms enveloped him in a familiar, sweet scent. Abigail. Gratefully, North buried his face in the warmth of her throat, drawing on the comfort and love she so freely offered.

A dark shape carrying a candle crept unerringly through the dim second-floor passageway that led to the library where Robert Dinwiddie, royal governor of Virginia, kept his papers. The sounds of music and merriment drifted from below. With everyone occupied at the ball downstairs, now was the perfect time to find those documents.

Confidently, the shadowed figure entered the book-lined room and glanced through the connecting door that led into his lordship's bedchamber. No one was there; as expected, all the servants were busy serving supper and seeing to the needs of the throng of guests.

Feet silent on the carpet, the enemy agent walked over to a desk in the center of the library, setting down the candle. A small instrument was produced from a pocket of the spy's formal attire and inserted by nimble fingers into the lock in the top drawer.

A tiny click, then a sliding scrape as the drawer was opened. A rustle of parchment.

And, at last, success. There, at the bottom of a stack of correspondence, were the documents. Proof of precisely how the colonial government of Virginia planned to oust the French from the Ohio Valley. Even the light of the candle could not soften the corrupt nature of the spy's smile. Ah, yes, the information in these papers would serve a purpose . . . but not the one the governor had intended.

Quick fingers reached for a quill pen and began to copy down the vital data, dipping into the inkwell time and time again until the task was completed. Then the original documents were replaced, the drawer relocked. The copy was sanded and folded and secured deep within the spy's pocket.

The library looked exactly as before; there was nothing to show that anyone had been there. Picking up the candle, the figure slipped out into the passageway and down the stairs, to rejoin the festivities in the ballroom.

Chapter Twenty-three

Elise lounged in a wooden bathtub before the hearth. As she lifted her hands to squeeze the water out of her freshly washed hair, droplets rolled off her skin and splashed into the steaming liquid that enveloped her. A hint of roses perfumed the air.

Lazily she ran a dripping square of cloth over her breasts. The rosy peaks were tight and faintly throbbing, for her thoughts had been centered on Troy. No longer did she doubt his desire for her; the look in his eyes revealed how much he wanted her. She'd been certain of it ever since the passionate embrace they'd shared three nights ago at the governor's ball . . . the same night she had come face to face with Northrup Kingsley.

Recalling her father, Elise felt a resurgence of anger, mingled with a distressing pain. Try as she might, she could not forget the flash of anguish in his eyes when she'd told him her mother was dead. He was only play-acting, she rationalized. He was a man who used people, and so he must have thought to benefit from her position in the Fletcher household. There could be no other

337

explanation for his interest in her.

Yet no matter how she denied it, the meeting had opened the floodgates of memory. Once again, she felt the bewilderment of a little girl trying to understand why her papa had left without even saying good-bye. Didn't he care that she loved him? What had she done to make him reject her so cruelly?

Elise stepped out of the tub, lecturing herself that it was foolish to feel a twinge of vulnerability after so many years. Northrup Kingsley no longer possessed the power to hurt her; she despised him with every ounce of her being. And he must have realized she meant every word she'd said to him, for he had not tried to approach her again.

Picking up a linen towel, she briskly dried herself off. The chemise she drew over her head was a froth of lace-edged lawn. She sat down on a stool beside the fire and began to comb her damp hair.

Elise felt a pang quiver through her heart. One thing was for certain, she reflected. The encounter with her father had reaffirmed her belief about marriage to an Englishman. Even though she loved Troy, she dared not trust him for fear he might someday leave her. She could not bear the grief of losing a husband. As his mistress, though, there would be a certain distance between them that would lessen the hurt.

A sudden weakness gripped her limbs. *Sacré Dieu*, how she longed to feel his warm hands stroking between her thighs, his lips suckling her breasts! And she wanted to touch him, to run her fingers over the strength of his chest, down his flat stomach to the essence of his masculinity. Her abdomen throbbed at the very thought of such sweet pleasure.

Soon, Elise promised herself with a smile. Soon she would complete her seduction. She would make Troy want her so badly he would forget his scruples and take her to his bed. Somehow she must wear him down and convince him that this talk of marriage was foolish. If he could torture her with ultimatums, then she would fight back by tempting him with every bit of sultry femininity she possessed.

She sat by the warmth of the fire until her waist-length hair was dry. Tossing aside the comb, she walked to the window to gaze out into the wet afternoon. Raindrops splashed from a leaden gray sky, running down the glass panes like tears. The Palace Green looked muddy and dismal. Only an occasional brave soul, hunched beneath a hooded cloak, ventured out in the chilly April drizzle.

The depressing scene failed to dampen her sense of anticipation. If Troy followed his normal routine, soon he would be returning home after a day spent at the Capitol building. When he came upstairs to change for supper, then she would have a chance to make her move.

Elise paced the length of the chamber, waiting for her quarry to appear. From time to time, she paused by the window to peer out, smiling as she contemplated her plan. At long last, she discerned Troy's familiar form riding on horseback toward the house, a tricorn hat and greatcoat protecting him from the driving rain.

Quickly she stepped into a gown of dark gold taffeta, deliberately leaving the back unfastened. In front of the looking glass, she arranged the bodice with trembling fingers, making certain the frilly decolletage revealed more than it covered.

Heart pounding, Elise hurried to the door and put her ear to the wooden panel. Soon she was rewarded by the heavy tread of a man mounting the stairs. Just as the steps were passing her room, she swung open the door, one hand clutching the slippery taffeta to her breasts.

Troy pivoted toward her and stopped, staring. He had shed his greatcoat and hat, and his tawny hair was darkened by raindrops. A white shirt, ruffled at the wrists, had been unbuttoned partway to reveal the broad expanse of his chest. Tan breeches covered his long legs and black leather riding boots came to his knees.

To her secret delight, his gaze dipped to the shadowed valley between her breasts. Elise could well imagine the sight she looked, with her unbound curls cascading over bare shoulders and the loosened bodice exposing creamy swells of flesh.

"Oh!" she exclaimed in artful surprise. "I thought you were Pandora."

She made a show of modestly rearranging the folds of her gown, by design uncovering the top of her chemise, where the tips of her breasts showed through the gauzy material. Troy didn't look at all fooled by her actions. Yet he made no move to walk off, and that buoyed her hopes.

"Dear me," she added nonchalantly, "I wanted to ask your sister if she could aid me in fastening my gown."

Troy's eyes again swept over her bosom as though drawn by magnetic attraction. Abruptly he pursed his lips and turned toward the stairs.

"I'll call one of the servants."

"Nay! They're all busy with supper preparations, and there's no one else around." Elise paused, as if an idea had just occurred to her. "Do you suppose I might trouble you to help me?"

"I hardly think—"

"Please," she begged, gazing at him through the veil of

her lashes. "'Twould take but a moment of your time, and I would be most grateful."

Troy saw through her prettily worded request. This was another of Elise's ploys to seduce him. For the past several days, she had been intent on wearing down his resistance, teasing and taunting him until his blood ran hot with lust. He ought to show her right here and now how strong-willed he was by turning and walking away from the enticing glimpse of her breasts.

"I'll help you," he found himself saying instead, the words coming out half-strangled.

Troy didn't miss the flash of triumph in her brandy-colored eyes as she swiveled around, leaving him to follow her inside like an eager puppy. Silently he cursed himself for a fool. What kind of masochist was he, to enter a bedchamber alone with a half-naked woman he dared not touch, a woman who made his loins tighten with almost unbearable heat?

"I cannot tell you how grateful I am," Elise murmured as she pulled her heavy mane of hair over her shoulder. "I was beginning to wonder what I would do."

"I'm sure you were," Troy said dryly.

He resisted an urge to plunge his hands into her lustrous mass of copper curls. God, what had he gotten himself into? The back of the dress gaped open to her waist, the gauzy fabric of her chemise doing little to conceal the tantalizing flesh beneath. She was so exquisitely beautiful.

Gritting his teeth to hold in a groan, Troy began his task. Of course, she hadn't worn a gown with only a couple of hooks to fasten, she had chosen one with a myriad of tiny buttons that would strain the limits of his fortitude. Trembling slightly, his fingers brushed her warm skin,

341

and he couldn't help but think of how easy it would be to slide his hands inside and encircle her breasts, to feel those ripe swells filling his palms as he had so many times before. He wanted to give her his love in every way a man could love a woman.

Perhaps he had been wrong to give her that ultimatum. If he forgot about commitment and marriage, then her sweet body could be his right now. . . .

Instantly Troy was angry at himself. By God, he was reacting precisely the way she wanted! His flesh was aflame with need, the longing in his belly almost a physical pain. Without even lifting a finger, Elise was controlling him like a puppet. Dammit, if he gave in so easily, she might never wed him!

A sudden idea brought a grimly wicked smile to his lips. Supposing he gave her a taste of her own medicine? It might just cure her of these seduction attempts.

Leaving her gown half-unbuttoned, Troy put his arms around her, pulling her close and rubbing his hips to hers so that she couldn't help but feel the hardness in his loins. His mouth gently nibbled the lobe of her ear. He noted wryly that it was not going to be difficult to make his voice sound tortured.

"Elise, my lovely angel, I've tried to resist you, but I haven't the willpower. Please, I must have you now!"

He felt a quiver run through her. She turned in his embrace to look at him, lifting a hand to his cheek. "You truly mean that?" she asked breathlessly. "You . . . you won't insist that I agree to wed you?"

"Nay, I should never have asked such a thing of you. I should have known 'twould be impossible to keep away from you."

"Oh, Troy, I'm so happy. . . ." With a sigh, she buried

er face in his chest, where his shirt was unbuttoned, and
egan to kiss him.

The moistness of her tongue on his skin was infinitely
rousing. Damn, he'd best get this over with quickly
efore his passion got the better of him. Already
rimitive instinct was overriding his sense of purpose.

"Come," he murmured, leading her over to the bed.

He pressed her down on the quilt, then positioned
imself beside her. Her sultry smile made his blood beat
vith hot passion as she reached for the buttons on his
reeches.

"Nay," he said firmly, pulling her hands away. "Allow
ne to do this in my own fashion."

She lay back without a protest, her brandy-dark eyes
vatching him with a heart-melting expression of love.
;od, why did she have to look so trusting? A flash of guilt
nade Troy pause, but relentless determination drove him
n.

Her taffeta skirt rustled as he delved beneath it,
moothing his palm up the bare length of her leg, seeking
nd finding her most secret place. As he'd suspected, her
ndergarments consisted of only a chemise, leaving the
ewy warmth of her desire vulnerable to his touch. He
lid a finger into her silken depths, stroking there as his
humb pleasured the outward folds of flesh, until she
vrithed and moaned in helpless need.

The intensity of her response was almost Troy's
ndoing. His breathing sounded rough and raspy as he
ought an urge to tear open his breeches and plunge into
he core of her. Only by exerting the limits of his
villpower was he able to resist the temptation. Dammit,
e was going to teach her a lesson if it killed him!

"Is this what you want?" he murmured hoarsely.

"Yes, oh, yes!" She pressed her hips against his hand, her eyelids heavy with passion. "Please, *chéri*, come into me."

Oh, Lord, he had to end this right now or it would be too late. Taking a deep breath, Troy dragged his hand from beneath her gown and sprang to his feet.

"No."

Elise rose on her elbow, cocking her head at him in bewilderment. "Don't tease me, Troy."

He stared down at her broodingly, hands on his lean hips. Her hair was tumbled around her face, and the bodice of her gown had slipped, revealing the lush swells of her breasts straining against the thin lawn of the chemise. Her lips were moist and red and inviting.

Raw, animal lust seethed inside Troy. Every fiber of his body felt the enticing lure of her femininity. He wanted to take her with all the savage passion of a wild beast.

But dammit, it was time she realized he would not back down!

"At the risk of repeating myself," he said unevenly, "I want a wife, not a mistress."

There was a long moment of silence, then her eyes narrowed. "You mean you deliberately deceived me?"

"I was but following your rules. After all, you tricked me into coming in here in the first place."

"English swine!" she spat, sitting up in stiff-backed rage. "How dare you humiliate me this way!"

"Oh, so we're back to name-calling, are we? I'm afraid I haven't the time for your tantrums." Troy strode toward the door.

"Tantrums!" She heaved a feather pillow that he just barely dodged in time. "You have nerve to accuse me of that after what you just did!"

His expression remained firm. "Come to my bedchamber when you're ready to pledge your troth to me. I'll make love to you then, and not a moment before."

"I'll see you in hell first!"

"As you wish, madam."

Troy walked out and slammed the door. There was a muted thud as something struck the wooden panel behind him, another pillow most likely. The determination that had steeled his spine drained away, and he slumped his shoulder against the cool wall of the passageway, his body throbbing with frustrated desire.

Aye, he had won the battle of wills, but it was a hollow victory. Whom had he punished more, Elise or himself?

Chapter Twenty-four

"Elise!"

The sound of her brother's voice drew Elise's attention from the sewing in her lap. Marc was walking into the drawing room, his cap in his hands. As always, his dark hair was slightly mussed and there was an air of restlessness about him.

Behind him, Troy lounged against the door frame, arms folded across his white shirt, the merest hint of a sardonic smile on his face. Elise flicked a cool glance at him, then returned her attention to the youth.

"Yes, what is it, Marc?"

"Troy says I must have your—how do you say?—your permission to go with him to the Capitol. Might I, please?"

Knowing how her brother hero-worshipped Troy, Elise was tempted to refuse. But she would not give Troy the satisfaction of thinking his easy relationship with Marc bothered her.

"Of course, you may."

"Bon!" Marc exclaimed, lapsing into French as he did

when excited. Over the past months, his mastery of the English language had grown by leaps and bounds, and now he spoke almost entirely in his adopted tongue.

With thoughtful affection, Elise watched him sprint out of the room, dragging Troy along with him. Marc's acceptance of his new life here in Virginia was vaguely troubling. Didn't he miss the wide-open spaces of the frontier as she did? Didn't he ever long for the uncomplicated life they had led before? Though, of course, she reflected, maybe he didn't see things precisely the way she did. After all, he wasn't suffering from damaged pride and an aching heart.

Her own emotions had been in a turmoil ever since the confrontation with Troy two days earlier. With a halfhearted sigh, Elise poked a needle into the white linen handkerchief she was supposed to be embroidering. Now that her initial rage and humiliation had subsided, she had come to a reluctant acceptance of the situation. Her vanity had been hurt by Troy's rejection. She hadn't wanted to admit that she could fail to overcome his iron will. And Troy had no intention of changing his mind; it was either marry him or live without his lovemaking.

Irritation washed over her. The devil take his confidence! He acted so certain she would come around to his way of thinking that she felt an urge to show him she could be as stubborn as he. And yet . . . something deep inside her wanted to see his ring on her finger, to know that he belonged to her as much as she to him. Elise shoved that madness out of her mind. She wouldn't, couldn't, shouldn't wed him. As soon as her passion for him died, she would leave Virginia and return to the frontier.

"Miss 'Lise, you gots a visitor." Standing in the

doorway to the drawing room was Ophelia, the stout old slave woman who worked for Jason and Mirella.

Elise frowned. Surely Ophelia was mistaken; it must be someone to see Pandora or Mirella, who were off visiting friends. "Who is it?"

"He say his name's Mistah Kingsley. You be wantin' me to show him in here?"

Elise jabbed the needle into her thumb, but the panic blinding her senses blocked out the pain. "Nay!" she said quickly. "Tell him I've gone out . . . that I've returned to the plantation . . . anything so long as you get rid of him."

"He sho' seem powerful anxious to see you," Ophelia said.

"I don't care. Send him away."

"I won't be sent away."

Northrup Kingsley strode past the housekeeper and into the room. Startled, Elise rose from the chair, the sewing supplies tumbling out of her lap and onto the Persian carpet, unnoticed. The tall, neatly clad frame of her father dominated the cozy chamber, and he swept a tricorn hat off his graying red hair.

"Get out of here," she said through gritted teeth.

"Elise, if you refuse to listen to me now, I'll only keep after you until you do."

Behind his quiet words, she read a steely determination. Tension tightened her limbs. What could he possibly have to say to her? This must be a trick to use her!

"You may leave us," he told Ophelia.

"Nay!" Elise exclaimed.

"Aye," her father countered firmly. Turning to the servant, he added, "If you don't mind, ma'am, I'd like a

348

word alone with my daughter."

The black woman looked him up and down, assessing him with speculative dark eyes. "Yessuh," she said, and waddled out of the chamber.

Fuming, Elise pursed her lips. He wasn't going to get away with this high-handed behavior! The instant the drawing room doors were closed, she turned on him.

"Mr. Kingsley," she said, saying the name with pointed emphasis as if he were a total stranger, "I thought I'd made it clear I never wanted to see you again."

"Aye, but I never agreed to stay away from you."

"You have the nerve to try to foist yourself upon me after what you did!"

"Elise, so many precious years have slipped by us. We need to get to know each other again, so the years to come are not wasted as well."

His quiet words slipped past her defenses. He looked so lonely, standing there in the center of the chamber, shifting the tricorn hat from hand to hand, his wide shoulders held with stiff dignity. Elise crushed the momentary softening. North Kingsley was a scoundrel. He was lying about his reasons for seeking her out.

"Then why have you let five days pass before coming to see me?" she taunted.

"Because I judged we both needed time to adjust to the shock of finding each other."

"Or perhaps *you* needed time to think up a scheme to use me," Elise countered coldly. "What is it you wish of me? Tell it to me quickly, so we can get this over with."

"All I want is the chance to be your father."

"My father!" she scoffed. "The devil himself would have been a better sire than you!"

A spark of torment flared in his dark eyes, eyes so like Marc's. Kingsley averted his face as he seated himself in a chair, placing his hat on a nearby table. When he looked at her again, there was no expression on his rough-hewn features.

"You hate me, and I can understand that ," he said. "But after I spoke with you at the governor's ball, I realized that your mother might not have explained to you my reasons for leaving. If you hear me out, perhaps you'll see why I acted the way I did."

"I have neither the time nor the patience to listen to your feeble excuses." Elise marched across the room and put a hand on the doorknob. "I must request you to leave."

"Not before I have my say," her father said stubbornly. "Perhaps I can't make you stop hating me, but I at least want to tell you my side of the story." He leaned forward, his big hands gripping the chair arms. "I love you, Elise. You're my only child, flesh of my flesh, blood of my blood. There's no one in the world who can take your place in my heart."

"But . . ." *But what about Marc?*

The question died on her lips. Stunned, Elise stared at her father. For the first time it occurred to her that he'd never asked whether she had a younger sister or brother. The bastard must have forgotten that her mother had been pregnant when he'd walked out on them!

He wouldn't find out about Marc from her, she decided swiftly. Not only was there no sense in subjecting her brother to this man's badgering, but deep in her heart she feared Kingsley might try to steal Marc away from her. Men were fanatical when it came to having a son and heir.

"Won't you listen to what I have to say, please?"

Kingsley asked again.

Elise left the door to sit down in a chair opposite him. Much as it galled her to give in, it would be better to hear him out now while Marc was gone rather than risk having him return another time when he might run into her brother.

Kingsley showed only a flicker of surprise at her abrupt acquiescence. Then the cool mask settled over his face and he leaned back, crossing one long leg over the other. "Before I speak of your mother and me, it might help if you learned a little of your English heritage. Other than Brigitte—your mother—I've never told anyone about my background."

There was a fractional pause, then he continued, "You see, my father, your grandfather, was the earl of Middleford, head of a very ancient and powerful English family."

That was the last thing Elise had expected him to say, yet it would explain so much—his noble bearing, his refined speech. Still, she kept her expression aloof. "I must commend you on your imagination, Mr. Kingsley. Pray tell, how could an aristocrat like yourself end up as a tradesman in the colonies? Or are you a bastard in blood as well as character?"

Her father regarded her with steady eyes that made her shift in her chair, ashamed of her scathing words. "I am no bastard, but my father's true son," he said. "I was born last of eight boys. My eldest brother was groomed to take the title, the second brother was destined for the military, and the third for the clergy. The rest of us were someday to inherit property of our own, but I found the life too stifling, and so I ran away when I was sixteen, searching for adventure.

"I spent a few years as a sailor, then jumped ship in Boston and worked a short stint with a silversmith there. It was a job I loved, until the shop burned down one night and I was accused of perpetrating the deed. I fled into the wilderness, but I never regretted it because that was where I met Brigitte." His voice gentled, and his gaze was focused somewhere over Elise's head.

"Your mother was a beauty to behold, with her long sable hair and sparkling eyes. Her father had a little trading post up near Lake Ontario, and he violently opposed our marriage because he didn't want her tied to a penniless Englishman. But we were in love and nothing could stop us from running off together. I became a fur trapper, and we bought some land and built a cabin . . . that was where you were born, Elise. Then one day I received a letter saying that my father had died and left me a wealthy man."

"And so you deserted my mother and me to claim the money," Elise broke in, anxious to deny the stirrings of sympathy inside her. It was absurd to get soft and sentimental about a man who had rejected his own family!

"That's not the whole story," her father denied. "Brigitte knew more than anything that I wanted to become a silversmith. For years I'd dreamed of saving up enough to open my own shop, and the inheritance finally gave me a chance. I tried to convince her to move here to Williamsburg with me, but she refused. She'd grown up in the wilderness, and she was as bound and determined to stay there as I was to start my own business."

"But we did move to the city . . . to Montreal," Elise pointed out. "That just goes to prove you were wrong about her."

Kingsley frowned. "So that's where you disappeared to! I tore the forest apart looking for you!"

"Are you trying to tell me you came back for us?" she scoffed, fighting an impulse to believe him.

"Yes, I did. We had a big argument one night, and I walked out on her. By the time I was onboard the ship to England, my anger had cooled, and I saw what a fool I'd been. I couldn't turn the ship back, so I conducted my business in England as swiftly as possible and returned to Williamsburg. All my letters to your mother were returned unopened. At last I tried to track her down myself. But no one could—or would—tell me where she had gone. Her father was dead, and she had no other relations so far as I knew."

"She had a distant cousin in Montreal."

"I didn't know." Stark sorrow shadowed his eyes, and his voice lowered, as if he were talking to himself. "It was too late when I realized what a mistake I'd made. Brigitte and I loved each other, but neither one of us would give an inch. We were both too proud, too passionate, too stubborn. And so we lost everything . . . everything." Staring down at the carpet, he massaged his forehead with his large hand.

Elise surged out of her chair and paced across to the fireplace, trying to digest what her father had said. His story sounded so reasonable, so logical. If he was telling the truth, that meant her mother had been as much at fault as he!

"I should never have left you." Kingsley's tortured voice drew her eyes back to him. "Can you ever find room in your heart to forgive me for being such a fool?"

Elise was at a loss to answer. Her mind was a muddle of confusion as the beliefs of a lifetime threatened to crumble. Was that truly remorse on his face or was he acting? Was he a monster or just a human being who had made a mistake?

"Elise, where are you?"

She froze as Marc entered the drawing room, his dark hair disheveled from the wind. Oh, no! Her brother was supposed to have been gone all afternoon!

"What are you doing here?" she blurted.

"*Pardon*, I didn't realize you had a visitor," he said politely. "Troy was called into a meeting and so I came back without him."

Nervously she dug her nails into her palms. Kingsley was regarding the boy with a faint frown of curiosity. He couldn't find out about Marc, not until she'd had time to think! "Run along to the kitchen," she urged. "There's some fresh-baked cherry tarts for you."

Marc started to turn, then shot Kingsley a suspicious look. "Are you here to . . . how do you say? To court my sister?"

"That's absurd!" Elise burst out. *Sacré Dieu*, this was going from bad to worse! "Marc, this is none of your concern. I want you to leave here this instant!"

Neither male acted as if they'd heard her. Kingsley sat very still, his hands gripping the chair arms, his eyes intent on Marc. "Your sister?"

"*Oui*. I know she is pretty, but you cannot marry her. She is going to marry Troy Fletcher."

Elise swept toward her brother, taking him firmly by the arm and steering him out the door. "Marc, you are being impertinent. I want you to obey me—"

"Let the boy stay." Kingsley had risen to his commanding height, a grim expression on his face.

"But he has no business here—"

With a quick slash of his hand, Kingsley cut her off. "I suspect he has as much right to be here as you do. Come back in and sit down, both of you."

His terse voice brooked no argument. Elise found herself swallowing hard as she walked back into the room. She perched on the edge of a chair, fingers laced tightly in her lap.

"How old are you?" Kingsley asked Marc, who had seated himself on a stool near the fireplace.

"Twelve years," the boy replied, with a touch of wary belligerence.

"And when is your birthdate?"

"The twenty-ninth day of *novembre*—November."

Kingsley uttered a harsh curse under his breath. His dark eyes bored into Elise, conveying an accusing message: *How could you have not told me I have a son?* Biting her lip, she looked away, both resenting and understanding his anger at the same time.

"Elise, who is this man?" Marc demanded. "Why is he asking me these questions?"

She parted her lips, but was unable to speak.

"I'll answer that." Kingsley strode over to the fireplace, his face softening as he looked down at Marc. "You see, I only just found out . . . you're my son."

For a long moment they stared at each other, then Marc jerked his eyes toward Elise. "He lies! Tell him . . . my father is dead!"

Mutely, Elise shook her head, wishing she were able to spare him.

"You are *mon père?*" Her brother's disbelief became anger, and he leaped up from the stool. "*Merde!* You are the *bâtard anglais* who left Maman! I should kill you!"

He launched himself at his father, hammering his fists

355

on the older man's chest. Kingsley seized Marc's arms and thrust him out of reach. The thin boy wrestled for freedom but was no match for his father's superior size and strength.

"For Christ's sake, calm yourself!" roared Kingsley.

Startled, Marc ceased struggling and glowered at his captor.

"If you'll kindly behave yourself, young man, I'll tell you why I left your mother." Kingsley released Marc, and the boy backed up, rubbing his arms and watching his father with wary eyes.

"What can you say to me?" he asked sullenly. "You left Maman all alone, even before I was born. You didn't want any of us!"

"I'm not trying to excuse myself, but for what it's worth, I had no idea she was going to have another child."

"You must have known!" Elise interjected. "She told me the very night you left!"

"I assure you, I didn't know," Kingsley repeated firmly. "I can only speculate that since Brigitte and I had been arguing for several weeks over my inheritance, she must have thought I'd use the fact of her pregnancy to convince her to leave the wilderness."

"Inheritance?" Marc asked.

"Aye," his father replied. "'Tis only fair I tell you everything I'd just finished telling your sister before you walked into the room. Now, sit down."

Scowling, Marc obeyed. Kingsley also seated himself, and proceeded to relate his tale. Listening to his deep, rasping voice, Elise felt a vivid wash of memory. Every night he'd held her in the rocking chair before the fire and told her stories. She recalled his tucking her into bed, kissing her goodnight. . . .

A lump formed in her throat. He really *had* loved her; that was why she had been so desperately hurt when he'd left so abruptly. She'd felt abandoned and confused, and the pain of it had gradually been buried behind a wall of hatred. But now she knew the reason why he had gone away . . . that was, if she could believe him.

Elise gazed at her father, feeling as if she were seeing him for the first time. He was leaning forward as he talked, studying his son. There was a serious expression on his rough-hewn features, though the laugh lines bracketing his eyes and mouth bespoke a natural good humor. With a pang, she realized she had not seen him smile since her childhood.

Hearing his explanation again, Elise was aware of the emotion in his voice. Surely such sadness and regret had to come from the heart. From the heart . . . was it possible that their separation had really been an enormous mistake, a cruel twist of fate?

"Why did Maman not tell us about your argument with her?" Marc demanded. "Why did she let me think you were dead?"

Kingsley lifted his shoulders. "I suppose she had good cause to think I was never coming back. We were so angry at each other that night. Likely she thought 'twas best you and Elise forget about me."

"I saw part of your fight with her the night you left," Elise admitted. "You didn't even stop to say good-bye to me, and that made me hate you all the more."

There was a long pause, then her father said heavily, "I regret that you had to witness such a scene. All I can do is beg your forgiveness. I know it does little good. . . ."

Abruptly he rose and walked to the window, leaning on

357

the sill as he stared out into the late afternoon sunshine. There was a slump to his shoulders that Elise hadn't seen before. Something twisted deep inside her, but she shied away from identifying it.

"Marc, I would like a cup of strong tea. Will you ask Ophelia to fetch us some?"

"*Oui*," he murmured.

She watched as her brother left to do her bidding. He looked so solemn, so troubled; it was best to give him a moment to himself. Like her, he needed time to absorb the shock.

A quiver of vulnerability seized her. Her fingernails dug into fragile gold fabric covering the chair arm. *Sacré Dieu*, she didn't hate her father anymore! That realization wasn't nearly as frightening as the one that followed: What *did* she feel for him?

Kingsley pivoted to face her, his large frame silhouetted by sunlight. "Elise, might I ask you one more thing before I go?"

Unsteadily, she nodded.

"Will you tell me . . ." He paused, and when he continued, his voice was hoarse. "Will you tell me about Brigitte's death?"

The naked grief on his face touched Elise's soul. He really *had* loved her mother! A shameful memory of her cruel words to him at the governor's ball flashed through her mind. *She worked herself to death and it's all your fault!*

Tears stung her eyes as she saw how wrong she had been. Her father had made a mistake, but so had her mother. They were both just people, with ordinary human failings.

Something broke inside of Elise . . . the shell of hurt and anger that had ruled her emotions for so long.

"Oh, Papa . . ." she cried, and ran across the room to throw herself into his arms.

Abigail paced the parlor floor in the neat frame house she owned on Francis Street. Through the window, she could see the deep blue of twilight. What was taking North so long? she wondered. He'd left hours ago! Unless he had forgotten he was supposed to stop by here afterward, and had returned to his own home. Perhaps his mind had been so full of his daughter that he had failed to remember his promise to come here.

Abigail dismissed a sudden flash of jealousy. It was wrong to resent Elise's unexpected reappearance in North's life. Of course, she was glad he had finally found the daughter he had lost so long ago! North was a fine, good-hearted man, and he deserved all the happiness in the world.

But if he managed to reconcile with his child, would he still need her?

Hands trembling slightly, Abigail reached for the tinderbox sitting on the fireplace mantel. After several aborted tries with the steel and flint, she managed to make a spark in the tinder and nursed it into a tiny flame, which she then used to light several candles throughout the parlor.

The moment the task was done, Abigail sat down weakly as thoughts of North again poured through her mind. They had been together for nearly five years now, since the year after her husband had died. North had brought a joy to her life unlike anything she had ever before felt. Her first marriage had been arranged, and though she had been fond of her husband, her feelings

359

for North ran much deeper. All that marred her contentment was the knowledge that he was already joined to another.

It was not, she reflected, that they had done anything wrong. For over twelve years North had been unable to find his wife. What was he to do? Remain celibate for the rest of his life? No matter what other people might think, Abigail knew in her heart that there was nothing immoral about the physical side of their relationship . . . as long as they loved each other.

Fear formed a tight knot in her stomach. At the governor's ball, North had found out from Elise that his wife was dead. His grief had been understandable, since Abigail knew how deeply he had loved Brigitte. But in the days since, why had he not even mentioned their future together?

She was being overly impatient, Abigail tried to tell herself. North was intent on reuniting with his daughter, and once he had resolved that problem, everything else would fall into place.

But what if it didn't? whispered a voice inside her head. What if North transferred all of his affections to Elise?

Abigail squeezed her eyes shut to keep the moisture in them from overflowing. Heaven forbid, but if that should happen, she still had her three married sons and her grandchildren. She would not be alone. But the brave reassurance failed to assuage the ache inside her. Dear God, please, she prayed. She couldn't lose North . . . it would hurt too much.

A sudden rapping on the front door jarred her heart into her throat. He was here at last! Hurrying into the hall, Abigail smoothed the sides of her silver hair and brushed her shaking hands over the lilac silk of her gown before opening the door.

North stood on the stoop, looking so strong and handsome that an ache gripped her chest. The smile on his face told her the meeting with Elise must have gone well. Firmly, Abigail tamped down the fear that gnawed inside her like a ravenous beast.

"Well, don't keep me in suspense," she said lightly. "What happened?"

His grin deepened. Stepping inside, he pulled her into his arms and twirled her around, planting a hard, exultant kiss on her lips. "Abby, it couldn't have gone better! Wait until you hear!" Seizing her hand, he pulled her into the parlor and onto a brocaded couch beside him.

"Have you been at the Fletchers' all this time?" Abigail asked.

"Aye, Elise even asked me to stay for dinner, but I thought 'twould be best to give her some breathing space. Oh, Abby, I was so afraid she would hate me forever! When I explained everything to her and Marc, it took a while, but they truly seemed to understand."

"Who is Marc?"

North squeezed her hands, his face jubilant. "He's my son! I have a son—can you believe it?"

"How can that be?"

"I didn't know it, but Brigitte was pregnant when I left. All these years and I didn't even know about him. Tomorrow he wants to come and see my shop. Who knows, maybe I'll talk him into becoming an apprentice. Just think, I'll have a son to work with me and someone to take over the place someday."

"Oh, North, I'm so glad." It was impossible not to catch his infectious good mood. And she *did* rejoice at his happiness, Abigail thought, despite the nagging fear of losing him.

"It scares me to think how close I came to not ever finding Elise and Marc," North went on. "Can you imagine how it feels, Abby? At last I have my daughter back. It took a lot for her to overcome her mistrust of me, and I can't help but admire her for it."

"She's a lovely girl," Abigail agreed softly. "You have every right to be proud of her."

"The only thing that bothers me is her relationship with Troy Fletcher," North mused. "He returned home while I was still there, and I'm afraid we had a few words before Elise could intervene. All I could think about was what she'd told me before—that she was whoring for him." His face darkened with rage. "Dammit, if Fletcher intends to sleep with my daughter, he'd best marry her first!"

"Do you think he's in love with her?"

"I don't know. Neither of them would talk about it."

"Give Elise a little time. She'll open up to you."

North ran a hand through his hair. "God, I can't help but feel so damn guilty for not being around when my children were growing up. They've been through so much pain because of me. I want to make it up to them, no matter how long it takes."

Abigail put a comforting hand on his arm, though a fierce desire to keep him all to herself made her almost tremble. Icy fingers of dread crept over her skin. Already he was so involved in the lives of his children. Would there still be room in his heart for her?

Suddenly she could not bear looking at him any longer without tears burning her eyes. Rising, she went to the window to stare out into the night. Against the dark glass, the candles scattered throughout the parlor formed glowing pinpricks of light that blurred before her misty gaze.

Footsteps sounded from behind, and then she felt North's strong arms come around her, molding her spine to his chest. The feel of him was both comfort and pain, and tears began to trickle down her cheeks, tasting warm and salty at the corners of her mouth.

"Is something the matter?" he asked gently. "I fear I've been so wrapped up in my own concerns that I've neglected you."

Abigail forced out a light laugh. "Don't be absurd. Naught is wrong."

"But you're trembling."

"I—I should light a fire. The night grows chilly."

He turned her around to face him, lifting her chin when she tried to bury her face in his chest. "Abby, you're crying! Tell me why. Is it something I've done?"

"Nay, I'm just . . . happy for you."

"Come now," he chided softly, wiping away her tears with his fingers. "You can't put me off. There is something bothering you, and I won't rest until I find out what it is."

"'Tis silly. . . ."

"It can't be silly if it troubles you so."

His tender reassurances broke down the last of her resistance. "Oh, North, I'm so frightened," she choked out. "I'm frightened that I'll lose you."

"Lose me?" he repeated with a short, disbelieving laugh. "Whyever would you think that?"

"You have your children now . . . you won't be lonely. I thought . . . you wouldn't need me anymore."

"Oh, Abby." His arms tightened, and he pressed her

363

face against the broadness of his chest, one strong hand stroking her hair. "How could I ever stop needing you? Yes, I'm happy I've found my children, but they couldn't ever replace you in my life."

Abigail looked up at him, afraid to believe he spoke the truth. "But . . . since they're Brigitte's children . . . I mean, I know how much you loved her . . . still love her—"

"Abby, I'm not still in love with Brigitte. Yes, I grieved for her, for the happiness I once shared with her. But she's my past—you're my present and my future."

"You truly mean that?"

"With all my heart," he softly reassured her. "To be perfectly frank, even if I'd found out Brigitte was still alive, I don't know that I could have left you for her. I love you too much to ever let you go."

"Oh, North, I love you, too."

Their lips met in a fervent affirmation of their feelings. Abigail felt a wild surge of elation as his arms hugged her close, his hands moving down her spine to press her hips to his. Eagerly she touched his tongue with hers, aware of a hunger for him that was deeper and richer than anything she had ever before felt. It was a hot desire that was a natural outgrowth of love.

North drew her over to the couch and laid her down, positioning his large frame atop her. "We're getting married," he murmured, planting kisses over her forehead, her cheeks, her jaw. "As soon as possible."

"Are you asking or telling?" she teased, overflowing with happiness.

"Telling," he growled. "And if you've any objections, don't bother expressing them. I've waited too long to call you wife. Far, far too long."

"Such an arrogant beast of a husband you'll be."

"Aye, one who'll keep his woman naked in bed and well satisfied."

Quickly he undressed the both of them. Abigail's heart soared as North again took her mouth in a masterful kiss. His hands touched her breasts, slid down her bare hips. The feel of his hard arousal probing the depths of her womanhood sent spasms of pleasure throbbing through her. Awash with joy, she held nothing back, caressing him, loving him, clinging to him as they drowned in a pulsating tide of passion.

Chapter Twenty-five

The Fletcher house in Williamsburg was dark and silent as Elise slipped out of her bedchamber. She stood for a moment in the hall, letting her eyes adjust to the gloom. The slick wood floor felt cold to her bare feet. Shivering, she wrapped the filmy silk robe more securely around her slender form. The muted chimes of a clock drifted up the stairwell, tolling the hour of two in the morning.

It was time to put an end to her estrangement with Troy.

Her heart fluttered. Ever since the previous day, when she had learned the truth about her parents, she had been comparing their tragic parting to her own relationship with Troy. The more she thought about it, the more she saw that no matter how hard it was for two people in love to resolve their problems, it was vital to make the attempt. Otherwise, a chance at happiness could be lost forever.

Taking a deep breath, she tiptoed through the shadows to Troy's bedchamber. But as her fingers gripped the smooth knob of the door, a flash of doubt made her pause. What about their political differences? If the French and English went to war, as seemed more and more probable every day, how could she live here in the midst of the enemy?

That was a risk she must take, Elise told herself firmly. She would not repeat the mistakes of her parents by letting pride and stubbornness keep her from the man she loved.

She twisted the knob and let herself inside the bedchamber, quietly closing the door behind her. Only a glimmer of moonlight through an unshuttered window relieved the room of total blackness. The faint glow cast patterned shadows over the large four-poster and the man sprawled therein.

Elise drew nearer, her feet silent on the thick carpet. At the side of the bed, she stopped, her pulse rate accelerating. In a restless sleep, Troy had kicked off the quilt, revealing his body in its naked splendor. Her gaze traveled up long legs to the nest of hair that cushioned his relaxed manhood, then roamed higher still, over a flat stomach and broad chest, contoured with lean muscles that gleamed in the pale wash of moonlight.

A thin, jagged scar marred the taut flesh at his waist, as did another one just below his shoulder, where Marc had made his aborted attempt to kill him. Twice Troy had been hurt because of her, and the thought of him dead made Elise shudder.

The ruggedness of his features was softened by slumber. A lock of tawny hair lay across his forehead, and she longed to touch its rough silken texture. She restrained the urge, for a long moment contenting herself with drinking in the sight of him and listening to the quiet sound of his breathing. Then her eyes drifted to his lips, and the memory of his kiss was too enticing to resist.

Sitting down on the edge of the mattress, she reached out to cradle his jaw in her palms, her fingers stroking the slight abrasiveness of his cheeks. Lightly she brushed her mouth against his. The familiar leather-and-sandalwood scent of him made a quiver of excitement run through her. Leaning more fully against him, she let her silk-covered breasts feather across the hardness of his chest, the loose fall of her hair slipping over her shoulders to tease his skin.

Troy shifted position, a groan rumbling inside his chest as his lips opened to her tongue. His arms crept around her, his hands sliding over her gossamer nightgown, tentatively exploring her feminine shape as if he believed her to be a figment of fantasy, a product of some erotic dream. Then he opened his eyes to look at her. Meeting his moon-silvered gaze, Elise pressed another soft kiss to his lips.

"Witch," he murmured against her mouth, his voice drowsy. "You shouldn't be here."

She kissed him again. "But you invited me."

With a sudden frown, he pushed himself into a half-sitting position. His jaw was set and hard, his chest rigid beneath her fingers.

"Elise, I don't know what nonsense it is you're spouting," he said coldly, "but I want to see your backside heading out of this room right now."

"But you don't understand," she cried. "You told me I'd be welcome in your bed under one condition, and that's why I'm here."

An eternity of silence stretched out, and Elise felt her heart pulse painfully. Was she doing the right thing? There was still time to retract her words, to laugh and say she jested. And oh, God, what if he rejected her? What if he'd gotten fed up with her refusals and had changed his mind about wedding her?

"You'd better tell me precisely what you mean," he commanded hoarsely.

She took a deep breath to shore up her courage. "I'm saying that . . . I'm ready to marry you."

Troy stared at her for a long moment, then a light came into his eyes, a light that made her heart give a wild leap.

"Oh, God, Elise." He pulled her tight against him and buried his face in her hair. His hands trembled as he held her in a cherishing embrace. "I must be dreaming. I'm going to wake up in a moment, aren't I?"

"Then we're both dreaming—together." Happiness surged through her as she laid her head against his chest. She wasn't making a mistake, she couldn't be! Surely the love that swelled her heart was enough to overcome any obstacle.

Troy lifted her chin. "What made you change your mind?"

"Talking to my father, realizing how bitterly he regretted leaving Maman. When Papa left us, Maman told me to follow my head and never my heart. For so long, I followed that advice, but now I know she spoke out of anger and hurt." Elise lay her hand against his cheek. "Oh, Troy, I don't want that to happen to us. I don't want to look back someday and wish that I hadn't been too proud and stubborn to share my life with you."

"And my being English—?"

"It doesn't matter anymore. My hatred for the English was because of my father, but now that I've lived in Virginia, I can see there are both good and bad people here, just as there are anywhere. How could I ever hate people like Pandora and Jason and Mirella?"

"What if the hostilities between England and France should come to war?"

Elise took a deep breath. It was the question that plagued her the most. "Let's not think such thoughts," she urged, seeking to distract him by sliding a hand over the taut muscles of his chest. "The outside world isn't important, not right now."

He caught her hand and kissed the palm. "Then what say you to setting a wedding date? How does tomorrow sound?"

"Tomorrow!" she exclaimed. "But the preparations—"

Troy released a deep sigh. "Then the next day, if you must force me to wait so long."

"But . . . oh, you're teasing." Catching the gleam of devilment in his eyes, Elise slapped at him playfully.

"Aye, I'll grant you a few weeks," he grumbled. "I know how you women must have your fancy wedding gowns and fripperies. You'll make me a pauper before I can even say 'I do.'"

"I shan't spend your money—"

He silenced her lips with his fingers, his face tenderly solemn in the moonlight. "Little angel, everything I own belongs to you, too. And the sooner I can announce to everyone in the colony that you're my wife, the happier I'll be."

An unexpected flood of misgivings overwhelmed her. What would his friends and neighbors think when he told them he was marrying a penniless Frenchwoman? She couldn't bear it if they shunned him because of her.

"Troy, are you certain—? There are so many other women more suited to you."

His arms tightened around her. "More suited? Who could be more suited to me than the woman I love?"

"But you deserve a lady—someone who knows how to do and say all the right things."

"Elise, you *are* a lady, the only lady I've ever asked to be my wife."

"But sometimes I feel as though I don't belong here," she continued doggedly. "The frontier is all I know. I don't know how to run a large household or give parties or . . . or even how to flutter my fan properly."

"I have Mrs. MacGuire to run my house, and Mirella or Pandora can coach you on the rest."

"I don't know. . . ."

"Well, I do," he countered. "What I *don't* know is why we're arguing when all I want is to make love to you."

He pressed her down on the pillows and his lips descended to claim hers. His tongue plunged into the depths of her mouth, filling her with the taste and scent of him. All of her uncertainties vanished in a rush of sensual and emotional awareness. How she loved this man!

Overjoyed, Elise yielded to his magic, returning his kiss with all of the frustrated need that had been bottled up inside her for weeks. She arched her hips to his, aching for the ultimate joining that would make them one. Beneath her exploring fingers, his flesh was strong and smoothly muscled, and through the gossamer fabric that covered her breasts, she could feel the quickened beat of his heart. The hard masculine fire that burned into her thigh lit an answering flame inside her.

He slid off her robe, sitting up to peel away her nightgown. "Lift your arms," he commanded softly. "I want to see you naked."

371

Wordlessly she complied, letting him draw the wisp of silk over her head. Then he sat back on his heels, his powerful chest lifting and falling, his eyes a dark jade in the moonlight.

"You're not going to suddenly tell me you were only joking, are you?" he asked, his deep voice half-teasing, half-serious.

In a flood of tenderness, she reached out for him, longing to feel his weight covering her. "Oh, Troy, *je t'aime*. I want to marry you more than anything else in the world."

"Praise God," he said with a glimmer of humor. "I was beginning to wonder how much longer I could last without having you in my bed."

He bent down and kissed her hard, his chest hairs rubbing her sensitive nipples. Flattening his palm over her stomach, he kissed a path down the delicate arch of her throat and to her breasts, where he suckled the hardened bud. She clasped his head to encourage the seductive sensation. When he slid a hand between her legs, caressing the warm wetness of her desire, she couldn't suppress a moan of unabashed pleasure.

"Sweet, sweet angel," he muttered hoarsely. "You're mine at last . . . forever."

She was too caught up in his magic to form a reply. With every stroke of his fingers, he was drawing her more deeply under his spell. He was so virile, so potent. In wanton eagerness, she writhed beneath him, her nails grazing his back. Just when she thought she could bear no more, he slid inside her, filling her so completely she cried out with the joy of it. The throbbing fire in her belly swelled with each thrust of his hard body until waves of release shattered her body, the rippling shocks washing her in the most intense pleasure she had ever felt. Weak and trembling, she clasped him tightly as he made his own final plunge into passion's sweet abyss.

Scattered raindrops swept across the Palace Green. In the distance, lightning flashed against a pewter-gray sky, followed a few seconds later by the angry rumble of thunder. Lined up along a white picket fence, late-blooming tulips bowed their scarlet heads under the onslaught of a sudden gust of wind.

Elise wandered down the street, feeling as though she were floating. The promise of rain in the air enhanced her feeling of exhilaration. She welcomed the thrill and excitement of the coming storm, so reminiscent of the passion she and Troy had shared the previous night. The satisfying ache in her loins was the fruit of long hours they'd spent making love before falling into an exhausted sleep wrapped in each other's arms.

As she turned onto Duke of Gloucester Street, she saw only a few people out shopping who were brave enough to risk the impending shower. Elise blinked as a raindrop struck her lashes. Pulling her cloak tight against the chilly breeze, she hurried down the brick walk to her destination, the silversmith shop with the small sign in a corner of the window that read: Northrup Kingsley, Propr.

A tiny bell tinkled overhead as she opened the door. From out of the back room came Marc, his thin frame swathed in a white apron. "May I help . . . ?" The polite smile on his face grew warmer. "Elise! What are you doing here?"

"I came to see you and Papa."

"Tiens! Come back here with me, then." As she stepped around the counter to follow him through the door at the rear of the shop, Marc added, "I wondered where you were at breakfast this morning. You must have slept late."

"I . . . yes, I did, as a matter of fact."

Elise knew he was only making idle conversation, yet a blush bathed her cheeks. Heaven forbid that her brother should learn where she had spent the night. Though she was far from ashamed of her actions, she preferred to keep private the intimacy she had shared with Troy. It was something close to her heart and very, very special.

The room they stepped into was large and airy. The venetian blinds had been drawn up to let in every bit of natural light the gloomy day had to offer. At the far end of the room was a forge, where two apprentices were hammering a silver ingot into a flat sheet. North Kingsley sat before an anvil on a workbench by a window, using a mallet to carefully shape a sheet of lustrous metal into a cup.

"Father, we have a visitor," Marc said.

Kingsley looked up, a smile softening his rough-hewn features. Quickly he set aside the half-finished vessel and strode over to them, wiping his hands on his apron. "Good morning, daughter. What brings you here? Let me take your cloak."

He reached for the garment, but Elise kept it on. "Nay, I shan't stay long because of the weather. I only stopped by to tell you there'll be a small party tonight at the Fletchers'. I would like it very much if you would attend."

"Of course, I will," her father replied. "Is there a particular occasion we're celebrating?"

Her lips curved into a mysterious smile. "Troy and I have an announcement to make."

"An announcement?" North queried, his dark eyes narrowed in speculation. "Come, you cannot keep me in suspense. Surely your own father deserves advance knowledge."

Elise only laughed and shook her head.

"*Eh, bien!*" Marc exclaimed. "Perhaps you and Troy will marry?"

Elise refused to give them even a hint. Still smiling, she wagged a finger at them both. "No one will know until the moment arrives, the both of you included."

"I should like to bring someone with me, if I may," North said, a hint of hesitation in his voice.

"The woman you were with at the governor's ball?" Elise guessed, remembering the petite lady who had entered on his arm.

"Aye. Her name is Abigail Banks, and I want you and Marc to meet her." He paused before adding, "I would be greatly honored if the both of you would come to our wedding next week."

Elise stared at him, startled. Her father was remarrying! She searched her heart for resentment, but found only happiness for him. After so many years alone, he deserved another chance at love.

Sensing that he feared her reaction, she sought to give him reassurance by putting her arms around him. "Oh, Papa, that's wonderful news. Of course, we'll come."

Marc seconded her words as he shook his father's hand. Elise was glad to see that the two of them were now getting along so well. Love, she mused, was a much more satisfying emotion than hatred.

"Are you certain you won't wait out the foul weather

here?" North asked.

"Nay, if I hurry, I can make it home before the rain starts. I have preparations to see to for tonight's party."

Reluctantly Elise took her leave and went back out into the growing storm. She stood before the shop, hesitating. The wind whipped the branches of a nearby oak tree and tugged at her hood, blowing it off her head. Lightning ripped across a charcoal sky and the growl of thunder rang closer now. As of yet only an occasional raindrop struck her cheeks.

An impetuous decision sent her scurrying down the walk, not in the direction of the Fletcher house, as she'd told her father, but to the Capitol building, some two blocks distant. This was about the hour Troy had thought his meeting with the council would end and, if she rushed, she might catch him on his way home. The prospect of spending a few stolen minutes with the man she loved thrilled her heart.

By the time she reached the stately brick building that housed the government of Virginia colony, chilly droplets were spattering her more frequently. Looking up, she saw a black-skinned servant on a narrow walkway high atop a white cupola, struggling to lower the British flag that flapped wildly in the growing gale.

Preoccupied with the slave's dilemma, she barely glanced at the man who emerged from a side door. Then the shock of his identity made her stop dead in her tracks. Brown eyes, brown hair, rigid posture, and the white coat and gold-trimmed blue waistcoat of a French officer.

It couldn't be . . . and yet it was.

"Yves Larousse," she whispered.

Chapter Twenty-six

At that very moment, the heavens opened to a deluge of cold rain. Yves snatched Elise's hand and pulled her inside the building, out of the downpour. Putting a protective arm around her shoulders, he steered her into the first door off the hall.

The handsomely paneled chamber they entered was that of a court of law. Two rows of wooden benches were lined up before a railing, beyond which the far end of the room was curved into a half-circle, where judge and jury presided. Rain lashed the trio of round windows in the wall behind the magistrate's high-backed chair. There were papers strewn about; the court must have recessed for the noon meal.

Yves turned Elise to face him. She gazed at him mutely as he untied the bow of her wet cloak, his fingers impersonal, his face solemn. When he had removed the garment and tossed it over a bench, he put his hands on his hips and returned her stare, his spine ramrod-stiff.

"I wondered if we would ever meet again," he said.

There was a thread of mockery in his voice, but Elise

was still too startled to take more than passing notice. "Yves, what are you doing here?" she choked out, automatically speaking in French as he had done.

"I've come on a diplomatic mission from the commander of the French forces. I volunteered because I wanted the chance to find you, to take you back with me. But you appear to be doing quite well for yourself."

With a hint of contempt, his dark gaze raked her costly gown of amber silk. Elise drew back as though stung. He implied she was a fallen woman, a whore! Anger blazed through her, coupled with a trace of hurt.

"How dare you pass judgment on me! You know why I had to come here to Virginia—to save my brother's life."

"And you threw away your own life in the process."

"What was I to do, let Marc rot in prison for attempted murder?"

"You should have let him suffer the consequences of his own actions, as any man must."

"He's not a man, he's a twelve-year-old boy!"

"That's old enough to be responsible for himself."

Elise had forgotten how inflexible Yves could be. "How ironic that you brought me in here," she said bitterly, waving a hand at the courtroom. "You've tried me and found me guilty without heeding a word of my testimony."

"If I speak harshly, 'tis only because I care what happens to you," he said stiffly.

"Then tell me this, Yves, if you were so concerned for my welfare, why has it taken so long for you to come after me? Why did a boy of twelve possess more courage than you in that respect?"

Yves had the good grace to look ashamed. A dark flush stole over his cheeks and he glanced away as if embarrassed. When he met her gaze again, there was a hint of pleading in his eyes. "I was given a specific order not to follow you," he said in a low voice. "I had to obey—I had no choice."

"You did have a choice, but disobedience would have meant a tarnish on your sterling military record," Elise taunted. "And that meant more to you than me."

Lightning slashed across the leaden sky beyond the windows, the eerie glow illuminating a mixture of regret and misery on his face. Her heart thawed. Yves could not change the man he was, so why did she bother arguing with him?

He stepped closer and grasped her by the shoulders. "Elise, I love you. I'm still willing to marry you, even though your reputation is sullied."

Despite her resolve, his slur on her character was annoying. "How generous of you, " she mocked. "But what makes you think *I* still wish to marry *you?*"

Yves looked genuinely startled. "What are you saying? That you would stay here with that Englishman rather than be my lawful wife?"

She twisted out of his hands and took a step back. "I happen to be in love with 'that Englishman.' He and I plan to wed next month."

For a moment the only sounds were the rain pelting the window glass and the booming of thunder. Then Yves uttered hoarsely, *"Pas possible?* You'll abandon your homeland, have children who will never know of their French heritage?"

The thought of bearing Troy's baby sent a thrill

through Elise. "Should I be so blessed, they will learn what is necessary." Quickly she told him the truth about her father, in hopes that Yves would better understand her position.

"*Alors,*" he said in disgust, "you've become a true English lady."

A twinge of guilt assailed her. "Nay, that isn't so."

"But you dress like one, act like one, and now you're even marrying one of the enemy."

"That doesn't mean I've forgotten I'm French."

"Then prove it."

"What do you mean?"

Yves eyed her speculatively. "This Monsieur Fletcher whom you plan to marry is an advisor to the governor's council. You could go through his papers and obtain information for me."

She gasped. "You're asking me to be a spy? To turn traitor against my intended husband?"

"Traitor to the English, but heroine to the French. Which shall it be?"

Elise swallowed hard, her nails biting into the thin silk of her sleeves. What he proposed was impossible! And yet . . . to which country did she owe her loyalty— France or Britain?

I've heard rumors that the French already have a spy placed high in the government," she hedged. "Why do you need me?"

"Should our other informant be uncovered, we'll need a substitute." Yves shrugged. "And who knows? You might be able to turn up something our other spy misses."

"Who is the other spy?"

380

He chuckled. "Nay, you'll never be privy to that secret—'tis for the protection of the both of you. So, are you willing, Elise? Or will you betray the country of your birth?"

She stared at him, her insides roiling with a turmoil that rivaled the storm outside. On the one hand, she felt sympathy for the French cause, but on the other, she despised the thought of deceiving Troy.

"Can you not leave me out of these political maneuverings?" she pleaded. "All I wish is to live my life in peace."

"There will be no peace for any of us in the months to come," Yves said. "We French must reclaim the frontier that rightfully belongs to us."

"Is there not enough land for everyone? Why must one side or the other have it all?"

"'Tis French land," he repeated adamantly. "We will not lie down like cowards and let English settlers steal it away."

"And you'll kill them if necessary," Elise said, feeling a shudder of revulsion as she recalled the scalped family she and Troy had encountered in the wilderness. "Innocent men, women, and children alike, whose only crime is a desire to eke out a living."

"'Tis regrettable, but that is the way of war."

She was sickened by his callousness. "It hasn't come to war yet."

"But it will soon. Already Lieutenant-Colonel Washington is mustering forces to march on the French." A satisfied smile touched his lips. "But the English haven't acted quickly enough. They built their puny Fort Prince George at the juncture of La Belle

Rivière, but we captured it a week ago. We renamed it Fort Duquesne, in honor of the esteemed governor-general of Canada."

Elise had mixed feelings about the news. At one time she had been so certain of her allegiance. Now she was no longer sure of which side she favored.

Restlessly, she walked to a window and gazed out into the rain. After a moment, the sound of Yves's footsteps approached from behind.

"If you aid the French cause," he said, "the conflict will be over so much the sooner."

She didn't turn. "I don't know that I can be a part of such death and destruction."

"I'll give you time to reconsider," Yves said. "Should you need to reach me, I'll be staying at the Raleigh Tavern for at least a few days. Just remember, you'll have to choose sides eventually." The firm step of his boots moved away, then the courtroom door closed with a quiet click.

Elise continued to look outside, watching as Yves's square-shouldered figure headed away from the Capitol building. Even in the slowing rain, he never abandoned that stiff military stance. Suddenly she realized that he might have been her husband by now had she remained at Fort LeBoeuf. The thought filled her with a faint sense of horror. It was not that he was such a terrible man . . . it was simply that he was not Troy.

Remembering her reunion with Troy the previous night, she felt a knee-weakening flood of emotion. Aye, she assured herself, she was doing the right thing in marrying him.

Yet a tiny seed of doubt flourished in her mind. She

could surrender to his love with all her heart and soul, but how could she embrace his political beliefs?

That night a throng of guests gathered at the Fletcher house to hear the happy couple announce their betrothal. Cries of congratulations filled the air. Snifters of brandy and Madeira wine were distributed by beaming servants, and the clink of glasses mingled with the buzz of excited conversation.

Caroline Whitman stood in a corner, feeling like an outcast. Her heart throbbed with shock and pain. She wanted nothing more than to slink away to some private place and give free rein to the tears that pricked her eyes. Troy really didn't love her! He was going to marry that copper-haired Frenchwoman!

Her hopes swirled away like ashes in the wind. Why did she have to hurt when everyone else was so happy? It just wasn't fair, Caroline wailed inside. Didn't anyone care about her? Couldn't they see she had been denied the only man she had ever wanted?

Feeling the beginnings of a righteous anger, she grabbed a glass from a passing servant, mutinously ignoring the fact that the brandy was meant for the men in the gathering. She took a healthy swig, nearly gagging as the liquor burned down her throat. At least it gave her an excuse for the tears in her eyes, she thought with dark humor.

Swirling the amber liquid in her snifter, Caroline stared through the crowd. Troy had his arm around that hussy's waist, and then he leaned down to whisper something in her ear. Elise blushed and touched him on the chest, murmuring something in reply.

Jealousy pierced Caroline like a burning sword. She couldn't let him slip away so easily. She had to do something to get him back. If only there were some way to discredit that woman in his eyes. . . .

A plan began to form in her mind. The corners of her mouth curled upward as she considered the possibilities. She brushed off a twinge of conscience, arguing to herself that she only meant to save Troy from a miserable marriage. After all, if war broke out, Elise would side with the French.

"Caro, I don't like that look on your face."

She whirled around to see a tall man lounging against the pale Chinese-papered wall, staring at her suspiciously. "Zach! You frightened me!"

"I hope I frightened away all thought of whatever scheme it was you were concocting in that pretty little head of yours."

She opened her fan and began to flutter it furiously over her hot cheeks. "Why, I don't know what you mean."

"I think you do. So let me give you a word of warning: Should I catch you doing anything at all to harm Troy and Elise's happiness, I'll turn you over my knee and administer the walloping your father should have given you a long time ago."

"You wouldn't dare!"

"Just try me." His piercing dark eyes bored into her for another moment, then he pivoted and strode away.

Caroline closed the fan with a snap. She gulped down the remainder of her brandy, firmly squashing the secret thrill that rose in her at the thought of Zach's touching her. The nerve of that man! Just because they'd been friends for so long didn't give him any right to tell her what she could or couldn't do.

As her midnight-blue eyes returned to the newly betrothed couple, Caroline pursed her lips stubbornly. Yes, she would follow through with her plan as soon as possible. There was too much at stake to worry about the consequences.

Chapter Twenty-seven

Twilight draped the woods on either side of the dirt road. The soft sigh of a breeze riffled the underbrush and swirled the scent of wild jasmine through the deepening darkness. A sleepy bird twittered in a dogwood, then swooped through the lavender shadows to seek out another perch, in the glossy leaves of a magnolia tree with milky buds about to burst into bloom.

Suddenly a foreign sound intruded the woodland scene; it was the rattle of a carriage and the clip-clopping hooves of four sleek horses.

Elise gazed out the window of the swaying vehicle, wishing she could feel as peaceful as the passing landscape. Tonight there was an engagement party for her and Troy at Thousand Oaks, the plantation that belonged to Caroline's father. Caroline had stopped by the day after the betrothal announcement to deliver the invitation, and Troy had deemed it a good excuse to leave Williamsburg for a short time and check out a problem on his own plantation that the overseer had notified him of.

Fleetingly Elise wondered if Caroline had some sort of mischief planned for tonight. Why had the woman given up on Troy so easily? Perhaps it was silly to be so suspicious, she chided herself. This party might simply be Caroline's way of yielding gracefully to an opponent's victory.

Elise was conscious of the reassuring warmth of Troy's large hand curled around hers, resting against her rose-pink silk gown. As they rode in companionable silence, his commanding presence captivated her senses. Somehow he had become intrinsically wound into her heart and soul. The happiness of these past weeks had assured her she was making the right decision in wedding him. And yet . . .

A sudden frown wrinkled her brow. Ever since the meeting with Yves, she had wondered uneasily if her love for Troy outweighed her loyalty to France. Though nothing had happened on the frontier since the French had seized the fort at the forks of the Ohio, the threat of war still hung in the air. Both sides appeared to be waiting for the other to make that final plunge into open conflict. Elise murmured a fervent prayer that some miracle would happen to end the hostility, before she was forced to make a choice between the country of her birth and that of her intended husband.

"Why the somber look?" Troy slid his hand out of hers and put his fingers under her chin, gently turning her face toward him.

Elise gazed into his jade eyes for a moment, at a loss for words. The deep purple light of evening illuminated the firm lines of his cheekbones and jaw, the strength in his broad chest and shoulders. The ruffles of the white shirt beneath his dark blue coat emphasized his rugged masculinity.

She swallowed painfully. Heaven forbid Troy should guess the doubts that wrenched at her heart. She hadn't told him of her meeting with Yves. When he had mentioned the Frenchman's presence in Virginia, she had pretended surprise, afraid to risk jeopardizing their newfound happiness.

"Something is bothering you," Troy stated with a frown. "Won't you tell me about it?"

A lie rose to her lips. "I—I was but wondering why Caroline would wish to give a party for us."

"What do you mean? She and I have known each other since childhood."

"But she wanted you for herself."

He shrugged. "In the past, aye, but she has sense enough to know when to give up."

"Are you so sure?"

A devilish grin tilted the corner of his mouth. "And are you so jealous you cannot cease worrying about a woman who means naught to me?"

His fingers stroked along her jaw and began to toy with an errant strand of copper hair. Arousal rippled through her as soft and warm as the breeze outside the rocking carriage. Elise drew in a deep, shuddering sigh.

"*Oui*, I am jealous," she admitted. She snuggled against his hard frame, tilting her head back to look at him, acutely aware of his male presence. "I'm jealous of any other woman who wants you. If Caroline still harbors plans to have you, she'll have to get past me first."

Troy chuckled, his arms tightening around her. "My sweet, fierce angel. I'm glad to hear I won't have to fight off the ladies all by myself."

"So you expect I will have some rivalry tonight, mmm?"

A twinkle lit his eyes. "Well, this party might be my last chance to sow some wild oats before you place the shackles of matrimony on me."

"Before I—!" she said in a huff. "*You* were the one who persuaded *me* to wed!"

"Be that as it may, you wouldn't begrudge a man one last love affair, would you?"

Elise pretended to consider the notion. "I suppose not—providing I have the same privilege."

"You'd doom some poor bastard to an early grave?"

The feel of his fingers doing delicious things along her lace-edged bodice was most distracting. "And what is that supposed to mean?"

"I mean," he growled into her ear, "I'd wring the neck of the man who dared touch you."

"Mmm. But then you'd be thrown into prison."

"True." He cocked his head, studying her with a crooked grin. "However, I did just have a thought. If we both want one last love affair before our wedding next week, what say you to having it together?"

"If you're certain that would satisfy your need for wild adventure," she teased.

"I've never met a woman who drives me as wild as you do."

He bent to kiss the milky swells of her breasts just above her bodice. The warm wetness of his tongue sent shivers of need cascading through her body. Weak and fevered, Elise clasped his shoulders for support.

"You'll disappoint all the other ladies tonight," she whispered.

"To hell with the other ladies. You're more woman

than any of them."

He reached beneath her hooped skirts, sliding a hand up the silk stocking that covered her calf, and caressed her intimately. The magic touch of his fingers made her twist and moan, her breath coming quicker. The depth of emotion she felt was stunning. She wanted him here, *now*.

She reached for his breeches, but at that moment, the carriage swayed sharply as it turned a corner. With a muffled curse, Troy stopped her fingers from venturing any farther.

"By the devil, this is poor timing," he said with wry humor.

Following his gaze through the coach window, Elise saw an imposing house outlined against the amethyst sky. Numerous candles glowed inside the panes of glass that dotted the stately brick facade. She released a sigh of acute disappointment. This must be Thousand Oaks, Caroline's home.

"It appears we shall have to wait until later," Troy said, reluctantly readjusting her skirts.

Elise remembered they were staying the night to avoid the long ride back in the dark. "Until *much* later," she grumbled. "I rather doubt Caroline will be so kind as to arrange for us to sleep in the same bedchamber."

He laughed and stroked her cheek. "My passionate angel. There'll be plenty of time for loving once we're married. In truth, you'll probably tire of me and wish you'd wed that Frenchman of yours."

There was a trace of vulnerability hidden in his light tone. Did he truly believe she might leave him? Suddenly Elise felt a sense of foreboding, dark and hideous. She caught at his chest.

"Nay, Troy, that could never happen. I can't lose

you . . . I couldn't live without you!"

"You won't have to." He pulled her close, pressing his lips to her hair. "I won't ever let you go. No matter what happens, I want you with me forever."

His deep, impassioned voice soothed her fears. Against her cheek, she felt the reassuring beat of his heart, and the comfort of his embrace lulled that peculiar feeling of dread. By the time the carriage pulled up in front of the house, she felt calm once more. Troy loved her and nothing could change that.

He opened the door and stepped out, taking her by the arm to aid her descent. His appreciative look bolstered her confidence.

"Darling," he murmured into her ear, "you're going to outshine all the other ladies tonight."

"*Merci, m'sieur.*"

Glowing with happiness, she smiled back at him. Then Caroline was gliding down the wide porch steps in a swirl of ultramarine satin that enhanced her lovely eyes and porcelain skin. A cluster of ribbons adorned one side of her fashionably powdered hair.

"Welcome!" she gushed. "I'm so very pleased you've arrived."

Inserting herself between them, Caroline took Elise and Troy by the arm, chattering gaily as they entered the house. Even after the months she had lived in Virginia, Elise couldn't help feeling a bit overwhelmed by the elegance of Caroline's house. Candlelight from a crystal chandelier in the foyer glinted off the Italian marble floor. A fine French tapestry adorned one wall, while gilt-framed portraits scattered the other walls. The sounds of laughter and the clinking of glasses came from the drawing room beyond.

Caroline guided them into the chamber filled with guests. When she clapped her hands for attention, the noise died down so that her voice could be heard.

"I should like to announce the arrival of our guests of honor, Troy Fletcher, our neighbor and friend," Caroline lightly tapped his arm with her fan, "and, for those of you who haven't yet made her acquaintance, on my other side is Troy's French fiancée, Mademoiselle Elise d'Evereaux."

There were a few scowls and mutterings amidst the cries of felicitation. Elise felt a flash of dismay. With war on the horizon, mention of anyone or anything French was like putting a flame to gunpowder. Not for a moment did she believe that the reference to her heritage had been by chance. Her suspicions had been correct; Caroline hadn't given up on Troy.

There was an almost nervous excitement about the woman as she fetched them glasses of punch. Her dark blue eyes seemed overbright, her voice a trifle too animated.

After a few moments, Zach strolled up and took the protesting Caroline by the arm to the next room, where a trio of musicians played.

Troy bent and whispered teasingly in Elise's ear, "Don't worry, it doesn't matter to *me* that you've suffered the misfortune of being raised a French-woman."

"And it doesn't matter to *me* that you were born a conceited beast," she retorted.

He chuckled; then other guests swarmed around to demand their attention. They greeted many well-wishers, including Pandora, who had traveled to the party with Jason and Mirella, and North Kingsley, with his new wife, Abby.

"I thought you two left for Alexandria," Elise exclaimed.

North enveloped her in a quick hug. "We turned around and came back so we wouldn't miss your wedding festivities."

"Aye," Abby agreed, giving her husband a look of adoration. "We decided to stay close to home for a while. There'll be time enough later for pleasure trips."

"And besides," added North, "so long as we're together, we can be happy no matter where we are."

As they strolled off arm in arm, Elise felt a lump form in her throat. Would the love she and Troy shared weather the storms to come? Or would he someday regret marrying a woman who hadn't been raised in his social class, a woman whose political beliefs clashed with his?

She was glad that Troy was at her side, speaking to a neighbor, when Richard Whitman approached. Caroline's father was dressed superbly, in tan breeches and a maroon coat with gold buttons. Yet despite his appearance of a gentleman, there was something in his dark eyes that made Elise shiver.

"I see congratulations are in order," said Whitman. "When is the happy occasion to take place?"

Troy slid an arm around Elise's waist and flashed her a warm smile. "The ceremony is at Bruton Parish Church on Thursday next. You and Caro should have received your invitation by now."

"Ah, well, I'm sure we have and my daughter simply forgot to inform me," Whitman said with a dismissing wave of the hand. "Of course, we'll come to the wedding. Let's only hope that war doesn't break out first."

"Have you heard any more news from the frontier?"

Troy asked.

"Only that the French have more than a thousand men at the forks of the Ohio. Compare that to the pitiful hundred and fifty-nine Washington was able to muster."

"Has he had any more luck getting horses and supplies?"

Whitman shook his bewigged head. "Nay, and not only that, the officers are protesting the low pay. Just yesterday the governor received a letter from Washington pleading for more funds to avoid mass resignation. I shall have to leave here early on the morrow to attend an emergency meeting of the council. I was to inform you tonight that Dinwiddie has also requested your presence."

"Damn right I'll go," Troy growled. "I'll do everything I can to influence the council to support Washington. If we have no troops, the war will be over before it even starts."

Whitman shrugged. "You must understand, our hands are tied. The people are already grumbling over what they call excessive taxation."

Troy gave a cynical laugh. "And so the politicians may well lose the war in their eagerness to win the next election."

"Perhaps," Whitman said noncommitally. "Be that as it may, I've a copy of Washington's letter locked in my desk, should you care to peruse it yourself."

"Thank you, I would."

Elise thought Troy had forgotten her presence until he turned and tenderly stroked a finger across her cheek. "Have you any objection, little angel? Word of honor, I'll return in just a few minutes."

"I'll be fine," she assured him with a smile.

As soon as they were gone, she went in search of another glass of punch. Refreshment tables were set up in the dining room. A supper would be served at midnight, but for now, there was an assortment of pastries and cakes, in addition to the finest wines and liqueurs.

Elise was sipping on an iced concoction of honey and brandy when she noticed something sounded different. Instead of the usual revelry, an angry buzzing of whispers swept the gathering. Even the music had stopped.

The crowd parted and Caroline came sauntering through, a smirking smile on her face. The glass slipped out of Elise's fingers and crashed to the floor. The stiff-shouldered man at Caroline's side was Yves Larousse!

A liveried servant leaped forward to wipe the puddle of sticky punch from the wood floor while another daubed at the liquid spattering the rose-pink silk of Elise's skirts. She scarcely noticed them. Whatever was Yves, a French officer, doing at a party for the cream of Virginia society?

Caroline answered the unspoken question. "Elise, dear, I met this French gentleman in town, and when I heard you two were once so well acquainted, why, I felt sure you'd want me to invite him."

"How very thoughtful of you," Elise said through gritted teeth. She glared at Yves, but he only regarded her with an impassive expression.

"Yes, wasn't it? Well, I'll leave you two alone. I'm sure you have plenty to talk about."

With a wave of the hand, Caroline swept away in a rustle of starched petticoats.

Elise felt her cheeks grow hot. Everyone was staring at them, and that was precisely what Caroline had intended. Fury rose in her. There was no graceful way out of the situation short of being rude to Yves, and she could not—*would* not—renounce him simply because that was what was expected of a lady about to wed one of the colony's most prominent businessmen. She motioned Yves over to a window opened to the cool spring breezes. Thankfully, the music began to play again, and most of the guests resumed dancing and drinking.

"What are you doing here?" she hissed for his ears alone.

He shrugged. "I was invited."

"That isn't what I mean and you know it."

"Perhaps I wanted the chance to approach you again and see if you'd changed your mind about spying for France."

"Hush! There may be people here who speak French." Elise glanced around, but there was no one close enough to eavesdrop. At least Yves had had the good sense not to wear his military uniform here; that might have been the spark that would have set off the powderkeg.

"I had to take the risk—for France and for your own good," he said urgently. "In a few days, I'll be leaving, as soon as the council meets and drafts a reply to the letter I delivered. Elise, you must do your part to help France regain its rightful lands! Taking the side of the British will make you a traitor to your own country. I cannot walk away and let you ruin your life so!"

It was the most impassioned speech she had ever heard from him. Doubts churned inside her head. Where was her strongest loyalty, to Troy or to her homeland?

"As I told you before, I will take neither side."

Yves regarded her shrewdly. "This Mademoiselle Whitman, she wants Troy Fletcher for herself, *n'est-ce pas?*"

396

Elise lifted her shoulders casually, denying the tiny jolt of jealousy she felt. "So what if she does?"

"So women like that will try and try until they get what they want. Is that the sort of life you want to lead, always wondering if your husband is being faithful to you?"

"I trust Troy."

"But you're from a different social class. Take a good look at yourself, Elise. You don't belong at such a fancy *soirée.*"

"My father is the son of an English earl."

Yves shook his head impatiently. "Blood doesn't matter—you were raised to live a simple life on the frontier. You're a diversion to Fletcher now, something new and different. What if someday he tires of you and wishes he'd married one of these ladies here?"

"That won't happen!"

She bit her lip and turned her eyes toward the window, seeing the elegantly dressed crowd reflected on the night-darkened glass. Despite her denial, Yves had touched upon one of her deepest fears. She had never felt as though she fit into Troy's life. Yes, she had learned enough to give the outward appearance of a lady, but she didn't *feel* like one inside. Would Troy see that someday and wish he'd chosen someone else?

Yves reached out and took her hands in his. *"Chérie,* I speak so frankly because I want only for you to be happy." He hesitated, then added softly, "If you won't agree to spy, at least return to the fort with me. My offer of marriage is still open."

Confused, Elise gazed into his dark eyes. The sincerity in his voice was unmistakable. He truly did believe he was helping her, she realized. For a fleeting instant, she was tempted to go with him, to escape this world where she would always feel like a misfit.

Then she saw Troy and Richard Whitman coming toward them through the crowd. Her doubts swirled away like smoke in the wind. Surely their love was strong enough to overcome any obstacles the future might hold. Pulling away from Yves, she reached out to Troy.

He slid an arm around her waist. "Elise, I've been looking all over for you."

Troy shot Yves a cool glance without relinquishing his possessive hold on her. He was jealous! Elise realized, half-amused, half-irritated. Did he really think she might be interested in another man?

Richard Whitman was also scowling at Yves. For a moment she fancied a peculiar look passed between the two men, then Whitman's voice cut through the air.

"Might I ask what a Frenchman is doing in my home?" he demanded coldly.

Yves' expression was inscrutable. "Mademoiselle Whitman, your daughter, invited me."

"If that is so, 'twas done without my permission. I must ask you to take your leave now, lest I be forced to take more drastic measures in ridding this house of you."

Yves accepted the insulting words with a brief bow. "As you wish. *Excusez-moi, mademoiselle, messieurs.*"

He flashed Elise a final piercing look before turning on his heel and marching away, his shoulders squared proudly. The crowd parted to make way for him, the gentlemen staring tight-lipped, the ladies whispering to one another behind their spread fans.

Elise felt a spurt of anger that mellowed to a reluctant understanding. Of course these Britishers mistrusted Yves. To them, he was the enemy.

And how did they see her?

She tossed her chin up. Whatever suspicions they murmured, she wouldn't let them bother her. Tonight was the celebration of her betrothal to Troy. Nothing anyone said or did could mar their joy in each other.

Then Troy whirled her away to the dance floor and there was no more time to think. With a sudden gaiety of spirit, she clung to him as he spun her in a dizzying round of dance steps. The jeweled hues worn by ladies and gentlemen alike flashed past, softened by candlelight. When no one was watching, he drew her out onto the terrace and kissed her until she was breathless.

"I love you," he whispered fiercely against her mouth. "Think about that in bed tonight . . . as I will be thinking of you."

Those words made her float through the remainder of the party in a haze of happiness.

It was long after midnight when, pleasantly weary, she headed up the wide staircase with a group of chattering ladies. Troy and some of the other men had sat down to a game of cards in an already smoke-filled room, their drinking and political discussions likely to go on until dawn.

Carrying a candle, Caroline escorted the women to the bedchambers they would share. Not even the knowledge that she was to stay in Caroline's room could destroy Elise's good mood. Two other girls, one as plump as the other was skinny, were also assigned to the frilly chamber with its gilt-edged furniture. There was a four-poster and a trundle bed to accommodate the four of them.

A little slave girl was waiting to unlace their gowns and help the women into their nightclothes. Caroline paced the rich Persian rug like a nervous cat. Briefly, Elise wondered what it was that was bothering the woman, then she shrugged off her curiosity and strolled over to the opened window to look out dreamily, only half-listening as the others discussed the party. Off in the distance, the James shimmered in the moonlight like a twisted ribbon of silver.

"Sadie, why are there only three nightgowns lying on the bed?" demanded Caroline. "Did you not unpack all of our guests' clothing?"

Elise turned to see the girl looked at her mistress with wide dark eyes, her hands pausing at the lacings of the plump woman's gown. "But Miz Whitman, you tol' me—"

"No excuses," Caroline interrupted. "Which trunk haven't you unpacked yet?"

Sadie pointed at Elise's leather trunk, which sat beside the hearth. "That one, jus' like you tol'—"

"That's enough. You go on with your business there, and I'll unpack it myself."

"Yes'm." Dutifully, Sadie turned back to her task.

Elise hurried over as Caroline swept across the chamber and opened the trunk. "Caroline, I'll do that. There's no need for you to bother."

The woman gave a tinkling laugh. "But I mustn't put you to work. 'Tis my duty as hostess to see that all guests are cared for properly."

Caroline bent to reach inside the trunk. There was a slight crinkling sound as she drew forth a shawl, and a sheet of parchment fell out of the fringed triangle of cloth and onto the marble hearth.

"Dear me, what's this?" Caroline picked up the paper, then her blue eyes widened. "Why, this is a letter from the governor to my father. Whatever is it doing with your things?"

400

"I don't know." Puzzled, Elise took the page from Caroline and frowned down at the unfamiliar handwriting. Her mind whirled. Where had this come from? One of Troy's servants had packed for her—

Suddenly Caroline pointed an accusing finger at her. "'Tis just as I thought! You're the spy who's been passing information to the French!"

Chapter Twenty-eight

Elise gazed at her in shock, her throat too dry to form a protest. This was impossible! How had that paper gotten into her trunk? Bewildered, she glanced down at the incriminating document in her hands as if to find the answer there.

Caroline marched to the door, then whirled back around. "Just you wait until my father hears about this! Ladies, don't let her get away." She swept out into the hall, the heels of her slippers clicking over the polished wood floor.

Elise realized the other two women were staring at her wide-eyed, as if they expected her to pull out a pistol at any moment. As if she were a criminal! Couldn't they see this was all some incredible mistake?

Caroline wanted them to look at her that way. . . . She had planned the whole thing!

Elise trembled with anger. Caroline had purposely planted that letter in her trunk so that Elise would be branded a spy.

Within moments the buzz of voices could be heard in

the hall. She walked out of the bedchamber, determined to prove her innocence. Troy and Zach were coming up the stairs behind Richard and his daughter. The men had shed their coats in favor of shirtsleeves. Several of the other guests already gathered held candles that cast wavering shadows over the walls. A few people peeked out of their doors to see what the commotion was all about.

"Now, daughter, what is this babbling of letters?" demanded Richard Whitman. "You interrupted the best hand of whist I've had in months."

"I'm sorry, Papa," Caroline apologized prettily. "But I thought you would want to know right away —I found a letter Elise stole from you hidden in her trunk. She's the French spy everyone's been searching for!"

Murmurs of shocked surprise rippled through the gathering. Richard started visibly, staring from his daughter to Elise and back again. "Spy! Where is your proof for such a serious charge?"

"Let me show you the letter." Caroline darted into the bedchamber and returned to present the piece of parchment to her father. "See? 'Tis from the governor to you. She must have rifled through your desk during the party."

"That isn't true!" Elise burst out. "How can you be so sure 'twas *I* who put it there?"

"Let me see that." Troy snatched the paper from Richard's hand and studied it for a moment. "This is absurd. Elise is right; anyone could have hidden it in her trunk."

"Now *that's* absurd," Caroline scoffed. "She's the only one here who would want to steal a letter like that. She probably planned to pass it on to that Frenchman, Yves

Larousse. I understand they were once very close." She put a pointed emphasis on the two last words.

"Elise, how do you answer these charges?" asked Richard.

"Of course, I deny them."

She looked at Troy and saw the barest flicker of doubt in his eyes. Shock coursed through her anew. A moment ago, he had acted as if he believed her! Was it the mention of Yves that had made him change his mind?

"If I were a spy," she went on bitterly, "don't you think I would have hidden the evidence more carefully?"

"And yet the letter was found in your trunk," Richard said, his graying brows drawn into a severe frown. "You must admit, circumstance weighs heavily against you."

"I believe I can explain what happened." Elise regretted having to do so, yet she was unwilling to take the blame for one of Caroline's tricks. "Caroline," she said, focusing her attention on the woman, "I think you know who placed that letter in my trunk, don't you?"

"Why, I don't know what you mean."

"'Twas you yourself." Ignoring the collective gasp from the crowd, Elise added relentlessly, "You made sure my things hadn't been unpacked so that you could 'discover' the hidden letter in full view of witnesses, didn't you?"

"Why, how dare you insinuate such a thing!"

Elise turned to the little black servant hovering at the edge of the group. "Sadie, did Miss Whitman tell you not to unpack my trunk?"

"She has naught to do with this! Sadie, you go on back inside and attend to your chores." Caroline tried to dart across the hall to shoo the girl into the bedchamber, but Zach grabbed her arm.

"Stay right there, Sadie," he called out.

The girl froze in place, watching the proceedings with ide chocolate eyes.

Caroline jerked futilely against Zach's grip. "Let go of e! Papa, make him release me!"

Richard turned his frown on Zach. "Let her go."

"Gladly—provided she can manage to comport herself an adult." Zach shot his pretty captive a stern look fore removing his hand from her. Rubbing her arm, e thrust out her lower lip at him.

"Now, Sadie," Zach said gently, "answer the question. d your mistress give you orders not to unpack Miss Evereaux's trunk?"

The girl glanced at Caroline and muttered, "Yessir, she ne tol' me don't touch. Ah din mean nothin' by it—Ah ly done what Ah's tol'."

"Of course, you did," assured Zach, before turning ck to Caroline with an expression of mingled disgust d fury. "My God, Caroline, you've stooped to new ws! Does it mean so much to you to have Troy that you uld destroy the woman he loves?"

Caroline regarded him petulantly. "This is ridicu- us!" she huffed. "I never gave any such order. Elise ust have bribed the girl to say that!"

"I heard Caro insist on unpacking Miss d'Evereaux's ings herself." The plump young woman who spoke ood in the doorway to Caroline's bedchamber, modestly utching together the unlaced halves of her bodice. Her eeks grew beet red as all eyes focused on her.

"I heard Caroline, too," piped the skinny girl beside er. "Miss d'Evereaux offered to unpack the trunk erself but Caroline refused to let her."

Bless you both, Elise thought fervently.

"Why, you two . . ." Caroline sputtered. She turned to her father and grasped his sleeve. "Papa, they're all lying! They're twisting everything around! You believe me, don't you?"

Richard took a long look at the muttering throng of people, then turned a regretful look at his daughter. "'Twould seem the evidence now weighs heavily against you, my dear."

"Papa! How can you say that!" When her father guiltily averted his eyes, she swung toward Elise. "This is all your fault! Why don't you just go back to the French where you belong!"

"That's quite enough!" snapped Zach, seizing her by the arm and propelling her toward the stairs. "'Tis time you learned what the payment is for acting like a spoiled brat."

She tried to wrench away. "Papa, make him let loose of me!"

"Come now, Zach, there's no need to—"

"With all due respect, Richard, you've had your chance," Zach cut in grimly. "I intend to put an end to her childish behavior once and for all."

Abruptly he took her waist in his hands, hefting her up and over his shoulder like a sack of grain. Caroline hung there, stunned into silence for an instant, as he started down the stairs. Then she beat on his back with her fists.

"You beast! You let me down! Papa, make him—Ouch!" she squawked as Zach's hand smacked her behind.

Richard hurried down the steps after them. "Here now," he protested, though his voice held none of its usual authority. "Don't you hurt my little girl."

Watching them go, Elise clutched the walnut railing

hat edged the stairwell. She knew she should feel ictorious, but instead there was only an emptiness nside her. One by one, the other guests shuffled away, ome returning to their bedchambers, some going ownstairs, until only she and Troy remained.

The candlelight from the wall sconces threw eerie hadows into the corners. A clock ticked loudly on a table t the far end of the hall. Troy's boots sounded on the loorboards, coming closer until he stood directly behind er.

"I'm sorry you had to bear the brunt of Caro's hildishness," he murmured. "I had no idea her feelings or me were deep enough to make her do such a thing."

"Caroline is the one who needs sympathy, not I." Elise ripped the smooth round wood of the banister, nwilling to face him. "She loves you, yet her love is not eturned."

There was silence for a moment, broken by the distant umble of laughter from one of the rooms downstairs. 'You're right, of course," he admitted softly. "How well remember the pain and frustration of loving you when I new you didn't feel the same for me."

His hands descended to her shoulders. She drew away nd turned to him. "You say you love me," she vhispered, "but you don't really trust me, do you? You hought for a moment there that I *had* stolen the letter, hat I planned to pass it on to Yves."

Troy heard the pain in her voice and felt a wave of hame. She was right. In spite of his love for her, a doubt ad crept into his mind. Yes, he knew Elise loved him, ut did that also mean she was now loyal to the English? eeing her hand in hand with Yves at the party had stung is heart. Jealously, he'd wondered if the Frenchman had enough influence over her to convince her to spy for him.

Could she forgive him that momentary lapse?

"Yes, I cannot deny it," he admitted heavily. "But you must know why. I feared you might still have feelings for Yves, feelings that he might use to remind you of your loyalty to France." He hesitated, then added, "Elise, believe me, 'twas only jealousy that made me think such foolish thoughts. I was afraid he might try to take you away from me."

Seconds ticked by in an agony of suspense. Her copper eyes studied him in the candlelight, giving no hint of her thoughts. When at last she spoke, her voice was so low he had to strain to hear it.

"Don't you know—? Yves could never, ever replace you in my heart."

The breath Troy hadn't been aware of holding rushed out of him in a groan. Roughly, he pulled her close, burying her face in his neck, his hand tunneling into her hair. He closed his eyes and drew in a deep breath of her feminine fragrance. It was an unbearable joy to hold her in his arms, to feel the fullness of her breasts pressing into him. If ever he lost her, his world would be an aching void.

And yet a tiny doubt clung stubbornly in his brain. He wouldn't relax until Yves Larousse was out of Virginia and gone from her life for good.

Caroline felt Zach's hard shoulder cutting into her stomach as he carted her out the front door and down the porch steps. Mortification churned inside her. How dare he treat her so, and in front of all those people no less.

408

Why, she had even heard a laugh or two from the crowd!

He had no right, no right at all. Angrily she pummeled his back and tried to kick her feet, but his arms snared her legs and skirts securely against his chest.

"Damn your soul, Zach Birmingham," she gasped. "You let me go this instant!"

He only chuckled darkly and kept on walking, his feet crunching purposefully over the shell path. The ground swayed before her eyes in rhythm with his pace. Glancing up, she saw they were heading toward a clump of trees beyond the formal gardens.

What did he plan to do? Her heart raced. Perhaps he would throw her to the forest floor and force her to kiss him. . . .

Fury surged through her anew. She didn't want him touching her! She wanted to get as far away from him as possible!

They plunged into the woods, where the soft May breeze carried the scents of blossoms and rich earth. A full moon hung high in the sky, sending shafts of silver light through the shuddering leaves.

Zach stopped and dropped her unceremoniously to the ground so that she stumbled backward into a tree.

"Damn you!" Caroline spat, breathing hard as she rubbed her middle. "My ribs will be bruised for weeks."

"That, my dear," he drawled menacingly, "won't be the only part of your anatomy to bear bruises. When I get through with you, you won't be able to sit down."

He advanced on her, his handsome features grim and hard in the dappled moonlight, his boots grinding over dried twigs and leaves. A jolt ran through her. He meant to spank her, just as he'd threatened to do if she meddled in Troy's life!

"You daren't touch me," she sputtered, backing away. "My father would kill you!"

"Your father made no move to stop me. Perhaps he's finally realized the mistake of giving you everything you ever wanted."

"What he does or doesn't give me is no concern of yours!"

"It is when you try to destroy the happiness of my friends, all so that you can satisfy your own selfish desires."

Guilt flashed through her, but she brushed it aside. She hadn't meant to hurt Troy, she reasoned, only to save him from more pain later, when that Frenchwoman dumped him. That excused her for hiding the letter, didn't it?

Zach was getting closer. Her heart thudded as she stepped backward swiftly, her slippers scuffling through the underbrush. A quick glance through the moonlit trees told her she was near the edge of the forest. It was now or never.

Turning, she broke into a run. Before she had gone more than a few feet, his hard hands were on her shoulders, spinning her around to face him.

"Oh, no, sweetheart, you're not getting off so easily."

Fury whirled up inside her. "Who do you think you are, Zach Birmingham? You're not my husband, to tell me what to do!"

"Maybe I'm your conscience," he mocked.

Before she could retort, Zack yanked her down with him onto a fallen log, draping her over his lap none too gently, her bottom pointed skyward. He thrust her voluminous skirts and hooped petticoats out of the way and smacked her on the behind.

Caroline cried out in a most unladylike howl of mingled rage and pain. Involuntary tears sprang to her eyes. How dare he! His broad palm met her backside again, the thin silk of her underdrawers providing little protection. She tried to wriggle free, but he held her firmly and ruthlessly in place, applying blow after stinging blow to her tender posterior. Distress flooded her with each resounding strike. After a few moments, she forgot even to struggle, lying limply on his knees, wrapped in wretched misery.

At last he pulled her skirts back down and let loose of her. She stumbled to her feet, her derriere throbbing and her pride in shambles. Tears coursed freely down her cheeks. She covered her face with her hands, feeling so woebegone she wanted to crawl into a hole and die.

Warm arms came around her. Beyond caring who it was that held her, she clung to him for support, sobbing against his broad chest until it seemed not another drop of moisture could be wrung from her. A handkerchief was thrust into her hand. Hiccupping, she used the square of fine linen to dab at the wetness on her cheeks.

"W-why did you h-have to d-do that?" she sniffled.

Zach smoothed back her tangled hair. "I never meant to make you cry, Caro," he said gently. "At the same time, though, I can't say that I'm sorry for what I did."

In a rush of humiliation, she propelled herself backward out of his arms. "D-don't you e-ever t-treat me that way again!" she said, disgusted with herself for sounding more pathetic than firm.

"If you behave like a child, I'll treat you as one."

"I w-wasn't acting l-like a child!"

"Yes, you were. And might I point out, in case you

411

hadn't considered it, you owe Elise an apology."

Deep down Caroline knew he was right, but her pride was too fragile to let her admit it. Driven by a blind need to deny a nagging sense of guilt, she snapped, "I'll n-never apologize to that F-French bitch! She s-stole Troy away from me, and I w-won't stand for it!"

Even as the words faded into stillness, Caroline regretted them. It was as if for the first time she really heard herself. Had she really sounded so infantile?

The expression of profound distaste on Zach's face cut into her like a knife. Never before had she seen him look at her like that.

"I never realized what a callous person you are," he said with cold contempt. "How I could ever have fallen in love with you, I'll never know."

Pivoting on his heel, he strode off toward the house.

Caroline stared after him until she was alone in the moon-dappled forest. Her knees felt weak. Without thinking, she started to sink down onto a log, but the sting in her backside made her straighten up with a gasp.

Despite the pain, joy soared through her.

Zach was in love with her!

Yes, she had always known he was attracted to her . . . but *love?* She wanted to laugh and cry all at the same time. A sudden thought made the buoyant feeling deflate like a pricked bubble. What if she had destroyed his love by her foolishness?

She shook off the silly fear. Zach was only a friend, she reminded herself. Troy was the man she wanted to marry.

So why did that prospect make her feel so hollow inside?

*   *   *

Lost in thought, Elise paced her bedchamber in Williamsburg. Since Dinwiddie had requested Troy return to the capital as soon as possible, they had set out that morning, directly after spending the night at Thousand Oaks. It was a relief to exercise her legs after that long, jolting carriage ride.

A sudden smile quirked her lips. Speaking of aches and pains, Caroline hadn't appeared to be in very good shape at the breakfast table. She'd seemed to have a distinct problem sitting down; it was plain Zach had given her a long-overdue disciplining. Caroline's usual spunk had vanished, and wonder of wonders, she had even apologized to Elise.

Elise's smile gave way to a frown. Still, a few hours had failed to erase her deeply ingrained mistrust of the woman. She couldn't help thinking the change was only temporary and Caroline would soon return to her old tricks.

Pensively, Elise continued to pace the soft Persian rug. Today on the ride into town she'd had lots of time to think. She couldn't forget how people had looked at her when they'd believed her to be a spy. Even after she had proven Caroline had framed her, she wasn't sure whether or not they truly believed in her innocence.

She was French and therefore a prime suspect for espionage.

How could she marry Troy with such questions hanging over her head? It simply wasn't fair to saddle him with a wife of less than sterling background.

Therefore, she must clear her name. She would discover for herself who the real enemy agent was.

During the long hours of the carriage ride she had mentally gone over lists of people, trying to figure out

413

who the traitor might be. Was it Will Granger, the French tutor? Or perhaps a member of the House of Burgesses? Or was it someone closer to the governor, someone on his select council, perchance? Who among all the people she had met here in Virginia would betray his country?

Then a startling idea had popped into her mind.

What if the spy were Caroline herself?

Bits and pieces of evidence fed the theory. Caroline had access to her father's government papers. She had once lived in France when her father had been ambassador, and so might have developed a sympathy for the French cause. Somehow she was acquainted with Yves, for she had invited him to the party. And she could go freely about her secretive business by pointing the finger of suspicion at Elise.

It was the best lead Elise had, and she intended to follow through on it. She knew the Whitmans had also come to Williamsburg that day. She had barely a week before the wedding, so tonight, after everyone was asleep, she would launch her campaign.

But much later, before she could make her departure, Troy entered her bedchamber and she was forced to shelve her plans. It made for a pleasurable night, but was not at all helpful in uncovering concrete evidence against Caroline.

The following evening, she thought it best to take precautions against another such interruption. She and Troy were standing near a window in the drawing room as Pandora played the harpsichord. The girl had arrived that day with Jason and Mirella, who sat arm in arm on a sofa, listening to the music.

"All these people," Troy groaned softly in her ear.

414

"Were it not for convention's sake, I'd carry you upstairs right now."

Elise lay a hand on his sleeve. "Troy, I wanted to speak to you of that." Haltingly, she whispered, "I've been thinking . . . perhaps we should cease sharing beds until we're married."

His mouth curved in amused disbelief. "'Tis rather late for this maidenly shyness, don't you think? Especially after what we shared last night."

The look in his eyes made her pulse quicken. It pained her to have to lie to him when she wanted him so badly, but there was no other way. She couldn't take the risk of his stealing into her room later and finding her gone. And she couldn't tell him of her plans, because he would stop her for certain.

"Let me explain," she murmured. "You see, if we spend this week apart from each other, 'twill make our wedding night so much more special. I'd like to come to you then with all the anticipation of a true bride, so that it isn't just another night like so many before."

"Our lovemaking has always been special to me," he said tenderly. "I cannot see what difference a few days of abstinence can make."

"It matters to me. Please, Troy, say you'll agree."

After a moment's reflection, he shook his head in good-humored frustration. "All right, little angel, you win You have one week alone, and then you'll share my bed every night for the rest of your life."

After everyone else was asleep that night, Elise clambered out of her second-story window and onto the thick branch of an oak tree. A cap covered her hair, and the breeches and shirt she wore belonged to Marc, who of course knew nothing of this midnight excursion.

She looked down and gulped. The ground seemed a long way off. Ignoring the urge to scuttle back inside, she crawled cautiously toward the trunk and began to feel her way down, making as little noise as possible.

Suddenly her foot slipped on the bark. She bit back a scream, frantically grabbing at the rough trunk. Steadying herself, she couldn't help a wry smile. She'd have a lot of explaining to do if she fell and broke a leg. And if the ladies of society could see her now, dressed like a boy and climbing trees in the middle of the night, they'd have an attack of the vapors!

Gritting her teeth, she concentrated on getting down with every bone intact. It was a relief to feel her moccasined feet touch solid earth once again. Elise brushed off her knees and took one last look at the darkened house before setting off across the Palace Green.

The moon was nearly full, but the scudding clouds captured most of the light. Thankfully, she passed no one in the few blocks to the sprawling two-story clapboard house on Nicholson Street where the Whitmans lived while in Williamsburg. She glided into the thick shadows of a magnolia. From there, she could see both front and back of the property, the house and its numerous outbuildings.

She settled down to wait. After one boring hour had passed and then another, doubts began to creep into her mind. Maybe it had been a mistake to assume Caroline would sneak out at night to do her spy work. After all, there were ways for her to pass along information during the day.

416

It was also possible she wasn't the spy.

No, Elise chided herself, she mustn't think negatively. Though there wasn't much concrete evidence to go on, Caroline *was* a prime suspect. All this job required was a little patience. She couldn't expect to catch the woman in one night.

The hardest part was staying alert. More than once her eyes started to close and she had to pinch herself to stay awake. At last the chirping of birds warned her of dawn's approach. Wearily she trudged home and scrambled up the tree, barely able to strip and hide her boy's clothing before falling into bed.

That night set the pattern for the ones to follow. Stubbornly Elise kept the secret vigil, until everyone commented on how tired and wan she looked. They fussed that she must rest up for the coming nuptials, giving her an excuse to sleep late each morning.

It was two nights before the wedding when at last she found success.

She was stationed in her usual spot beneath the spreading leaves of the magnolia when a movement near the stables caught her eye. All her senses came alert. The faint light from the quarter-moon made it difficult to see. Then suddenly her ears picked up the clop of horse hooves.

A rider was heading out of the stables!

Elise edged closer, straining her eyes. The black-cloaked figure crouched low over the horse's neck as the pair cantered off. She ran after them, darting from shadow to shadow, only to see her prey vanish into the forest at the edge of town.

A low cry of frustration left her lips. Oh, to fail when she had been so close to catching Caroline in the act!

Then a thought took hold in her mind. She hadn't failed . . . yet. Caroline had to come back sometime, and Elise planned to be there waiting.

Guided by the pale moonlight, she returned to the Whitmans' and went to the stables at the rear of the property. The door squeaked as she slipped inside, and she froze for an instant, fearful of awakening a servant. But all that greeted her was the aroma of horses.

If it was dark outside, it was pitch-black in there. Elise felt her way down to the other end of the building and into a corner behind a sack of grain, where she settled down to wait.

Time dragged. A horse snorted in a stall nearby. Something scurried across the rafters, then all was silent. So silent that Elise fancied she could detect the beating of her heart.

It took a minute for her to realize it was not her heart she was hearing but the clip-clop of approaching horse hooves. The animal stopped just outside the stables.

As the door opened with a squeak, every muscle in her body tensed. Her ears caught the sounds of someone leading a horse inside, then the scratching of flint on steel. Suddenly a light bloomed, creating macabre shadows in the corner where Elise hid. There were more sounds that told her the horse was being stabled for the night.

Her fingers dug into the rough weave of the grain sack. The time had come to confront Caroline.

Slowly she raised her head, squinting as her eyes adjusted to the light of a lantern that hung from a post at the opposite end of the stable. The black-cloaked figure was emerging from the stall, hood thrown back.

Elise swallowed a gasp. It was Richard Whitman!

Quickly she sank back down behind the sack. So it wasn't Caroline who had ridden off to some unknown assignation, it was Caroline's father! *He* couldn't be the spy . . . could he?

Why would a man ride into the forest in the middle of the night clad in a black cloak? Unless he had something to hide. . . .

Swiftly her mind assembled other pieces. Richard Whitman had access to important government papers. He had once lived in France. And now she recalled the strange look that had passed between him and Yves at the party. Yes, he had thrown Yves out, but wouldn't he do that if he wished to convince people that he hated the French?

She was mistaken, Elise tried to tell herself. After all, what motivation could he have? He already had plenty of wealth and power. No, Richard Whitman was too important a personage in Virginia politics to be a traitor.

But a gut-level instinct told her she had stumbled onto the real spy.

Cautiously she lifted her head above the grain sack in time to see Whitman extinguish the lantern, then he strode out the door, the cloak swinging from his shoulders. Without stopping to think, Elise got up and tiptoed after him. She waited in the stables until he was through the dimly lit gardens and into the house.

Her moccasined feet flew across the path and up the back porch steps. She slipped inside the darkened hall and paused, waiting for a clue that would tell her where he'd gone.

The faint sounds of movement came from behind a pair of doors. Creeping through the gloom, she reached out and put her hand on the cold brass latch.

Now that the moment was at hand, she felt a ripple of misgiving. Was she wrong about him? And even if she wasn't, could she really confront him?

Suddenly anger burned inside her. If he was the spy then she was paying for his clandestine activities with the ruin of her good name.

Lifting the latch, she opened the door and walked boldly into the lion's den.

Chapter Twenty-nine

The room she entered was a library. Rows of books lined the walls and the air bore the mingled scents of leather bindings and beeswax. Two wingback chairs faced each other across the brick hearth, where no fire burned on this balmy night in late May. At one end of the chamber was a mahogany writing desk with a straight-backed chair behind it. Richard Whitman was standing there, using a tinderbox candle to light a silver candelabrum that sat atop the polished wood surface.

He turned as she walked inside. He still wore his cloak, and the glow of the candles threw his features into sharp relief. Never before had she noticed how much his eyes looked like a ferret's. Without his customary white wig, she could see that he was balding. He cast a startled glance over her and his graying brows drew together in a frown.

"What the devil are you doing here?"

Elise closed the doors behind her and stepped fully into the room. "I was out there watching you," she said, striving for a coolness that went only skin-deep. "I saw you ride off into the forest and I saw you come back."

Whitman stared at her for a long moment, the frown still on his thin face. A clock on the mantel ticked softly in the silence. Then he casually blew out the taper in his hand and set it aside. Lifting a hand to his neck, he untied his cloak and dropped the garment on a nearby bench. The breeches and shirt he wore were of a dark-colored fabric, undoubtedly part of the disguise meant to help render him invisible.

He sat down behind the desk and waved her into a chair on the other side. "Sit down, my dear, and tell me. What is this you're babbling about? Yes, I went for a ride. I couldn't sleep and fresh air often makes me drowsy."

His patronizing tone enraged Elise, implying that he was humoring this slightly mad young woman who had burst into his library in the middle of the night dressed like a boy and talking gibberish. Ignoring his suggestion to sit, she marched across the room to stand over the desk.

"A man like you doesn't ride off into the woods in the dead of night clad in black unless he doesn't want anyone to see him. What is it you're hiding, Monsieur Whitman?" When he merely stared at her, his hands steepled beneath his chin, she went on furiously, "You're the spy everyone's been looking for, aren't you?"

A faintly contemptuous smile lifted a corner of his mouth. "My, what an active imagination you have. All right, I admit it—I was lying about not being able to sleep. But perhaps the deep, dark secret behind my riding out was to keep a lovers' tryst."

"If that is so, you returned rather swiftly."

He continued to study her with those dark ferret eyes,

his. It was impossible to tell what he was thinking. With stubborn courage she kept her gaze locked to his, unwilling to show weakness by glancing away. Then abruptly he laughed, a menacing sound that sent a tiny shiver down her spine.

"I could give you a score of plausible explanations for my actions tonight. None of which, I might add, I owe you." He paused, his eyes roaming over her until she felt vaguely unclean. "However, it occurs to me you're one of the few people to whom I can admit the truth. Yes, I am the spy who's been passing information to the French."

He said it almost proudly. Elise was jolted by his attitude. How could he sit there so calmly and announce he was betraying his country?

"Why?" she whispered.

"I have my reasons, none of which are any of your concern."

"But what you're doing may cost lives—English lives. Doesn't that matter to you?"

He shrugged. "Lives are lost in any war. And think of it this way—what I'm doing will cost fewer lives, because once the war begins, I mean for it to come to a swift conclusion. None of this dragging things out for years and years."

"You truly *want* the French to win the frontier?" she asked incredulously.

"Why not? Nothing out there but bears and savages. The French are welcome to it."

She shook her head in disbelief. "How can you be so blasé about this?"

"How can you ask so many questions?" he countered. "I should think you of all people would be happy to see the French cause served so well."

Elise felt a familiar conflict tug at her insides. Which side *was* she on? Why did she have such ambivalen feelings, when at one time she would have whole heartedly applauded Whitman's actions? Now she wa appalled by his treachery—and as outraged as any tru Virginian.

Folding her arms across her breasts, she swung aroun and walked blindly to the hearth, staring down at th clean-swept grate.

The truth was too earth-shattering to face. Elis pushed it to the back of her mind, focusing on the fac that Whitman was letting *her* shoulder the blame for hi deceit.

She whirled toward him. "I can't let you go on lik this. People are only too willing to think 'tis I who skulk around and spies for the French. By your own actions you force me to expose you to the governor."

Far from looking shaken by her threat, Whitma lounged in his chair, amusement twisting his thin lips

"But, my dear, that's why I said you're one of the few people to whom I can admit the truth. No Englishma would ever believe the word of a Frenchwoman Especially not when she accuses an outstanding citizen o such an outlandish charge."

"Troy will believe me," she insisted stubbornly. "He' help me convince Dinwiddie."

"Then might I also point out, you have no proof. I'l deny everything, and you'll end up appearing even les trustworthy than ever."

Elise knew with a sinking feeling that he was right Silently she cursed her ineptness. She should have tol

Troy and forced him to accompany her on this vigil. Unless another Englishman actually saw Whitman handing a document to a French courier, no one would believe he would do such a thing. And undoubtedly, Whitman would lay low for a while so that she would not be able to get any such proof.

There was so little for her to fight him with. Still, there might be one last feeble chance to stop him.

Elise walked to the double doors, then turned back, her hand on the latch. "Don't think I'm giving up," she said coolly. "You haven't won yet."

His sardonic laugh followed her out into the gloomy hall. "I'll be waiting, my dear."

In the faint predawn light Elise crept out the back door of the Fletcher house. Reaching the street, she walked fast, clutching the shawl around her simple gray gown to ward off the slight chill of the morning. It was imperative that she accomplish her mission and return quickly before anyone discovered her absence.

Already there were people out at this early hour. Shopkeepers readied their wares for sale, housewives hurried to market, a few ragged children ran laughing down the street. From somewhere drifted the succulent scent of frying ham. The windows of many of the stores were still dark, including her father's silversmith shop.

At last the Raleigh Tavern loomed ahead, its white clapboard washed a pale pink by the early dawn. A young woman in a mobcap and aproned gown stood on the front stoop, yawning as she halfheartedly shook a braided rug.

"Miss, do you work here?" Elise asked.

The girl stilled her hands and focused bleary blue eyes on her. "What's it look like? D'ye think I'd be standin' out here so early if I wasn't?"

Tactfully, Elise ignored her rudeness. "If you would, I'd like you to deliver a note to a man who might still be staying here, a Mr. Larousse. If he isn't here, I want you to tear it up and throw it away. This is for your trouble."

She handed the girl a coin, then drew from her pocket a folded piece of paper sealed with a glob of wax.

Staring at the silver in her palm, the girl suddenly became more respectful. She slipped the coin into her bodice and took the letter. "Aye, miss, right away."

Pivoting, she disappeared into the tavern, her feet moving swiftly for one who had acted so sleepy just moments earlier.

Elise started back toward home. She frowned, hoping her scheme would work. For all she knew, Yves had returned to the frontier. Fervently she prayed that he hadn't yet left and would meet her that night in the churchyard, as she had asked in the note.

She managed to steal back into the house unnoticed. All day she was on edge, her mind on the encounter with Richard Whitman and the coming rendezvous with Yves. Luckily, everyone laughed at her indulgently, mistaking her anxiety for bridal nerves. Mirella and Pandora fussed happily with the final preparations of the trousseau and wedding gown. Elise's bedchamber was strewn with silks and satins, laces and velvets. Downstairs, Ophelia bustled about, directing the army of servants who polished and cleaned and cooked, getting the household ready for the crowd of wedding guests.

Elise wandered through all the confusion like a little

lost waif. Her heart gave a tug as she thought of the next day's nuptials. She had to find a way to clear her name—if only for Troy's sake.

The moon was a sliver of silver against the starry sky as Elise climbed down the oak tree with the nimbleness of a week's worth of practice. After dropping quietly to the ground, she adjusted the cap that covered her copper curls and then hurried out the gate in the white picket fence. She moved from shadow to shadow, making her way down the street to the Bruton Parish Church.

As her eyes adjusted more fully to the darkness, she could see the brick building ahead, silhouetted against the night sky. There was a low brick fence surrounding the church and a wooden gate that opened to a touch of her hand. Slowly she walked into the deserted courtyard, her moccasins making an occasional slight scraping sound on the path.

She paused to peer into the gloom. The only movement in the shadows was the fluttering of leaves in the wind. Yves must not have arrived yet . . . unless he was waiting on the other side of the church.

Cautiously Elise stepped around the rear of the building, eyeing askance the ghostly-pale shapes of the gravestones that scattered the yard. She had forgotten there was a cemetery back here. A cold prickle ran over her skin. The faint scent of damp earth hung in the air, bringing to mind unwilling thoughts of dark deeds and decaying bodies.

She jumped as an owl hooted in a nearby tree. Chiding herself for being foolish, she continued along the murky

427

path to the opposite side of the church.

To her great relief, she found Yves there, slowly pacing back and forth in the faint moonlight, his hands clasped behind his back. He turned at the sound of her footsteps and hurried over to seize her by the shoulders.

"Elise! Why is it you wished to see me?" he said urgently. "Have you changed your mind about going back with me?"

She shook her head. "Nay, I've come on another matter. Yves, you must put an end to this spying. Too many people are becoming suspicious of me."

He stared at her for a moment and then abruptly let her go. "So, you've decided to take the side of the British," he said flatly.

"I haven't decided any such thing. I want only to live my life in peace. It isn't fair to Troy that his wife should be the object of suspicion."

"Then you fully intend to go through with this wedding tomorrow."

She was disheartened by his coldness. "*Oui*, but please, Yves, cannot you try to understand—?"

"What I understand is that you're abandoning your heritage. I suppose you've become such a true English-woman that you'll even be wed here by an English minister in this English church." Angrily, he jabbed a hand at the brick building beside them.

"We'll marry here, yes, but we'll have a second ceremony before a Catholic priest," she said defensively.

"And you think that makes it all right?" He shook his head in disgust. "Your good mother would have been ashamed of you."

Elise felt an uncomfortable flare of guilt. He was right; her mother would have moved heaven and earth to stop her daughter from marrying an Englishman.

But she wasn't making a mistake, Elise cried out inside. How could there be any wrong in loving Troy?

"All I want is to wed the man of my choice," she said passionately. "Why must it matter what country he's from?"

"It matters when his country is at war with yours. Elise, just hours ago I received word that the first shots have been fired. The conflict is no longer conjecture but fact!"

As she froze in shock, he went on, his eyes dark and grim in the moonlight. "A few days ago, the English Lieutenant-Colonel Washington came upon a party of French soldiers in the forest. He and his men attacked, killing ten brave Frenchmen."

"Nay," she whispered, "it cannot be true."

"Rest assured, it is," Yves said harshly. "Washington even let the Indians who traveled with him scalp the men as they lay dying. Is that the sort of country you wish to adopt?"

Sickness coursed through her. Still, she couldn't help a bitter retort: "And the French pay Indians to scalp innocent settlers who are not even soldiers!"

"I might have known you would defend the English!" Yves growled contemptuously.

Elise paced back and forth in the gloomy churchyard. "I neither defend nor condone either side! Can you not understand that I have no wish to support any bloodshed, be it done by English or French?" She stopped in front of him. "What I *do* wish is for you to tell Richard Whitman that you no longer need his services as spy!"

There was a flicker of surprise in his Yves's eyes before a blank shutter came down over his face. "Whitman? I don't know what you mean. Where did you come by a tale so *incroyable?*"

"There's no use in pretending with me, Yves. Monsieur Whitman admitted it to me himself, after I saw him riding off into the woods last night to leave a message—probably to you."

The silence that followed was disturbed only by the sigh of the wind ruffling the leaves overhead. At last Yves spoke, his voice stiff and cautious.

"And what do you intend to do with this information?"

"Nothing," Elise admitted with a trace of bitterness. "I have no proof other than my own eyes and ears, and regrettably my word would count for little beside Monsieur Whitman's."

Yves relaxed visibly. *"Bon.* This is for the best, *petite,* you'll see. With the information Whitman is giving us regarding the plans of the British troops, the war should be over in record time."

"Indeed? And should that excuse Whitman for betraying his country?"

"May I remind you, Elise, you are as much a traitor as he."

His harsh words cut her like a knife. Cold and heartsick, she stepped blindly to the church and laid her forehead against the rough brick. Yes, in a way, he was right, she *was* a traitor to the French. Even though it had been done in the name of love, there was no escaping the fact that she had abandoned her homeland to live in the midst of its sworn enemy.

Yves came up from behind and placed his hands on her shoulders. *"Chérie,"* he urged softly, "don't do this, don't forsake your country. Forget Troy Fletcher and

eave with me tonight. Now that war has come, I can
delay my return no longer. It isn't too late for you to go
with me."

"I cannot leave the man I love," she whispered.

"*I* love you, Elise," he said in a low voice. "Please, at
least consider it one last time. After I collect my things,
'll come back here and wait. You'll have until dawn to
meet me here should you change your mind. *Adieu.*"

His footsteps moved away, toward the gate. Elise
slumped against the side of the church for a moment.
This meeting had been a waste of time. Not only had she
failed to end Whitman's spying, now she felt more torn
and confused than ever. War had begun! How would that
affect her relationship with Troy?

Slowly she walked through the darkened churchyard
and out the gate, heading toward home. Their wedding
was just a few hours away. Suddenly love washed
through her like a ray of sunshine. No matter what
happened, Elise told herself, she had made the right
decision. Worry she might feel, but not doubts. Her love
for Troy would be enough to overcome any obstacle.

With a resurgence of energy, she climbed up the oak
tree and scrambled into the open window of her
bedchamber. The room was dark, the bed empty. A soft
smile touched her lips as she realized this would be her
last night to sleep alone.

Against the armoire at the opposite end of the room
she could see a gleam of white, the wedding gown of satin
and seed pearls that hung in readiness, a veil of rich
Belgian lace beside it. In just a few short hours, she would
walk down the aisle to speak everlasting vows to the man
she loved.

Tears misted her eyes. Yes, she wanted to be his wife

with all her heart, to be at his side for all of eternity—

A sudden sound from the shadows in the corner made her whirl around with a gasp. Troy's hard voice lashed through the air.

"Well, well, so the deceitful angel returns. Does tha smile mean you're pleased with your evening's work?'

Chapter Thirty

He stepped out of the darkness and into the patch of light in front of the window. Only a pair of breeches and an unbuttoned shirt covered his tall, imposing form. The faint aroma of brandy pervaded the quiet air. In his hand was an empty glass, and he turned slightly, setting it down with a tiny *clink* on a table.

There was a deliberation to his movement, as if he were barely containing some inner wildness beneath a veneer of good manners and civilized behavior. The pale moonlight gleamed over his tightened lips and angry eyes. A jolt of dread pierced Elise. What must he think, seeing her dressed like a boy and sneaking back into the house so late at night?

Hesitantly, she whispered, "What . . . what are you doing here?"

"I should think that would be obvious. I was waiting for you."

She moistened her dry lips. "I can explain. I couldn't sleep, so I went out for a walk—"

"Don't lie to me." His harsh words exploded through

433

the air. "I came in here earlier, wanting to speak to you but instead I saw you climbing down that tree. So I decided to follow you, only to see you meeting Yves Larousse in a churchyard in the middle of the night!"

"It isn't what you think—"

"Do you even care what I think?" There was a note of anguish in his voice that stunned her into silence. He took a step closer, hands on his hips, his face raw with emotion. "Do you even care that you lied to me? You said you wanted to sleep apart from me this week in order to make our wedding night more special. Instead, I find that was only a cover for espionage!"

"That isn't true!" she cried desperately.

His eyes raked over her in cold contempt. "I can see now why you've been so tired lately—from these nocturnal meetings. Is that the real reason you were so nervous today—because you were afraid of being caught with Larousse? Afraid that someone would find out you're the spy who's been betraying Virginia?"

"Nay," she murmured, shaking her head numbly. "How can you even think that? You must have heard what I said to Yves!" But then she remembered he didn't speak French.

"I saw you run up to that bastard, but then I turned and left. You probably spoke French, anyway. I was afraid I'd throttle you right then and there. How could you do this to me . . . to my family?"

Seeing his hands clench and unclench at his sides, Elise felt a sick horror rise in her throat. Did he truly believe she would betray him like that? She had to make him see the truth!

She ran across the room to grasp at his shirt. "Yes, I *did* lie to you. But only because I wanted to find the spy

434

nd clear my own name. And, Troy, I *did* discover his identity—'tis Richard Whitman!"

His look of scorn was so withering that she recoiled, instinctively withdrawing her hands.

"You expect me to believe such a tale?" he said cathingly. "If you're so intent on discrediting someone else to save your own hide, you could at least have thought up a more likely suspect."

"Richard Whitman *is* the spy! He admitted it to me himself."

Troy gave a bitter laugh. "I'd as soon believe the spy is Dinwiddie himself. Why would one of the colony's most prominent citizens pass information to the enemy?"

"He—he wouldn't say," Elise stammered. "Perhaps he has gambling debts—?"

"Impossible," Troy denied flatly. "I've never seen Whitman risk more than a few pounds at an occasional game of whist. Nay, you'll have to come up with a better tale than that one."

His icy skepticism tore at her heart. In a paralysis of fear, she tried again.

"You must believe me," she pleaded. "Tonight I arranged to meet Yves near the church so that I could beg him to stop Monsieur Whitman from spying. I did it for you, Troy! I wanted to wed you with no suspicions hanging over my head." Her voice softened, entreating him. "I did it because I love you."

"Love!" He snarled the word like a curse, and the disillusionment in his eyes cut her to the quick. "Why don't you admit the truth? Your loyalty to France is far stronger than anything you could ever feel for me." In the moonlight, his face twisted with sudden agony. "I should have seen this coming . . . if I hadn't been such a besotted fool. . . ."

Abruptly he stormed past her to the armoire. Elis
watched in wide-eyed horror as he snatched at he
wedding gown, ripping the fragile fabric as he yanked
with a vicious jerk off the hook, flinging the gown to th
floor.

A searing pain spurred her into motion. With a sob
she darted across the room and sank to the rug, lifting th
gown with trembling hands.

"*Sacré Dieu*," she cried out in anguish. "I'll never b
able to repair it in time."

"You needn't bother. There'll be no wedding."

His cold, controlled words sent a shiver down he
spine. She stared up at him in shock, the satin slippin
from her fingers into a pale puddle on the carpet, he
throat so constricted with pain that she couldn't speak

"I won't have a wife who uses her position as a cove
for espionage," he went on relentlessly. "You don'
really love me and you never will. Thank God I foun
that out now, before I gave you the honor of my name.

Pivoting, he strode out of the room and slammed th
door behind him.

Elise sat on her heels, numb with disbelief. He couldn'
mean that . . . she must have misunderstood . . . thi
was all a tragic mistake! An excruciating despair began t
squeeze her heart, knotting tighter and tighter until sh
could scarcely draw a breath. Troy didn't want he
anymore. He was calling off the wedding.

Moisture splashed onto her fingers. Woodenly lifting
hand to her face, she realized that tears flowed in
torrent down her cheeks. *Why, why, why?* chante
through her mind like a litany. Why could he not see tha
she had acted out of love?

436

She should have confided in him earlier, Elise chastised herself bitterly. How damning the evidence must have appeared to him! Catching her stealing out in the dead of night, seeing her meet Yves in a deserted churchyard, realizing she had lied to him. . . .

By her own folly, she had destroyed Troy's trust in her. By her own folly, she had shattered her radiant future into a thousand worthless shards.

And there was no going back. Even now, the frigid finality of his words drummed inside her head. Troy had thrust her from his heart and soul forever.

Moving as slowly and painfully as an old woman, she reached out and fingered the ruined bridal gown that lay pooled before her. Perhaps she had never belonged in a gown so splendid, anyway. Perhaps now Troy would wed a real lady.

Swallowing a sob, she scrambled up and walked swiftly to the door, wrenching it open. There was only one course of action for her to take.

She would return to the frontier with Yves.

Chapter Thirty-one

A hawk wheeled against the blue sky. Sunlight filtered through the trees and hung within the forest like a shimmering hot blanket. A squirrel ran chattering along a branch overhead, while crickets sang in the underbrush.

Listlessly, Elise wiped the moisture from her brow with the back of her hand. As she trudged along the Indian path behind Yves, sweat trickled between her breasts, dampening the homespun shirt that had once belonged to Marc. Pain washed through her as she thought of her brother, who had remained in Williamsburg working as an apprentice in their father's silversmith shop. It hurt to think that she hadn't had the chance to say good-bye to either of them.

Melancholy settled over her like a shroud. The trek through the wilderness had been long and wearisome. The days dragged by, each seeming to stretch out before her like an endless tunnel. Elise focused her mind on putting one foot in front of the other so that she would not have to think. Thinking hurt, for it brought back the emory of that final night with Troy.

Every now and then, pain burst through the stone ound her heart. Odd things would remind her of that ng-ago journey through the frontier with Troy—a ction of trail that looked familiar, the flicker of the mpfire at night, even the far-off howl of a wolf. Once e had caught sight of a cabin in the distance and ought for a poignant moment that it was the place here she and Troy had first made love.

But Yves was leading her on a slightly different route rough the wilderness than Troy had, to avoid countering any British troops. They were heading orthwest, toward Fort Duquesne, where Yves had been assigned. She knew he was anxious to reach the safety that garrison, but she felt no worry herself. The ospect of death roused no fear in her. Why should it, e thought dully, when she felt dead already?

"We'll stop and rest here for a few minutes."

Yves's voice penetrated her stupor. He had come to a lt in the trail and was gazing at her in concern.

"I can go on," she said, with a hint of her old ubbornness.

"It's all right, *petite*," he said gently. "We've made good me today. We should arrive at the fort in just a few ore days."

With a sigh, more of lethargy than relief, she lowered r leather pack to the ground and then dropped down side it, leaning back against a tree trunk. Birds wittered in the branches overhead. The nearby bushes stled as a rabbit scampered by in search of food.

Yves walked across the clearing to a brook, where he lled his canteen. He was clad in the garb of a ontiersman, the fringed buckskin breeches and rough

439

linen shirt more practical for travel than his French officer's uniform.

He came back and crouched beside her. "Would you like a drink?"

Wordlessly she took the leather pouch from him and tilted it to her lips. Droplets of cool water ran down her chin and throat, reviving her body but not her spirits.

"You'll forget him in time, Elise."

She looked at Yves without much interest. "I don't want your sympathy."

"But I care about you, *chérie*. I can't bear to see you so unhappy."

"As you said, 'twill pass."

To discourage conversation, she glanced away into the surrounding forest. A cardinal flew by in a flash of scarlet. A hot breeze ruffled her braided hair and skimmed across her skin. Absently, she took another swallow from the canteen.

At times like this, it was easy to imagine she had never even met Troy. Aside from a permanent throbbing ache buried deep within the empty shell of her heart, no tangible proof remained of their love. Not a lock of hair . . . not a ring . . . not a child. . . .

Suddenly the canteen slipped from her hand and thumped to the dirt, spilling its contents in a brown spreading stain at her feet.

The fog cleared from her head. *A child.*

"You should be more careful next time," Yves chided, picking up the canteen. "I'll have to refill this."

Before he could rise, she turned to him, urgently grasping at the rough weave of his shirt. "Tell me, how long have we been traveling?"

"Nearly three weeks. Why?"

"Three weeks," she repeated, her mind making a rapid calculation. A surge of bittersweet wonder swept away the apathy that cloaked her senses. At least two months had passed since her last woman's time. That would explain the occasional bouts of sickness she had felt these past mornings. . . .

"Oh, Yves," she said eagerly. "I've only just realized—I'm going to bear Troy's baby!"

His dark, disbelieving eyes bored into her. Then, abruptly, he shot to his feet and stalked to the edge of the clearing, presenting his back to her as he stared off into the trees.

Embroiled in her own emotions, Elise paid little heed to him. A child! The knowledge was both pleasure and pain. She would never feel the joy of seeing her beloved husband holding their baby in his arms. But at least there would be the comfort of having a part of him with her always.

Stiffly, Yves marched back and towered over her, hands on his hips. "Have you given any thought to how you'll support this child?"

"Nay; I suppose I'll find work—"

"My offer of marriage is still open."

Pain wrenched her heart anew. "Please understand," she murmured heavily, "if I cannot have Troy, I will never wed another."

Yves tightened his lips. Then his grim look faded and he sank down on his haunches, taking her hands in his.

"But think, *petite!* You cannot properly care for a baby on your own. And surely you do not want your child to grow up a *bâtard*, to endure the taunting of the other children? Consider all the pain you'll spare him if you let me claim him as my own."

She gazed searchingly into his face. Could she let another man raise Troy's son or daughter? Her entire being rebelled at such a sacrilege. Yet Yves was right about the stigma of being born out of wedlock. Could she let her child suffer so, only because she herself had no desire to let another man touch her?

"I love you, *chérie*," Yves persisted, his voice low. "I know that you don't love me now, but you might learn to in time. Please, Elise, say you'll be my wife."

Still, she hesitated. *Oh, Troy!*

To bind her life to anyone else would be agony. But she had her baby's future to consider.

She drew in a deep breath and spoke, her voice soft and sad. *"Oui*, I'll marry you."

Troy slumped his shoulder against the window frame in the dining room, gazing out into the garden behind the Fletcher house in Williamsburg. Brick walks wound between clumps of flowers and boxwood hedges. The tulips and daffodils of spring had given way to hollyhocks and daylilies. Though the morning was young, Mirella was already outside trimming the rosebushes, a wide-brimmed hat covering her ebony hair.

With her back turned, he could almost imagine that slender woman was Elise.

Elise. His heart gave a familiar, painful wrench. Oh, God, why had he driven her away? If things had worked out, she would have been his beloved wife for a week already.

Now that his hot fury had dwindled to ashes, he could think back on their confrontation with a clearer head. A deep shame gripped him as he recalled his blatant disregard for everything she had said. He had been so hurt and angry, thinking her to be spying behind his back, that he'd been unwilling even to consider that she might be telling the truth.

Could Richard Whitman be the true spy? Nay, the notion bordered on the absurd. Perhaps Elise had misunderstood Whitman—or maybe Whitman had merely been playing some sort of strange joke on her.

Troy shook his head. None of it made any sense. If it weren't for this damn war, he'd have had time to pull Whitman aside and have a talk with him.

"Lawdy me, Massah Troy. You ain't even touched that breakfast Ah done made special for you."

Ophelia's scolding voice came from the doorway. He turned to see the old black woman come waddling into the room, a white turban over her graying hair and an apron over her broad front.

"I'm not hungry."

"You be worryin' 'bout that Miz 'Lise?"

"That's none of your business," he said testily.

She threw up her hands. "Yes, suh! Ain't none of my bizness if you be too weak from hunger to go after that gal of yours. Now sit down here," she ordered, pulling out a chair at one end of the long mahogany table. "You ain't so old that you can't listen to your mammy."

"Good God," Troy grumbled. Yet Ophelia meant well, and he couldn't bring himself to hurt her feelings.

With a grimace, he settled himself in the chair and looked askance at the china plate set on the snowy white tablecloth in front of him. Eggs and ham and biscuits. Ordinarily, he would have dived in with gusto, but of late, his appetite had been nonexistent. The sight of food made his stomach turn.

Ophelia was glaring at him, hands on her ample hips. To placate her, he picked up his fork and started on the fried eggs. A piece of parchment would have tasted as appetizing.

With a satisfied "hmmph," the slave woman left the dining room. The moment she was gone, Troy threw down his fork with a clatter and rose from the table. Hurt feelings or not, he couldn't bring himself to eat another bite.

His boots thudded purposefully across the pine floor as he strode into the hall and out the front door. Walking through the gate in the white picket fence, he headed across the Palace Green toward the Capitol several blocks away. The early morning sunshine made him squint. Today the House was voting on appropriating money to raise more troops, and he wanted to sit in on the debate beforehand.

Oh, God, Elise was somewhere out there in the wilderness with that bastard, Yves Larousse.

He buried the haunting thought. He mustn't let himself think about her. After his colossal show of jealous mistrust, she was probably overjoyed to be out of his life for good. Deliberately he locked the pain inside his heart and turned his mind to the day ahead.

As he approached the brick Capitol building, Zach Birmingham was hurrying out the side door. He hailed Troy urgently, his face grim with worry as they met beneath the spreading limbs of an oak tree.

"I was just on my way to your house," Zach said. "Troy, you won't believe the news. Late last night, Richard Whitman was caught stealing some private papers from the governor's library!"

Troy felt a jolt of shock. "Papers? What do you mean?"

"They were secret dispatches Dinwiddie had received from Washington—information about the movements of our troops. Whitman was in the middle of copying the data when Dinwiddie himself walked in on him."

"My God," Troy said slowly. A sick feeling twisted his gut. So Elise had been right, after all.

He didn't voice the thought; no one, not even his closest friends, knew the real reason why she had vanished on the eve of their wedding. Out of respect for both her and Whitman's reputations, he'd let it be known only that they'd had a difference of opinion. Now it seemed Whitman hadn't deserved such courtesy.

"They're questioning him in the conference room, and I thought you'd want to be there," said Zach. His face saddened. "Meanwhile, I'd better inform Caro before she hears about this from someone else."

He strode off toward the Whitmans' house a block away. Troy entered the building alone and walked swiftly upstairs to the conference room, where he slipped inside.

Morning sunshine streamed in the windows and onto the gathering of colony officials. His Majesty's royal governor, Robert Dinwiddie, presided at the near end of a long oval table that gleamed with polish. In his powdered wig and brown frockcoat, he looked even more sober and businesslike than ever, and a frown darkened his paunchy features. Eleven equally stern-faced council members were scattered on either side of the table.

At the far end sat Richard Whitman. Troy was struck by the change in the man's appearance. The once debonair gentleman now bore signs of dishevelment. His stock was tied ineptly, and without his usual wig, his gray hair was sparse and mussed. His fingers nervously twirled a quill pen.

Everyone was intent on the proceedings as Troy

quietly entered the room and took a seat.

"Mr. Whitman," the governor was saying, "to whom were you intending to sell those papers?"

"Did I say I was selling them?" Whitman replied, his tone bordering on the insolent.

"A poor choice of words on my part," Dinwiddie admitted stiffly. "To whom, then, were you planning to *give* those papers?"

Whitman remained silent, staring sullenly down the table at his superior, his fingers fidgeting with the pen.

The governor's frown deepened. "Mr. Whitman, may I remind you that you are here under charge of treason, and 'twould behoove you to cooperate more fully with this panel of inquest. Now, I shall ask you once more, to whom were you intending to transmit those papers?"

Whitman slammed the pen down on the table and leaped up. "The French, damn your hide! You know that as well as I. Why don't you just try me and get it over with!"

"I shall tolerate no more of these outbursts. Sit down, sir."

Whitman glowered, but slowly he sank back into his chair.

"I believed you one of the colony's most loyal and respected citizens," Dinwiddie went on sternly. "I should like to know, what cause have you for perpetrating such a treasonous act?"

"Because I wanted to see you lose this war!" Whitman hissed.

Shocked whispers buzzed through the chamber.

"Silence!" Dinwiddie warned the council members. "That does not answer my question, Mr. Whitman. Tell us, why would you wish for Virginia's defeat—"

"Not Virginia. I said, I wanted *you* to lose the war."
Hatred contorted Whitman's thin features as he pointed
down the table at his adversary. "I wanted *you* to be
discredited and thrown out of office, Dinwiddie! Then
the king would appoint *me* governor, as he should have
done years ago!"

Before anyone could stop him, he jumped to his feet
and darted down the length of the chamber, lunging at
the governor. His hands throttled the folds of flesh at
Dinwiddie's neck.

Troy leaped up to help another man drag Whitman
away. Shouting slurs, the spy twisted and fought his
captors with surprising strength.

At that very moment, Caroline burst into the room.
Her chestnut hair was unpowdered and her gown was
mussed, as if it had been hastily donned. She stopped
short for an instant, staring in wide-eyed horror, then
flew across to her father, Zach at her heels.

"Papa! Papa, stop it! What are you doing?"

At the sound of her voice, Whitman calmed his
struggles and the momentary madness faded from his
dark eyes. "Caroline?" he asked hoarsely. He shook his
head as if to clear his vision. "You shouldn't be here,
daughter."

She threw her arms around him. Troy and the other
man holding him let go, though eyeing him watchfully.

"I had to come." Her voice caught in a sob. "Oh, Papa,
how could you have done such a thing?"

Whitman bowed his head, his shoulders slumping like
a defeated old man. "You couldn't understand," he
muttered. "Nay, you were never poor as my parents were
when I was a child. I didn't want you to have to work
hard, as I did. That's why I gave you everything you

447

ever wanted."

"Tell me you didn't steal those papers," she whispered, clutching at his shirt. "Tell me this is all a horrid mistake."

His eyes glazed over as though he were lost in his own private world. "I only wanted to be governor. I wanted my daughter to be proud of her father."

"But I *was* proud of you!"

Whitman stared straight ahead, as if he hadn't even heard her, mumbling under his breath.

Tears rolled down Caroline's pale cheeks. "Oh Papa . . ."

Dinwiddie cleared his throat. "I am afraid, Miss Whitman, 'tis time to remove your father to the jail where he shall await trial before a jury of his peers."

"Nay, you mustn't do that to him," she sobbed brokenly. "He didn't mean any harm, he didn't. . . ."

Zach put his hands on her shoulders and gently steered her aside, letting several of the men take Whitman away. With Zach's arm around her, Caroline followed as her father was led out of the chamber.

A somber mood prevailed over those who remained. Hushed murmurs of conversation were exchanged as Dinwiddie gathered up his papers and departed along with the members of the council. Troy hung back, needing a moment alone.

He walked to the window and stared out into the sunshine. It seemed odd that the day could look so bright and cheery when his insides were a churning mass of dark despair. To witness one of his peers sinking to levels of madness, to see Caroline so devastated . . . and worst of all, to learn that he had been so very wrong to doubt Elise.

Oh, God, if only he could turn back time and relive that fateful night! If only he could tell Elise that it was jealousy that had blinded him. . . .

But guilt weighed down his spirit.

It was too late to tell her anything; now he must live with the consequences of his actions. He had thrown her love away—and his life along with it.

Numbly, Caroline hung onto Zach's arm as they mounted the stairs to the white clapboard house that had been the Whitman's town home for as long as she could remember. Moving like a sleepwalker, she let him guide her into a sunny yellow drawing room, where he pressed her down onto an elegant Chippendale sofa. Then he went to a sideboard and poured a brandy from a crystal decanter.

Zach sat down beside her on the cushion and put an arm around her, lifting the glass to her lips. "Drink some of this," he murmured. "'Twill make you feel better."

Dutifully Caroline took a swallow. The brandy burned down her throat, making her cough. She felt the first stirrings of life in her body since that horrifying moment when she had watched her father being locked in manacles in a cell at the town jail.

Oh, God, this was a nightmare! Her dearest Papa, chained like a common criminal . . . and because he was a traitor to his country!

Pain washed through her, and she pushed the glass away. "Please, no more," she choked out. "'Twill do no good to fog my mind with spirits. I must face up to what my father did and accept it."

Zach put the glass on a walnut tea table, then turned to

draw her close to him. "I know how hard this must be for you," he murmured gently.

"Oh, Zach, I can't help but think this is all my fault somehow," she moaned, her dark blue eyes tortured. "Why, I expected my father to give me so many things. He was only trying to please *me* by becoming governor."

"Don't blame yourself," he said roughly. "You never encouraged him to pass secrets to the French. His ambitions are not your fault."

"If only I had known . . . if only I'd been able to stop him before he . . ." Her throat tightened, strangling her words.

"There was naught you could have done. Don't torment yourself with what might have been."

She gripped his shirt in sudden fear. "Oh, Zach, what do you think they'll do to him?"

"We'll just have to wait until the trial and see. Try not to think about it now."

He nestled her head against his hard chest, smoothing the tangled chestnut hair away from her face. His sympathetic support was a soothing balm to her ravaged heart, the feel of his arms around her a comfort. Caroline felt his strength flowing into her, making her anguish more bearable.

Guilt suddenly made her sit up straight in his arms. "God above, and to think I tried to make people think Elise was the spy. All the time, the traitor was my own father!"

Inexplicably, Zach's dark eyes turned cool and his muscles went taut and tense beneath her fingers. "Perhaps this will teach you a lesson, then. You cannot use other people to get what you want."

"I know that now," she admitted miserably.

450

"I hope to God you do. If you will excuse me, I'll take my leave."

He rose from the sofa and started toward the drawing room door, his shoulders set rigidly. With a small cry, Caroline leaped up and ran after him. She grasped his arm to bring him to a halt.

"Where are you going?" she asked in bewilderment.

"Back to the Capitol."

"But . . . but I thought you'd stay with me for a while."

"Don't fret," he said with a trace of mockery. "I'll find Troy and send him over. I'm sure you'd be more satisfied with his company, especially now that Elise is out of the picture."

The confusion that blurred her mind vanished like a puff of smoke. Of course—he believed she was in love with Troy!

But she wasn't, Caroline realized with abrupt clarity. She loved *Zach*, this handsome brute of a man with the smoldering dark eyes who had been her friend for so long that she hadn't realized how much he meant to her.

Vulnerability washed over her. Dare she hope that he was jealous? That she hadn't destroyed his feelings for her, and that he still cared? She had to take the risk and find out.

"I don't want Troy here," she murmured. "I want you."

A muscle in his arm jerked, as though he'd been stung. "You don't know what you want," he said harshly. "You can't have us both, Caro."

She hesitated, then answered softly, "I want only you. My feelings for Troy were a girl's infatuation. What I feel for you is a woman's love."

451

He seized her by the shoulders, and Caroline could feel the trembling in his fingers. His eyes searched her face. Disbelief ruled his features—then the grim lines of his expression gentled.

"My God—"

His mouth closed over hers, moving urgently, seeking her sweetness with the frantic hunger of a starving man. Caroline responded joyously. The outside world vanished until there was only this man and his arms . . . the home she had been seeking all of her life. Dizzily, she pressed herself against him, drowning in a need as desperate as his own.

When at last he lifted his head, she was breathless and quivering.

"Marry me," he demanded, his breath hot on her forehead.

"Yes, oh yes, I do so want to. But are you sure? People will talk about what my father did—" Her voice choked off in anguished pain.

The touch of his fingers on her cheek assured her that he understood. "I love you. I don't give a tinker's damn what anyone else thinks on the matter."

Still troubled, she frowned up at him. "Oh, Zach, I don't deserve you. I want to make it all up to you, all those times when I acted like a child."

"Ssshhh. 'Tis over and done with. All that matters is that you love me now."

He lifted her face to kiss her again, a long and tender melding that that left her aching for more. Her hand traced his rugged features, so dear and so familiar. His arms were warm and welcoming—how could she have gone so long not recognizing her love?

"Do you know, I just had a thought," she said. "There

is one thing I can do to redeem myself."

His smile was tenderly indulgent. "I told you, it isn't necessary to prove yourself. I believe in you."

"But listen. To make up for all the suffering I caused Troy and Elise, I can at least try to convince him to go after her. I don't know what made her disappear on the eve of their wedding, but it can't be allowed to keep them apart forever." Her voice softened as she gazed up into his warm eyes. "People in love belong together, don't you think?"

His embrace tightened with pride and affection. "Absolutely, my dearest love, absolutely."

Fort Duquesne was located at the tip of the peninsula where three mighty rivers converged: the Ohio, the Allegheny, and the Monongahela. Critical to the French defense, the fort controlled wilderness land claimed by both Virginia and France. The smaller and cruder Fort Prince George had been captured from English forces in April and, ever since, swarms of men had been busy erecting a larger and mightier fortification. Now, at the end of June, the walls and essential buildings had been completed and the work crew was busy putting the final touches on the officers' quarters and soldiers' barracks.

Elise removed the last of the laundry from a line strung between two poles, then slumped wearily onto an overturned bucket that doubled as a stool. She gazed out over the forest of bark huts that provided temporary housing for the troops until permanent quarters were ready. The outer stockade, where she was sitting, was surrounded by a twelve-foot wall and guarded by sentries. In the week since her arrival, the banging of hammers and the grating of saws had drifted from the inner stronghold of the fort.

Perspiration dampened her gown. The late afternoon was hot and humid, and she longed for the cool breezes of evening. Already cooking smells filled the air as Indian women prepared supper for the soldiers. Elise had grown accustomed to seeing the squaws in their buckskin dresses attending to tasks around the camp.

She rose, picking up the basket of clothing on her way back to the small hut she occupied alone. It was only one of the many little comforts Yves had provided for her despite the overcrowded conditions here at the fort. He would make a good husband and a good father, Elise told herself for the umpteenth time.

She should be anxiously awaiting the day when the chaplain would arrive at the fort and speak their wedding vows. She should be . . . and yet she wasn't.

Her soul mourned for Troy. Each night, she wept herself to sleep, missing his presence beside her, wanting to share with him the joy of their coming child. The awful futility of it tore at her heart. They were hundreds of miles apart, enemies on opposite sides of a war.

Elise placed the clothes inside the dim interior of her hut. The thought of bending over a campfire when she was already so hot and tired held little appeal, but after all Yves had done for her, the least she could do in return was to prepare his food. With a sigh, she picked up a wooden pail and headed into the inner stronghold to fetch water.

The postern gate stood open, the scent of new-hewn lumber perfuming the air. Men swarmed around the long log barracks, some hammering on the roof, others going in and out the doors as they finished the interior. The

lace was at least twice the size of Fort LeBoeuf, and Yves
ad promised her their own snug little cabin once they
ere married.

She neither dreaded the prospect nor welcomed it.
nside her, there was simply . . . nothing. Her heart was
n empty shell.

Slowly Elise walked to the center of the fort, where the
eur-de-lis fluttered from a tall flagpole. After filling the
ucket at the well, she was heading back across the
ompound when a commotion near the front gate caught
er eye. A crowd began to gather—workers, men in
niform, Indians. Mangy dogs raced around, barking.
he air rang with excited murmurings, and a few
natches of conversation caught Elise's ear.

"Soldiers riding from the east . . . a prisoner . . . an
nglish cur. . . ."

The tiniest spark of curiosity broke through her
thargy. An English prisoner—could it be one of
Vashington's men? Perhaps even someone she knew?

Setting down the bucket, she peered through the
illing crowd, shading her eyes against the late
fternoon sun as several French soldiers rode through
he gate on horseback. A rope tied to one of their saddles
ailed behind, tugged taut by the man stumbling on foot
fter the party.

The light blinded Elise's eyes for a moment, then the
aptive came into full view. He was a tall, shaggy-bearded
aan clad in grimy buckskins.

Her heart jolted to a halt.

The prisoner was Troy!

Chapter Thirty-two

She gasped in shock, but everyone around her was too intent on Troy to notice. Jeers and hoots hurled through the air as the residents of the fort released the tension built up over weeks of waiting for battle. This one hapless Englishman would bear the brunt of their abuse.

Elise stood paralyzed, fingers balled into fists. In a shining bolt of lightning, understanding dawned. Troy had been caught coming after *her!* He had risked life and limb for *her!*

Joy see-sawed with fear. Troy must still love her . . . yet now he was a prisoner.

Helplessly she watched as he stumbled after the horseman leading him toward the prison in a corner of the fort. She prayed that he would turn and see her through the crowd, but his eyes were fixed straight ahead. With a pang, she realized that he probably believed she had returned to Fort LeBoeuf. Oh, how wretched he must feel, thinking himself deserted by her and at the mercy of the enemy!

"*Merde,*" spat a grizzled old soldier standing beside her. "Them dirty redcoats ain't got no right trespassin on our land."

He turned away before Elise could reply. And that was probably a blessing, for she might have tossed caution to the wind and leaped to the defense of the English. No longer did she think of them as "dirty redcoats." The man she loved was one of the enemy, and their child quickened inside her belly. Yet logic warned her she must keep that knowledge quiet, else risk losing the chance to see Troy.

The crowd trailed along after the prisoner, still taunting and shouting. Elise could catch only glimpses of Troy as he was untied and yanked into the sturdy log prison behind the cadets' barracks. The instant he was out of sight, she abandoned her water pail to go in search of Yves, driven by desperate need.

She didn't have far to look. As she hurried across the compound, he emerged from the commander's lodging, along with two other officers, all resplendent in military uniform. They walked swiftly toward the prison.

Elise ran after them and caught him by the arm. "Yves, I must speak to you."

"*Plus tard*," he murmured. "I have duties to attend to right now."

Elise felt a flash of frustration. Didn't he know by now that she wouldn't disturb him like this if it weren't absolutely necessary?

"This cannot wait!" she snapped. Seeing the other two officers eyeing her curiously, she lowered her voice. "It is a matter of vital importance. Can you not spare me a moment?"

He pursed his lips with a trace of impatience. "*Oui*, one moment, then."

"Alone," she said, glancing pointedly at the other two men.

"If you must." Turning to the officers, he ordered,

"Go on to the prison. I'll be along shortly." He looke
back at her and asked, "Now, what's bothering you
petite?"

Her irritation vanished at the thought of Troy, an
quickly she glanced around to make certain no one wa
close enough to hear.

"It's about the British prisoner who was just brough
in. Oh, Yves, that man is Troy!"

Yves started visibly. "You're saying 'twas Fletche
who was captured by our soldiers?"

"*Oui.* Yves, you can't hold him here! You've got t
help me free him!"

He stared at her for a moment. Then stiffly he said
"You ask the impossible. I haven't the authority t
release a prisoner of war."

"But this is no ordinary prisoner! You know he didn'
come here to spy or even to fight, he came to find me!"

Yves turned away, his shoulders rigid. "I'm sorry.
can't help you."

Ignoring her pleas of protest, he marched swiftly away
his uniformed figure disappearing into the prison.

Elise slumped in despair. How could she alone secur
Troy's release from a heavily guarded fort filled wit
French soldiers? Not to mention making sure that no on
caught them in the process!

Firmly she bolstered her sagging spirits. Just becaus
Yves refused to help didn't mean it was hopeless. Th
odds might be impossible, but something would come t
her. She would rack her brain for a plan . . . and pray

Troy stumbled and almost fell as the French soldier

458

oved him inside the prison. His shoulder slammed
infully into the hard log wall, and he had to grit his
eth to hold back an instinctive urge to retaliate by
irying his fist in the man's face. He reminded himself it
as better to save his energy for escape later, than to
aste it all now, when there were too many of the enemy
r one man to fight off.

A soldier crouched down before him. There was a
anking sound and then a feel of heaviness on his ankle.
sick horror slashed through Troy as he watched the leg
ons being locked into place. By God, he felt like a rat
ught in a trap! He wanted to yank at the thick metal
anacles even though logic told him it would be a waste
effort. Now he understood why a wild animal would
ght the snare until bloody, sometimes even killing itself
the effort to escape.

To calm his nerves, Troy studied the prison. It was a
rge, square chamber with manacles along the walls for
any captives. The air was stifling, but at least the place
oked and smelled new. A few tiny barred slits high in
e walls let in light.

Two more men came into the narrow prison door. By
e braid and cut of their uniforms, Troy judged they
ere officers. They motioned the other soldiers out, then
ood together across the room, speaking in French and
ooting Troy an occasional sharp glance.

Wearily, he slumped against the wall, wondering what
ey intended to do with him. Oh, God, to have come all
is way only to be captured a hundred miles from Fort
Boeuf! If he hadn't been pushing himself so hard to
ach Elise, he wouldn't have fallen into such sound
ep last night. He would have heard the French soldiers

459

as they'd crept into his camp.

Silently he cursed his luck, and a wave of despondenc washed through him. Was he never to see Elise again Never to have the chance to repair the damage he ha done to their love? How the devil was he to get himse out of this predicament and back into her arms?

The door swung open again and a stiff-shouldered ma strode into the prison. He said something to the two othe officers and they went scurrying out the door.

Troy stood up straight, unable to believe his eyes. was that damn bastard, Yves Larousse!

His heart beat swiftly as a sudden hope swelled insic him. Elise had left with Larousse. Could that mean sh was also here at Fort Duquesne?

"Where is Elise?" Troy demanded.

Yves's face was impassive, exhibiting no surprise, n anger, no hatred, no gloating. There was simply . . nothing.

"So, *mon ami*," he said, "we meet again."

"Where is she?" Troy repeated more forcefully.

"Why should it matter to you? You hurt her wit your—how do you say?—your accusations. She deserve a man who will treat her with kindness."

"And I suppose you see yourself as that man."

Yves regarded him stonily. *"Oui*. She has agreed to l my wife."

The news hit Troy with the force of a fist slammir into his gut. With a roar of disbelief, he lunged for Yve But the leg irons caught at his ankles before he coul reach the Frenchman's neck. In the nick of time, h caught his balance and steadied himself, his finge clenching into fists as he glared in furious frustration a

460

is opponent, who stood just out of reach.

"Come closer, you lily-livered bastard!" Troy taunted.
"I'll tear your heart out and serve it to Elise on a platter."

"You would have to travel far to do so," Yves snapped.
"Elise is in Montreal. I sent her there to be safe."

Troy felt the fight drain out of him. So she wasn't here
after all! And Montreal—that was a hell of a distance.
God above, if only he weren't chained like a damn dog!
Somehow, some way, he had to break out of here and get
to her, try to make her forgive him before she was lost to
him forever.

"I see no need to question you any further," Yves said
crisply. He wheeled around and strode to the door, the
two other men following him.

"Wait!" Troy called out impulsively.

His hand on the latch, Yves turned and looked back.

Troy gritted his teeth, hating to humble himself, but
forcing the words past his pride. "Would you at least let
me write a letter to Elise? I'd like to clear up the
misunderstanding between us."

Yves stared at him measuringly. "I will think on it," he
said, then marched out of the prison.

Hearing the door shut and the bar slam into place,
Troy let his weary body slide down to the dirt floor. He
leaned his head against the wall and stared up at the
rough plank ceiling. It galled him to no end to have to rely
on that bastard's good nature, but the long shot was
worth the humiliation if it meant reuniting with Elise
sooner.

His palm struck his thigh in an outburst of painful
frustration. For a few brief moments, she had seemed so
near. Now it looked as though the waiting might last

461

months, even years.

Unless, of course, he could escape. Resolutely, he began to plan.

As the sun dipped lower in the western sky, fingers of darkness crept across the land. The air cooled to a more tolerable temperature and stars began to wink to life in an ebony sky. The creatures of the forest launched into their nightly chorus: bullfrogs croaked, insects buzzed, owls hooted.

Elise was oblivious to it all. Cloaked in shadows, she paced back and forth before her hut, her gown swishing impatiently. Hers was the only dwelling without a campfire glowing before it, for in her distress all thought of cooking dinner had flown out of her mind.

A few of the Indian women cast sidelong glances at her, but she was too embroiled in thought to pay any heed. She had to find a way to get to Troy, she just had to! Yet her brain had rejected one desperate scheme after another.

At last she decided it would help to reconnoiter the prison and see how many guards were on duty. Only then would she know what she was up against.

Quickly she left the camp and circled the high wall of the inner stronghold. A half-moon crept slowly up over the forest, laying a sheen of silver over the silent black waters of the river. Sentries paced the outer bulwarks so that an alarm could be raised in case of an attack.

Elise found the postern gate closed, but a wicket enabled her to slip inside. Cautiously, she began to make her way toward the prison, but the sudden hum of voices made her shrink into the shadows of the new-built barracks. Her damp palms pressed against the rough log wall as a trio of soldiers sauntered by, talking and laughing.

When they were gone, she took a swift glance around and then resumed her way. Pinpricks of candlelight wavered in a few windows here and there, identifying the commander's lodging and the officers' quarters. Quietly she stole as close to the prison as she dared and then paused in the murky darkness to assess the situation.

To her great relief, only one guard was posted before the single door. The long black shadow propped against the dark log wall must be his gun. A tiny red glow flared and dulled, and the faint scent of burning tobacco drifted through the air.

Absently brushing away a mosquito, she began to plan. She had no idea how long Troy would be interned here, so swiftness was of the essence. At the same time, she couldn't risk playing her hand until she was sure—

"What are you doing here?"

She whirled with a gasp to find Yves standing behind her. The gold buttons on his uniform glinted in the moonlight, though his face was shadowed. With the memory of their parting that afternoon still fresh in her mind, anger boiled inside her, prompting her to hiss sarcastically: "I'm here to help Troy escape, couldn't you guess?"

"Don't do anything foolish, *petite*."

Elise lifted her chin. "What do you expect me to do? Let him rot in there?"

"Do you love him so much, then?" he asked quietly.

She caught at his sleeve. "*Oui*, I do, you know that. I would do anything to get him out of there. Anything."

He was silent for a moment, then he said stiffly, "I've

done some thinking since this afternoon, and I've decided it wouldn't hurt to let you see him for a few minutes."

She stared at him in astonishment. "You mean that?"

He gave a curt nod. "Wait here."

Yves pivoted on his heel and marched over to the sentry on duty in front of the prison. There was a low murmur of conversation, then the guard walked off toward the main gate. As soon as he was gone, Yves beckoned to her.

Elise scurried over to him. "How did you get rid of him?" she whispered.

"I told him I needed to ask the prisoner a few more questions, and that he should return in fifteen minutes. You have exactly fourteen to speak to Monsieur Fletcher."

He lifted the bar on the door. Elise's heart pounded as the heavy planked panel swung open, and she took a few tentative steps into the black interior. The door closed quietly behind her, further darkening the chamber. Several barred slits placed at regular intervals high in the walls provided only the faintest of light. The scent of new-hewn lumber pervaded the air.

A slight rustling to her left was all that warned her. Abruptly a hand clamped over her mouth, a steel arm yanked her spine close against a hard-muscled chest. There was a muted clanking of leg irons.

"Whoever the hell you are, mam'selle," growled a familiar voice in her ear, "you're going to help me get out of here. I hope to God you have a key to these damn manacles."

Elise tried to speak, but her frantic words were muffled against his palm. *Sacré Dieu*, didn't he know who she was?

She wriggled against his iron grasp, but he only tightened his grip. Their silent struggle left her panting—and from more than just lack of air. The feel of his body was sheer heaven.

After a moment, she found herself moving with more sensuality, undulating her hips against his loins, pressing her breasts against his enclosing arm. When she managed to slip her tongue out to taste his fingers, he jerked in surprise. His heart thundered against her back, telling her that he was as affected as she.

"Damn you, wench," he cursed under his breath.

Sensing his momentary confusion, she yanked her head aside, out of the stifling gag formed by his hand. He moved in swift retaliation. Making a grab for her, he inadvertently pulled a few strands of hair, bringing tears to her eyes.

"Troy!" she croaked just as his fingers closed over her mouth again.

He stiffened. She was aware of the pulsing of his heart, the heat of his breath on her nape. Then he was swiveling her in his arms, his hands closing over the sides of her head, angling her face to the faint moonlight. She could just barely make out his bearded features in the ebony darkness.

"My God—Elise?" he uttered hoarsely. "Is it really you?"

She nodded mutely.

The breath came out of him in a rush. He pulled her to him, his hands moving up and down the length of her spine, tunneling into her hair and dislodging the pins that held the curls in place. His beard rasped against her cheek as his lips pressed hot kisses against her forehead and cheeks. She clung to him in a dizzy exhilaration.

465

"Angel, little angel, forgive me . . . I had no idea . . . that damn Frenchman told me he'd sent you off to Montreal for safekeeping!"

It took a moment for his words to penetrate her joy. She pulled back slightly, straining to see him in the gloom. "Yves? He told you I'd left the fort?"

"Aye, he said so this afternoon." His hands cradled her cheeks, touching her as if he couldn't believe it was really she. "My God, Elise, I've found you . . . I thought I'd lost you forever . . . drove you away with all those awful things I said to you."

She caught her breath. "Do you believe me, then? That I wasn't a spy?"

"Not long after you left, Richard Whitman was caught stealing some secret government documents. And he's dead, Elise. After they jailed him, he went berserk and wrestled a knife away from a guard and killed himself."

"Oh, no," she whispered in shock.

"It still seems like a nightmare. I should have trusted you, Elise. 'Tis something I'll regret for the rest of my life."

The deep anguish in his voice tore at her heart. "Don't," she cried out softly, wreathing her arms around his neck. "Don't torture yourself about what's past."

"I can't help it," he muttered. "How could I have been so cruel to you, so unfeeling? I was so afraid that Larousse would take you away from me that I made it become a reality."

"But I was wrong, too, you know. I should have confided in you from the first about my plans to find the spy. Oh, Troy, I love you, and now that we're together again, all is forgotten, forever."

His hands burrowed into the rich mass of her hair,

tilting her head up to his shadowed face. "Forever. I like the sound of that word," he whispered hoarsely. "And I love you. God, how I love you!"

Their lips met in a tender kiss that sent the whole world spinning away into nothingness. The feel of his powerful shoulders beneath her fingertips, the warmth of his encircling arms, were like a haven in the midst of a storm. Hot and impatient, she pressed herself to him in an instinctive need to link their bodies.

A foreign noise intruded on her senses—the rattle of the door opening. It brought her crashing back to earth.

"Elise?" called Yves's voice. "Come, you must leave now. The guard is returning."

"One moment," she hissed back through the darkness. Standing on tiptoe, she slid her hand around Troy's neck and whispered in his ear, "Oh, Troy, I haven't yet told you—I'm going to have your baby!"

He drew in a breath, his hand gently splaying over the slight rounding of her stomach. "A child," he murmured. "Sweet angel, you've just given me one more reason to love you."

"I'm going to help get you out of here," she promised fiercely. "As soon as I can."

"Nay! I won't have you taking any such risks."

"And I won't have the father of my child imprisoned," she retorted. "We both need you."

Troy laughed softly in amused resignation. "All right—knowing you, I'd best not even waste my time trying to talk you out of it."

"Elise, hurry!" Yves called again, more urgently.

Their mouths met for one final, swift kiss. Reluctantly she pulled herself out of Troy's arms, their fingers touching until the last possible moment. Then her feet flew across the dirt floor to the pale slit of the opened door. There, she paused and looked back at Troy, a tall black shadow against the ebony interior.

She slipped outside and dragged the heavy plank door shut behind her.

Yves grabbed her by the arm and gave her a push toward the shadows of a nearby building. "Go, *vite!*" he hissed. "Wait over there for me, out of sight."

Obediently she scurried toward the murky patch of darkness a short distance away. And only just in time, for it was but a few moments later that the sentry sauntered back across the compound to the prison. Her hands pressed against a rough wooden post as she heard the murmur of voices drifting through the night air.

Then Yves walked toward her. When he reached the spot where she was hiding, he whispered, "Come, *petite*. I'll take you back to your hut."

She didn't argue, too grateful to him for letting her see Troy. Silently she fell into step beside him as they headed through the sleeping fort toward the postern gate. The memory of Troy's embrace made her heart sing. He still loved her! He wanted to spend the rest of his life with her!

And yet he languished in prison, bound by leg irons like a wild beast. *Sacré Dieu*, it was her fault! If she hadn't run away, he wouldn't have been forced to come after her. How was she to get him out of there and past the guards who prowled the outer perimeter of the fort?

She wanted him with her, free, so desperately that tears of frustration pricked her eyes. It wasn't right that he should be a prisoner, all because he loved her.

As they slipped out the wicket in the postern gate, Yves touched her on the arm, halting her in the shadows of the bastion's towering wall. His hand tilted her chin up to the

468

oonlight. For a long moment he studied her face and
e tears that glittered in her eyes.

"You love him far more than you ever could me, don't
ou?" he said heavily. It was a statement filled with pain,
d it sounded as if he had just now realized the
reversible truth of it.

Shame rushed over her. In her single-minded focus on
roy, she had forgotten that Yves loved her, too. She was
pposed to be marrying him, and here she was, making
ans to run away with Troy without even considering
ow that would affect Yves.

Elise lifted a hand and touched his cheek. "Oh, Yves,
ve been so selfish. I don't know what to say to excuse
yself—except that I'm truly sorry. I owe you a debt of
ratitude for helping me when I needed you the most."
he took a deep breath, seeking a painless way to say the
ords that would wound him. "I think you've guessed
at I cannot wed you," she said as gently as possible.
'Twouldn't be fair to you when I love another."

He nodded slowly. "I can see that now. This afternoon,
hen I saw him, I hated him, I wanted to hurt him for
oving you. But then I realized I would only be hurting
ou, too." He paused for a moment as if wrestling with
ome inner demon. Then he took her hands in his. "I
ant to help you one last time, *petite*. I want to help the
wo of you escape."

Hope flared in her like a new-lit torch. The generosity
f his proposal touched her heart, for she knew what a
reat risk he was offering to take for her, what it would
ean to his career should he be caught freeing a prisoner
f war.

"You would do so much for me?" she asked humbly.
After what I've done to you?"

469

He shrugged. "I want you to be happy."

Impulsively she drew his hands to her mouth and kissed them. "I owe you so much. How can I ever repay you?"

"I don't expect repayment," he said roughly. "Now you'll have to allow me time to arrange things. Will you promise to be patient?"

Eagerly, she nodded her head.

Chapter Thirty-three

Those days and nights of waiting proved to be the
ngest, most difficult hours of her entire life. She found
rself counting the time in minutes and even seconds.
ie hours plodded by on weary feet, trudging along with
e slowness of a child being sent to do a dull and boring
sk.

Elise alternated between dark despair and radiant
pe. How she wanted Troy beside her! Although they
re separated by only a few hundred yards, she hadn't
en him since that clandestine visit.

On a rainy evening three nights later, the long-awaited
oment finally arrived.

Elise stood outside the postern gate, shivering more
om excitement than from the warm drizzle that
rinkled her hooded cloak. A blanket of clouds covered
e sky and obscured the moon; she prayed the gloom
uld enable them to slip past the sentries unnoticed.

With anxious impatience, she peered through the
cket and into the night-darkened fort. Yves had
rbidden her to go with him as he released Troy from the

prison. Only his explanation that the fewer peop[le] involved, the better his chances of getting Troy o[ut] undetected kept her at the appointed post. The plan w[as] for Yves to knock out the guard from behind so that t[he] next morning it would look as though Elise had done t[he] deed. That way, no suspicion would fall on Yves and ru[in] his career. She had insisted on that part, feeling it was t[he] least she could do for him in return.

At last she saw the dark figures of two men hurryin[g] through the gate. Despite the moonless night, sh[e] recognized Troy's tall form. Swallowing a cry of joy, sh[e] went catapulting into his arms.

He hugged her tightly, stroking his hands into her hai[r], pushing the hood away from her face as if he could n[ot] believe it was really she. She tilted her head to ga[ze] hungrily at his shadowed features, the warm ra[in] spattering her cheeks.

Then he snatched up her hand and they followed Yv[es] down the path that led to the river. Stealthily they cre[pt] through the mud, the hiss of raindrops all around the[m]. Elise's heart lodged in her throat as she saw a shadow[y] figure on the ramparts in the distance. A sentry. *Sac[ré] Dieu*, what if one of the guards were to see them and rais[e] an alarm?

She saw Yves glance around, ever watchful. At t[he] high picket wall that formed the outer barrier of the for[t] he stopped and silently lifted the bar from the gate s[o] they could pass through to the path cut into the slopin[g] embankment. Yves led them the short distance down t[o] the river and onto a wooden pier, where several cano[es] were tied.

"I've put provisions in the last one there," h[e] murmured to Elise, pointing to the canoe that bobbed i[n] he murky waters at the end of the pier.

The point of final parting had come, and with it, a giddy sense of freedom. Looking at Yves through the darkness, she felt a rush of profound gratitude. She owed him so very much.

On impulse she threw her arms around him and hugged him. Mere words seemed inadequate to express her appreciation and, in the end, all she could whisper was, *"Merci."*

For an instant, his arms tightened around her, then he was thrusting her away. "You must go, *now!*" he hissed.

Solemnly Troy shook Yves's hand, and a look of understanding passed between the two men. They were enemies, yet united in their love for one woman. Turning away, Troy took Elise by the arm and drew her over to the boat, carefully stepping in first, then reaching out to aid her boarding.

The slender birch-bark vessel bobbed in the water as Yves bent to untie the line. Wielding the paddle, Troy steered the canoe out into the middle of the black river, where the current carried them swiftly downstream. Elise couldn't help gazing back as the fort and Yves vanished into the night.

Warm raindrops pattered against her face. She picked up her paddle and began to help Troy. She felt saddened for having to hurt Yves, but the farther down the wide river they paddled, the more that somber mood lifted. They were free! She said a fervent prayer that Troy's absence wouldn't be discovered until morning, when they were long gone.

It was difficult to see through the gloom. On shore, the shadowy outlines of trees rushed past. The only sound was the splash of their paddles. Elise's cloak hung damp and heavy on her shoulders, and though it was hot, at least it provided some protection against the drizzle.

She had lost all track of time when the rain finally stopped. The clouds began to clear, giving an occasional glimpse of the star-pricked heavens and an almost-full moon. Its pale light helped them see their way down the river.

After a while, the adrenaline that had boosted her spirits faded, and weariness began to take its toll on Elise. Her shoulders slumped and it took more and more effort to wield her paddle. Troy must have sensed her exhaustion, for he turned to her with concern in his voice.

"Why don't you take a break and let me manage on my own."

"I can help," she insisted.

His grin gleamed through the darkness. "Stubborn to the last, aren't you? Rest for our child's sake, then, if not your own."

That logic Elise could find no argument with, and so she meekly drew her paddle into the canoe. She threw off her stifling damp cloak, determined to stay awake even though her eyelids were drooping.

The next thing she knew, a scraping sound woke her. She was curled into a cramped position in the bottom of the canoe. Raising up on her elbow, she saw a forest of reeds waving gently in the warm breeze. Dawn painted the sky in pinks and pearls.

Troy was standing in shallow water beside the canoe as he towed the birch-bark craft up the embankment. With a glint of a devilish smile, he reached in and swung her up in his arms.

"I can walk!" she protested.

"Humor me. I've been deprived of holding you lately."

Tenderness washed through Elise, and she melted against his hard chest, looping her arms around his neck. "If you insist, m'sieur," she said demurely.

"Good." He slanted a sly look down at her. "A woman must learn to obey her future husband."

"Obey!" she sputtered. "I have a mind of my own, I'll have you know."

Troy laughed. "Believe me, I *do* know."

Water splashed around his boots as he carried her up the sandy bank to a thicket of trees, where he laid her down on the soft grasses, beneath the draping branches of a willow.

Troy bent to plant a warm, possessive kiss on her lips. "Wait here, little mother, while I fetch the provisions."

Head propped on her hand, she watched him walk back to the canoe. He was so tall and gloriously handsome that she could never get enough of looking at him. Warmth pulsed inside her at the sight of those powerful muscles and long legs. Though his buckskins might be dirty and his beard unkempt, she wouldn't trade him for any other man in the world.

He returned with a large bundle and knelt down to unwrap it, finding blankets and food. "Damn," he growled, rummaging around in the pack, "I'm so hungry I could eat a bear."

Elise couldn't keep from reaching out to run her fingers over the soft, supple buckskin that covered his thigh. Troy looked at her hand, then tossed the pack aside with a wry grin.

"How very strange," he mused, "of a sudden I find I have a different appetite entirely."

He spread out a blanket and lay down to draw her close.

His hands molded her against him, his mouth seeking o
the warm crook of her neck. A rush of heat course
through her—until a worry intruded on her joy.

"Troy? She touched his shoulder, and he lifted h
head inquiringly. "Should we be stopping for long? Wh
if we're followed?"

"I doubt they'll bother pursuing us. Still, for safety
sake, we'll stay here until darkness falls tonight, to avo
the risk of running into Indians or anyone else."

"But what if someone stumbles upon us?"

"No one will—in case you hadn't noticed, we're on
small island out in the middle of the river." That devilis
glimmer lit his green eyes. "'Tis most private fo
whatever endeavors we might wish to engage in."

"Lusty beast," she grumbled indulgently. "Yo
planned things this way, didn't you?"

"Blame yourself, lovely angel—you're too enticing fo
a man to ignore."

His fingers made short work of the ribbon that held he
bodice in place. Then he peeled away her chemise so tha
her breasts were bared to his view. Cradling one rip
mound in his palm, he bent and suckled the peak unt
she trembled with pleasure. Her hands threaded into h
hair to press him closer and encourage the delightfu
sensations.

"Ah, Elise . . . your breasts are fuller . . . swollen fo
our child."

"I'll soon grow fat and ungainly."

Troy caught a hint of worry in her voice, though sh
had spoken lightly. Sensing her need for reassurance, h
gathered her close, burying his face in the fragrant clou
of her hair.

"You'll be as beautiful to me in your ninth month a

476

ou are right now," he whispered fiercely. "I love you, nd don't you ever forget that."

Her arms tightened around him and he felt her smile gainst his neck. "Aye, m'sieur. I love you, too."

Tenderness enveloped him, along with a rush of aching desire, the two feelings irrevocably entwined. Slowly he undressed the both of them until the warm breezes caressed their naked flesh. Then he stopped to drink in he sight of her. God, she was gorgeous, with her copper hair tousled and those brandy-hued eyes dark with onging. Her breasts were the color of creamy satin, with honey-rose tips. And her belly was slightly rounded with heir child.

A wave of almost unbearable desire inundated Troy. Yet he subdued his own physical needs, wanting to give her the most exquisite pleasure she had ever known. His mouth moved over every inch of her, lingering on her breasts and then between her thighs, rousing her passion with infinite care until she was wild with need. They came together in an explosive release, a perfect joining of body and soul.

For a long time afterward, he held her nestled in his arms as the birds trilled sweet melodies and rays of early morning sun drifted through the trees to dapple their skin. Judging by her soft, even breathing, he guessed she was drifting to sleep. He was weary himself after their long night, but holding her close was a delight he wanted to cherish for just a little while longer. Very gently, he brushed a wayward curl off her forehead.

"Mmmm," she murmured, stirring against him. "I'm so glad you found me. I was afraid I'd lost you forever."

"You can thank Caroline that you didn't."

"Caroline?"

477

He grinned as she shifted her head to look up at him in obvious puzzlement. "Aye. You see, I was convinced that you would never be able to forgive me for doubting you. She told me that if I truly loved you, I couldn't allow myself to give up. If Zach had given up on her so easily, she said, they would have lost a lifetime of happiness together."

"Zach and Caroline—?"

"They're marrying as soon as the mourning period is over with."

"I'm glad," she said with soft sincerity.

Then a look of sadness stole over her face, and he knew she was remembering Richard Whitman. Wanting to see a smile return to her lovely face, he changed the subject to one he had devoted great thought to during that long, lonely journey through the wilderness.

"Elise, do you think you might ever want to leave my plantation and live on the frontier?"

An expression of startled interest lit her face, then she turned away as if she were afraid to let him see it. "Is that what you want?"

Gently he drew her chin back to him. "Come now, don't answer a question with a question."

Elise stared at him uncertainly, unsure of whether or not to express her true feelings. Oh, if only she could live a simple life, without having to worry about all the proper things a lady must know! She didn't need fancy gowns and parties to make her happy—just the man she loved. But what if Troy were only making idle conversation?

"I—I think I'd like it—would you?"

Her expression spoke volumes to Troy, assuring him that he had guessed right about her feelings.

"I was hoping you would," he said, running a hand

own her bare arm. "You see, I own land in the Shenandoah Valley, land I'd always intended to settle on someday. Elise, you'd love it there. 'Tis so very beautiful—there's a soft blue haze over the mountains that looks like smoke."

"It sounds wonderful," she said with a trace of wistfulness.

"Then you wouldn't mind leaving the comforts of civilization for a rugged life in the wilderness?"

Her eyes were shining with repressed excitement as she shook her head emphatically. "Nay, of course, I wouldn't. But oh, Troy, don't tease me. Are you truly serious about this?"

He nodded. "What say you, then? Shall we make the move? We'll have to wait until the war's over, but—"

He never got the rest out because Elise threw her arms round him and kissed him on the mouth. Her enthusiasm was gratifying. Chuckling, he hugged her close, reveling in the taste and touch and scent that was uniquely and wonderfully hers.

"The frontier will be a perfect place to raise our baby daughter," he observed.

"Daughter!" Elise huffed. "I'm giving you a son!"

He denied it with a shake of his head. "Nay, a little girl with copper curls and brandy-colored eyes, just like her mother."

"A little *boy* with tawny hair and devilish green eyes."

He looked at her hopefully. "We could compromise on twins."

"I think we'll just take what we get. Knowing, of course, that we can always try again . . . and again . . . and again."

Her hand stroked over his chest and wandered

enticingly down to his stomach. His body flamed i
instant response, a reaction he tried to subdue withou
much success.

He drew in a ragged breath. "Aye, there is that," h
murmured. "Now don't you think you and baby need
little sleep?"

She smiled lovingly as her hand dipped lower stil
"There's plenty of time for sleep—later."